OVER YOU

KYRA LENNON

Copyright

Trigger Warnings

If you have no triggers, please feel free to skip the following information as it does include some spoilers.

However, if there are things that have the potential to be upsetting to you, read on. This isn't a dark romance, but it DOES have some dark elements scattered throughout.

This story includes mentions of domestic and emotional abuse, fertility issues, SA/abuse-related PTSD, and abduction of an adult from a school event (no child witnesses).

Please, please proceed with caution. <3

Dedication

For Uncle Peter,
Without you, many things were never quite the same again – Dawlish
Carnival being one of them.
The brightest smile, the one who was always there to help with a friendly
word and to give a burst of laughter to any situation.
Even after all this time, it's impossible not to smile when I think of you.
Miss you always.
P.S. Thanks for the free entry to the carnival discos too.

Contents

# Chapter 1

Gaby

I CARRIED MY BOX full of gifts into my flat, then kicked the door closed behind me, huffing out a sigh of relief. Carefully placing it down in the hallway to sort out later, I headed for the kitchen to make a strong cup of black coffee to satisfy my rapidly increasing caffeine craving.

The end of term was always bittersweet. I was excited we'd reached the conclusion of another school year, but seeing my little ones leave hurt. They came to me for their first foray into full-time schooling, and watching them spread their wings and fly away, headed for a new class, never got any easier, even after six years.

I flicked the kettle on and walked into the attached living room to grab my latest read from my bookshelf. My living room basically doubled as a mini library, with two wide bookshelves at either side of the large fireplace, packed with a mix of chick-lit, dark romance, classics, and a whole array of personal development books I'd used at various points in my life.

Reaching for the rom-com I'd become engrossed in, I placed it on the desk that stood in front of the large sash window. Once I'd finally settled, coffee beside me and book in hand, a contented smile crossed my face. The rest of the day was mine, as were the next few weeks, and I planned to start it off right with a takeaway and probably even more reading. I'd deal with anything else I needed to do in the morning.

I'd only read a few pages before my phone beeped. It was tucked into my skirt pocket, and I pulled it out, my eyes widening slightly in surprise as I read the message on the screen.

> Shannen: **Hey, do you want to ride down to Penzance with Guy? Saves you both taking a car each, though I totally understand if you want to be able to escape on your own :p xx**

In two days, my work colleague, Shannen, and I, plus her partner, Cal and his son, Aiden; my other colleague, Nova, and her other half, Donovan; and Cal's friend, Guy, were going to Cornwall for a week. Donovan was a travel blogger, and while he'd been away in far sunnier climes for most of the year, he'd invited us on a group holiday; a holiday he got for free because of his status as a social media influencer.

The resort we were staying at was luxurious in the extreme. We would be spending the week in a large lodge together, with our own private deck with a hot tub.

I was going to relax my arse off.

I laughed as I re-read the end of Shannen's message. There *would* be a lot of us in one place, including one wild kid. I had considered asking Shannen if I could ride with her and Cal, so we weren't all rocking up in separate cars. However, I'd surmised it'd probably be too cramped with all the stuff Shannen and Cal would need to take to entertain Aiden, and I did *not* travel light. I was a 'pack everything in case you need it' kind of girl, so I decided I'd drive down on my own. I hadn't thought that Guy would be driving alone too.

However, if I went with him, as Shannen pointed out, I wouldn't have my own transport to get around if I wanted to.

But if I go with Guy... I get to spend time with him.

The thought both surprised me and made me roll my eyes at myself.

A couple of months back, Guy and I had exchanged numbers after Shannen's car accident. Since then, we'd stayed in touch, speaking on the phone a few times, but mostly texting. We'd been out for drinks twice—something I hadn't mentioned to anyone—and each time had been fun. Guy was funny, kind, and ridiculously attractive, but he had also not long ago got out of a serious relationship. As much as I'd started to like him and enjoyed the flirty banter, I didn't want to be his rebound girl. So, while we'd continued to text now and again, I hadn't seen him in person for about six weeks.

Not that I was counting.

Aware Shannen was waiting for my answer, I thought fast.

Did I want to spend two hours in a car with Guy when I could drive myself? While Cornwall itself was gorgeous, the drive there was fairly dull, and having someone to talk to would make it better.

Buying myself more time, I text back:

Have you already asked him? xx

If she hadn't, I could think it over for longer. If she had, I'd need to answer faster.

Shannen: **He brought it up, but I wasn't sure how you'd feel about it since you don't know him that well. xx**

A sliver of guilt crept across my skin. There was no good reason I hadn't told her or anyone that I'd hung out with Guy. Nothing had ever happened. It just felt like the wrong time to mention it with everything Shannen and Cal had been going through back then.

Thinking practically, it made sense to go with Guy. When we were doing stuff as a group in Cornwall, we'd probably travel in as few cars as possible anyway. Worst case scenario, I could find a nearby bus route if I wanted to go somewhere on my own.

Me: **Tell him yes please. It'll be more fun than driving solo! xx**

My phone buzzed again right away.

Shannen: **Okay. He says he'll text you later to sort out what time to leave. So excited!! xx**

I chuckled. This would be a fun week. The start of a summer of friendship and good times. And maybe, if I was lucky, I'd have a chance to get to know Guy a little better.

Chapter 2

Guy

I LOOKED AROUND MY flat one more time to ensure everything was switched off, the doors were closed, and then double-checked my pockets to ensure my phone, wallet, and keys were in there.

I was actually going to miss the place. I'd moved into the flat I'd bought for Cal to rent from me the second he and Aiden had moved into Shannen's apartment. I'd lived in a three-bedroom house for the past eight years, but once I was the only one there, I didn't need that much space. I never had, really. It had seemed like a smart investment for the future, but the future I'd imagined had gone to shit at the beginning of the year, and I wanted out. Shortly after, Shannen and Cal had made an offer to buy my house without me having to put it on the market, and we were just finishing off the decorating before they moved in.

With a final glance back, I picked up the bag I'd packed to take to Cornwall for the week and headed out of the apartment to pick Gaby up.

It had been a while since I'd seen her, and over the last week or so, she'd been creeping into my thoughts more and more. Maybe it was because I knew I'd be seeing her soon, or perhaps because I'd missed hanging out with her. Not that we had done that often. Most of our communication had been via texts and calls, and when it stopped, I didn't know if it was because she didn't want to talk anymore, or if we'd just reached a natural ending point and neither of us had picked it back up again.

Maybe you should ask her out on an actual date.

Had enough time passed now that I could do that without feeling like I was cheating on my ex?

Helen and I had split up almost six months ago, after almost seven years together, so being alone, even if it was for the best, was strange at first, but I was finally through the worst of it. Maybe not ready to start seeing someone new, but I wasn't going to close myself off to the possibility, either.

When I pulled up in front of Gaby's apartment building, she was already waiting outside for me.

Along with a gigantic suitcase and two smaller bags, as well as a handbag slung over her arm.

She looked incredible, even dressed casually. She wore a denim skirt that stopped at the mid-point of her thighs, showing off her long, toned legs. She had a pair of simple white slip-on sandals on her feet, and her toenails were painted a soft pink. Her blonde hair was tied back in a loose ponytail, and her top half was covered by a grey vest top.

I was already laughing at the amount of luggage she toted as I got out of the car. "You know we're only going for a week, right?"

She gave a slightly sheepish grin. "Listen, a girl needs the essentials when she goes away. And this is all essential."

I continued to chuckle as I rounded the back of the car to open the boot, where I held out my arms in the manner of Will Smith presenting his wife at an awards ceremony, indicating my solitary bag. "Essentials."

With a roll of her eyes, Gaby picked up her two smaller bags and walked towards me. "Men don't need makeup, hairdryers, hair straighteners, hair curlers... and lots of other hair things. A couple of changes of underwear and shirts, some deodorant, and you're set."

I lifted one of her bags into the boot and then over into the back seat while she did the other. "I'll have you know I change my underwear every day."

Gaby snorted. "Still, underwear doesn't take up much room. I *need* everything I've brought with me."

My eyes studied her face for a moment. Didn't look to me like she had much makeup on right then. She had the most intense green eyes, full lips, and her skin was so smooth she looked like she'd been Photoshopped.

"You don't need makeup," I told her. "And your hair is fine as it is." Her cheeks flushed a little, and her shy smile at my words made me smile too. "Get in the car. I'll get your case."

"Thanks," she said, glancing up at me for a second before going to the passenger side to get in while I picked up the last of her luggage.

Once it was secured in the boot, I jumped back into the car and put my seatbelt on. I turned my head to look at Gaby, who had already taken off her sandals, her feet resting on top of them. Considering we hadn't had much contact in a while, she looked totally relaxed in my company, with one ankle crossed over the other, her smile still in place. For a second, I was slightly blinded by how good she looked with the sun beaming in through the window, illuminating her.

Shaking my head so I stopped staring, I said, "I thought we could drive for an hour, then find the nearest service station and get some coffee and something to eat before going the rest of the way."

"Sounds good to me," Gaby answered, then pressed the button on the passenger door to open her window. "Let's do this!"

Seven hours later, everyone was together in the place Donovan had booked for us, and I was still a bit in awe. The lodge we were currently lounging around had four bedrooms, two of them with ensuite bathrooms. The living area housed three large sofas in a horseshoe shape, facing a gigantic television. The design of the lodge was light and inviting, the kitchen big enough for four or five people to easily move around in. We also had a huge deck with sun loungers and a hot tub, and the main bathroom had a jacuzzi bathtub, a double shower, and a load of fancy-looking toiletries. While there were other lodges around, there was a pretty big distance between them, so it felt private. On the way into the resort, we'd driven down a long, winding lane, and there were small, wooded areas which looked like places people could walk around. We also passed what we later found out was the bar and entertainment area, plus the gym, and a few of the outdoor activities like tennis and badminton. There was a pool and spa somewhere around too.

And we were there for free.

Nova, Donovan, and Shannen had gone out shopping for food earlier. We'd all pooled our money to buy everything we would need for the week, and they came back with more than necessary, but at least we wouldn't go hungry. Nova and Donovan cooked for us; they'd made a Chinese feast that would have made our local takeaways jealous. Now, we were all suitably stuffed and sitting around, chatting in the living area.

Aiden sat on the floor, playing on his iPad, Shannen and Cal were on the sofa behind him, Nova and Donovan were on the sofa in the middle near the sliding doors that led to the deck, and Gaby and I sat at opposite ends of the sofa across from Shannen and Cal.

I glanced sideways at Gaby, but she wasn't looking at me. She had her feet tucked under her, chatting with the others about plans for the next few days.

Our road trip had reminded me how much I enjoyed her company, and even though I didn't offer her a lift to Cornwall so I could make a move, I couldn't deny my attraction to her.

Cut it out. This isn't why you came here.

Dragging my gaze away with a sigh, I put my focus back on the conversation, although there was a slight lull now.

Maybe this is my chance.

I had been waiting for an opportunity all day to share some news. Since splitting from Helen, I'd thought about what I wanted my life to look like, and moving out of my house was step one. I had a successful business, and I still wanted to have a family one day, but while I waited for that to fall into place, I needed a focus. And it had appeared to me almost accidentally. I wouldn't say I acted on a whim exactly, but I'd taken a big risk a few months back, and only now was I in a position to tell people about it. Now the keys were firmly in my hands.

"Are you okay?" Shannen asked. I hadn't noticed her eyeing me from across the room, a look of amusement on her face. Christ only knew what my expression had showed.

Suddenly, everyone's eyes were on me, and I nodded. "Yeah, I just... there's something I've been wanting to tell you all, and I've been waiting for the right time, but..." I paused, glancing around the room. "I guess that's now."

Cal's dark brows furrowed, concern on his face. "What's going on?"

I grinned at my mate. "This will interest you. I have a proposition for you too."

There was a strange change in the atmosphere of the room, like I'd got everyone's interest now, and it made the whole thing feel much more real.

"Okay," I said, taking a breath. "So, you all know that I run Hue Got It, and it's going well. We've had consistent work for years now, and while I still love it and plan to keep it going, I needed a new challenge."

Shannen and Cal exchanged a curious look, and I could feel Gaby's eyes burning into the side of my head. Nova and Donovan, who I knew the least well out of everyone, simply sat waiting patiently.

"I bought a bar," I blurted out, glad to finally speak to someone about it who wasn't an estate agent or a solicitor. "It's in a bit of a mess, though not so much that it'll cost a fortune to fix up. I spent a long time weighing up the costs, but if I fix it up right, then I'll be able to sell it on for a lot more than I paid for it. So, I'm going to hire some people in to help with the things I can't do, which isn't that much." I looked at Cal. "And I want you to help me. I figured, with the baby coming, it'll be easier for you to always be in the same place, plus you will always know what hours you're working, and you'll be able to get away fairly easily if you need to."

Cal stared at me for a moment before his face broke into a grin. "You mean, no more painting for people who can't decide what the hell they want?"

I laughed. "Yeah. For a while, anyway. If we focus and get the right people in, it could be ready by Christmas, and if things get quieter in the main business, I can get our guys to chip in."

"I'm in," Cal said, and Shannen smiled.

"This is amazing, Guy," she said. "It'll be great for you."

I smiled back at her. "Yeah, I think so. I know exactly what I want to do with it too. It's a good space, mostly open-plan, and there is a lot of backroom space that could be turned into a kitchen if the new owner wanted to. Equally, though, it would work fine just as a bar. It's near the university, so students will probably use it more than anyone."

"Sounds great," Donovan chipped in, and I looked over at him. His large frame had straightened slightly with his interest, and he ran his fingers across his short beard. "Can I have a look at it before Nova and I leave for the Philippines?"

I nodded, surprised. "Sure. You planning to become a bar owner?"

He laughed, though Nova offered him a questioning look. "No. That's more work than I can handle. Plus, I have a lot of commitments to fulfil in the next year or so. But I'd love to see the space."

Nova's face fell slightly at his words, and I felt a bit bad for her. They hadn't even been together for a year, and for most of it, they had been at opposite ends of the world. Maybe one day, Donovan would settle down in the UK, but it was clear he loved travelling and was in no rush to stop anytime soon.

"I'd love for anyone who wants to see it to come and have a look," I said, glancing around at everyone.

When I reached Gaby, I saw she was also smiling. "That's why you wanted my brother's law firm details."

"Yup." Gavin Davis did a great job of representing Cal a few months ago when he'd been wrongfully arrested, so I wanted to see if he had someone in his firm who could help me with the things I needed to know. "Without their help, I'd still be stressed out."

She chuckled. "My brother has a brilliant team. I'm glad he could help. And if you do decide to keep the bar and want some help creating cocktails, I'm your girl!" Her eyes lit up at the idea of compiling a drinks menu.

I shook my head. "I'm not keeping it. Running a bar is way too complicated." There was a moment when I saw myself owning the place, standing behind the bar and chatting as customers came in in droves. But while I had plenty of experience of running a business, I had zero clue how to manage a bar, and juggling two lots of books and employees, plus all of the learning I'd have to do to make it work was more than I wanted to take on. I'd bought it solely to revamp and make a profit.

Gaby shrugged. "Fair enough. But I'd like to take a look too."

"Of course. We'll figure something out for us all to see the place."

"Speaking of drinks," Gaby said, standing and bouncing on her toes as she grinned. "Shall we crack into the wine and go sit out on the deck for a bit? Seems a shame to waste such a nice evening indoors."

Shannen smiled at her friend, a hand on her baby bump. "I'll join you on the deck. If I can haul my ass off this sofa."

The rest of us nodded in agreement, and as everyone shuffled around, some heading outside and some helping to carry glasses, snacks, and the wine from the kitchen, I couldn't help thinking this felt like the start of a great summer.

⤌⤏

Nova and Donovan seemed to have taken on the role of designated chefs, and I woke up on Sunday morning to the smell of bacon, eggs, and mushrooms. When I'd thrown on a T-shirt and a pair of shorts and headed out to the main living area, my eyes widened. They'd laid up the table like an all-you-can-eat buffet. There were plates of every breakfast food imaginable, including pancakes, waffles, toast, pastries, and cereals.

No wonder they'd brought so many shopping bags back with them yesterday. This breakfast alone must have accounted for most of it.

"Are you planning to open a B&B at some point?" I asked, staring at the spread with wide eyes. "You could make a fortune."

"I love cooking," Nova said with a smile as she added various condiments to the table. "And since it's our first morning, I thought we'd go all out. Don't expect it every day, though." She giggled, and I shook my head, amused.

Just then, one of the bedroom doors opened and Aiden walked into the room in his favourite Toy Story pyjamas, rubbing his eyes. "What smells nice?"

"Nova made... everything," I said, reaching out my arm towards him. "Come and sit down."

Never one to decline the offer of food, Aiden rushed across the room and hopped up onto a seat at the table. He turned his head to look at Nova, his eyes as wide as mine had just been. "I can have whatever I want?"

She glanced at me for confirmation, and I nodded. He didn't have any allergies to worry about, and he had so much energy, he burned off any excess food he ate. "Yes," she said. "Would you like some orange juice?"

"Yes, please!" Aiden swivelled back towards the table, glancing at the food laid out before him.

"What would you like?" I asked him, picking up a plate for him.

"Pancakes, bacon, and syrup, please!" he practically shouted with glee.

I passed the syrup to him before stacking up a couple of pancakes and some bacon on the plate. As I placed it in front of him, I heard another door open and glanced behind me to see Gaby padding barefoot across the room.

Fucking hell.

She was wearing an oversized white T-shirt that hung over the tops of her thighs, and a pair of light blue sleep shorts that ended slightly above her knees. Her blonde hair was tousled in a way that looked like she'd been tossing and turning all night, and it put a whole other idea in my head that it took me a minute to shift.

"Morning," I said, trying to stop imagining her underneath me, with me messing up her hair in a different way.

Her eyes fell on me, and she ran them slowly down my body before looking back up at my face, blinking. "Hi." She shook her head, her hair falling in front of her face as she walked closer to the table, and I tried to conceal a grin.

Did she just check me out?

"Who wants hot drinks?" Donovan asked from the kitchen area.

"Coffee, please," Gaby and I said in unison. We looked at each other again, and she gave a small smile as she sat down next to Aiden.

"Morning, kiddo," she said to him, reaching for a plate as I took a seat too. "Are you looking forward to spending the day with me?"

Lucky kid.

I tuned out their conversation as I piled my plate with food. Gaby had planned to watch Aiden for the day and night so Shannen and Cal could have some time alone. They needed this, and Gaby had offered to entertain Aiden while they were gone. Nova and Donovan were planning to stay in and around Penzance for the day, and I hadn't decided what to do yet. I'd scoped out places to go before I left home, but I wasn't against staying in the lodge for the day, maybe heading to the gym or for a swim.

"Guy?" Gaby's voice broke through my thoughts, and I turned my head to look at her. "I was thinking of taking Aiden swimming in the pool here. Do you want to join us?"

"Did he tell you he can't swim?" I asked.

Gaby smiled. "Yes, but we can still play in the pool for a while."

I paused since their plans somewhat matched mine. "If you want, we can go somewhere in the car. There's a lot to do around here."

"Can we go to the beach?" Aiden asked, hacking into his pancakes with a fork.

I glanced at Gaby with a raised eyebrow. From the sun streaming in through the glass doors, it looked like the ideal weather for a beach trip, and if we did that, there would be some level of swimming or paddling involved. We'd have to make sure we had some sunblock for Aiden, but if Cal hadn't brought any, it would be easy enough to find some.

I wasn't sure how I'd handle seeing Gaby in a swimsuit, though.

The thought made me choke on the mouthful of toast I'd just scooped up from the table, and Gaby laughed.

"Do we need to get you a bucket and spade?" she asked with a grin, mistaking the reason for my 'excitement'.

With a cool nod, I said, "Actually, yeah. I'd like that." She rolled her eyes, still smiling. "Beach day, it is!"

Chapter 3

Gaby

AFTER THE BEST BREAKFAST I'd had in a long time, I got dressed, ready for a day at the beach. Even though it was only half past ten, it was already scorching outside, and thankfully, Shannen and Cal had the foresight to bring sunscreen for Aiden, just in case. As a realist, I wasn't expecting it to be quite so hot.

I left my room wearing a jade green halterneck bikini with high cups on my top half, and a pair of high-waisted short-ish denim shorts with my bikini bottoms underneath, though they were also more like shorts than regular bikini bottoms. I'd also tied a long-sleeved green and black checked shirt around my waist in case it got cooler later. I had a small handbag over my shoulder containing my phone and my key for the lodge, and as I walked across to the kitchen area, Shannen slathered Aiden in a layer of sunscreen. He already had a pretty good tan, and he looked so cute in his white shorts and a Newcastle United football shirt.

"Aiden, are you sure you don't want to wear something cooler?" Shannen asked him, putting the cap back on the bottle and handing it to me, and I secured it in my bag. "You're going to cook in that."

He shook his head. "I can take it off if I get too hot." He looked up at her with a grin, and she shook her head. "Fine. Make sure you drink lots of water and do as Gaby and Guy tell you."

Guy must have told her we were all going out together, but he was nowhere to be seen. In fact, the three of us were the only ones in sight.

"Where is everyone?" I asked, looking around as Aiden ran off to put on a pair of flip-flops.

"Nova and Donovan have already gone out, Guy is outside loading the car up with bottles of water, and Cal is getting ready."

"Are you looking forward to today?" I asked, and she smiled.

"Yeah. It'll be nice to have a bit of time to ourselves. I can't wait." She reached forward and gave me a hug. "Thank you for watching Aiden. We really appreciate it."

"I know." I hugged her back, her ever-growing baby bump pressing against me. "Be careful out there today. Stay in the shade."

She chuckled. "Yes, Mum."

I poked my tongue out at her as Cal came out of his and Shannen's room. Shannen's eyes lit up as he approached, and when I looked back at him, his eyes were the same as they fell on her.

Man, they're a good-looking couple.

"Right then," I said, clapping my hands together, a weird habit that stemmed from having to round up a class of thirty kids on a regular basis. "Are you ready to go, Aiden?"

"Yup," he called out, rushing back towards us and wrapping his arms around Shannen and Cal's legs.

Cal reached down and ruffled his hair. "Be good," he said. "Me and Shannen are going to be gone until tomorrow morning, but we'll be home early. I'll ring you later, though, okay?"

Aiden nodded and smiled up at Shannen and Cal. "Okay. See you to-morrow!"

"Come on, then," I said, holding my hand out for him to hold. "Let's go and find Guy and we'll go on our own adventure."

He beamed at me as he walked over to take my hand. I looked back at Shannen and Cal. "Have a good time today, and we'll see you in the morning."

They both said goodbye, and Aiden offered them a wave before we headed out to the car, where Guy was shutting the boot.

When his eyes fell on me, they widened slightly as his gaze dropped to my legs then back up to my face before swallowing hard. I bit my lip to stop myself from smiling at the fact that he was checking me out. I couldn't keep from doing the same to him. He was absolutely gorgeous with his short honey-blonde hair and blue eyes. He was the only person I knew who looked like he worked out as hard as I did. His knee-length shorts allowed me to see how strong his calves were, and while his grey T-shirt wasn't designed to cling to his body, his arms were bulky enough to make it happen anyway.

If he takes that off later, I am so screwed.

Shaking my thoughts away, Aiden and I walked closer. "Are we good to go?" I asked.

Guy nodded. "Yeah. I already said bye to Shannen and Cal. I checked where the nearest supermarket is, so I thought we could go there and get some stuff for lunch, and then head to Godrevy."

I furrowed a brow. "What's there?"

I knew a few places in Cornwall, but that wasn't one of them. I'd been to Newquay, and I'd been to Penzance before too. Both places were super cool and had lots of things to do, but I wasn't sure about Godrevy.

Guy grinned. "Godrevy is a National Trust area, and there's a beach, and a lighthouse, and a cafe that does really nice food. Although, if we take a picnic, we won't need that part."

I grinned. "Can we go to the lighthouse?"

Guy shook his head. "Sadly not. It's not reachable, but the views are incredible. I figure we can hang out there for a couple of hours and then we could come back and use the facilities here."

I nodded. "Sounds like a plan!"

⁂

Within an hour, we had got our picnic and packed it into the car. We'd also remembered to get buckets and spades and a cheap football in case there was space to have a kick around on the beach.

Godrevy was stunning. The beach was busy, the sea full of surfers of all ages and abilities. The backdrop of the lighthouse perched on a tiny island in the sea took my breath, and as I sat on my towel in the sand, the hot sun beating down on me, I was pretty sure I was in heaven.

Guy sat on his own towel beside me, shirt still on and sunglasses covering his eyes as he helped Aiden build a sandcastle. As a fully grown adult, it only made sense to me to get my own bucket and spade so I could play too.

This was my summer holiday, and I was going to have as much silly fun as I could.

"When I went to the beach with Donovan and Nova before, we looked for shells and pebbles," Aiden said as he heaped sand into his castle-shaped bucket. "Can we do that today too?"

"Sure," Guy said. "We can use them to decorate the castle."

I smirked. "On holiday and still thinking about decorating, huh?"

Turning his head, Guy grinned at me with a smile that highlighted exactly how beautiful his face was. "It's hard to turn that side of my brain off. At least I don't have to do any painting today, though."

He turned back to Aiden, and I watched as Guy helped him pack the sand into the bucket and then carefully turn it over to make the first bit of the sandcastle.

A small sigh left my lips. The wistful kind, and I hated how quickly my mind had flicked.

In a different life, I could have been sitting on a beach with my own kid, playing in the sand, thinking about what a great summer we were going to have together. My choices, though, had meant that wasn't the case.

Would never be the case.

I'd chosen to have a termination in my final year of university after a very unexpected pregnancy, thinking it wasn't the right time to have a baby, especially with the man I was with then. I told myself it was 'sensible' because I was getting ready to graduate, had my whole life ahead of me, but that wasn't really it. My ex was toxic, and even before he reached his most disturbing, violent point, I was already firmly under his thumb. I could never have raised a child *with* him, but he'd conditioned me to doubt my own ability to do anything, let alone raise a child by myself. At the time, I'd been so messed up that I'd been unable to see another option.

There hadn't been a single day of my life since I'd made the decision to end my pregnancy that I didn't feel guilty about it. It was more than ten years ago, yet it still weighed on me. Years of counselling had made it just about manageable to live with, but even after so long, I still sometimes berated myself, wondered how different my life would have been if I'd taken another path. Maybe I would have lived in a different place. Chosen a different career that would have made being a mum easier. Maybe I would have met someone to share my life with.

Guy, however, would one day make an amazing father. The way he guided Aiden and the banter between them was adorable. I had seen him around Aiden before, and each time, it struck me how fatherly he was. Probably because he had been there for a lot of Aiden's life and they had a good bond. But it wasn't just that. From what I'd learned about Guy, I

19

knew he was a good person. He was a hard worker, loyal, and one of the most physically attractive humans I had ever seen, and fun too. The whole package.

You, however, are not *the full package.*

I rolled my shoulders, shifting uncomfortably.

You are *the full package. There may be a couple of pieces missing, but that doesn't affect your value as a person. As a woman.*

In order to stop myself before I could let my head take over, I leaned forward, running my fingers through the warm sand. At the exact same moment, now Aiden had got to grips with what to do, Guy shuffled back, and I could feel his eyes on me.

"You okay, Gabs?"

His use of the nickname my friends used for me sent a tiny thrill through me. And the fact that he had sensed my change in mood only enhanced my feeling that it would be good to have him in my life. Within the short time I'd known him, he'd often noticed the tiny things about me that most people didn't see. That was useful because if I wasn't called on it, I wouldn't bring it up.

And there was no denying that there were times I needed to talk about things.

I glanced at him from the corner of my eye and nodded. "I am. I was just wondering if it's too late to become a mermaid so I can swim out to that lighthouse and have a look around."

It wasn't an absolute lie. If I had the ability to encase my feet into a tail, I would have.

Guy laughed, but I also got the impression from the way his shoulders loosened that he might not have believed me, but he wasn't going to push it. "Did you have dreams of being Ariel as a kid?"

"Oh, yeah." I nodded solemnly. "I also think having animals as sidekicks would be great."

"I want a monkey," Aiden piped up, shovelling more sand into his bucket. "My dad says we can't, so I asked him for a dog. Then he asked me what kind of monkey I wanted." He looked up at us, his brow furrowed. "But I don't know why he said that because I think a dog would be much easier to look after apart from having to clean up their poop."

Guy and I looked at each other and burst out laughing.

"Maybe when you move house, you can have a dog," Guy said. "There's no room at the flat."

Aiden shook his head. "Dad and Shannen said maybe one day, but not until the baby is a bit older."

"Are you looking forward to having a new brother or sister?" I asked him, moving the sand in front of me into a small pile.

He twisted his lips to the side as if thinking. "Maybe. Dad says that if I have a brother, then I can teach him how to play football, but then Shannen said that I could also teach a sister, but I would be afraid I might hurt a girl if I kicked a ball at her head."

"Girls can be pretty tough," I said. "Though I wouldn't recommend kicking a ball at anyone's head."

"But what if we're practising headers?"

Guy snorted. "It'll be a few years before you'll be able to do that anyway. For a long time, the baby won't be able to do very much."

"Yeah," Aiden said. "I hope Dad and Shannen will still play with me as much when the baby comes."

My heart.

Shannen had told me Aiden had expressed these concerns to her before, and to Cal too. I figured until the baby arrived and he could see for himself, it would be hard for him to believe that things wouldn't change in that area. They might get less time all together with him sometimes perhaps, as they would both need to get their rest with a newborn, but Shannen loved that boy with every breath in her body and she would never stop spending time with him.

"They will," Guy said, ruffling Aiden's hair. "When the baby first comes, it'll probably sleep a lot."

"And cry a lot," Aiden said, scooping more sand into his bucket. "Aria and Avery said their baby brother cries all night and all day."

"Not all babies cry that much," I told him, pushing my pile of sand towards him, which he quickly dug into. "I bet you'll be a really good big brother."

Aiden stopped shovelling and looked up at me. "Do you think so?"

"Of course," I told him with a smile. "You can teach them all about *Toy Story* and *The Brave Little Toaster* and show them how to build a sandcastle."

He nodded enthusiastically. "Yeah, and when the baby is really little, maybe I can hold them and make them feel better if they get sad."

Exchanging a smile with Guy at how cute Aiden was being, I said, "I'm sure you'll be able to do that. See? It's going to be lots of fun."

Aiden nodded again, a big smile on his face. "Yeah, it is." Dropping his spade down, he said, "Guy, can we play football now?"

Now his concerns had been settled, Aiden was ready to get moving again, and Guy said, "Sure, buddy. Do you think Gaby will look after your sandcastle while we're gone?"

Aiden looked at me expectantly, and I laughed. "Yes, I can look after it for you. I might even make one too!"

# Chapter 4

Guy

I SHOOK MY HEAD in amusement as Aiden handed me my phone and shot back outside the lodge, where a fairly intense water balloon fight was happening. Cal and Shannen had just called to check on Aiden, and while I knew he missed them, he was also eager to get back outside and have fun.

I left my phone on the coffee table, knowing it would get soaked if the water fight continued as it had been, and went outside to join the others. Instead of getting right back into the midst of it, I watched for a moment, smiling at the scene in front of me. Aiden was giggling so much he could barely hold his water balloon steady as he crept up behind Nova. Moments ago, he initiated a sneak attack on Gaby while she'd been quietly reading a magazine on one of the loungers, and the scream she let out made Aiden and me fall to the ground, laughing.

Seeing Aiden like that, no cares in the world, was pretty new. That kid had always had so many things he kept inside, so many feelings and fears, that even when he was having a good day, it seemed to drag him down. Over the past few weeks, he'd lightened up more and more, coinciding with Cal also slowly letting go of some of his own baggage.

For the first time in years, I saw him and Aiden changing. It was especially noticeable in Aiden, though. He smiled so much more now. He had friends, and he got in far less trouble at school. Football had become a big thing in his life too, but more than anything, he finally had stability. This was the first time he'd been on holiday, and he was definitely making the most of it.

"Are you hiding, you big wuss?" Gaby shouted to me from her position behind the hot tub. She crouched, her head peering over the top to look for anyone coming for her. She'd tied her hair back in a high ponytail, but a few strands had fallen out around her face. She smirked at me, her green eyes holding a challenge.

"You're one to talk," I said, stepping out onto the deck. On the grass around the decked area, Aiden, Nova, and Donovan were locked in a stare-out, each of them watching the others to see who would make the next move. A bucket full of water balloons sat by the steps that led down to the grass, and I picked one up and slowly walked towards Gaby.

She held her hands up as I approached. "Wait, I'm unarmed!" she said, straightening up and backing away around the hot tub.

"You should have thought of that before you provoked me." I smirked in return, and her eyes widened as I picked up my pace towards her.

"Would you really soak an innocent woman?" she asked, lowering her hands and fixing me with puppy dog eyes. However, behind the facade, amusement shone through, and I laughed as she continued to back away, both of us now circling the hot tub.

"Innocent?" I asked, shaking my head. "I'm not buying that."

"Yeah, you shouldn't."

Before I could react, she darted back the way she'd come, bent down, and then launched a water balloon at me. It hit me on the shoulder, cold water exploding down my arm and across my chest.

"Argh!" I shouted, her laughter as she ran past me to grab another balloon the only thing I could focus on. I launched my balloon at her and caught her bare feet, making her squeal as she took cover behind my car.

I whipped my wet T-shirt off over my head and dropped it on the deck before taking another balloon and gunning for her again.

Gaby shrieked as she saw me coming, and this time, she wasn't fast enough to get away. As my next balloon hit her ass—not my intended target but still where it landed—she cried out. As she ran, though, she slipped, landing on the grass and on top of the balloon she was holding so it burst all over her front.

"Shit," she said, though she was still laughing as she got to her feet, wiping her hands on her skirt. Behind us, I heard more screams and shouts, where the others had clearly broken their stalemate, but my focus remained on Gaby.

"Are you okay?" I asked her, though I couldn't stop myself from laughing. The vision of my water balloon hitting her arse and then her toppling forward and effectively soaking herself through was like a scene from a comedy sketch.

"Yeah," she said, mock scowling at me. "No thanks to you."

The strangest urge to pull her into my arms hit me, and I had to stop myself. However, looking at the way her wet, green bikini clung to her top half, her nipples peaking from the cold, made it difficult.

Shit. Stop looking at her nipples, you fucking pervert!

I blinked quickly, but apparently, I didn't need to worry because her eyes were fixated on my chest, as if she'd only just realised I'd taken my shirt off. She swallowed as she lifted her head to look at me, and I tried to conceal a grin.

I'd spent most of the day with her trying to figure out whether there was any potential for me to ask her out. Whether she saw me as anything other than a friend. I also didn't want to make things awkward. We were going to be in fairly close proximity for the next week, so I didn't want to ask her out if she wasn't interested and make her and maybe everyone else uncomfortable.

"Hey," I said, attempting to break the rising tension between us, "you were the one who baited me into this. You have nobody to blame but yourself!"

"Oh, is that so?" Gaby quirked an eyebrow, and I tried to keep my eyes on her face.

"Yup. That."

Tilting her head to the side, she shrugged with fake nonchalance. "Okay. Well, I guess I'll have to take my punishment."

I closed my eyes for a second as my dick stirred, and I willed it to calm down because there would be little way to hide a boner in the shorts I was wearing.

Licking her lower lip slowly as if she knew exactly what she'd just said, she grinned and began to walk past me, back towards the lodge and the rest of the water fight, which was still in full swing. I kept my eyes on her as she walked away, slightly mesmerised by those toned legs again. She had the most incredible figure, but she never showed it off. She wore clothes that looked good on her, but she never seemed to wear anything that emphasised how fit she was. She didn't need to. Gaby oozed sexiness just by being herself.

"Guy!" Aiden shouted, and I focused my gaze on him. "Help!"

Gaby grabbed a water balloon and ran towards him with it while he charged at me, grabbing onto my leg as he swung around behind me to hide as Gaby yeeted her water balloon. Instead of hitting Aiden, who was safely behind me, the balloon hit me square in the nuts. The impact plus the cold water made me shout out, and I doubled over before hitting the ground. Gaby covered her mouth with her hands, her eyes wide, but a laugh spilled out of her. Aiden had fallen onto the grass too, lying on his back with his hands on his stomach, giggling.

"Are you okay?" Gaby asked, repeating the question I'd asked her only a few minutes before. She kept a distance, tears of amusement streaming down her face, and Nova and Donovan paused their own water fight to join us.

"What happened?" Donovan asked, and I curled up in a ball dramatically.

"She's evil." I pointed at Gaby. "I think I just lost a testicle!"

As Nova took in how much Gaby and Aiden were laughing, she joined in too. "Unlucky," she said. "I'd ask if you need some ice, but the... *area* is probably cold enough already."

"Any comments about the cold and dick size and I'm out of here," I said, laughing as I pulled myself up to my feet, then reached down for Aiden's hand to lift him back up too.

He jumped up and ran back to the bucket of water balloons as I shook myself off. "We really should have filmed this for Cal and Shannen to watch when they get back," I said. Aiden had hung up the phone before I could say goodbye to them, but I knew hearing how much fun we were having would make them wish they were with us.

"We'll just have another water balloon fight sometime during the week," Nova said.

"Any chance to hit you in the nutsack sounds good to me," Gaby added with a wink as she let her hair down from her ponytail and shook it out. The wet strands hung around her shoulders, and she combed her fingers through them.

"Okay, I've had enough of you today," I said, glowering at her, but my lips still turned up at the corners.

"Never," Gaby said. She lifted her skirt a bit, walked around behind me, then placed her hands on my shoulders and jumped up on my back, her legs wrapping around my hips and her arms around my neck. Instinctively, I moved my arms back, supporting her thighs in the unexpected piggyback.

"You said you wanted to spend the day with me and Aiden, so you're going to have to see it through!"

I glanced sideways at Nova and Donovan, and Donovan wiggled his eyebrows at me, while Nova giggled, totally used to Gaby's wild side.

"I mean... I could just drop you," I pointed out.

The feel of her pressed up against me, her hands on my skin, meant there was no way I was going to, but I couldn't resist messing with her since she had just mounted me without invitation.

Not that she needed one.

Before she could answer, I started to run towards the lodge, and she screamed at the speed I'd suddenly moved at. She clung to me tighter, and I sped through the doors, swinging around quickly and dropping her on one of the couches.

I turned around to her with a grin, and she lay on her back, laughing as I sat down on the coffee table. Her green eyes were bright and her cheeks pink.

"All right, you win," Gaby said. "I release you from your day with me." She smiled up at me, but I shook my head.

"Nah, I've re-thought things, and I've decided I'll see it through."

"You changed your mind in the last ten seconds?"

"Yup. We're going to eat together, hang out with Aiden a bit before he goes to bed, maybe read him a bedtime story, and then... I guess we'll see what Nova and Donovan are doing."

I heard the words I'd just said and realised that, although it wasn't intentional, I'd had the perfect family day with Gaby.

Memories of days like that with Helen flicked through my head. She and I had had a lot of fun times with Aiden. Very few days out, but we'd taken him to the beach once or twice, and we'd taken him shopping and out for food. When the three of us went out together, it really reinforced how much I wanted a family. How much *we* wanted a family. I just didn't want it as badly as Helen... or so she said before she walked out.

That wasn't true, though. I just didn't want to be used as a personal sperm bank that she could take deposits from when it suited her. She made sex a chore, and she was so on edge all the time that the more she wanted it, the less I did. No matter how much I tried to make the relationship fun again, she wasn't interested. I'd tried so damn hard to be there for her when she needed me. Instead of letting me, she used me as her verbal punchbag until it reached the point where I stopped trying.

I still wanted a family one day, but because there had been so much pressure from Helen for so long, I was in no rush now.

Was six months after a break-up too soon to want to try being with someone new? I was over my time with Helen, but maybe not all the way over how she treated me and the things she'd spat at me when she left. They still crossed my mind occasionally, but it was getting less.

Gaby carefully rose into a sitting position, then moved from the couch to sit next to me on the coffee table. From the way she rubbed her hands down the back of her skirt, I figured she was worried about making the sofa wet.

"I don't like how serious your face just went," she said, though her words were light. She wasn't berating me, just trying to bring me back to the good time we'd been having. "Surely the idea of spending the rest of the day with me isn't that bad."

"Sorry," I said, pushing a hand through my hair. "It's not bad at all."

She smiled. "We're on holiday, Guy. This is when we take a break from real life and just exist. No work. No drama. No overthinking. The only thing we're doing this week is whatever the hell we want to."

I wondered if she'd still feel that way if she knew the thing I wanted to do the most was be around her. The way her eyes lingered on my chest again told me that she might.

Aloud, I said, "You're right." I could almost feel my eyes light up as I added, "In that case, there is a bucket of water balloons outside, and some of them still have our names on them!"

Chapter 5

Gaby

THE FEW TIMES WE'D all sat around together as a group at the lodge, we'd found our own designated seats. Nova and Donovan on one sofa, Cal, Shannen, and Aiden on another, and Guy and me on the third. The difference was, the couples sat snuggled close, and Guy and I sat at opposite ends of our couch.

The evening of the water balloon fight was no different. Nova, Donovan, Guy, and I were in the large living area in our usual seats, watching some random thriller movie since Aiden had gone to bed. Essentially, we were having an adult sleepover, as we'd all changed into our bedtime wear. I presumed that what we wore wasn't everyone's typical sleepwear; mine wasn't. I usually slept only in my underwear, but that wasn't appropriate around so many other people, so Shannen, Nova, and I had gone shopping and bought some semi-matching summer PJs. Mine consisted of a pair of white shorts with tiny strawberries on them, and a long vest top with thick straps that had a large picture of a strawberry on the top. Nova's set was blue with blackberries on, and Shannen's were yellow with a banana on the front. Donovan wore a baggy white T-shirt over a pair of long grey shorts, and Guy... was a gigantic distraction. He was also wearing shorts, black ones, and his hair was still a little damp, as he'd taken a shower shortly before the movie. He'd thrown on a Newcastle United football shirt too, and for some reason, that made him look more attractive than ever. He had the right stature to be a footballer; tall, lean, but super muscular.

I didn't even watch football, but seeing him in that shirt tempted me.

If it was only about his looks, I could probably have handled being around him. But we'd had the best time together that day. I couldn't remember the last time I'd been around a man for so long and hadn't found myself drained at the end of it. I was tired, sure, but the good kind. From the sea air and the amount of laughing and playing, not because I'd used all my energy looking out for red flags. Most of the men I'd been on dates with had waved their red flags around openly, and the ones I'd had more than one date with... I'd always got a feeling deep inside that they weren't the kind of men I could depend on or trust with all of my baggage.

Guy felt different. Probably because he was never a date, so I'd never had to try to hold anything back. I wasn't scoping him out to see if he could handle my leftover trauma. Not that there was much left, but enough that it was always a consideration.

The part of my brain that had begun to look at him as a friend, and maybe something more, had marked him as 'safe'. Not safe as in boring. Safe as in he wouldn't rip my heart out of my chest and kick it around until it ceased to work.

And *that* was dangerous. That meant that I might want to dip my toes into dating again. I hadn't done so in around eight months after all the ridiculous fiascos I'd gotten into with men I'd met on dating apps, or the occasional guy at the gym or on a night out.

The thought caused my stomach to tighten, but I shrugged it away. No point in stressing about things that might never be an issue because he might not even be interested in me.

Except, I was beginning to think he might be.

You are thirty-five years old, Gabriella. Stop acting like a highschooler. What happened to no fear, no stress?

That was one of many mantras I'd created for myself while going through therapy after my last long-term relationship, which had destroyed both my mind and my body. I had sworn to myself that nobody would ever take away my voice or my dignity again. That if I wanted something, after being stifled for years, I would go for it. That I would never have anyone tell me to squash down my wild side. If I wanted to dance on a table, I would. If I wanted to take a second out of my day to tell another woman that her outfit was badass, I would. If I wanted to dress up like a cowgirl for a night out, I would do that too, because I lived life on my terms now.

So, why was I causing myself so much confusion about what I wanted with Guy? It came down to a series of simple questions.

Did I like him? Yes.

Was I attracted to him? Fuck, yes.

Could I imagine dating him? Yes, but slowly.

In spite of my 'go get 'em' attitude, I didn't let just anyone have access to my body. Though, there had been a short time many years ago when I had. Another side effect of having freedom after being with a man who barely let me go anywhere without him, and who used me whenever he felt like it. Sex on my terms had been a novelty, even though it should have always been my right, as it should be for all women. Now, though, things were different. Now, I wanted someone who would take his time and show me he was willing to wait, put the effort in before he tried to put his dick in me.

Unfortunately, I hadn't met that many men who'd been interested in going slow. And the few who were didn't stay around for too long once they'd got what they wanted.

I blinked as I realised the end credits of the movie we were watching rolled across the TV screen.

I guess I'll never find out if she escaped the crazy stalker...

I turned my head towards Guy and saw a knowing smile on his face. Clearly, he'd noticed that I'd tuned out some time ago, and I gave him a sheepish grin in return.

Stretching her arms over her head with a yawn, Nova said, "I think that's me done for the day. We're going to be doing a lot of walking around tomorrow, so I'm going to get some sleep."

Donovan gave her a flirty side-eye that clearly said, 'After we've had sex,' and Nova's cheeks flushed at the silent suggestion. She gave him a playful slap to the thigh, then stood and reached for his hand to pull him up.

Swiftly changing the subject, Donovan said, "What time are Shannen and Cal expected back in the morning?"

"Before ten, I think," I answered. We were all going to Land's End, and though it wasn't too far from where we were staying, we didn't want to leave it too late to get there. The next evening, after our day out, the guys were planning to go out for a boys' night, and they would also want to chill for a few hours before they headed to the nearest pub they could find. The girls weren't getting left out, though. Shannen, Nova, and I were having our own night out later in the week, though it would be far tamer than the boys' night since Shannen couldn't drink.

"Okay," Donovan said, wrapping an arm around Nova's waist. "We'll be ready to go for nine o'clock and then we can head more or less straight out."

I smiled. "Okay."

The travel blogger in him was pretty organised. Although he had been used to living on his own schedule for more than ten years, the job he'd taken on over the last six months meant he'd had to do more planning. Nova had told me that he wasn't as keen on a strict schedule, but when it came to planning out what he would be blogging about, he was always meticulous, and I guessed he was going to use this week away to put some more UK-based content out there. Land's End was a great place to do that.

Land's End was the most westerly point of England's mainland, and one of the most popular tourist attractions in the UK. It was often the start point of the famous Land's End to John O'Groats walks that people did for charity or just one hell of a challenge. I'd never been there before, but I was excited to see it.

After saying goodnight, Nova and Donovan headed to their room, leaving Guy and me alone.

"Movie not your thing?" Guy asked, looking at me, and I turned to him, lifting my knees and wrapping my arms around them in front of me.

"Nah, it was good. I think I'm just a bit tired." Not a total lie, but not the whole truth either.

Guy's eyes stayed on me for a moment, as if contemplating speaking, so I sat quietly, waiting. Eventually, he said, "Thanks for asking me to hang out with you today. I had a good time."

I nodded. "Me too. It's been a while since I built a sandcastle and had my toes in the sand."

"Same. I don't get much time to do things like that."

"You should make time," I told him with a smile. "Like I said earlier, this is the time to do whatever you want. And I highly recommend doing something ridiculous every now and again."

Guy relaxed against the back of the sofa with a chuckle. "Like what?"

Stretching my legs out a little, I shrugged. "I don't know. Hasn't there ever been a time when you've wanted to do something crazy in the moment but talked yourself out of it?"

He glanced up, catching my eye for a second before chuckling again. "Yes. Lots of times."

"Well, Guy, my prescription for you is to do at least one thing a week that makes you happy, even if it seems crazy at the time."

"Thanks, Doctor Gaby." He grinned. "I might just do that."

"It's the least I can do. Besides, if it weren't for you, I wouldn't have seen a lighthouse today."

Seeming to relax more, Guy dropped his head back onto the headrest. "I've always loved Godrevy. I used to surf there when I was younger."

The visual that brought up in my mind, of his wet body riding the waves, made me swallow. "I didn't know you could surf."

"I'm a man of many talents," he said with a wink, and I laughed.

"Are you flirting with me, Guy?" I asked before I could stop myself. I hadn't meant for it to slip out, and now it had, I had to disguise my nerves with a flirty grin.

"What if I am?" he asked, his face turning slightly more serious. "Would that be okay with you?"

My cheeks warmed at his words, and usually, I was not a woman who blushed. I was confident, great at banter, and as such, nothing really embarrassed me.

But I wasn't embarrassed. I was... flattered, and my insides squirmed with something I hadn't felt in years. That tingling of excitement you get when you find out the person you like likes you back.

"That would be okay with me," I said, then bit my lip. If I didn't, I was certain I would have let out an uncharacteristic squeal.

It wasn't like I'd spent months mooning over Guy, desperate for him to ask me out. With him, it was more of a slow learning of who he was and a realisation that rather than trying to 'match' with someone on a dating app based on a list of likes and dislikes, this had happened naturally. Far better than seeing a photo and hoping they matched up to who they said they were in reality. Guy already matched up.

With the words now out in the open, though, it was as if we'd both become stuck for what to say. He hadn't asked me out, he'd asked for permission to flirt. If he was this respectful of my feelings at this point, there was a strong chance it would spill over into everything.

Hopefully, a date wouldn't be too far away, though.

"Maybe we could..." Guy's sentence was cut off as his phone started vibrating across the coffee table. He frowned. It was after ten, so pretty late for a call. As he leaned over for it, he groaned then muttered, "For fuck's sake." He cut the call off and said, "It was Helen."

Heaving out a sigh, he tossed the phone down in the space between us on the couch.

"You could have answered it," I said gently. "I wouldn't have minded."

"I don't have anything to say to her." His eyes were still on his mobile. "I don't know what she could have to say to me that she didn't say when she left."

"Maybe it was a butt dial."

He laughed, but his shoulders slumped, and I shuffled across the sofa to sit a little closer to him. Resting my hand over his on his lap, I said, "I feel like I can't really offer too much advice here because..." I gave a small shrug, then gestured between the two of us with my free hand. "I don't want to feel like I'm influencing what you do just because I want you to keep flirting with me." Guy smiled, and I continued, "Perhaps it was an accidental dial, or maybe she really does want to talk to you, but if she tries again, maybe you should let her know where you stand."

"We broke up. Isn't that enough?"

I gave a nod, conceding that that was a fair point. "It should be. But you were together for a long time. Maybe she's realised her mistake in ending things."

Guy's eyes dropped down to my hand on his, and I began to pull it away, thinking I'd done the wrong thing, but he flipped his over and held mine in place gently. "I had more fun with you today than I had with Helen in years. I don't know where this flirting thing is going, and I don't want to think about where it's going right now. I just want to have more days like today before I have to go home and get back to work and deal with the reality of the most gigantic business decision I've ever made." He grimaced slightly, making me laugh, and I realised he was referring to his new bar.

"You don't strike me as someone who makes decisions without being completely sure of them."

"That's true. But that doesn't stop it from being scary."

"All the best things are at first. It just means you care about them."

Once again, Guy glanced down at our now joined hands and nodded. "That's also true."

Before things could become awkward, even though I enjoyed the warmth of his hand in mine, I leaned forward and dropped a kiss on his cheek. "Get some sleep. I'll see you in the morning."

Letting my fingers slip from his grasp, I smiled, and he said, "Goodnight, Gabs."

# Chapter 6

Guy

ALMOST AS SOON AS Shannen and Cal got back the next morning, we were back out the door to head to Land's End. The weather was amazing again, and to save taking more cars than necessary, I travelled with Cal, Shannen, and Aiden, and Gaby went with Nova and Donovan.

Once we arrived at Land's End and parked the cars, we all got out, and the breeze from being right on the sea was a welcome relief in the heat. As expected, it was busy, and we all took a slow stroll down towards the main entrance. On the way, Donovan took out his phone, filming the walk, speaking to explain that he was going to be showing his followers around the place. We all watched him, keeping quiet as he did his thing. I'd followed him on social media, and his way of speaking and talking about the places he'd been was entertaining enough that I'd spent a solid hour watching his reels. He had a sarcastic but engaging way of talking, and I laughed out loud a lot of times while watching him. I didn't know him well yet; neither did anyone really since he was away so often. But the short time I'd spent with him had shown me he had a dry sense of humour, but he was an all-round nice guy, and I hoped to get to know him better while we were in Cornwall.

"What can we do here?" Aiden asked, looking unimpressed by the view.

Shannen laughed. "There's lots to do when we get all the way down the path. There are shops, and a small farm, and also some craft workshops where you can see people making things."

"What is with you and art galleries?" Cal asked with a grin, and he pulled her closer into his side. He'd told me that while he and Shannen had been in St Ives, she had dragged him in and out of art galleries, trying to engage him, but it wasn't his thing.

"It's not art galleries," she said, playfully shoving him in the side. "There's all different kinds of crafting. It's interesting!"

Cal and Aiden exchanged a sceptical look, and the rest of us laughed.

"The website said there's mini golf here," Gaby said, and Aiden's eyes lit up.

"Can we play?" he asked, jumping up and down and tugging Cal's hand.

"Yeah, if you want to," he said. "But let's look around first."

When we were inside the main area of the resort, I paused to look around. It made up of a lot of white buildings of various sizes, housing entertainment and shops, but the thing people came to see more than anything else was the views. Mostly, the point that stuck out into the sea; the southernmost point in mainland England. I couldn't wait to get down there, but there was a lot more to look at first.

Gaby insisted on grabbing a coffee, while Aiden asked for an ice cream. How she could drink coffee on such a hot day baffled me, but she seemed pretty addicted to it. Once she had grabbed a drink and Aiden had got a vanilla ice cream with a flake, we wound our way down the path towards the farm situated next to the craft workshops Shannen had been so excited about.

Once again, we all made small talk as we walked down the winding path, weaving between other visitors on the way.

Cal, Donovan, and I ambled slowly behind the girls and Aiden, and Cal said, "So, you and Gaby..."

My head flicked sharply towards him, and Donovan smirked beside him. "What about me and Gaby?" I asked, and Donovan laughed out loud.

Cal looked at Donovan, a grin on his face before turning back to me. "You're into her."

Not even a question. However, I couldn't figure out how he'd reached that conclusion. I'd been looking at her before Cal had started talking, but I wasn't exactly staring or making it obvious.

Hopefully.

"Doesn't take a genius, mate," Cal said. "You said before you think she's attractive, and she looks at you like she wants to pounce on you. And then you spent yesterday taking care of Aiden together..."

"Not to mention she threw a water balloon at your nuts," Donovan added, and Cal burst out laughing as I winced at the memory.

"She what?" he asked.

"That was an accident," I said, shaking my head, but I smiled. "Yeah, I'm into her, and she knows."

"Did something happen last night after we went to bed?" Donovan asked, the male banter levels lowering to a more serious conversation.

"Not really. I just asked her if it would be okay if I flirted with her."

Cal shook his head, laughing again. "You are a pussy. This from the man who took the piss out of me for saying Shannen was sweet the first night I met her!"

I flipped him the middle finger, rolling my eyes. "You were the king of one-night stands. I do long-term relationships. We are not the same."

"Nah, I get it," Donovan said. "I've been both of you at different points of my life, but with some women, you need to take your time."

Throwing him a grateful smile, I then looked at Cal. "At least one of you knows how to treat a woman."

With a cocky smirk, Cal said, "Ask Shannen right now if she's satisfied."

"We know she's satisfied, mate. We have the room next to yours!"

Donovan's words made me bark out a laugh, and Cal shook his head. If this was how the conversation was going at ten-thirty in the morning with no alcohol involved, I could only guess how it would be once we had a few beers inside us.

My laugh caught the ladies' attention, and they and Aiden stopped and turned around.

"What's so funny?" Gaby asked, tilting her chin in question.

"Donovan's got jokes," I said as we continued to walk, catching up to them.

"Do tell." Shannen looked up at Cal as he took her hand, and he shook his head.

"Boy talk," he told her, and she gave a knowing nod. Probably better if he didn't inform her that Donovan had just implied she was loud in the bedroom. I was pretty sure he was kidding about that. Shannen was way too reserved to make noise when she knew other people were close by.

At least the heat was back off me now.

I found myself beside Gaby as we walked. It was the natural thing to do since the others were in their own couples, but it was also where I wanted to be.

"I don't know what we've been doing," Gaby said, linking her arm with mine, "but apparently, we're giving off a 'vibe'."

Her smile as she looked up at me was cheeky, and I smiled back. "Oh, yeah? What vibe is that?"

"The vibe that we want to bang each other."

I raised an eyebrow in amusement as she took a sip of her coffee. "Yeah, I had a similar conversation with Cal and Donovan. What I haven't worked out is how we've been giving off a vibe when we've hardly been near each other all morning."

"Ah, well," Gaby held up her index finger. "As it turns out, we've been the subject of a study since we got to Cornwall."

That was news to me, and I felt my forehead wrinkle. "A study?"

"Mmhmm. I've just been informed that when you suggested giving me a ride to Penzance, Shannen told Cal that she thought you might like me, and he said he already suspected it. And then, when we arrived together, Nova asked Shannen how that happened, and she shared her theory, and Nova then told Donovan, so... we've been under observation the whole time. Basically, we're two lab rats thrown together to see whether we mate or kill each other."

"Man, do you have a way with words." I shook my head, then grinned. "I'm pretty sure I don't want to kill you."

Reading the extremely unsubtle subtext in my words, her cheeks flushed, but she winked at me exaggeratedly, making me laugh again. After she took another drink from her coffee cup, she said, "Let's see how you feel by the end of the week."

"I would place a bet on the fact that I won't change my opinion of you. But also... I don't think we'll be 'mating' either."

A flicker of hurt flashed in her pretty green eyes, but she disguised it with a shrug. "You couldn't handle me anyway," she teased.

I stopped walking, and because we were still linked at the arm, Gaby had to stop too. Looking deep into her eyes, I said, "Gabriella Davis, not only could I handle you, I would make you feel so good you'd never want to let me go."

She swallowed hard at my words, staring up at me with wide eyes for a second. "Is that a promise?" she asked, quirking her eyebrow.

Making a slightly bolder move than I'd intended to, I unlinked my arm from hers and gently placed my hands on her waist, pulling her closer to me. I didn't press her against me, just took a small step closer so my meaning was clear. "How about we start with a date?"

She looked around where we stood. We were on the edge of the path that led down towards the farm and shops, and there were people everywhere. Our friends were still walking on ahead, having not realised we'd stopped, and when Gaby looked back at me again, she said, "Can this be a date? Right now?"

The bubbly side of her had overtaken her softer, more vulnerable side again, and she bounced on the balls of her feet, making me laugh.

"You are so not as cool as you pretend to be," I teased her, and she laughed.

"I'm exactly as cool as I 'pretend' to be," she said, smiling. "I just also happen to really like the idea of being on a date with you." She softened again, her face flushing a little, and she slowly leaned her forehead against my chest with a sigh. "I like you."

Those simple words made me feel ten feet tall. What a difference it made to hear something so real and honest.

As she slowly looked up at me, I thought for a second about kissing her. About pressing my lips to hers for the first time to see how I felt.

However, since we'd only a moment ago established that we were on a date, I didn't want to move too fast. I couldn't say why, but something told me that going slow with her was a good idea.

She had kissed me on the cheek the night before, just before she went to bed. I leaned down and returned the gesture, letting my lips linger for a fraction longer than necessary, then whispered in her ear, "I like you too."

She looked up at me from beneath her long eyelashes, and even though she wasn't mine—yet—I felt like the luckiest man in the world. That this woman had just confessed to 'liking' me was better than a last-minute goal in a cup final.

"Come on," I said, taking her hand again, and as our fingers linked, we followed the others down to the little farm area.

Once we caught up with our friends and they saw our intertwined hands, there was a lot of smirking going on, but nobody said anything, even though I knew Cal and Donovan were going to give me shit for it later. I didn't care, though. This was the first time in... I wasn't even sure how long that I felt some kind of energy in my body.

Not that I'd been completely lifeless through the end of my relationship with Helen, just that... being with her drained me. The only thing she wanted was a baby, and with every month it didn't happen, she got angrier, mostly with me. I really had tried hard to understand, to be there for her. There were times when she was receptive to it and times when she would scream at me. There were also times when I shouted back. Times I begged her to try going to couples' counselling to see if we could fix whatever had gone wrong between us, but she didn't want it. I'd tried to explain that even if she did get pregnant while our relationship was breaking down, it wouldn't fix *us*. Just having a baby wouldn't make us the family she wanted if she and I were broken. It went over her head. It was all just words that distracted her from her only goal.

I was lucky that I had a business and good friends around me because without them, I would have found it much harder to bounce back. Buying a bar had given me back a sense of purpose, but holding Gaby's hand was like reconnecting with feelings that had been dormant inside me for so long. I was standing next to a woman who once bought a wedding dress for fun. She loved life and she lived it every single day. Everything in my world had been dark and stagnant for so long. Gaby had breezed in, upbeat, and thrown some clarity on the rut I'd been sinking into, and I hadn't even realised it had been happening.

We strolled around the farm area together, spending a long time with the miniature ponies, with Gaby wondering if she could smuggle one into the car. Aiden liked the goats and ferrets, and he almost had a meltdown when Cal told him it was time to move on to the shops.

Gaby didn't let go of my hand the whole time we were walking around, and it was amazing how quickly I got used to it being there. Donovan filmed some more and talked about the things he was looking at. He even filmed all of us as we stopped to have our photo taken by the famous signpost. It stands near to the end point of the land and displays the distance to John O'Groats and New York, but underneath, the words are interchangeable so people can use their own hometowns or whatever they want on the sign. Visitors have to pay for the privilege, but it's worth it for such an iconic shot.

Once we'd finished there, we walked further down, to the First and Last House. It wasn't so much a house as a shop, but very aptly named, and we all took photos there too. Shannen and Cal took Aiden into the shop to look around, and Nova and Donovan were busy taking photos for Donovan's blog, leaving Gaby and me to stand as close as we dared to the edge of the cliff, looking out at the expanse of sea in front of us.

In spite of the hot day, the breeze down there made it a bit cooler, and Gaby stood close beside me, her blonde hair blowing with the wind. She smiled up at me, then looked back out at the sea. "It's pretty cool to be standing at the end of the world."

I laughed at her word choice. "Yeah, I've always called it that too. My mum used to say it's *not* the end of the world, but when you're standing here, looking out... it feels like it."

"It does. It's peaceful. Even though it's busy and there are lots of people here, it's relaxing." She paused, then said, "I like being near the water. I didn't grow up by the sea, but the first time I ever went to a beach, it became my happy place. This, although not a beach, is perfect. I wish I could build a house here and look out at this every day."

I smiled. "Yeah, I like the water too. There are some really nice properties in Dawlish that have a view over the sea. I've done some work on a few of them, and I never wanted to leave. One of the days I was there, a storm came in. It was incredible. The lightning flashing over the sea, lighting up the dark clouds. The lady who owned the house said I could stop working to watch it because it was such a beautiful sight."

Lost in the memory of it, I didn't realise Gaby hadn't responded, and when I looked down at her, she was already watching me, awe on her face.

"What?" I asked.

"Nothing. You just... you watch football and do manly things like fixing up people's houses, and you like being with the guys, and working out, but... you also see the beauty of a storm over the sea. I like that."

"Oh, you thought I was just some meathead who lifts weights and kicks a football?" I teased, and she laughed.

"No. I have it on good authority that you are a lot of other things too. But I guess... I don't know. I just didn't think you'd be so captivated by the beauty of nature."

I dropped my arm from around her shoulders and shifted around so we were face to face. "I'll have you know, I'm quite the expert when it comes to what's beautiful. And right now, I'm surrounded by it." Lowering my head closer to hers, I said, "Spoiler alert, I don't only mean the view."

I heard a sigh fall from her lips, and as I moved my head back a little, she said, "Damn, that was a good line."

Her green eyes sparkled, and I said, "That wasn't a line. That was a fact."

Her body swayed slightly as if my words had knocked her off balance, and she stepped the slightest bit closer to me. I wasn't sure where the words were coming from. I sounded like an overly sentimental bellend, but I wasn't lying.

"Guy," she said, "how come you stopped calling me? After we'd had drinks a couple of times, you just stopped reaching out."

The question was neither accusing nor spoken with any level of hurt. She asked like she was simply curious, and I twisted my face into a grimace. "I'm sorry about that, Gabs. I don't even have a good answer. I guess I thought if I always called first, then maybe you were only seeing me because you felt like you had to. And then you never called me either, so I figured I was right."

It was Gaby's turn to grimace. "I felt like, if I called you as often as I wanted to, you would think I was a weirdo, but also... you hadn't been single for long, and I didn't want to be a rebound thing."

46

I nodded slowly. "I think it would have been too soon for me to get into anything. We both made the right choices, but that doesn't mean I forgot about you."

"I didn't forget about you either."

"So, as a first date," I said, "how do you think it's going?"

She grinned. "Good coffee, miniature ponies, ice cream, sea views, excellent company. A solid ten out of ten. How about you?"

"Since I've used my quota of cheesy words for today, I'm going to just say that I agree with everything you said."

Gaby laughed lightly, and I stared at her for a moment, taking in her high cheekbones, her pretty smile, those green eyes that were so bright, and her blonde hair still rippling in the breeze.

I wanted to do a *lot* more than only flirt with her.

Before I could speak again, Gaby slipped her arms around my waist. "This is shaping up to be the best holiday I've ever been on, and I've been to Disneyland."

"Well," I said, gently resting my hands on her hips, "Let's see if we can make it even better."

Chapter 7

Gaby

Take it easy.

I said the words in my head, reminding myself to breathe, but with Guy's eyes on me, it was difficult.

I'd thought about Guy more often than I'd been willing to admit to myself. Not in a starry-eyed 'Oh, how I wish he was mine' kind of way. But out of all the men I'd been around in recent years, he was someone I felt a pull to. I had a reasonable number of male friends, but they remained very much at arm's length. I was comfortable with them, but I never wanted to cross the friendship lines. With Guy... there was something there, but after we'd seen each other a few times and then it had fizzled out, I just assumed he wasn't feeling it. And I was fine with that. Years of clinging onto something I should have let go of taught me that wasn't the way to live my life.

But as I stood in his arms, on a clifftop, the setting somehow felt very fitting. It wouldn't take too many steps to fall over the edge, not knowing if I would land safely in the water or end up with my heart and body battered by the jagged rocks below. Likewise, the slightest movement of our heads, and Guy's lips would be on mine. Same risks. Could I guarantee a soft landing, or was I about to get my emotions torn to shreds again?

There was no way to know unless I took the leap.

Since the day before, the water fights and the pre-bedtime chat, I was running out of ways to tell myself I could breeze through this 'crush'. And when he'd taken my hand earlier, kissed my cheek, I'd started to allow myself to want something more. When I'd called this a date, even though we were out with our friends, it hadn't made me want to back away. I wanted to lean into it.

I liked being with a man who didn't mind that I had many times been labelled 'a bit much'. After being suppressed and made to feel 'less than' for a long time, once I was free and began to rediscover who I truly was, I found out I wasn't someone who wanted to tone myself down for fear of what people might think. Not in an obnoxious way; I didn't get in people's faces. I just knew that after I used to not wear a certain type of clothing or refused to spend money on things I enjoyed in case people thought me frivolous, I was done caring about the opinions of others. Someone had taken everything from me, including my personality, and I didn't fight to get away only to live my life in the shadows.

Guy seemed to like that about me. When he laughed at something I did, he wasn't laughing *at* me. He was laughing with surprise and what sometimes looked like admiration or awe. A refreshing change from men who never quite seemed to know what to make of me.

Now, I stood at what I'd called the end of the world, my arms around Guy's waist. Looking up at him, I saw the warmth in his gaze as his eyes found mine. He smiled at me in a way that was sexy and made me feel safe at the same time. Time seemed to slow down as he leaned in, his eyes remaining on mine as if ensuring I definitely wanted this. If I backed away, he'd have let me go, and that made it so much easier to stay.

His lips pressed against mine, lightly brushing over them in a kiss that made me remember how good a simple kiss could be. It was gentle, unhurried, and I could tell from the slowly deepening rhythm that he had been wanting to do this for a long time.

And the feeling was entirely mutual.

As his lips finally and slightly hesitantly pulled away from mine, I let out a small sigh, making him chuckle.

"That was totally worth waiting for," he said, pulling me in even closer to his firm body.

"Yeah." I laughed. "It was." Unwilling to look away from him, I added, "Do you think any of our friends saw that?"

His eyes shifted sideways, in the direction of The First and Last House, where Shannen and Aiden were. When he moved his gaze back to me, he winced. "Shannen and Aiden saw. And I think I'm going to owe Aiden a lot of sweets from the glare he's giving me."

"Why is he glaring at you?" I asked, tilting my head to the side.

"It's kind of a running joke between Shannen, Cal, and me that Aiden has a crush on you." My eyes widened, and Guy burst out laughing. "You didn't notice?" he asked, and I shook my head.

"He's five!" I said. "He does not have a crush on me."

Guy laughed again. "Not a proper full-on crush. But he's always asking Cal and Shannen when he'll see you again, and he looks really unhappy with me right now."

"Oh, no!" I closed my eyes, though a small giggle slipped out. Aiden was only little, and I knew his annoyance with Guy wasn't going to cause him any major upset, but I still didn't like the idea of him being sad in any way. "I'm sure we can find a way to make it up to him. Also, way to make me feel guilty about our first kiss."

Guy slid his hands down my waist to my hips before letting go of me and taking my hands in his. "We'll just have to have some more later to make up for it."

My insides melted at his words and the way he was looking at me, like the time he'd get to kiss me again couldn't arrive fast enough.

I couldn't disagree.

The rest of our time at Land's End was spent with all of us together, and we played mini golf and had another wander around the shops. Guy took Aiden to the side for a while before we all got in our cars to go back to the lodge. Aiden was much happier when they rejoined us. When I asked Guy what he said to him before we left, he told me that they'd had a quick heart to heart and that Guy had told him I would still be his friend outside of school time, and that if I was spending more time with Guy, then Aiden would also see me more often too, which had cheered him up.

We spent the remainder of the afternoon relaxing in the lodge. Nova and I used the hot tub, Shannen took a nap, and the guys had a kick around on the grass where we'd had our water fight. Even though we weren't doing anything overly exciting, it was still a great afternoon spent in the best company.

Later that evening, after the guys had left for their night out, I was curled up on the sofa reading. Nova had gone for a shower, and Shannen and Aiden were sitting at the large dining table, drawing together

"Shannen?" Aiden's tone was filled with such curiosity that it was hard not to listen in, but I tried to keep my focus on my book. "Are you my mum now?"

If it was possible to hear someone's heart clench, I was sure I'd have heard Shannen's do so. There was a noticeable silence, like they had both stopped drawing and were waiting to see what would be said next.

Cal had talked to Aiden about his mum some time ago, once he'd spent some time coming to terms with her death. With the new baby coming, knowing Shannen would soon be addressed as 'mum' herself made him realise that Aiden needed to know about where he came from, and where his mum had been all his life. Shannen told Nova and I that she had sat with Cal while he told Aiden about Katie. It was a lot, especially having to cover the concept of death with him too, but Aiden had dealt with it really well. Having never met his real mum, I supposed that might have made things easier for him. At least for the time being. Perhaps when he was older, he would feel differently and want to know more about her, though.

"Erm," Shannen stuttered. "Well... your dad told you all about your real mum, remember?"

"Yeah, but I didn't know her. And, well, you know when I go to Aria and Avery's house?"

I could only assume Shannen nodded, but I didn't want to turn my head to see. I already wished I'd chosen to read outside on the deck, but I was too afraid to move now and draw attention to myself. I stared at the pages of my novel, trying to take in the words in front of me, but there were no other sounds in the room, so it was impossible not to overhear.

"Their mummy is really nice," Aiden said. "And she plays with them, and she takes them to fun places, and she makes them food, and she buys them things. And you do those things for me. Also, you read me bedtime stories and you like it when I tell you about my friends, and you always look after me when Dad's at work. So, does that mean you're my mum?"

This is too cute. Aiden had changed so much since the beginning of the year. He used to be such a troublemaker, but he'd calmed down a lot. Shannen loved him, and I could only imagine her expression as he waited for her response. A smile pulled at my lips.

"Well, I..." Shannen began, and I knew she was weighing up her words carefully. "You will only ever have one real mum, but if your dad and I get married one day, I would be your stepmother."

"Like in Cinderella?"

Biting my lip to conceal a snort, I bowed my head, carefully turning a page, even though I hadn't read the one I was on.

"Sort of," Shannen said. "Except I'm nice to you."

"Yeah." There was a short silence, then he continued, "I would like it if you were my mum."

I closed my eyes, still grinning to myself at the sweet innocence of his words. I knew exactly how much it meant to Shannen too. Even the slight twinge in my chest at the word 'mum'—a name I'd deprived myself of—couldn't dim how happy I was for my friend.

"Do you mean you want to call me mum?" Shannen asked carefully.

"Can I?" The eagerness in his tone made me imagine his eyes were wide with excitement at the idea.

Shannen let out a gentle chuckle, and I heard the legs of her chair moving. I shifted my eyes sideways and saw she had moved her chair closer to his and had wrapped an arm around him. "I would like that," she said. "But... let's talk to your dad about it first. We'll see what he says."

I was still smiling to myself a couple of minutes later when Shannen joined me in the living area. Aiden was still at the table, immersed in his artwork, and I looked up at her over the top of my book. She carefully sat down on the other end of the sofa from me, resting both hands on her stomach, a contented smile on her face.

"Well, that was fucking adorable," I said quietly, and she laughed.

"Gabs, I can't..." she trailed off, shaking her head. "I can't believe this is my life. This time last year, I was getting ready to start a new job, spending every Saturday lunching with Jade and avoiding the nightmare men she kept trying to set me up with. Now..." She shrugged, shaking her head again. "None of this would have even come close to what I imagined for myself. At least, not at this speed. I mean, really, this is all your fault."

I threw my head back, laughing, and I closed my book and placed it on the coffee table. I wasn't paying attention to it anyway. "All I did was encourage you to loosen up. And by loosen up, I meant having fun and letting go of expectation. I didn't mean getting knocked up within two months and buying a house with a man within six months. I told you to chill, not go extreme!"

Shannen chuckled, turning to put her feet up on the couch, facing me. "It's crazy. I didn't see having a family by the end of the year as something that would ever happen to me, but then... my whole life is upside down now." Her face fell slightly. "I spoke to my mum yesterday. She told my dad she wants a divorce."

This was not a surprise to me. Shannen's mum, Annie, was the kindest woman, but when her husband went rogue and started messing with Shannen's life, Annie went full mama bear on him, and as much as it was clear she still loved him deeply, she couldn't get over the shock and hurt of what he did. This was all exacerbated by the fact that her best friend, Judith, whose almost son-in-law had been part of it all, had also tossed her aside. It was as if she somehow blamed Shannen's family for the fact that her daughter's betrothed was the puppetmaster behind most of the bad things that had happened to Shannen and Cal. He was certainly behind, if not personally responsible for the death of Aiden's real mum. However, he was still awaiting trial, and it was still a long way off, which meant the full truth of the sick things he'd done wouldn't be uncovered for a while.

"I'm sorry," I said. "How do you feel about it?"

She sighed. "Not sure yet. I think I always knew this would be the decision, but now I have to work out exactly how to navigate it when Cal doesn't want to have anything to do with him. It means that, between us, we have to work out how it'll be when the baby comes. Whether we want my dad to be a part of their life."

"Well, you have a couple of months before decisions need to be made. But I'm here if you want to talk it through."

"Thanks." As she looked at me, her expression turned to one of mischief, and I guessed she was ready for a subject change. "So... you want to tell me what's going on with you and Guy?"

I'd been waiting for this. I'd ridden back to the lodge with her, Cal, and Aiden, but Aiden had gotten cranky and misbehaved in the car, so there wasn't really an opportunity to discuss it. Plus, it wasn't a long journey, so any conversation around it couldn't happen, and it was more than Aiden needed to hear anyway. Now, he was still in the room with us, but he'd just put something on his iPad to watch while he was drawing, and Shannen had lowered her voice as she'd asked the question.

Dropping my head back again, not in amusement but in slight apprehension this time, I said, "There was kissing."

Shannen laughed as I looked at her, and she said, "Yeah, I noticed that. So... are you two... what are you?"

"Well... I don't think we're in a position for labels yet. But I called today our first date, and I'm thinking that we will have some more of those and see where it goes."

Nodding slowly, Shannen said, "Sounds like a good plan to me."

I thought back over the day with him, how it had felt to kiss him. How it had felt to have him pull me against him, and how easy it had all been. I hadn't enjoyed something as simple as holding hands with a man in a really long time, and when we'd had to separate when it was time to go back to the lodge, I wished we could have stayed longer or had an hour or two more on our own.

He had, however, pulled me into his room shortly before he went out with Cal and Donovan, so we could steal a few minutes to ourselves. He'd smelled incredible and looked even better in black jeans and a deep blue button-up shirt. I'd mostly only seen him casually dressed, so to see him ready for a night out was a pleasant surprise. It had floated through my mind that, looking like that, he could easily pick up a random woman in a bar somewhere, but when he'd kissed me again, I remembered the feeling of safety he gave me. Realistically, he didn't owe me anything, and if he wanted to get it on with someone else, he was well within his rights to do so.

But I knew he wouldn't. Something deep inside me told me he was going for a night out with his friends, not to pull women.

With that thought, though, came a tiny ripple of fear.

Getting close to a man meant there might then come a time when I needed to open up about things even Nova and Shannen didn't know the depth of.

In fact, it was a certainty that I would have to.

One step at a time. You've kissed twice and been out once.

Still, though, this was different to other men I'd been out with. With them, I hadn't set off knowing where they stood on what they wanted from their futures. With Guy, I had some insider knowledge, and I couldn't help second guessing whether being involved with him at all was a smart plan.

"Gaby," Shannen said softly, and I dragged myself out of my thoughts to look at her. Empathy filled her eyes, and she said, "I know your last serious relationship was... well, you know. But Guy... he's good."

Bless her.

Shannen knew I'd had an abusive partner, and I guessed she'd concluded that those concerns might come back now I was seeing someone new. It *was* always a consideration, no matter who the person was because in all honesty, some of the most abusive people were the ones nobody would suspect. But I was one hundred per cent sure Guy wasn't one of those men.

"I know," I told her. "I'm not worried about that."

"But you are worried about something." It wasn't a question.

I sighed. "Yeah. A bit. It's just that... there is a lot from my past that I haven't told anyone before, and also... it's just been a while since I've been really interested in someone. I don't know if I remember how dating works."

I screwed up my face in mock confusion to cover the genuine concerns that kept trying to make themselves known, and Shannen laughed.

"I felt a bit like that when I started seeing Cal," she said, "but it comes pretty naturally once you start."

"Yeah, I suppose so. I don't want to overthink it or anything. Let's just see how things play out."

And maybe when he comes back later, there will be more kissing.

Guy

THE WEEK IN PENZANCE went way too fast. I'd needed the break more than I'd realised. The seven of us had made the most of every second of the holiday. As well as Land's End and having several epic water fights, we'd been to Newquay Zoo and St. Michael's Mount as a group, and Gaby and I had also taken a couple of days to ourselves and visited the small fishing village of Mousehole, and the Cornish Seal Sanctuary.

Spending time with Cal, Shannen, and Aiden was always great, but to be included in a trip that was more their friends than mine had meant a lot. I'd enjoyed getting to know Donovan and Nova. Nova's sweetness balanced out Donovan's dry sense of humour, and it was pretty damn clear how much they loved each other. I got the impression that being apart so much was a strain, and I wondered if Donovan might one day consider moving back to the UK on a more permanent basis to make things easier.

However, Gaby made the trip for me. One of the reasons I'd asked her to ride down to Cornwall with me was to see how things would be between us after not seeing each other for a while. And yeah, I'd hoped to feel out whether there might be a chance of her going out with me sometime. I hadn't expected us to have a date while on holiday, and I had expected even less that she would be the one to suggest it. I wasn't sure why because she was always so upfront, but somehow, I'd assumed it would be on me to instigate things.

Being with Gaby felt... different, but in the best way. I'd spent years of my life with Helen, who was familiar. I knew her and mostly knew what to expect from her. I hadn't done the getting-to-know-someone-new thing in forever, but it felt good. It wasn't just getting to know Gaby, though. I was getting to know myself again. To remember who I was outside of a relationship. I'd gotten lost somewhere along the way. While I had my own business, everything else had been tied to Helen, and anything left after that was tied to Cal and Aiden. I needed something for myself again; that was why I'd moved and bought the bar. I wanted an entirely fresh start.

I took Donovan and Cal to look at my bar on the Sunday morning after we got home to show them my newest project. Every time I walked in there, I felt like I'd won the lottery because... that was mine. The thing I would work on and hopefully make a massive profit on too. The money wasn't my top priority; it was the challenge. The excitement of turning a place that needed a fix-up into a place that someone would be proud to own. But until that day came, *I* owned it, and I was going to make it the best it could possibly be. It went beyond the realms of just painting and decorating, but my dad had taught me a lot about home renovation over the years; that used to be his thing, and I learned everything I knew from him. I was confident I could do the bulk of the work with Cal's help.

"This is a great space," Donovan said as we walked on the creaky, worn-down wooden floorboards.

I nodded. "It is. It needs a lot of work, but at the same time... it doesn't."

Donovan nodded in response, as if he knew exactly what I meant. The entrance doors led into the main area of the space, a long, wide room that had two slightly raised seating areas at each side of the doors, surrounded by chipped and tarnished wooden banisters. The bar ran the full length of back wall, and that also needed repairing. The walls were all exposed brick, by design, and in good condition. There were a couple of doors behind the bar that led to what could become a kitchen and what I imagined was once used as a staff room. On the right were the male and female toilets, and they needed an entire refit and replacement. A large, square dance floor lay in the left corner, and there was also a small, raised platform that could be used as a stage once it had been fixed. On the left side of the room, a wide archway led to a short corridor, which led to another set of toilets, but there was also a set of wooden double doors, and I grinned as I pushed them open.

"Wow," Cal said as we stepped inside.

"Yeah." I laughed, and Donovan let out a low whistle.

The smaller room behind the double doors had ugly, olive-green-painted walls and an old-fashioned, threadbare carpet on the floor. A few old and battered tables were stacked up in one corner, but there were also four old-school arcade gaming machines lined up against one wall, table football in the middle of the room, and a piano gathering dust close to the door.

"Was all this included in the price?" Cal asked with a laugh as he approached the piano and drew a line in the dust with his finger.

"Yeah. I asked the previous owner if he wanted to clear it out, but he told me he'd taken everything he wanted, so... I'm not sure what to do with it all, but I have it for now. I was thinking about getting rid of it and then making this room into a dining area. I'd keep the bar as more of an entertainment area since it has the stage and dance floor."

"Do these work?" Donovan asked, walking over to the gaming machines.

"They do," I said. "I tested them before the electricity was cut off. I could probably sell them and the piano for a decent price on their own."

"Don't get rid of them yet." Donovan placed his hands on the joysticks of one of the games and gave them a wiggle around. "The nostalgia is strong."

"Do you reckon Nova will let you move one into her house?" Cal asked with a grin, and Donovan laughed.

"Unlikely." He turned to me. "Before you make a decision on them, can you let me know first if you want to get rid of them? I definitely want at least one of them. Just need to find a home for them."

"When I move into Guy's old house, I can probably stash one for you," Cal offered, and Donovan smiled.

"Perfect." Donovan looked at me again. "I'm gutted I won't be here to see you fix this place up. It's great, Guy."

"I just hope I can do it the justice it deserves."

Donovan paused for a moment, then said, "Will you send me updates on how it's going while I'm away? If you're looking to sell this place, I know someone who might be interested in it. A mate of mine is itching for a new project, and this is right up his street. He owns a couple of bars in London, and he's always looking to expand."

My eyes widened. Not even a dent had been made in the renovations and Donovan had a potential buyer already? My luck definitely seemed to be changing. First Gaby, now this? Excitement shot through me, and I said, "Of course. Let me know the best way to contact you and I'll keep you in the loop."

The three of us spent a little more time looking around the bar, and I explained the ideas I'd had. Cal and Donovan also pitched in some ideas, some of which were better than mine, and then we went to Wagamama for lunch before we went our separate ways. Cal had to get back to unpacking from the holiday, and Donovan had to go back to Nova's so they could get ready for their trip to the Philippines. He said he was unlikely to be able to get back until Christmas after this, though he would try to snag at least a few days in October if he could.

And I... didn't have any plans. I'd sorted out my washing from the holiday that morning, and I'd been in touch with my employees through the week, so I knew I wasn't in for any nasty surprises when I got back to work. That meant I was free for the rest of the day. Naturally, my mind went to Gaby. I'd spent the past seven days in her company, and I missed having her around all the time. After I'd dropped her home the previous afternoon, the post-holiday blues kicked in almost immediately, but we had messaged a few times during the evening. It wasn't quite the same as our late-night chats on the sofa, though, during which we'd sat closer and closer to each other with every day.

It's probably too soon to see if she wants to meet up again.

I was still sitting in my car in the nearest multi-story car park, trying to decide whether to go home, for a drive, and now, whether I should call Gaby.

I had to go back to work the next day, and since I'd been away and was helping Cal finish up the decorating on his soon-to-be home, not to mention that I would have to catch up on a ton of paperwork, I probably wouldn't have much free time until the following weekend. And that felt like too long to wait to see her again.

Fuck it.

I picked up my phone and called Gaby's number.

Chapter 9

Gaby

I HADN'T BEEN TO the gym nearly as many times as I'd wanted to while I'd been in Cornwall. I'd popped in and used the onsite one twice, as well as having a swim in the pool, but I'd spent most of the week with my friends, out and about, and enjoying the sunshine and the freedom of being off work.

The summer break was usually my time to de-stress, and I would often hang out with Nova, some of my other friends, or my brother, and go on nights out, but I also enjoyed my own company. I could read a *lot* of books throughout August, sometimes at home in my flat by the sunny window, or other times I'd drive to Exmouth and read on the beach. The change of having an actual holiday with people I was either close to or getting close to had been a much-needed experience, but I was also pleased to get back to my own space and routine.

And that was why I was in the gym on Sunday afternoon, sweating it out on the rowing machine. I was just finishing up when I saw my phone light up and start vibrating across the wooden floor. Wiping the sweat from my forehead with my towel, I reached for my phone and saw my brother's name on the screen.

I rolled my eyes. I'd been home for twenty-four hours and he was check-ing on me already. Honestly, it was a minor miracle he'd waited this long. Gavin, my brother, was... let's call it overprotective. Not in the 'stay away from my sister or I'll kill you' way. He just worried about me, even though I'd more than proved I was capable of looking after myself. Such was his protective nature that he moved from Maidstone, Kent, to Exeter so I wasn't alone, not realising that being alone was exactly what I needed and wanted. Still, that was a good few years ago now, and I'd—mostly—for-given him for choosing to set up his law firm here instead of back home, closer to our family.

I reached for the phone and pressed the button to answer it. "Hey," I said. "What's up?"

"Are you okay? You sound out of breath." Immediately, concern filled his tone.

"Yeah," I said facetiously. "Just trying to outrun a serial killer down a back lane, but don't worry. I've been able to run in heels for years."

"Is there any need for your sarcasm?" He said the words, but a small laugh still bubbled out of him.

"A little. It's two o'clock on a bright summer's day in Devon. What harm do you think I could come to?"

"I didn't think you were in danger. Maybe you're sick."

Rolling my eyes, I said, "Maybe I was having an afternoon bean-flick. That would also get me out of breath."

"For God's sake, Gaby!"

I let out a loud laugh, making the person on the next rowing machine cast a quick glance in my direction, and I waved a hand in apology. "I'm fine, Gav. I'm at the gym, that's all."

"Great. Next time, please just get to the point." Gavin sighed, but I also heard him chuckle again, which made me smile. "How was the holiday?"

"Amazing," I said, unable to resist thinking about Guy.

The time we'd spent on our own together was... peaceful. Guy was someone I could be around and not have to second-guess anything. He was so straightforward and honest that I never once felt confused about where I was with him. He liked me. He wanted to be around me so we could learn more about each other. That was it. No games. No fuckery. I was thirty-five years old. I didn't want someone who was going to piss around and waste my time. Guy was not like that.

I internally swooned at the thought of him.

"Care to elaborate on that?" Gavin asked. "Where did you go? What did you do?"

"We went to lots of places. Lots of beach time and warm evenings sitting around together on the deck of the lodge, just taking things easy. I had a really good time."

"How are Cal and Shannen?"

My brother had represented Cal when he'd been arrested. Shannen and Cal often enquired after my brother as he had been such a support to them at that time. We'd been out for dinner together once, a little while after everything had been cleared up, but that was several months ago now.

"They're great," I said, smiling. "They had a night away together so they could rest and talk and enjoy some child-free time. Shannen said they spent most of the time sleeping and eating."

"Good for them," Gavin said. "Send them my best when you speak to them next."

"I will. Maybe we should try to get together again sometime."

"Yeah, we can do." There was a short pause, then Gavin said, "Gaby... I need to tell you something."

His tone had become extra serious, and it instantly set me on edge. As a solicitor, he was already relatively serious, but I knew the changes in the way he spoke, and that tone never meant anything good.

"What is it?" I asked. "Oh, God. Are Mum and Dad coming to visit?"

Most people I knew liked their parents visiting, but I was not one of them. My dad was, for want of a better word, scary, and my mum was as opposite to him as she could possibly be. She was an artist. She dressed like the exact stereotype of an art teacher in long, flowy skirts and tops, her hair falling all the way down her back in blonde waves. I loved them because they were my parents, but spending any length of time with them was hard work.

When he didn't laugh at my comment, my anxiety deepened. Usually, that would have elicited a chuckle, but nothing came.

"It's not that," Gavin said. "It's... a friend of mine who works for the police in Manchester reached out to me last week. He's been keeping his ear to the ground for me for the last couple of years, and he... Gaby... Flynn is out of prison. He was released about three weeks ago."

A shudder rippled through my body from head to toe. Flynn Burton. My ex. The man who had almost ended my life.

"Okay," was all I could manage.

"I'm not telling you this to worry you," Gavin said. "There's no way he can know where you are, and you're a long way from where you lived with him. But I still felt like you should know."

Knowing he was out didn't change anything for me on the surface, and I could have lived quite happily without the information. But I knew my brother. He wouldn't have felt good keeping it from me.

"Why were you keeping tabs on whether Flynn is still in jail?" I asked him, though I already knew the answer.

Gavin sighed. "I knew you wouldn't be happy about it, and I'm sorry. But I also knew there was a chance he'd be out earlier than he should be. I don't think he'll come looking for you, but I'm also not willing to risk the chance that he might. I want to be able to find him."

Yep, that was exactly the answer I'd expected.

Gavin had been the one to come to me when Flynn had beaten me to within an inch of my life and I'd had to have surgery to save me. Gavin was the one who'd stayed with me until I was allowed to leave the hospital, and he'd taken me back to the family home in Kent, where he and my parents—mostly my mum—had helped with my recovery. My parents, though, weren't really the kind of help I needed. Gavin had offered me the most support in terms of my mental health and confidence. My mum had taken care of me physically, helping me get around while I recovered from surgery and my broken bones healed, but she didn't know how to talk to me. She just looked at me with pity and sadness, and while I understood that it can't have been fun for her to see her daughter so broken, the more she looked at me that way, the more of a disappointment I felt. Like I would no longer be able to fulfil all the dreams she had for me. Like because one man had done so much to me, no other man would ever want me and her dreams of me one day having a perfect family were over.

And my dad? I knew he loved me in his way. In fact, the only time I'd ever seen a hint of emotion from him was the day I arrived back at their house, barely able to walk, parts of my skin still bruised or cut. That day, I'd seen him both devastated and the angriest he'd ever been. But once that additional show of feelings passed, the support he provided me was mostly financial. We'd exchange small talk over the dinner table, but he couldn't look me in the eye for a long time. So, he made sure there was always money in my bank account instead, and when I'd made the decision to move to Exeter for work, he gave me more than enough to get settled there. I appreciated it, but what I'd needed from both of them was emotional stability and to feel like they didn't see me as damaged goods.

Everything I needed had fallen on Gavin to provide, but the downside was that he took his role so seriously that he barely allowed me space to breathe. Getting away from all of them was the only way I could imagine having a life of my own again, so when he said he was moving to Exeter too, I was fuming. We had so many arguments over it, but in the end, I was glad for him. Grateful, because starting up somewhere new was harder than I could have imagined, especially when my mental scars continued to pop open whenever they damn well felt like it.

Over time, Gavin's protectiveness had calmed down a lot, but it didn't surprise me that he'd been staying alert for news of Flynn's release.

"Do you know if he's still in Manchester?" I asked.

"He is for now. I can get someone to keep track of where he is to put your mind at ease."

"No," I said quickly. "No. Please don't waste any more time and money on that, Gavin. He's still in Manchester. That's all I need to know."

"Okay," Gavin said, his seriousness easing a little. "But if you change your mind, I will find him and make sure he's nowhere near here. I'm sorry to drop this on you when you've just got back. I just... I felt like you should know."

"I know. Thank you."

I sighed, trying to calm the waves of discomfort that were still washing through me just at the thought of him.

Because I never thought of him. Not the man himself anyway. He'd turned into some kind of looming, shadowy figure that had once darkened every aspect of my life, and small elements of his presence still lingered. Most of it had been banished, talked out in years of therapy, but some very literal scars remained.

I glanced down at my stomach almost without thinking. The scar that ran from my belly button downwards, meeting a wide horizontal scar that ran along my pelvic area was fully encased beneath my gym clothes, but when I thought of him, it felt like everyone around me had X-ray vision and could see the result of the things he'd done to me.

You are stronger than the physical scars. Stronger than the damage he did.

Another of my mantras, and I chanted them hard to myself for a moment, reminding myself of the facts. I'd always known he would get out eventually. He'd been sentenced to fifteen years, and he'd served ten of them. I knew he might not serve all of his sentence, so the time had to

68

have been coming that he would be released. It only felt different because I knew for sure he was free now. But realistically, it *didn't* change things. He didn't know where I lived, and I doubted he'd give a shit. He hadn't when we were together, so it seemed unlikely he'd be interested now.

"Are you all right?" Gavin asked.

"Yeah," I said with a shake of my head. "I really am. It was just a bit of a surprise to hear his name, that's all."

"I can imagine. Gaby, if you change your mind and you want me to track him, I can make it happen so you can sleep a bit easier if it does start to bother you."

I smiled to myself. I gave my brother a lot of crap, but I really did love him and appreciate his support, even if it had been excessive at times. "I know, Gav. Thank you, but I'm okay."

"Okay. Well, I will let you get back to your workout, but let's get together soon."

I sighed as I hung up the phone, but I was glad I had a big brother who took care of me. I would never tell him in a million years that I needed him, but I was grateful for him all the same.

I lifted myself off the rowing machine, slung my towel over my shoulder, then took a long gulp of my water before heading back towards the changing rooms so I could shower and change. On the way, I felt my palm vibrating and realised my phone was ringing again, but this time it was Guy, and I smiled as I answered.

"Hey, Guy," I said brightly. "What's up?"

"Hey. I'm at a bit of a loose end this afternoon, and I was wondering if you want to do something if you're not busy."

"I've just finished up at the gym, so I'll be free once I've showered." I paused. "If you want, you could meet me here and we could use the facilities. There's a great coffee shop here and we can sit outside near the pool. I can sign you in as a guest."

"I'm already in town, so that could work. What gym are you at?"

I told him the name of the gym I was a member of, and he laughed. "Yeah, I won't need signing in. I'm a member there too."

"Wow. How have we never bumped into each other here?"

"Timing, probably. I either go in first thing or later in the evenings, even at the weekends."

As I reached the locker I'd stored my things in, I opened it up. "That makes sense since I prefer a daytime workout! Okay, I'm going to hit the showers. I'll meet you by the coffee shop in about half an hour or so?"

"Okay, I'll see you in a bit."

I hung up with a huge, dopey grin on my face at the idea of seeing Guy again. Sure, we'd only parted ways the day before, but the fact that he wanted to see me again so soon put a spring in my step, overriding my brother's news as I grabbed my things and headed for the showers.

Exactly thirty minutes later, I'd changed into a pair of blue, loose-fitting jeans and a long chiffon top in shades of orange. The combo looked cute with my slip-on sandals, and I'd left my damp hair to hang over my shoulders; it would soon dry sitting out in the sun.

Guy was leaning against the wall by the entrance to the coffee shop, looking at something on his phone as I approached, and I took a moment to appreciate his strong frame. He also wore blue jeans, and his T-shirt was black, but not tight-fitting. He looked super casual, and I'd come to love all of his styles over the last week. The only thing I hadn't seen him in were his work clothes. The idea of him in overalls, covered in paint splashes, brought to mind a vision of one of those calendars of hunky models designed for bored, thirsty housewives.

I held in a chuckle as I approached, and he looked up and smiled when he saw me. Straightening up, he said, "Right on time."

"Always," I answered with a wink, and he laughed.

Once I was directly in front of him, a moment of slight awkwardness descended over us. Would he hug me? Should there be a hello kiss? This hadn't been a consideration while we were on holiday as we'd been together the whole time anyway. Now, though, we'd been apart, and I wasn't sure what to do.

As if sensing my hesitation, Guy reached for my hand and linked his fingers with mine. He didn't comment on it, just started walking into the coffee shop, and I smiled at how easily he read me.

"So, coffee and a cake?" he asked as we got into the queue alongside the display cases of sweet treats. There were also healthy options available, but I'd just done a two-hour workout, so a juice and a boring snack wouldn't cut it.

"Absolutely." I eyed the offerings, and my gaze flitted between several things that looked appealing. I eventually settled on a large slice of banoffee cheesecake, which was 'helpfully' labelled with the calorie count per slice. I never understood if it was to make people feel guilty or simply for informational purposes, but I wasn't going to let a number stop me.

I used to be a lot more conservative with my food choices; another mental scar from my ex. He had frequently told me I was getting fat, and I was a size twelve back then. The paranoia made me cut out fat and sugar as much as possible, and I managed to get myself down to a size ten, but that still wasn't enough for him. I had just about enough strength left in me to remain at a healthy weight and not try to lose more, but it was hard to maintain and one of the reasons I still worked out a lot; to eliminate the possibility of someone else saying I was overweight. I remained a size twelve now, but if I went up to a fourteen, it wouldn't have been the end of the world for me.

"What do you want to drink?" Guy asked as we got closer to the counter.

I didn't need to look at the menu for that one. "Latte, please."

Once we'd got our refreshments, Guy carried the tray of goodies outside, where there was a kind of patio area with picnic tables for people to sit. Only one available table out of the ten there was free; no surprise considering the heat and sunshine. Cheerful music played over the outdoor speakers, and there was a real summer, cheery vibe out there, making me glad Guy had called. Otherwise, I'd probably have gone home and done nothing with the day.

When we were settled and had our drinks and cakes in front of us, I said, "So, what have you been up to today?"

He grinned, his smile lighting up his face. "I took Cal and Donovan to look at my bar."

"Oh, exciting! Will you be starting work on it soon?"

He nodded. "Pretty soon. I'm going to be with my guys at my old place making sure the last few things are ready for Cal and Shannen to move in for the next week or so. Then, the week after they've moved in, I'm going to go back into the bar with Cal and start putting together all the plans and making sure we definitely have everything in the right order to get done. I've been over things a million times, but it'll be good to have an extra set of eyes on it to ensure I didn't forget something or misjudge estimates and timings. I want it ready by Christmas. I don't think it'll be sold right away, although Donovan said he has a mate who might be interested in buying it, so... who knows? In December, I might have enough money to buy a new property or just retire."

"If I could retire before the age of forty, I think I would," I said with a laugh, although that wasn't totally true. I loved my job too much to give it up yet. On the other hand, the idea of having enough money to be set for life appealed to me. I'd grown up with a pretty well-off family, but I was rarely given anything freely as an adult. I had to make my own way, so did Gavin, but I didn't care for money as much as I cared for peace.

"I think I would get bored," Guy said, taking a sip of his black coffee. "I always need to have something to work on. I don't think I was built for sitting around and living a life of leisure."

"Same. It's okay for a week or two, to recharge, but I couldn't do it long-term. I'd lose my mind. Although..." I paused as a thought jumped into my head. It wasn't a new thought; it drifted through my mind semi-regularly. I supported of a couple of charities that raised money for women who needed help after escaping abusive relationships, but I often felt like I could do more.

"What?" Guy asked, curiosity written across his face.

"I've always thought about getting more involved in charities that support survivors of domestic abuse," I said. "I don't know how exactly, but it's something I'm interested in. I just... while I have standing orders to help them with money, I've always steered away from getting in any deeper. I think because, as much as I want to help, when I think about it for too long, I feel like it would be hard to be around people who have such upsetting stories. My own is bad enough, and I'm very conscious of not opening up old wounds for myself. But then that thought makes me feel selfish, and... it's just a whole thing."

I gently pressed my fork into my cheesecake and broke off the pointy end piece, thinking about what I'd confessed. Two seconds ago, we'd been having a fun conversation about living a life of freedom, and I'd soured the mood with my bullshit.

"Sorry," I said, looking up at him. "Didn't mean to get so serious."

Guy shook his head, his eyes filling with that look he sometimes got when he'd homed in on something I hadn't meant to give away. Shannen had the same look, but while she rarely called me on it, preferring to wait for me to speak in my own time, Guy sometimes asked. "It's okay," he said.

My brother's call had clearly affected me more than I realised. It always threw me how that happened. On the surface, I was simply given a piece of information, but internally, my brain was processing it without my permission, and often, my knowledge.

"Gavin called me just before you did," I told him. "My ex, Flynn, has been released from prison."

Guy's eyes widened slightly. "He was in prison?"

I often forgot to mention that part of the equation. Or maybe I didn't forget. Perhaps I left it out because that information would have given a clue to just how serious his attack on me was. Of course, there is no such thing as 'mild' domestic abuse. It's all awful and wrong, but when a lengthy prison sentence is involved, it indicates that the level of abuse was taken up another notch.

"Yes. For ten years."

Guy placed his coffee cup back down on the table, and said, "Gaby... what did he..." He shook his head, "You never told me he'd been locked up."

"I never tell anyone," I said, meeting his gaze. "Because I'm worried they'll look at me like that." I nodded in his direction, indicating the exact look of sadness and pity in his eyes.

With another shake of his head, he said, "Sorry. I didn't mean to look at you in any way that makes you feel bad, it's just... a surprise, that's all.

Putting my attention back on my cheesecake, I scooped the piece I'd broken off onto my fork. "It's okay. I still don't like to talk about it. I mean... I *can* talk about it, but I haven't in a while, and I didn't intend to mention it today."

"I'm sorry," Guy said again. "Really."

"It's not your fault." I looked up at him. "I brought it up. And I hate it because as soon as the past throws itself into the present, I forget that I can cope and I feel like I'm going to spiral. It pisses me off that the thought of him can sometimes still take me back."

It really didn't happen every time. Most of the time, if I mentioned it, it was just that. A quick hit, a fact of my life that I had dealt with. It was a little harder when he came up out of nowhere, as he had when Gavin phoned me. A thread of uneasiness had woven itself inside me because, when you've lived with so much fear, even when it's over, sometimes the memories can be overwhelming.

"Gabs, we don't know each other that well yet, but if you need to talk about anything, ever, I'm here. I know you have Shannen and Nova too, but I'm just saying. You can talk to me if you want to."

"I know. And I will. But for now, please can we go back to enjoying cheesecake and coffee?" I raised an eyebrow, and Guy chuckled.

"Sure."

Chapter 10

Guy

GABY TURNING SERIOUS OVER coffee and cake was unexpected. I liked that she felt comfortable enough to share things with me, but it had also allowed me to see something about her she likely didn't share with many people. She was vulnerable. Undoubtedly, she was a strong woman who had overcome a lot to be happy, but there was an underlying fragility I'd seen glimpses of and hadn't realised the depth of until that conversation.

I hadn't learned a lot about the specifics of things, but I had been shown that perhaps her cheerful side hid more than she let on.

Her confidence wasn't fake. She wasn't showing a false persona to hide the parts she didn't want people to see. It was more like she had a tiny piece of herself tucked away and it only came out when triggered.

And her brother seemed to have pulled this particular trigger without realising the effect it would have.

I refused to push Gaby to talk more about this event from her past that had seen her ex put behind bars. She didn't seem in the right frame of mind to delve into it, but I'd felt it important to let her know that she could trust me. I believed she knew that already, but I didn't want to let it go without reminding her she was safe with me.

> **Helen: Guy, answer the fucking phone! I miss you. xx**

I huffed out a breath as the message came through on my phone early on Monday morning. She'd called the evening before, when I'd been on my way home from Gaby's, and then again first thing, though I was asleep when that came through. The text didn't exactly make me want to rush to have a conversation with her either.

As I got ready for the day, I thought about what to do about her. With every day that passed, I wanted to talk to her less. We'd done all of our talking the day she walked out, and I couldn't see how rehashing it would help either of us.

Once I was dressed and ready to head over to my old house for work, I typed out a quick message back:

> I don't think there is anything left to say at this point. It's been six months. I don't want to talk.

With that done, I headed out, hopping into my van.

On arrival at my former home, I saw Cal's van already parked outside, and a couple of my other guys' cars too. I was having the electrics re-checked before everyone moved in, and another couple of my team were finishing up the tiling in the bathroom while Cal and I worked on the nursery.

Shannen was going to sort out the arranging of the furniture, but Cal and I had to finish the painting and wallpapering, then rip out the old carpet so the new one could be laid in the morning. The stairs and hallway carpets were being changed the following week, once we were done with what would be Cal and Shannen's room and the living room. The only rooms that hadn't had an overhaul were the kitchen and Aiden's room, which he'd had since he and Cal moved in with me and Helen. We'd asked him if he wanted new wallpaper, but he said he didn't. The only thing he wanted was the bed Cal had bought for him when they moved into the flat. Everything else was to stay the same, which would make the transition easier for him.

As I entered through the front door, I breathed in deeply the scent of paint and the new carpet that had been laid in the office; the best smell ever. The hallway walls were a light grey, with wallpaper on one wall and painted grey on the other and all the way up the stairs. It looked so much better than before. It had desperately needed a refresh for a long time, but as with anyone who works in a business, they tend to neglect their own stuff in favour of doing a good job for everyone else.

I could hear voices and a radio upstairs, coming from the bathroom, where the tiling was happening. As I climbed the stairs, the telltale sound of a scraper was going in what would be the baby's room.

I called out to let everyone know I'd arrived, and three voices returned greetings as I made my way to what used to be Cal's bedroom, where he was scraping the old wallpaper off the wall. Luckily, only one wall had paper on, so it wouldn't take too long.

"Hey," he said with a smile, then nodded to the bucket full of water and cloth near his feet. "I saved you the messy job."

Laughing, I said, "It's only messy because you slop water everywhere. That's why we don't usually let you strip wallpaper."

He was good at his job, but already, he'd managed to get water down the front of his work jeans, and a few flecks of wallpaper were stuck to his white T-shirt.

I went straight for the cloth, rubbing the wallpaper down to make it easier to remove. "You're on it this morning."

"Well, Shannen's pretty eager to get the baby furniture in here, so the quicker we get this done, the better. We still don't have any other furniture in most of the rest of the house, but this is what she deems most important."

He rolled his eyes, but I wasn't fooled. Cal was as excited as Shannen about not only getting the nursery ready but about having a baby. Even though the nursery wouldn't be used for a while, I guessed that having things set up in preparation made it feel more real.

A fleeting memory of Helen and me discussing what we would have in this room for our baby when the time came crossed my mind. I'd always joked that Newcastle United colours would be great, but she'd always quashed the idea. Obviously, a black and white room as a nursery was a bit bleak, but it was non-negotiable for me that, girl or boy, our baby would have a tiny football kit and would be on my lap watching the games from birth. Helen would always just shake her head in exasperation, but back then, she still used to smile fondly at the idea.

We'd come so close to having it. The dream family life.

That was the one thing I *did* miss. The *possibility* of the life we'd wanted. When she was still with me, even at her worst, it was always just within reach. Now, I was back at square one.

"It won't be long until you have everything in here," I said to Cal. "And this time in two weeks, you'll be living here."

He grinned. "Yeah. I can't wait. It's funny how this house was the one that helped me get back on my feet, and now it's mine."

"I tell ya," I said, dunking my cloth back in the water then squeezing it out, "I didn't see this coming."

"What, me getting my shit together?"

"No." I laughed. "This not being my house. But there is nobody else I could imagine living here but you and Shannen. It's perfect for you." As I began to wet the next bit of wallpaper, I said, "How are you feeling about everything?"

"Honestly?" he asked, pausing in his scraping to turn to me, and I nodded. "Like I'm dreaming. Even though some of the year was more like a nightmare, that felt normal to me. It's pretty much how I always expected my life to be. Being happy is weird. But it's getting easier to enjoy it.."

Since the day I bumped into him a few years ago, when he was at his lowest point, I'd wanted to hear that he was happy. He was no angel, but nobody deserved a break more than Cal. When Aiden's real mum was murdered, it set off a whole load of trauma in Cal's head, like her being gone gave him the permission he needed to lose his shit. He'd reached his limit of what he could handle, and while he was coping on the surface, that was about all he was doing. Now, there was a light at the end of all that darkness.

"I'm happy for you, buddy," I said. "You deserve this."

He dropped his head for a moment, a small smile still on his face. "Well, not to get all soppy and unmanly, but I would never be in this position if it weren't for you. I couldn't have turned my life around without your foot up my ass."

Cal was the least sentimental person I knew; at least on the outside. He felt deeply but didn't show it. The fact that he said this out loud caused a lump to form in my throat, which I swallowed down quickly.

Laughing to cover it, I said, "You would have got there eventually. And anyway, Gaby is the one you have to thank for all this. If she hadn't told Shannen to talk to you, none of this would be happening."

Gaby had been the one who'd encouraged Shannen to stay and chat to Cal after seeing how obviously attracted to him she was. She couldn't have guessed Shannen would take him home that same night; we would all have lost money on that bet. But Gaby was the one who had got the ball rolling in the beginning.

He nodded. "That's true. I really should thank her sometime." His face morphed into a smirk. "Unless you've already done that for me."

I flipped him a middle finger, but I couldn't help laughing again. "I have done no such thing with her."

Not that I hadn't thought about it.

"So, when are you seeing her again?" Cal asked, getting back to work, scraping away at the stubborn paper. "Don't leave it too long, mate. She's into you."

"I saw her yesterday. After I left you and Donovan, I called her, and we had coffee and then went back to her place for a few hours."

Cal turned his head to look at me over his shoulder. "Okay..." He threw me a questioning look, waiting for me to elaborate.

"There's nothing much to tell," I said, dunking my cloth again and squeezing out the excess water. "We're just getting to know each other. We talked, watched a movie, had a takeaway."

"And you haven't had sex with her yet?"

"I'm not you!" I flicked the wet cloth in his direction, the water splashing him and making him flinch and swear at me. "I'm not in a rush to get serious."

"Sex doesn't mean serious," Cal pointed out. "Not that I'm suggesting you should mess around with Gaby. I'm just saying, if you both just want a bit of fun, there's nothing wrong with that."

I shook my head. "I don't just want a bit of fun. I like her a lot. I want to not stress over where it's going. I want to take my time and see where it goes. And she seems to want the same. We haven't really had a conversation about it, but we're going to see each other again during the week."

Cal shrugged. "That's fair. You don't need to rush. For what it's worth, though, I think you two would make a good couple."

With a nod, I said, "Yeah. I think so too."

Chapter 11

Gaby

THE FIRST FEW DAYS of my summer post-holiday were spent mostly at Shannen's flat, helping her pack. Her mum had come over to help and also to ensure Aiden was occupied because, for him, this was boring. But with Cal and Guy at work, there wasn't anyone else to look after him. For a while, we'd made a game out of the packing, asking him to go and find things on a list and box them up carefully, but he soon got bored of that, and when the weather was so nice out, he didn't want to be inside drawing or playing on his iPad. He wanted to go outside.

So, on the Friday, as a treat and a break for all of us after working so hard, Shannen and I bundled Aiden into her car and we went to Dawlish for the afternoon. It was Dawlish Carnival Week; one of the most fun carnivals in the South West, in my opinion. I hadn't grown up around it, but Nova had told me about it as she'd lived there most of her life. She was surprised to hear that not everywhere had a regular week of fun in their towns when I'd said I wasn't familiar with the concept. In order to show me what I'd been missing out on, the year before, she'd invited me to stay at hers for a few days, and I had to admit, it was a good time. I pretended to be a tourist, and we watched the pram race, the duck race, played a few games of evening bingo, and of course, watched the procession that ran through the town on Friday evening.

Nova was gutted that she would miss it. She'd never missed a single carnival procession, even when her family had moved to Exeter. They always came back for it, but I argued that she was going somewhere substantially more exotic with the man of her dreams. While excited about the trip, the small-town girl inside her was a little heartbroken she would miss out on the fun of carnival week. She had informed me that they streamed the procession live on social media, though, so I expected she would still catch it that way since she couldn't be there in person.

From my memory of the previous year, the town was always packed on carnival day, and the car parks filled up quickly. Nova said we could park at her place and walk into town, and that was what we did.

At just after five, Guy and Cal joined us, and the four of us wandered around the town for a while, enjoying the excitement that permeated the air. I hadn't seen Guy since Sunday as he'd been catching up on work, but we'd spoken on the phone a couple of times, and we were planning to spend some more time together once we got back to Exeter after the carnival since Guy didn't have work the next day.

As we sat together on the sea wall after we'd finished eating fish and chips, I felt his eyes on me while I was looking out at the sea. Shannen, Cal, and Aiden had wandered along the wall a little way and were taking photos.

"Yes?" I said, turning my head towards him with a curious smile, and he laughed.

"Nothing. Just..." He shrugged, his head tilting as if what he was about to say was no big deal. "You're really, really beautiful."

I shifted my position to face him, offering a flirty grin. "Oh, really?"

"Yes," he said, more seriously now, and he moved in closer to me on the wall. "I've been looking forward to today."

"Me too," I told him, looking up into his eyes. "And for the record, you're not bad to look at either."

Laughing, he wrapped his arm around me, and I breathed deeply as I rested my head on his shoulder. "So, what do you want to do later?"

What I wanted was something I was a bit afraid to voice.

The previous Sunday afternoon, Guy and I had been wrapped around each other for hours, either kissing or while watching a movie, and I'd grown to enjoy the feel of him against me. I wasn't sure why he hadn't attempted to take things further with me, though I guessed it was because he followed my cues a lot. If I *had* tried to move things on to another level, he probably would have gone with it, but I didn't. So, he didn't.

I didn't know if I was ready to have sex with him yet, but what I did know was that after being so close to him for so long the previous weekend, I'd had to relieve the tension on my own once he'd gone.

He was so considerate, and I loved it. Needed him to be that way. But I also hadn't been able to stop thinking about how it would feel when his hands were on my bare skin. Even if we didn't take things all the way, I wanted more.

"I don't know," I said, looking up at him. "Maybe we could go to your place for a while?" The words 'Netflix and chill' lingered on the end of my tongue, but I swallowed them down. I didn't want to come across as desperate.

Although, I couldn't imagine any woman who had looked at his muscles and his angular face hadn't imagined shagging him.

Guy's eyes sparkled as he smiled at me. "Sure. I have movies and pop-corn." A tiny glimmer of mischief lurked behind his words, and it made my skin tingle with goosebumps at the thought of what might happen later. It was like he had heard the subtext I'd tried to conceal.

Plus, I hadn't yet had the pleasure of seeing his new place. I hadn't been there when Cal lived there, and I wanted to see what it was like.

Guy tilted his head forward slightly and brushed his lips lightly over mine. The sensation was gentle yet filled with so much, and I said, "Is the carnival over yet?"

"Not yet," he said, kissing me again. "But we should get ready to make a move soon."

I nodded. When Nova had told us to park by her house, she'd also told us that the main road by her place was where the carnival procession lined up, and it would be better to watch it from there, so we could get home earlier. She knew Aiden would likely get tired if he had to wait in the town.

After a short walk to the car park, we all piled into Guy's car, and I gave him directions to Nova's place. All the way up, there were cars parked in places they shouldn't be; on grass verges, up on the paths of narrow roads, and it was a bit of an obstacle course getting there. Nova's street, thankfully, wasn't packed with cars. Guy parked directly behind Nova's car, and as we all got out, Shannen said, "Look, there's June!"

"Who's that?" Guy asked as Shannen and I waved back to her.

"Donovan's nan," I said.

"If you want to know what Gaby will be like when she's in her seventies, you should go and say hello," Shannen teased, and I burst out laughing before looking back up at Guy.

"I mean... she's not wrong."

Guy shook his head, slight confusion on his face. "What does that mean? Has Donovan's grandma got a secret life as a pole dancer or something?" The corners of his lips tipped up into a grin, and I slapped his arm, still laughing.

"Hey, if I'm still as flexible in my seventies as I am now, I might consider it!"

Cal was also laughing beside me, and at that moment, June's front door opened and she stepped out and said, "Hello! Nova said you might park up here for the carnival. I was wondering, would you mind if I joined you?"

I smiled, as did Shannen, and Shannen said, "Of course not. We can wait here while you put your shoes on."

"Thanks, love," she said. "I won't be a minute."

She left the door open while she popped back inside, and I said, "Well, Guy, I guess you'll find out exactly what Shannen meant now!"

Fifteen minutes later, our now slightly larger group stood at the top of Oak Hill with a bunch of other people who were waiting for the procession to begin. On the way along John Nash Drive, we'd passed the lined-up carnival floats and groups of walkers and other display groups, and it was hard trying not to look at it all before the carnival began. At the front was the fire engine, led by Dawlish Fire Brigade; they and some local bagpipers were always the leaders of the procession.

As we stood at the edge of the road, June tapped Aiden on the shoulder. He'd been bouncing up and down on the balls of his feet in anticipation, and he turned around to look at her curiously.

"Did you know that at the carnival, there are going to be lots of people collecting money so they can make sure there's a carnival next year?" she asked him, and he shook his head. June reached into her bag and pulled out a small money bag filled with copper coins, which she handed to him. "When they come along, make sure you put some of these pennies into the collection buckets."

Aiden smiled as he took them. "Cool! Thanks!"

Then she leaned down to him and whispered, "If you have any left over, you can take them to the arcade next time you go."

His grin widened, then he turned back around to look towards the road, now even more excited for things to start.

"Thank you," Cal said to her. "That was kind of you."

"It's no problem, my love. I used to do this with my daughter when she was younger. I always make sure I have something to give to the carnival, and I thought your lad might like to be the one to give out the donations."

"He will," Cal answered, smiling at June.

She threw him a wink. "Besides, if I'm too busy worrying about putting money in buckets, I won't be able to dance as much."

I flashed Guy a bright smirk; that was *exactly* what Shannen had been talking about. June wasn't quite as steady on her feet these days, but she would still have a little boogie to the music when she could.

"Yes, June!" I cheered, wrapping an arm around her. "I will dance with you too."

"I knew you wouldn't let me down." June grinned, put her arm around my waist, and gave me a squeeze.

With that, the siren on the fire engine let out a loud wail, making everyone jump, and I guessed signalling that things were about to get moving.

The engine revved up and the fire engine came slowly around the corner.

"Here we go!" I said.

Guy was standing behind me now, and he chuckled. "You really aren't cool at all."

"Piss off," I said, but with humour in my tone. "You like my excitement over ridiculous things and you know it."

His hands slipped around my waist, and he pulled me lightly back against him. "I do," he said, resting his chin on my shoulder. "It's one of my favourite things about you."

"You can tell me the others later," I said, looking at him from the corner of my eye, and he kissed my cheek.

"I can do that."

As the bagpipes grew louder, the chatter stopped because it was impossible to hear each other over the noise. Aiden slipped his bag of coins into the pocket of his shorts and put his hands over his ears; they *were* super loud for someone as small as him. However, once they passed, and the fire engine had let out a few more blasts of the siren, Aiden relaxed again and got his money back out.

The carnival procession was so much fun. We watched in amazement as the Rampage Mas band with their huge and extravagant outfits danced and got the crowds fired up even at the start, where there were fewer people than in the town. We saw Dawlish's 'royal family' on their float, and a whole lot of people in fancy dress as various well-known figures ranging from pop stars to cartoon characters and more. There were also displays from local Tae Kwon Do and dance groups, and more still people who'd taken the time to make up their own dance routines for the joy of making people laugh and smile. June, Aiden, Shannen, and I danced whenever some particularly loud music passed us by, while Guy and Cal looked on with amusement.

It wasn't too often we got to be silly just for the sake of it, and I always took any chance I got.

By the time the parade had ended, I was high on life, while Shannen and Aiden looked ready for bed. It was only half past eight when we got back to our cars, the duration of which was spent with June and me singing our heads off to *Dancing Queen*. That woman was a blast, and I imagined as a youngster, she was a riot. Her mind and spirit were those of a twenty-year-old with her quick wit and ability to have a good time.

After we'd said goodbye to June, the rest of us hugged before going our separate ways, Shannen, Cal, and Aiden in her car, and Guy and me in his.

Chapter 12

Guy

BECAUSE THE TOWN'S ROADS were closed due to the carnival, we took the back road out of Dawlish to head back to Exeter. As we wove down the country lanes, I cast a sideways glance at Gaby, who was still dancing in her seat to what I assumed was a song playing in her head, as the car radio wasn't on.

"I never thought I would have so much fun at a small town carnival," Gaby said, smiling across at me. "The first time I went with Nova was also good. We stayed in town for a while, drinking and watching the shows on The Lawn. I had such a hangover the next day." She grimaced at the memory.

"It's a shame she and Donovan weren't here," I said.

"It is, but that woman was in dire need of a long holiday with just Donovan. I don't know how they've lasted months barely seeing each other."

"I can't imagine long distance is easy, especially for a new relationship. Donovan said they only got together at Christmas."

Gaby nodded. "Yeah. Shannen and I met him before they got together, and it was pretty obvious they were hot for each other. I really hope they enjoy the next couple of weeks together."

"I'm not sure how anyone could have a bad time in the Philippines."

Gaby sighed, stretching her arms out in front of her. "I could use a holiday in the sun." She paused. "Well, a different country's sun. Penzance was great, though."

"It was," I agreed. "I didn't realise how badly I needed the break."

There was another pause, then Gaby said, "Have you heard any more from Helen?"

With a groan, I said, "Yeah, a couple of times. I text her back to tell her to stop, and she did."

"Is it strange that she waited for six months to realise she misses you?" Gaby asked. Her face was neutral. She had never met Helen, so anything she knew about her came from me, and maybe Shannen and Cal, none of which would have been very favourable.

"Helen is stubborn," I said. "I can't say if she missed me right away, but I doubt it because she hated me when she left. But whenever she started to feel it, she probably would have tried to pretend it wasn't happening. She'd usually rather die than back down, so if she says she misses me, I believe her. But my feelings remain the same as they have for the last few months. I'm done."

With a slow nod, Gaby turned to face the front again. "So... you're not going to randomly call me and let me know you've changed your mind and you're going back to her?"

I chuckled. "Gabs, there is nothing that would make me consider going back there. I like it here. With you. I'd like to do more of that. And if you're not doing anything tomorrow, maybe we could spend the day together."

A smile formed at the corners of her lips. Running her hand over her hair, she bundled it all up and pulled it over her shoulder, combing out the ends with her fingers. "How would you feel about an escape room?" she asked, her eyes lighting up.

Most girls would have suggested somewhere nice for lunch, or bowling, or something super relaxed. An escape room as a date idea had never even crossed my mind.

"I don't know," I said, thoughtfully. "That's a pretty big commitment this early on. A test of communication and teamwork."

She shrugged. "Well, I figure it's also a good test of compatibility. If we can't manage to get out of a room together, there's probably no hope for us in the long-term."

She was only teasing, but it was still a decent point. One of my employees took his girlfriend of eight months to an escape room, and they'd had such a big fight that they'd split up afterwards. I couldn't envision that being the case with Gaby, though.

"Okay," I said. "You're on. When we get back to mine, we can have a look and see if we can book something, but that won't take up the whole day."

"The whole day, huh?" Gaby said. "That's also a commitment."

"We spent a week together, Gabs. I think we can manage a few hours."

Instead of going straight back to my flat, I asked Gaby if she wanted to go for a drink at On The Waterfront on the Quay, and she agreed and insisted on buying the first round. While I waited for her, I picked up my phone and scrolled through the photos I'd taken through the afternoon and evening. There was a great shot of Gaby and me sitting on the sea wall, the waves shimmering in the background, and I couldn't help thinking how good we looked together. Not only that, though, there was a distinct happiness in my eyes that I hadn't seen in a long time.

"I love that," Gaby said as she looked at the photo over my shoulder before walking around to sit down opposite me and placing our drinks down on the table. I quirked my brow at the bright yellow drink in front of her.

"That's why I paid," she said. "Cocktails are not the cheapest."

I was driving, so I'd just got a Coke, and I shook my head. "I wouldn't have minded. What's in that?"

"Rum, passionfruit, lime, and pineapple, but you can't taste the alcohol that much. It's more fruity."

We'd been lucky enough to bag an outside table, and it was the ideal weather for it. There were a lot of people walking up and down along the canal, and some people were still canoeing in the water too. On The Waterfront was lively, with lots of groups of youngsters, probably students, drinking and having fun.

It made my thoughts turn to the bar I'd be starting proper work on in just over a week. These kids were likely to be the kind of people the place would be full of when it was taken over with it being so close to Exeter University. Whoever took it on would have to be well-versed in dealing with not just drunk people, but young drunk people, and students at that.

"You look lost in thoughts," Gaby said, and I smiled up at her.

"I was thinking about this place and how busy it is, and then about my bar. I'll be starting work on it soon with Cal. I hope whatever we do with it makes it nice enough for people to want to spend time there."

"You will," Gaby said confidently. "You have a plan, right?"

I nodded. "Yeah, and Cal and Donovan helped me make it better, but I'm still not sure if I want to change my mind on some things."

"Like what?"

"Well, my plan was to keep the decor relatively generic. I want it tidied, fixed, and all the plumbing and everything working again before I sell it. That way, whoever takes it on can do whatever they want with it. But it's all wooden flooring and brick walls. There needs to be a decent heating system in place too, but I could maybe leave that to the new owners as I don't know about the costs on that yet." I shook my head to get myself back on track. "I feel like with the way it's already set up, it would make a cool country and western kind of bar, and since Beyonce did that country song, it seems to be making some kind of comeback. But I think that would be too restrictive to sell on at a good price as they would then need to redecorate if they wanted a different theme."

Gaby chuckled to herself. "Has anyone ever told you you're an over-thinker?"

"No," I said with a chuckle of my own. "But mostly because I tend to keep my overthinking to myself. That was what I did when I was buying the bar."

"Why?" Gaby asked, crossing one leg over the other and pushing her hair behind her ear. "You don't trust other people's advice?"

"I do. With the bar, though, I wanted to do that with no other input. I wasn't able to do much without getting Helen's opinion, and once I was on my own, I wanted to see what kind of mad ideas I could have now I was free to have them. And the bar was the first thing I decided on. I spoke to solicitors, as you know. And I do have a business advisor. But I really just wanted to do this by myself."

"I can understand that. When I left Flynn and I'd started to get my life back on track, it was the same for me. When you've lived with someone who hasn't given you a lot of freedom—or none in my case—it's normal and necessary to put your own decisions to the test."

I nodded slowly. "That makes sense. But now I get to second-guess those decisions."

Gaby laughed. "Well, you don't have to do that part alone. And I don't think there is anything to second-guess. You made your plan knowing that you were going to make the bar better but without steering it in any particular direction. I don't think that needs to change. Talk to Cal and some of the guys you work with. See what they think."

I nodded. "Yeah, I will. I do still think the original plan is good, but... sometimes I just need to let some of the other ideas out."

Resting her arms on the table, Gaby said, "Well, let's say for argument's sake you could design the bar a certain way, what would you do with it?"

Leaning forward too, I said, "I do think the country theme would be good. I had this idea that there could be theme nights where people dress up, and maybe something really nineties like line dancing nights and maybe country themed karaoke." I smiled at the idea because I had fully mapped it out from decor to ways to run the place. I had no intention of keeping it, but if I *did*, that was what I would do.

"Oh my God," Gaby said with enthusiasm. "*Please* can you keep it and do that? I'm not even a big fan of country, but that sounds fun. You could have country-themed cocktails like, Man, I Feel Like A Mojito or a Jolene-a Colada."

I threw my head back. "Those are amazing. If I change my mind, I will happily hire you to make up some more cocktail names."

Gaby grinned. "I like a good pun. And also, I like cocktails."

Gaby sat back, relaxing into her chair and turning her head to look around at the people slowly wandering by. A smile spread across her face, and she let out a contented sigh. "I love evenings like this," she said. "The weather is good, it's still warm and light, and everyone is so unhurried. Everyone looks happier in the summer."

She was right. There was a lot of laughter, and a feeling of freedom and possibility seemed to fill the air. Many of the people walking past and even some of the patrons of the bar were likely tourists, checking out the area. They'd stumbled on, in my opinion, one of the best spots in the city. I was glad Gaby had wanted to go out for a drink before we went back to mine. Although, it was getting late. I would offer to take her home when we left in case she'd changed her mind about coming over, but I hoped she wouldn't. Being in her company was a breath of fresh air in the stuffiness of my life.

I loved how easy it was to talk to her. It made me think of something Cal had said about Shannen when he was getting serious with her. How easy everything felt around her, when before, it had always been a struggle to feel comfortable with someone. I had never felt this much ease with a woman. Of course, we both had an advantage in knowing small things about each other from before. The door had been cracked open a little back then, and we'd left it, ready to walk through when the timing was right.

We spent another hour at the bar before getting into my car again. I asked Gaby if she still wanted to come over, and to my surprise, she'd said that she did.

As we entered my apartment, I flicked the light on, and Gaby looked around with interest. We were only in the hallway and there was nothing much to see there apart from a coat and shoe rack. I toed off my trainers and put them on the shoe rack, and then edged past Gaby and said, "This way."

I opened the door on the right that led into the living room, then turned off the hall light and switched on the living room light instead, closing the door behind us.

"Do you want a drink?" I asked her as she, once again, glanced around. I had changed nothing of the decor when I'd moved in because it had only been decorated earlier in the year. It didn't need a refresh, so the grey walls with the geometric wallpaper on one side remained the same as when Cal lived there.

"No, I'm good, thank you."

I gestured for her to sit down on the sofa, and I sat down beside her. "So, what shall we do?"

Gaby tilted her head to the side as if in deep thought, then as she looked back at me, she said, "This might sound anti-climactic, but I like talking to you. Maybe we could do more of that."

"We can," I said, "but on one condition."

"What's that?"

"I would like to put my arm around you."

She smiled warmly. "You don't always have to ask permission, you know?"

"I know," I told her seriously. And there were plenty of times when I hadn't and just jumped in for a hug, a kiss, or to hold her hand or put my arm around her. "But this is your first time here and I'm not the guy who makes assumptions about what you want."

Gaby stared at me for a moment, her eyes softening on me, then she said, "Are you real? Or maybe I fell asleep last night and haven't woken up yet."

"What do you mean?" I asked.

I understood that she was referencing the way I treated her, but had she really met so few men who had considered what she would be okay with that my behaviour was a surprise? Or maybe other men hadn't been aware of the abuse in her last relationship and didn't know to take things slowly.

"Well... I know you know a little about my past, but not enough that you need to be this considerate."

"Gabs," I said, shuffling a bit closer to her, "I don't know everything that happened to you, but before we thought anything might happen between us, you let me in on some stuff you might not have if we'd met with the intention of dating. When it didn't matter to you how I viewed you. I may have filled in some of the blanks incorrectly, but one thing I'm certain about is that you used to be with someone who didn't give you a lot of choice in the things you did. So, I just want to be clear on the fact that I'm not like that. I don't mind how you dress, if you want to go out with your friends, or how you spend your money. As long as you know you can trust me."

Closing her eyes, Gaby sighed and rested her forehead on my shoulder. "I hope you never realise how much of a catch you are, Guy. I'd hate for you to use these powers for evil."

I chuckled. "Well, I have some huge downsides," I said, gently running my fingers through her hair. "I'm really boring. I like simple stuff like drinks at the local pub, watching football, and spending time with people I care about. I guess the upside to that is that I'm open to trying new things, but I don't have any weird hidden quirks or well-buried secrets."

Leaning forward, Gaby kissed me softly. "You're not boring at all. I saw you having a water balloon fight, and the way you, Cal, and Donovan were laughing with each other when you came back from your night out. I've seen how passionate you are about renovating the bar, and how your eyes light up when you talk about the people who are important to you. You're not boring."

I let her words sink in slowly. I *saw* her, but apparently, she saw me too. I wanted everything Gaby symbolised. Happiness, grabbing life by the bollocks and living it with as much energy as it deserved, and the peace of being with someone who wasn't afraid to say what she wanted instead of expecting me to keep up with her ever-changing moods and desires with no explanation.

"Guy," Gaby said softly, and as I looked at her face, her eyes were slightly hooded as she gazed up at me. "Please can I stay here tonight?"

My heart picked up its pace slightly at her words, but I didn't want to take that the way I hoped she meant it. I didn't *need* to have sex with her tonight. If she didn't want to, I would be ecstatic to just be around her for longer. But her eyes flicked from mine to my lips, and as she gently put her hand on my thigh, my dick woke up and jerked slightly.

I nodded. "You can, but-"

Gaby interrupted by pressing her lips against mine again, this time a little more forcefully, and I moved my free hand and placed it on her arm, gently pulling her closer.

"I want to," she said quietly. "I want you."

After taking a second to look into her eyes for absolute confirmation and getting a single nod, I kissed her, and she wound her arms around my neck.

Gaby and I had kissed a lot. We'd never taken things much further, only because I was conscious of not rushing her, but this felt different. She'd already given her consent, but something had shifted even before that. From the first time she'd kissed me on my sofa, there was more urgency to it. Like she'd made a decision, and had maybe even made it before we got back to my place.

Pulling away from her slightly, I said, "Come on."

I got to my feet and took her hands to pull her up with me, then led her through the living room to the hallway that led to my room.

Once we were inside, I took her gently in my arms again and pulled her to me, my hands running from her waist to her hips. Gaby wasted no time moving her hands underneath my T-shirt, and the feel of her soft touch on my back made my heart beat faster again. As she slid her hands higher, it felt like she was trying to explore me, to trace over every part of my body, feel every muscle. And that was a sensation I hadn't had in a long time.

"Gaby," I murmured before moving my mouth over hers again and pulling her hips into mine. She had to be able to feel what she was doing to me because, with every stroke of her fingers over my skin, my dick struggled harder against the confines of my jeans.

"Touch me," Gaby whispered against my lips. "I need you to touch me."

I didn't need a second invitation to that party.

As gently as she had, I slipped my hands underneath her T-shirt and glided them around her back. Her body was firm and toned, and it felt incredible. Unfamiliar for now, but I wanted to make it familiar. Wanted to make it mine.

I wanted all of her to be mine.

Gaby's hands moved back around to my stomach, and she pushed at my top, forcing me to move back from her so she could take it off. While her hands were free, she whipped her own shirt off, and I couldn't stop my eyes from widening as she dropped it to the floor.

Gaby wasn't just toned; she had the most exceptional curve to her waist, her stomach flat and smooth. Her tits were encased in a red lace bra, and they were full enough that they slightly peeked out over the cups, but perfectly proportioned for her frame. Her shoulders were also strong-looking, and as her cheeks flushed slightly under my perusal, I had to fight back the urge to growl like a caveman because fucking hell... she had the body of a swimwear model and the face of a goddamn angel.

"Red lace, huh?" I teased, and she grinned.

"It's not for you," she said with fake nonchalance. "I just like pretty underwear." Her grin told me she was lying a little. I didn't think she'd planned for this, but she had perhaps been aware it was a possibility and dressed for the occasion.

"Well, I can't wait to see what else you have in your collection," I told her, reaching out for her waist to pull her to me again. Looking into her sexy green eyes, I said, "Jesus, Gaby." I wanted to tell her how beautiful she was, but I couldn't get the words to come out, so I hoped my eyes conveyed what I couldn't say.

She reached up to put her arms around my neck, and I pressed my lips to hers again. The kiss was slow, our tongues moving together as she trailed her hands down to my ass, then slowly up my back again, making a shiver run through me. My fingers reached for the clasp of her bra, and she gasped as I successfully unclipped it. I felt the soft weight of her breasts press against my chest, and I slid the straps down her arms, her chest rising and falling faster with the anticipation.

In the bedroom, I'd expected her to be a bit less bold, but she grinned as my eyes fell to her breasts. No hiding, no self-consciousness. She took my left hand, her eyes intent on mine the whole time, and rested it just to the side of her breast as if daring me to make the move.

Has any woman in history been as sexy as her?

She pushed her hips against mine, but she was leaning back enough that I could touch her if I wanted to.

And I wanted to.

Lowering my right hand to her ass, I pulled her as close to me as she could get as my left hand closed around her breast, my thumb rubbing across her pebbled nipple. She let out another gasp that went straight to my dick, making it twitch again. My lips brushed across her cheek and down to her neck as she reached in between us to undo my jeans and shove them down before doing the same with her own. Now, only our bottom halves were clothed, and only in our underwear. A glance down showed me red lacy shorts-style knickers covering the part of her I was now desperate for.

Without warning, I slipped both hands to her hips and lifted her up. When she wrapped her legs around me, her warm pussy against my cock, I muttered a curse word before turning to lay her on the bed.

She circled her arms around my neck again and pulled me down so I covered her body with mine. My knees rested at the sides of her closed legs so my full weight wasn't on her, just my chest against hers as I kissed her more fervently, driven by the way her hands gripped my shoulders and how her hips rose slightly with the rhythm of our kisses.

I lifted my head for a second, just to look at her beneath me, her blonde hair splayed out across the pillow and a look of need in her eyes. Dipping my head, I closed my lips around her nipple, and she arched her back as I hungrily circled my tongue around the bud, alternating between lightly nipping then sucking to soothe the sting.

The small moans and cries coming from her only made me intensify my movements, sucking harder and then moving my lips across the creamy skin of her breast, into the valley between, and then repeating the actions on the other side.

"That feels so good," she murmured, her fingers moving into my hair and running through it as I continued to provide pleasure to her.

It was no longer enough for me, though. I needed more of her, to touch her everywhere, and as I began to leave a trail of kisses down her firm, flat stomach, I couldn't wait to see all of her. Straightening up, I shuffled back a little, moving my knees back then running my hands down her waist to the top of her lacy knickers.

Looking up at her, the rise and fall of her tits as she panted, watching me, I wanted to dive right into her and make her moan in a way she never had before. Wanted to feel her pussy around my dick and watch her face as I made her come.

And then, I wanted to do it again.

Carefully, I pulled the lacy material down over her hips, taking my time because, as desperate as I was to be inside her, I wanted to ride out the anticipation for as long as I could.

Just as I moved the material to her thighs, I noticed a faint scar running almost the full width of her pelvis, with a small line going up to her belly button, and I paused.

Her body tensed beneath me as she saw where my eyes had fallen, and I looked up at her, hoping she didn't think I was horrified by it. I assumed she'd had some kind of surgery, and it had merely taken me by surprise on her perfect, smooth skin.

"I...." She closed her eyes, her head thudding back into the pillow, and I felt like such an arsehole. My hesitation had made her self-conscious and killed the mood in one fell swoop. "I know it's ugly," she said vacantly, her eyes fixed on the ceiling. "I should have mentioned it before, but..." she trailed off, covering her eyes with her arm and breathing deeply.

"Gabs, no," I said, moving to lie beside her, her knickers still only halfway down her hips. "Hey." I gently lifted her wrist to move her arm so I could see her face. "I didn't mean to make you feel like that. It's not ugly. I just wasn't expecting it. Shit. I'm sorry."

She shook her head. "It's not you. I... I had to have an operation a long time ago, and I really hate that bloody scar." Something in the way she refused to look at me told me she didn't want to go into it, and I didn't need her to.

"It's just a scar, Gabs," I said gently. "It's no big deal. If you want to stop, we can do that. It's up to you. Everything is up to you."

Chapter 13

Gaby

EVERYTHING IS UP TO you.

I had always wanted a man who would say those words to me. Not because I wanted to call all the shots, but because I wanted someone who would let me call some of them. And when it came to feeling free in a situation like this... that was the kind of shot I *had* to be able to call.

The fact that Guy had immediately stopped when he'd sensed my upset was another gigantic point in his favour because I needed that. Someone who wanted *me* more than they wanted my body. Before I freaked out, Guy had made it pretty clear that he liked the way I looked, but I was more than that for him. He actually gave a shit about whether I was okay, and on determining that I wasn't, that mattered more to him than what we'd been doing.

And what he'd been doing to me was so good that my body was still sensitive from the sensations he'd created within me.

If you want to keep seeing him, eventually, you're going to have to tell him the truth about what happened to you.

I knew that day would have to come, and if the way he made me feel continued, it would need to be sooner rather than later. But bringing that up could change everything for him. It could change how he viewed me, and whether he wanted to keep on seeing me.

"Gabs," Guy said softly, and I shook my head, realising I'd been zoned out for a while.

I didn't want to spiral now. Not now I'd actually found myself with a man I liked a lot, and who I felt like I could trust.

"Sorry," I said quietly. His eyes were full of unspoken questions, but more than anything, patience danced in his blue gaze, and I clung onto that like the lifeline it was. A silent promise that he wasn't going to push me on the tough stuff. "I hate this. I hate that you're seeing me like this."

"Like what?" he asked, his thumb stroking my cheek.

I shrugged, unsure of a suitable word for how I felt. "I don't know how to explain it. I think... it's just that this isn't who I am. Now, I feel like all you can see are my flaws, or you feel like the person you've been getting to know was a lie and, underneath all the fun, I'm nothing but a mess of hidden trauma."

"That's because that's how *you're* seeing yourself right now. You think I'm judging you as harshly as you're judging yourself because you know the story behind that scar. But I still just see you. There's nothing wrong with getting upset about things that you have a reason to be upset about. You've seen me get upset or pissed off when I've talked about Helen, and you didn't see me any differently. At least, I don't think you did."

The unsure look on his face made me laugh. "I didn't. But still... it's a bit different."

He nodded. "I know. I'm just saying, I thought maybe... when I told you about the stuff with Helen and the issues with her getting pregnant... I thought one of the reasons you never called me was because I seemed like an insensitive prick who had handled everything really badly because I would never fully be able to understand how she felt."

Shaking my head, I said, "No. That was never the reason."

But maybe I should have stayed away. I will never be able to give him everything he wants.

"So," Guy said, dropping a kiss on my forehead. "You want me to take you home? Or shall we get dressed, have a cuppa, and then get some sleep?"

He's so sweet. As ill-advised as it might have been, though, I didn't want to leave him. When I felt safe and as connected to someone as I felt to Guy, I wanted more of it. Even if it might not last in the long-term. Even if we had too many differences to go the distance.

"I don't want to go home," I said. "I want to stay."

He smiled softly. "Okay. So... tea?"

I stared up at his face, all sharp lines and gorgeous eyes that showed so much warmth that I wanted to bathe in them. I wanted to be near him because he felt like... *home* was too cheesy for me. The phrase was overused to the point it made me gag. But with him was definitely a place I treasured.

"I don't want tea," I said, my eyes on his. "I want to stay here, with you. I want to finish what we started."

His eyes narrowed slightly with concern. "You do? I thought the moment was over."

"Well," I said, moving the cover from over us and leaning up on my elbow. "That's the thing about moments. They pass." My eyes fell onto his sculpted torso, then back to the lips that had been kissing me so expertly a short time ago. Just the memory of how they'd felt as he'd licked and sucked on my nipples made my core clench. I lifted up more and wound one of my legs across both of his and then shifted so I was kneeling, straddling his muscular thighs. His eyes on me only aroused me more. "And then..." I continued, leaning down so my breasts lightly brushed his chest, my lips a breath from his, "another moment replaces it. A better one."

I felt his dick jump against my stomach, his breathing shallowing.

"Gaby," he said, meeting my eye. "Are you sure?"

I nodded, my hands moving around to the back of his neck. "I'm sure."

Once again, my eyes traced over his face, hoping he could see how much I meant that. I hadn't felt so much for anyone in a long time. I wanted to make the most of it before it slipped away.

His eyes lingered on mine for a moment longer as if really checking my certainty. Once he'd gotten the answer he was looking for, he leaned in and kissed me, his lips capturing mine gently at first. Brushing softly and then slowly increasing in pace and intensity, and finally, his hands landed on my skin again, making me shiver as he ran them down my waist to my hips.

Offering him one more kiss, I moved back up onto my knees and smiled teasingly as I slowly moved my hips from side to side, lowering my knickers. He watched intently as I pushed the material down further and further until I was fully exposed to him, and his Adam's apple bobbed as he swallowed.

This time, his gaze didn't falter at my scar. It swept from my face, down my chest, and between my legs, and as his eyes darkened with need, I leaned towards him again, kissing him once more, then doing the same thing he'd done to me earlier.

My lips danced along his jawline to his chin, then to his firm, toned chest. I kissed down his abs until I reached the waistband of his boxers. I hadn't taken the time before to look at the bulge there, but I was not disappointed with what I found. Rising back up onto my knees, I pulled his boxers down over his dick. He lifted his hips so I could pull them off before taking my own underwear all the way off and dropping them on his bedroom floor.

Moving back over him, I smiled up at him, right before sinking my lips over his length. He let out a sharp breath as I circled my tongue around the tip, then took him deeper into my mouth, my hands firmly on his hips.

"Fuck," he murmured as I alternated between gentle strokes with my tongue and taking more of him further down my throat. My aim wasn't to make him come in my mouth—not that I was against that—but to have him desperate to be inside me, and as I worked him, I could feel his body begin to tremble.

I released his cock from my hungry mouth and grinned up at him again, licking my lips. His eyes were hooded now, his breathing ragged. Seeing him like that, so turned on from watching me, only increased the slickness between my already damp thighs.

"Do you have any idea how sexy you look right now?" he asked, his voice husky.

My cheeks heated, but I was pretty confident I *did* know. Scar aside, I worked hard to have a body that was strong and lean, and the result of that was that I knew I looked good. However, not many people were allowed to see it, so when I showed it, I was unashamed to use it. If someone got this far with me, they'd earned it, and I wanted Guy to enjoy every second of it as much as I would.

I didn't offer him a verbal response, I just winked, and he held onto my hips again, gripping them with his strong hands as I leaned over him, his dick pressing against my stomach as I kissed him again.

His arms circled around my back, and he held me close to him, his tongue darting into my mouth, and Jesus Christ, he was a great kisser. I was pretty sure I could have got off from his kisses alone.

I needed to feel him inside me. My body tingled from the way he stroked my skin with his hands and teased my lips with his.

"Gaby, I need to..." he murmured, and I looked up at him, breaking the kiss. He nodded downwards, and I chuckled, realising he'd interrupted me to get protection.

"Sure," I said, kissing him once more, then rolling off him and onto my back while he leaned over to his bedside cabinet.

"There had better be some in here," he said, his voice strained.

As I looked over at him, staring at the muscles in his back as he searched in the drawer, I wondered if he'd had any need for them since he'd moved here. He'd been single the whole time, but I supposed that didn't mean he hadn't had a few one-nighters here and there. He was a man, after all. And a super attractive one at that.

"I'm..." I began, then stopped. Regardless of my circumstances regarding accidental pregnancy, condoms were something I always required, and I would have placed money on the fact that Guy was the same.

I wasn't sure he'd heard me, as a couple of seconds later, he turned back over, a condom in his hand and a smile on his face. "Thank fuck."

Laughing again as he opened the packet and rolled the condom into place, I said, "Just once tonight, huh?"

Guy chuckled. "Yeah, but we can rectify that tomorrow. If you want to," he added, looking over at me, and I laughed again.

"I'm confident that is going to be a yes."

He smiled as he shuffled closer to me, and as he raised his leg as if to climb on top of me, I stiffened slightly.

Not now, I begged my brain, but it was too late.

Instead of letting my internal protection system blare out its usual 'stranger danger' warning when I was with someone new, I lightly pressed against his chest, moving him onto his back so I could take up the dominant position and straddled him again.

"Okay," he said with a smirk. "I like this." His eyes were both soft and on fire as he raked his gaze over my face with a fondness I hadn't been prepared for.

And I liked it.

His hands reached out for my waist, and I slowly sank down onto his length.

A tiny moan fell from my lips at the sensation, and I closed my eyes as I began to move.

Even through closed lids, I could feel him watching me as I lifted and lowered myself over and over, slowly at first just to enjoy how it felt. His hands moved to my hips, not trying to control the pace, just holding me, and when they slipped around to my ass, I sighed at the feeling of him lightly squeezing.

It made me move faster, and I leaned down towards him so I could feel his lips on mine again. As I did, his hands moved up my back, and I propped myself up on my arms so I could balance and ride him harder.

Guy's hands roamed to any part of me he could reach as my core fluttered around his dick. I was getting close now, and my breathing became heavier with the need to reach that release that I knew was going to be so damn good. Guy's breathing also increased, as did the strength of his grip on my skin as he raced to his own climax. With him supporting my hips, I moved over him a little more, and he lifted his head so he could capture my breasts with his mouth.

I cried out as he sucked on the soft flesh, his hips bucking to meet mine, my body coiled and ready to erupt.

"Guy, I-" I couldn't get any more words out as the bomb inside me detonated, and I moaned out my pleasure into the room, still riding him harder and harder until his dick throbbed inside me. His body stiffened, his hips meeting mine with ferocity and then slowly unclenching as his body relaxed, and I fell onto his chest.

He was still inside me, but I didn't care. I wanted to bask in the feeling of what we'd just done, and he wound his arms around me, our skin hot and sticky.

"Yeah," he said, his voice husky. "I would like to do that again."

Chuckling against him, I said, "So, we'll add condom shopping to the agenda for tomorrow."

He held me tighter. "Good idea." There was a pause, then Guy said, "Gabs?"

"Mmhmm?"

"I really like you."

I lifted my head from his chest to look him in the eye, and I could see how much he meant it. Nodding, my hair brushing against his skin, I said, "I really like you too."

I liked him so much that I knew that, if we were going to go from 'seeing each other' to becoming a couple, I was going to have to open up about the things in my past a lot sooner than I wanted to. He deserved the truth from me.

The truth that might put an end to us before we'd really begun.

Chapter 14

Guy

WHEN I WOKE UP the next morning, I was pretty sure I had dreamt that Gaby had spent the night with me. However, her arm was laying across my chest, one leg hooked over both of mine. Still naked.

And the sight of her still took my breath away.

Gaby Davis was, without a doubt, the most incredible woman I'd ever met. Beautiful and sexy, and she also had this sense of inner strength and passion that had always caught my attention. I'd never truly expected for us to get this close. I'd hoped, but I didn't think it would happen. Slowly, over time, she was learning to trust me. It was clear she had a lot of defence mechanisms in place, and I hadn't set out to break them down. Maybe that was the difference. That I had no expectations of her. The mutual attraction had been obvious right away, but that didn't mean it would lead anywhere.

But it had, and apparently, the confidence she showed day to day fully extended to the bedroom.

The memory of how Gaby had looked in her red bra and knickers, how she'd looked naked on top of me, were seared onto my brain. She had taken control, and not in an 'it's all about me' kind of way. She wasn't selfish. In fact, she'd known exactly how to turn me on, to take me to the edge until I was ready to lose my mind.

Her skin was so soft and smooth, and her body was perfect, even down to the scar she didn't want to talk about. And the sounds she made as she got closer and closer to her own climax rang in my ears long after we'd showered and she'd fallen asleep.

The best thing about it, though, was that it was fun. We'd even had a moment of laughter when we realised there was only one condom.

I couldn't remember the last time sex had been fun. With Helen, it was functional and on her terms, and it had been that way for a long time.

Being with someone who didn't want to control every aspect of it, and who cared whether or not I had a good time, was a refreshing change. I couldn't help hoping that this wasn't going to be some kind of summer fling. Not because I thought she was that kind of woman, but because a small part of me felt like she might still be cautious of anything long-term. Gaby hadn't been in a relationship for ten years, and if that was by choice, then I wasn't sure why she might suddenly be ready now, or why I was the one she wanted to take the step with.

I almost laughed out loud at my own negativity. Seemed I had a few scars of my own. No surprise since I'd felt little to no affection from Helen for a while. I'd been the person she took her frustrations out on, and almost everything was my fault. I was 'uninterested in her,' 'wasn't doing enough to ease her stress'. Wasn't good enough in bed, like that was the standard for getting someone pregnant. I was used to being run down, so being with someone who didn't do that was the change I needed.

Gaby's hand drifted from my chest to my stomach, her body moving slowly as she wound her leg tighter around me, pushing her pussy into my thigh. As she shuffled closer, her tits pressed into my chest, fully awakening my dick. She tilted her head on the pillow to smile sleepily up at me. Her hair was messy, as if we'd been thrashing around all night, and more blood rushed to my cock at the idea of me being on top of her as she writhed beneath me, those sexy moans falling from her lips as I made her come over and over.

"Good morning," she said, her eyes on mine. As if she knew what I was thinking, she shifted the leg that was draped over mine and climbed on top of me. She wiggled her hips against my dick. "I see someone's awake."

The grin she gave me made me let out a frustrated groan. "There should be a law against anyone being this sexy first thing in the morning," I murmured, making her laugh.

"You're one to talk." I could feel her nipples hardening against my chest, and I rolled my hips against her, wishing I could be inside her.

"Are you always this horny right after you wake up?" I asked her, in between kisses.

"Nope," she said, pulling away from me slightly. "But I've never woken up beside you before."

My chest swelled at her words, at the smile she gave me, and I moved my hands down to her ass, pulling her hips even closer to me before rolling us over so I was on top. "I want you so much right now," I told her, my voice low.

She moaned at my words, grinding her hips against mine once more. "I want that too," she breathed, but her body stiffened slightly beneath me. She wiggled her hips, then slipped out from underneath me, turning me so I was on my back again so fast I wasn't even sure how she'd done it. The flush on her face sent another signal down to my dick as she climbed on top of me, but I knew we had to slow it down, no matter how badly I wanted her.

"Gabs," I said, my voice strained. "You're going to have to stop tormenting me."

"If it's any consolation, I'm also tormenting myself." Her hips were rocking slowly against me, her voice heavy with desire, and I circled my arms around her.

"Tonight, we will make up for this," I promised, kissing her lightly. "But right now, I need a cold shower before my balls explode."

Gaby grinned. "I'll hold you to that."

⊱✦⊰

I wasn't sure how I made it through the weekend. It was like some kind of dream. An image of a perfection I hadn't experienced or believed could be real before. And yet there I was, having breakfast with the most incredible woman on Saturday morning, followed by a fun trip to a detective-themed escape room, which we managed to escape from with seven minutes to spare. Saturday night was spent at my place, and thankfully, we had kept our promise of going condom shopping.

Then, on Sunday, we went to Corfe Castle in Dorset. Gaby was especially excited about it because Corfe Castle was the inspiration for Enid Blyton's Kirrin Castle from the Famous Five books. For a bookworm such as her, it was the ideal day out.

I hadn't expected one weekend to make me feel so much for someone. Everything was going at a good pace, and walking around, holding her hand made me feel like I'd won the lottery.

We'd finished Sunday with her once again riding me into another mind-blowing orgasm, but she'd insisted on going home because I had to work in the morning. However, if she'd wanted to stay with me for one more night, I wouldn't have minded at all. Not just for the sex but because having her with me, feeling like I was part of something again, felt really good.

Once I was back at home, all alone, I pulled my phone out of my jeans pocket, where I'd left it for hours unopened. I'd used it a few times that afternoon to take photos, but after that it had stayed where it was because I was too busy enjoying the time with Gaby.

"What the hell?" I muttered as I saw there were five missed calls from Helen, and underneath, a string of text messages.

> **Helen: Why are you on Facebook with your arm around some woman? Who is she?**

That was the first one, and I rolled my eyes. She must have seen the post from the escape room on their Facebook page. They took photos of people who had attempted the rooms, and Gaby and I had agreed to having ours taken.

The next message was only a preview, and it said:

> **Oh my God. She's that teacher from Aiden's school! Are you and Cal...**

Then it tailed off.

The messages and calls had all happened that day between half past three and six, when she'd presumably given up. It was close to ten p.m. now. Out of sheer curiosity, I unlocked the phone to see what the end of the message said, and the two others that had followed it.

> **Are you and Cal trying to work your way through the whole school's staff? Who's next, Mrs Braithwaite?!**

Mrs Braithwaite was the headmistress of Oakwood Lane Primary School, and I shook my head. Helen was acting like a jealous girlfriend, and she had absolutely no right to be blowing up my phone, asking questions that didn't concern her.

The next message said:

> **Answer the phone, Guy. I need to talk to you. It's important.**

And the next:

> **Fuck you.**

115

Shaking my head as I deleted the messages, I sighed. If what she wanted was so important, texting me *fuck you* ten minutes after the previous message she'd sent wasn't helpful. Why not just tell me what she wanted?

My guess was that she didn't have anything important to tell me at all. Instead, she wanted to quiz me about Gaby, and I wasn't up for that conversation.

My phone vibrated in my hand, but this time, it was Gaby.

Thank you for the best weekend xxxx

Smiling, I let out a sigh. It *was* the best weekend. I'd enjoyed every minute of it. No awkwardness, no lulls in conversation, no discomfort.

And going back to work, even though I was excited to start work on the bar, was going to seem boring in comparison.

I had the best time too. Can't wait to see you in a few days xxxx

Truer words had never been written.

And this was turning into the most interesting summer I'd had in a long time.

Chapter 15

Gaby

I LAY IN BED on my own after the most amazing weekend, wishing I had stayed at Guy's for one more night. He'd asked me to, but I was conscious of the fact that he had work in the morning, and I didn't want to monopolise so much of his time that he got sick of me. I'd gone into Friday thinking I'd spend that evening with Guy and then go home, and if I was lucky, maybe see him some time over the weekend too. I didn't anticipate staying over on both Friday and Saturday night, and spending two whole incredible days with him. The summer was always my favourite time of year, and Guy was making it so much better.

When we'd been in Penzance, we'd moved slowly while getting to know each other. We'd made as many plans together as we could without feeling like we were breaking away from the group too much, but when the others were doing couple-y things, we did couple-y things. I'd wondered then how that would translate when we got home. Whether it would fizzle out the way it had before. But this weekend proved that fizzling wasn't an option.

Sizzling, however...

My stomach fluttered at the memories of the nights we'd spent together.

Jesus. Something about him made my body come alive in a way it hadn't since I met my ex; the awful one. I was having to work really hard to control my inner monologue that told me a man couldn't be this amazing without hiding some dark secret or flaw. Not that I believed *anyone* was perfect, obviously. Just that my ex had started off fine. Allowing me time to myself and to be with my friends before the subtle digs began. I knew deep in my heart that Guy wasn't going to be that way, but my defence mechanisms had been in place for years and were always there to spot any possible red flags. And apparently, it had decided that no red flags was a red flag. I'd pacified the noise by reminding myself that it was possible to enjoy being with someone while still being alert, and that was what I would do.

But that wasn't the whole issue for me. *I* was the one withholding a secret. Two, actually. One of the other reasons for taking a break for the night was because I had discovered I still had a pretty gigantic issue with sex. And while I would have to address it eventually, I still wasn't ready to lay myself open yet.

The truth was, if I told him about that issue, I would have to tell him why, and I hadn't told that story in... forever. Not even to Nova and Shannen. I'd told the story to police officers, to my parents and my brother, and one guy I liked in the past who subsequently decided I was too damaged for him to date. I probably was back then. He was the first man I started seeing after I moved to Exeter, so around eight years ago. Before I'd finished the therapy I needed to get myself properly on track.

I was worried Guy would think the same. That when he knew everything about me, he'd realise that we needed to end this thing before it got too serious.

I squeezed my eyes closed.

What the hell did I have to do to be happy? Fully, totally, completely, and allowed to have all the things I'd ever wanted. Or at least, most of them.

I heard my phone buzz on my nightstand, and I reached over for it to find a message from Nova in our WhatsApp group chat. She, Shannen, and I had had the group since just before Christmas, and we used it for all kinds of things from silly memes to an SOS when one of us had something important to chat about. Thankfully, an SOS was rare.

> **Nova: Hey, is anyone still awake? xx**

I did some quick time zone maths in my head and realised it was just after seven-thirty in the morning in the Philippines, where she was currently having the time of her life with Donovan. She'd been sending us photos from the beach, from the cute hut-apartment they were staying in, and Shannen and I good-naturedly told her how much we hated her for being in such beauty while we were stuck at home.

I typed back:

> **I'm here. You're awake early. Donovan can't have run out of morning wood already! xx**

I grinned as she immediately sent a tongue poking out emoji then started typing again.

> **Nova: He had a super early start this morning. He wanted to catch the sunrise, and then he had a few jobs to do for his bosses here. Was hoping for a lie-in, but that's not happening. I miss you both, though, and was wondering if you fancied a video call. xx**

I was typing back that I was up for it when a message popped up from Shannen.

> **Shannen: I'm awake too. Aiden's asleep and Cal is heading to bed, so I have some time xx**

Once I had confirmed I was good for a call, I turned on my bedside lamp and sat up a bit, quickly throwing on the first T-shirt I could reach that was balancing on the chair by the window. When I was suitably clothed, I joined the call and smiled at seeing my favourite girls before me.

Nova was also obviously still in bed; I could see the headboard of her bed behind her, and she was wearing the blackberry pyjamas she had bought to go to Cornwall. I idly wondered why she'd even taken them with her as I imagined she and Donovan had intended to spend most of the two weeks they were together naked. Shannen was in her living room, on the sofa, and I could see stacked boxes behind the couch, all ready to start taking across to their new house over the next few days. She was still dressed, and her long, dark curls were thrown up in a messy ponytail.

"Hi," Nova said brightly. She looked fantastic considering how early it was for her. Her cheeks had a lovely tan, and her hair was down over her shoulders. Her eyes held a happiness in them that told me how much she needed this time with her man, and I smiled back at her. When I glanced at Shannen, she was also beaming at our friend.

"Hi," Shannen said, and I waved with a grin. "How's it going over there?"

Nova dropped her head back for a second, laughing. "Oh my God. This resort is insane. That's why I've sent you so many photos, although it's impossible to do it justice. It's huge, and there is so much to do here, and the beach... I am not looking forward to coming home. Apart from to see you two, of course."

Shannen and I laughed.

"I'm glad you're having fun," I said. "You look great."

"I've been in the spa a lot," she admitted with a giggle. "Donovan isn't doing much work at the moment, but anytime he's gone, I've had my ass in the sauna, or I've gone for a massage or a facial. The perks of him working here are that I don't have to pay for anything. I was expecting things to be discounted, but Donovan's bosses are so nice, and they said I'm Donovan's guest, and therefore, I can use whatever I want. So, I'm taking advantage of that."

"Good for you," Shannen said. "I don't blame you at all!"

Nova smiled, then said, "How are things with you two?"

Shannen wiggled her eyebrows. "Everything is normal here. Ask Gaby what she's been doing this weekend!"

Nova laughed, and I couldn't help joining in. "What do you know about my weekend, Shannen?" I asked with an arched brow.

"Just that you were with Guy for most of it," she answered, smiling. "Cal text him to see if he wanted to go for a drink last night, but he said he was with you. And I know you were with him on Friday night so..." she trailed off, tilting her head to the side as if waiting for me to fill her in.

"All weekend?" Nova teased. "Tell us more!"

"Oh my God," I said, shaking my head as my friends waited expectantly. "Yes. I was with Guy all weekend. I stayed over on Friday night and last night, and I've only been home for about an hour."

Looks of mock scandal crossed their faces, and then they both burst out laughing again. In that moment, I was struck by how much they both meant to me. To have such close friends was something I'd missed out on for years. I'd been close to Nova for a while, but Shannen and I had known each other for under a year, yet the three of us had such a great bond. I wished we were all together in person, maybe having another one of our sleepovers.

"So, what did you do all weekend?" Nova asked, and this time she wiggled her brows.

"Minds in the gutter, both of you," I said, but I snorted out a laugh. "Yes, we did some of that, but we also went out for lunch and drinks, and we did an escape room, and yesterday, we went to Corfe Castle. It's been a good weekend."

I could see their smirks, and if I were the one questioning them, I would have undoubtedly asked them if the man they'd spent forty-eight hours with was any good in bed.

"Yes, he was fucking phenomenal," I told them, and they both lost it, their laughs loud at my answer to the unspoken question.

"I did *not* need that information," Shannen said, "but I'm glad you enjoyed yourself."

"Oh, like you haven't wondered!" She gave a slow one-shoulder shrug, and soon, we were giggling like teenagers, but the thoughts I'd had before they called still lurked on my mind.

"What is it?" Nova asked, as both she and Shannen seemed to feel my change of mood.

"Eh," I said, "It's nothing really." I shuffled, adjusting my position in the bed, then blew out a breath. "I like him a lot, but I... I'm worried about how to tell him about the stuff with Flynn."

Actually, they didn't know about the things I needed to tell Guy either, but they did know about the abuse.

"There's no rush to tell him. Obviously, Shannen knows him better than I do, but Guy seems trustworthy to me, and he seems like he would be understanding."

"He is trustworthy," Shannen confirmed. "I wouldn't have encouraged you spending time with him if he wasn't. But I guess it still isn't going to be easy to explain the things that happened to you."

"I trust him," I said. "More than I probably should after such a short time. But I still also don't want to throw it all at him yet. But... I also need to. I feel like I owe it to him to be honest about everything. I don't want to keep it from him. And I don't want to keep it from you either, but... it's hard to talk about."

"Gaby," Nova began tentatively. "Do you remember when Shannen first met Cal and she was worrying about things she couldn't know the outcome of yet?" I nodded. "Well, maybe you should take your own advice. I know it's not quite the same and you have something you need to explain to him, but this is really new between you. You've already said you trust him, so why not just enjoy being with him until you're ready to share?"

She was right. It *wasn't* the same as Shannen debating whether or not to keep seeing Cal. Mine was something that could change everything about how he viewed me. But she was also right that it was early days and maybe I didn't need to be tying myself up in knots over this already. Maybe in a few weeks, things would stop between us like it had before.

Deep in my gut, though, I knew that wasn't the case. Something had shifted over the weekend, and unless something huge occurred, I was in this now, and I wanted to stay in it.

With a sigh, I said, "Yeah, you're right. I like him a lot, but I don't want him to look at me differently."

"Guy is the most understanding, patient man I've ever met," Shannen said gently. "And if you'd met his ex, you'd realise how much of an impressive feat that was because I consider myself patient, and I found her almost impossible to be around. I don't think you have anything to worry about, Gabs. He'll understand."

Chapter 16

Guy

"ONLY YOU COULD DECIDE to move house on the hottest day of the year," I said to Cal as we lifted his sofa off the back of the removal van and carried it up the driveway of his new home.

It was just after ten in the morning and so warm that Cal, Luke, Johnny, and Mike who worked for me, and I, had already shed our shirts. Luckily, the kitchen appliances had all been set up a few days ago, so the fridge was stocked with cold drinks and the freezer had ice lollies and ice cream for us to help keep us cool. Gaby was helping too, and Shannen's mum, Annie, her sister, Sadie, and her husband, Stefan. Shannen was out in the back garden with Aiden and her four-year-old nephew, Alexander.

Aiden had almost cried with joy when he saw what they'd set up for him out the back. They'd got a swing set, a trampoline, and they'd also put up a goal for him to practice football. Because of the heat, they'd also opted for a paddling pool, which they'd put water in first thing so he and Alexander could keep cool.

"I didn't exactly check out the long-term weather forecast before we picked a moving date," Cal said, rolling his eyes. "At least with so many people helping, it won't take too long to get everything in."

Aiden's room, the kitchen, and the bathroom had already been set up in full, as had Shannen's office and most of their bedroom except for the bed. Those rooms being ready helped immensely, but there was still the nursery stuff, the living room items, and bits and pieces for the spare room to deal with. Also, Shannen, like Gaby, had a crap ton of books and bookshelves, which were going to be a pain in the arse to get into the house and set up.

"It's a shame Donovan isn't still here," I said. "He and Nova would have been a great help."

Cal nodded, grimacing slightly as we twisted the couch to get it through the front door. "Yeah, they would. Still, at least we can look forward to a few beers and a barbecue later. We'll send them photos so they can be jealous." He snorted, both of us knowing that Donovan and Nova were too busy on their holiday to be envious of our day.

We silently manoeuvred the sofa into place in the living room, where Gaby was sorting out some of the boxes that had been dumped in there already and preparing to take them to the relevant rooms. She'd flung all of her blonde hair back into a scruffy bun, and she was wearing a white vest top and black shorts, her feet bare. She had a gorgeous tan from being out in the sun, and as she moved a box from one stack to another, I couldn't stop myself from staring at her strong, toned physique.

"Focus, dickhead," Cal teased, and I turned around to see him smirking and shaking his head.

His words seemed to shake Gaby out of whatever thoughts she was lost in, and she turned around and smiled. As she did, she reached up to her ear and pulled out an earbud. She only had one in, presumably so she could hear if anyone called to her, and I smiled back at her as her eyes fell to my bare chest.

"Okay," Cal said, dragging out the word as he saw the obvious connection between Gaby and me. "I'm going to leave you to it."

He left the room, and I walked over to Gaby and pulled her into my arms. It wasn't like this was the first time I'd seen her that morning. We'd had a few sneaky kisses before we got started on the moving process, but she looked so cute concentrating on the task she'd been given that I couldn't resist her.

"Hey," she said, circling her arms around my neck and dropping a kiss on my lips. "How's it going?"

"Good," I told her, my hands dropping to her ass. "We need to get a few more of the bigger items out of the van, but after that, it's just boxes of mostly books, which Shannen has already warned me must be placed on the shelves alphabetically."

Gaby laughed. "I prefer a genre system, but whatever works! I'll be glad when it's all done. I'm psyched for a big greasy burger in a bun, covered with onions and slathered with ketchup."

Only Gaby could make a beefburger sound sexy, helped by the distant look of longing in her eyes, and I groaned. "How? How did you make that sound so good? Did you work for M&S in a past life?"

With a laugh at my reference to Marks & Spencers' overly erotic TV ads which had been labelled as 'food porn', Gaby said, "What can I say? I like food!"

She did too. She didn't put junk food into her body constantly, but she didn't shy away from it either.

"I'm also looking forward to seeing you on chef duty," she added, grinning.

"I do make a mean burger." I'd briefly practised my barbecuing skills while we were in Penzance on one of those camping barbecue things. But the one in the back garden was way better, and since I had no need for it in an apartment, I'd left it for Cal and Shannen.

"Is it still okay for me to come over to yours tonight?" she asked. "Heaving furniture around all day is exhausting, so if you want to take a rain check…"

I silenced her with a kiss, and she chuckled into my mouth. "I don't. Besides, to get the full Premier League experience, you need to start the day off right!"

Against her better judgement, Gaby had agreed to watch Newcastle's first match of the season with me. The first games were on that afternoon, and Cal and I were planning to have everything done by the time the five-thirty game kicked off. We'd reluctantly accepted the 12.30 game wouldn't be an option, but we were going to put the TV on anyway so we could see it while we were lugging stuff around.

"And what does this include, exactly?" she asked, her head cocked to the side with curiosity.

I was totally bullshitting because I wanted her to stay at my place. I'd only seen her once during the week, and that wasn't enough for me. "A full English breakfast with a beer, followed by a re-watch of the best Premier League goals scored in the last ten years. Then, I'll give you a guide to Newcastle United's team, so you know who to cheer when they're playing well. And finally, I will personally sing you the team's most popular chants and songs. Then, it should be time for the match."

She stared at me, and I was only able to keep a straight face for a moment longer, at which point, she slapped my arm. "I may have known you were joking, but none of that would actually surprise me!"

Grinning, I kissed her again. "The only part of that I will fulfil is the full English breakfast. If you want. If not, I can make something else, and I'm sure we can find a way to entertain ourselves until game time."

"I would like the full English breakfast," she said. "Maybe we could go to the gym after for a quick workout and lunch?"

I could think of other ways I wanted to burn off the calories we were going to be eating, but instead of saying so, I just nodded. "We can do that. But for now, I'd better get back to work so we can get this place finished up."

Our attention was caught by the sound of Aiden, Alexander, and Shannen laughing out in the garden, and we turned our heads to look out through the patio door. Annie was looking sheepish, but her shoulders were shaking with laughter too.

"Well done, Mum," Shannen said, heading for the back gate. "Maybe no more football for you."

Aiden, still giggling, ran to the goal and said, "No, keep playing! You just need to practice."

A moment later, Shannen returned, carrying Aiden's football, and I assumed Annie had fired it over the fence and into the paved area behind the garden gate. Shannen tossed the ball to Aiden and said, "I'm going to go inside to help Gaby for a while, but I'll be back!"

Shannen padded across the patio area and inside, shaking her head. "I think my mother is ready to join the Lionesses," she said with a laugh as she came to stand beside us, then grinned because Gaby and I were still wound around each other.

"Aiden will have her trained up in no time," I said, then dropped a kiss on Gaby's forehead. "Right, back to work for me. I'll see you both in a bit."

Gaby and Shannen were smiling as I left the living room and headed down the hallway, stopping briefly by the kitchen to grab a bottle of water from the fridge. I was opening the bottle as I walked out of the open front door, and my feet stumbled as I took in the scene in front of me.

When I'd last been out front, everyone was moving furniture back and forth, sharing a laugh on the way. Now, all activity had stopped. Luke and Mike were standing on the path by the removal van, holding one of the bookshelves, Stefan had paused at the back of the van carrying a box, and Cal was standing on the front path, staring at Helen.

She had her back to me, and my heart stopped at the sight of her. What the hell was she doing here, now? Of course, she didn't know I'd moved, but her just showing up was not okay with me, especially when I'd made it clear that I had nothing to say to her. I was also not thrilled that she'd come when Gaby was in the house. Helen was aware I was seeing her, but I didn't need her kicking off about it.

What I didn't understand was why silence had fallen and everything had ground to a halt. Cal glanced over Helen's shoulder when he saw me standing on the front step, and his eyes were wide and his face a little pale.

"What's going on?" I asked, walking down the steps.

At the sound of my voice, Helen turned around, and I stalled in my movements as my gaze fell on her.

She looked good. Her blonde hair was longer, and she had left it hanging over her shoulders. She was wearing a pale blue dress that ended just above her knees.

And she was pregnant.

I knew her body. I'd known it for years, and it had never changed. Helen was slim and lean, with very few curves. It didn't matter what she ate or drank, she never gained weight. Now, though, her stomach was protruding from the front of her dress, and the bump didn't look too different in size from Shannen's.

My own eyes widened, and the world seemed to spin around me for a second.

"Hi," Helen said, her eyes on me, watching for a reaction.

Maybe the child she is so obviously carrying isn't yours. That would be a reason for her not to have mentioned it at any point in the last six months.

But it *was* mine. I could feel it deep in my bones, and it rendered me speechless and unable to move.

And clearly, everyone else felt the same way.

"Guy, can you..."

Gaby's voice rang out from behind me, and that snapped me out of the daze I was in. I spun around to look at her, but she had also spotted Helen and had frozen in place on the front step, her mouth dropping open.

Almost instinctively, I flicked my head to look at Helen again, and she was glaring in Gaby's direction.

Say something. Move!

The potential confrontation between my ex and the woman I was now seeing forced my feet to turn back towards Gaby. All I could think of was that she was going to either think I'd kept this from her, or she would assume whatever the hell was going on here would mean I would go back to Helen.

And while I didn't have any answers on anything, the one thing I was sure of was that I didn't want Gaby to think I was a liar.

As I approached, her gaze flicked to me, and apparently, I was showing my own shock pretty clearly because instead of flipping out, she said, "You need to get out of here." The words sounded confident, but she swallowed hard, and I could practically see her heart pounding in her chest. Her eyes flitted around the garden, where everyone remained motionless, watching to see what would happen next. While Gaby was pretty happy to be in the spotlight when she chose it, she wasn't so keen on it when it was thrust upon her like this. It wasn't just her who was under scrutiny, but the feeling was almost palpable. "Go somewhere and talk to her."

I shook my head, the shock and speed of everything still rushing through me. "Gabs..." But I didn't know what the end of the sentence was. What I wanted was to get in my car with her, not Helen, and have a drink while I processed what was going on.

Gaby put her hands on the tops of my arms, her thumbs stroking lightly across my shoulders. The move pulled me out of my own head, and I focused on her eyes. She took a long, slow breath, then said, "Don't worry. There are enough of us here to help Shannen and Cal. And I'll... I'll be here when you get back, okay?"

Her eyes were sparkling very slightly with moisture, but behind that, it was clear she meant it. That she would stay. Even if they finished moving everything in, she would wait for me.

I didn't want to go, though. I didn't want to talk to Helen any more than I had before.

But I *needed* to talk to her. To find out what the hell was going on and why, instead of telling me sooner, she'd been texting me to say she missed me.

Nodding, I placed a quick peck to Gaby's lips before looking at her one more time and then turning back to Helen. Her face was stoic, but I saw the twitch in her jaw that let me know she wasn't happy with what she just saw. Perhaps I should have been more considerate of Helen's feelings, and usually, I would have been, but her appearance, complete with baby bump, had thrown me off. A strange whooshing sound filled my ears, and I felt like I was floating outside my body for a moment.

I still had the bottle of water in my hands, and I chugged some of it back, hoping the icy liquid would awaken my senses again. It did, and I looked at Cal. Everyone else was *still* in the place they'd been when I came out into the garden.

"I need to..." I began, once again unable to finish the sentence, and Cal nodded.

"Go," he said. In his eyes, I could see his concern and surprise at this turn of events, and he added, "Come back when you're done."

That wasn't an order to get my arse back to work, it was the request of a friend who knew I was going to need someone to talk to once I'd heard all I needed to from Helen. And all the people who knew me the best were there, at Cal's new place.

"Will do," I said, then moved my focus to Helen. "Where do you want to go to talk?" I asked her.

She shrugged. "I hadn't thought about that. I wasn't expecting this." She gestured to all the people moving Cal and Shannen's stuff in.

"It might have been better if you'd called first."

"You don't answer my calls, Guy," she said dryly.

I couldn't argue that point, and if she'd text me to tell me she was pregnant, that wouldn't have been ideal either. But still... it grated on me that she'd waited so long to tell me. Helen went through pregnancy tests like most people go through toilet paper. She would have known about this the earliest it was possible to know, so why not tell me the second she found out?

I was drawing a blank on where to go with her. I didn't want to go to wherever her place was, and I equally didn't want her at mine. It was too hot to take a walk anywhere, and even though it was early, pubs and beer gardens would be packed when the weather was so good.

Shit. My place made the most sense, but I didn't want her inside.

"I've moved into Cal's old flat," I said. "I'll meet you over there."

I didn't wait for her response as I put my hand in my pocket and took out my car keys.

On the drive home, my mind whirred with possibilities of what she might say. What reason could she have for keeping her pregnancy from me?

Unless the baby wasn't mine, but if it wasn't, she had no reason to tell me about it at all.

That thought quietened all my questions. She said she missed me and wanted me back in her texts. Was the unborn child someone else's and she wanted me back to pick up the pieces? To be the father of a child that wasn't mine?

Nah. Helen would never ask that of me. There was no way I would be able to do it after all we'd been through, and difficult and demanding as she could be sometimes, she would know that.

Which meant... I *was* going to be a father.

I blinked as my vision blurred. The last thing I needed was to pass out behind the wheel and cause an accident.

Instead of my probable impending parenthood, my thoughts shifted to Helen again.

What did she want from me? Was she thinking that we might get back together now? Was it something I would consider?

Any time she crossed my mind lately, all I could hear were the cruel words she'd barked at me the day she'd ended things.

"You're so fucking weak! You let people walk all over you, but when it comes to what I want, it's a whole different story!"

She was, of course, referring to Cal. And the crazy thing was that while I did give him a lot, I also called him out on his shit when it was necessary, and when I felt he was taking Helen for granted, I told him so.

But regarding her? In reality, I had allowed her to have her way on almost everything, from the way she decorated my house, to where we went on holiday, to what food we ate... I didn't even realise how many things weren't my decision until I had to do my own shopping and found myself buying things I hadn't had for years. They might not have been healthy, but screw it. If I wanted to binge on junk food, I would.

"Be honest, Guy! You don't want me anymore, and you don't want a family!"

Only part of that was true. By the time that conversation occurred, I wasn't sure I wanted Helen anymore, but I *had* wanted a family. I still wanted that.

The day we broke up, I *did* still love her. If I was honest with myself, though, it wasn't the same kind of love I'd had for her before. It was... not less, but a lot of my feelings for her had been worn down by her actions.

I wasn't perfect. Our break-up wasn't all her fault. But I never gave her the level of disrespect she gave me.

"I fucking hate you! I hate that you made me waste so much of my life on you!"

That was the remark that had made the biggest impact on me. On how I felt. It hurt more than her leaving.

It didn't feel like a waste to me, even now. I knew she probably threw it out in the heat of the moment, but the fact that she could was painful because as unhappy as I was, I didn't hate her. I could never have said I hated her, even when I was angry, because it wasn't the truth.

My palms were sweating as I drove into the car park at the front of my apartment block. Helen had left after me, so I had a few minutes to compose myself.

It was at that moment I realised I hadn't even put my shirt back on before I drove away. I could have run up to my flat to grab one, but I didn't want her to arrive and come inside. I'd made that space mine, no trace of her there, and the conversation we were about to have would be one I didn't want lingering. I'd worked hard to keep my home stress-free, and I wasn't prepared to change that.

I got out of the car, grabbing my water bottle from the passenger seat where I'd dumped it, then locked the car. There was a small communal area by the car park with a picnic table, and it was sheltered by a couple of trees. That would have to do as a place for us to talk.

Until Helen arrived, I stood by my car, tossing my bottle of water in the air and catching it while I tried to get my brain to catch up with what the hell was happening. Twenty minutes ago, I was having the ideal day. Sure, I could have done without lugging furniture around in the heat, but I had my favourite people around me, and I was looking forward to relaxing with them all once the hard work was done.

God, what the hell was Gaby thinking now I was gone?

We'd been together officially for a week, although with the time we'd spent getting to know each other, it felt like longer. She knew the major reason Helen and I split was because Helen thought we were on different pages regarding having a family and I couldn't deal with feeling like my dick no longer belonged to me.

But now... Helen was pregnant, and Gaby had to be wondering what that would mean for her and me. I wanted to get back to her, to talk to her, but I needed to figure out what I was feeling first.

I had loved Helen for a long time, and while I didn't anymore, could I love her again now she had the one thing we'd both always wanted?

I fucking hate you.

That shot of hurt rushed through me like it always did when I remembered Helen spitting it at me. Was there any coming back from that?

The sound of a car approaching alerted me to Helen's arrival, and she parked in the space next to mine.

My mental shields were up because even though I was a pretty big guy who probably looked relatively tough to strangers, on the inside, I *was* still damaged from my time with her. Even though I knew she wouldn't make a scene here, that didn't mean she wouldn't be harsh with her words.

As she got out of the car, I tried to subtly wipe my hands on my jeans, and she walked towards me. My eyes fell on her enlarged stomach before moving up to her face. I couldn't deny she looked good, and when she smiled at me—a rare occurrence—for a second, I saw *my* Helen. The one who knew how to have a laugh. The one I loved.

Without a word, I began walking towards the picnic table, and she followed. Once we were both sitting down on opposite sides, I placed my water bottle on the table, keeping my hands wrapped around it.

Silence fell for the longest time because even though I had questions, I didn't know where to begin.

"So, you moved," Helen said after a while.

Glancing up at her, I nodded. "Yeah. Cal, Shannen, and Aiden are moving into my old place."

"Another gift?" she asked with a hint of bitterness in her voice. She had always hated that I'd helped Cal with things, such as buying the apartment I now lived in for him to rent from me. Admittedly, it was a huge thing to do, but I had the money, and Helen had wanted Cal out of our house. It was a no-brainer as far as I was concerned.

"They bought it," I said.

"Shannen bought it," Helen corrected. "Cal can't afford shit."

I shook my head. "Seriously? You come to me to, presumably, tell me you're pregnant, and still, making shitty comments about Cal is the first thing you do? Some things never change, do they?"

Helen at least had it in her to look embarrassed when I called her out, and she sighed. "Sorry. Old habits. What prompted the move?"

"Shannen is also pregnant," I told her. "Due in November. On Aiden's birthday."

She raised her eyebrows. "Wow. Well, good for them." Her eyes glazed over slightly, and she said, "How's Aiden?"

Helen and Aiden used to be so close, but her moods had even affected him towards the end of our relationship. When we first broke up, he was upset, and at that time, Cal had also split from Shannen, so he was left without two people he was close to. Losing Helen was harder for him because she had almost been a substitute mum for him. He used to talk about Helen a lot when she first left, but over time, he got used to her being gone. I knew she had missed him too, but even if she had asked if she could remain in his life, Cal wanted her out. Not just because of how much she'd hurt Aiden the last time she saw him, but because he hated her. If Aiden had struggled and asked for her, Cal probably would have given in, but the fact that he didn't made life easier.

"He's great," I said. "Doing well at school. He's made friends now, and he's really into football training too."

She nodded slowly. "I'm glad. Sounds like everything is more settled for him now."

"It is."

Another silence fell, and eventually, Helen sighed. "This wasn't quite how I imagined you finding out I'm pregnant," she said. "Not with so many people around, and especially not..." she trailed off, and I knew what she'd stopped herself from saying.

Not with the woman you're dating there too.

"So," I began, turning my water bottle around in my hands, "I... what the fuck, Helen?"

Sensible words had failed me as all the questions I had collided in my mind, and again, she sighed.

"I know this is going to seem all kinds of weird," she said. "So, I'm going to talk you through everything you need to know because I owe you one hell of an explanation."

No kidding. I took a deep breath, waiting for her to begin.

Placing her hands flat on the table in front of her, she said, "After we broke up, I was... a lot of things. Angry, hurt, lonely. It was my choice to walk away, and I didn't even blame you for letting me because I was a mess. An angry, self-involved mess. And while I'm not going to sit here and take on all the responsibility for how we ended, I know a lot of it was down to me. Anyway, after a few weeks, I realised my period was late, but I was so dejected that I didn't even bother worrying about it. A year of disappointment told me that there was no point in getting excited. But then it still didn't come. So, I took a test." She let out a small, slightly bitter laugh. "Can you imagine how it felt to finally see those little lines on the pregnancy test just over a month after we broke up? The irony."

"And you didn't think to tell me right away?" I asked, my glare cutting through her. Because... how different everything could have been if she had. The likelihood was, at that time, I would have moved heaven and earth to fix what had gone wrong between us so we could have the family we'd always wanted. It wouldn't have been easy. In fact, it would have been one of the biggest struggles I'd ever faced. But I would have done it for her. For our family.

"I did," she said. "I picked up the phone a million times. And then I remembered all the horrible things I said to you. Part of me wanted to tell you right away, and the rest of me felt like I deserved to be on my own. Like I forced you out of my life, so it was on me to deal with it. I knew I would have to tell you eventually, but... my head was in such a mess. I was happy when I found out I was pregnant, but it wasn't just the baby I wanted. I wanted us to be a family. But I broke that dream. And then I thought, if I told you, and you said we could try again, it would only be because of the baby and not because of me. That's why I wanted to talk to you, to see if there was any way we could bridge the gap. To see if you still felt anything for me, and if you did, I would know it was about you and me and not because you felt a responsibility to take care of me."

I ran a hand through my hair. She was wrong for not telling me right away. But she also had a point. At least, she did the longer she waited. I *would* have worked on our relationship if she'd told me as soon as she found out because, back then, I still cared enough. Hurt as I was, I would have still wanted it. I could understand her worries as time passed, though. Because the longer she left it, the more I got over her, and the more likely it would be that she'd see any decision I made as being less about her and more about the baby.

"So, why now?" I asked. "Why today?"

She lowered her head and blew out a breath. "You're moving on," she said, looking back up at me. "And this is monumentally selfish, but if I ever have any chance of getting you back, I need to ask now, before you fall in love with someone else. I still love you, Guy. I just needed some time away to realise that."

"Would you still have told me you love me if you weren't pregnant? Or if I wasn't seeing someone else?" I knew the words sounded harsh, and I spat them out without thinking, but it was a fair question. Helen was stubborn. She never backed down, even if it would ultimately hurt her. If things were different, if she thought she could get me back anytime she wanted, would she be making this confession at all?

Helen sighed, letting out another puff of air that made her fringe flutter. "I've been thinking a lot lately. I've been reflecting on everything that happened between us, and about the things I said and felt and how it all got so... big." She looked up at me, her blue eyes showing honesty and openness like I hadn't seen from her in probably years. "I owe you a lot of apologies, Guy. For the way I was with you, and for shouting you down and trying to control every aspect of our lives because I became so single-minded. I turned into a monster, and I didn't even see it. But I always loved you. That never stopped. My hand was forced when I found out I was pregnant, and again when I saw a photo of you with someone else. But I think I would have told you anyway."

Helen hadn't told me she loved me in a long time. I could barely remember the last time she said it, but it was a while before we broke up. Maybe Christmas or New Year. Before things got really bad.

I'd said it to her, but she had stopped saying it back.

Her eyes remained on me, hopeful, and I felt the tiniest glimmer of something for her. I didn't like the way my brain was flicking backwards, all the way back to the woman I'd first met. Bright-eyed and mischievous, and who looked at me like I hung the moon. Back then, I was certain she was the one for me. I just hadn't seen that Helen in a long time. I didn't want to see her now because I had made my peace with our relationship. I was moving on.

But she was having my baby. We hadn't even fully got into any of that yet, and I still had questions I needed answers to.

"When is the baby due?" I asked.

She smiled softly. "November 25th." *Shortly after Cal and Shannen's baby*. Helen reached for her bag and pulled out a photo. A scan photo. "It's a girl."

As she passed it to me and my eyes fell on the black and white image, for a second, everything else vanished.

I was holding in my hand a picture I'd wanted to hold for so long and sitting across from the woman who made it happen, who was carrying my baby daughter.

I was going to have a daughter.

"I know I have some work to do if I want to have you in my life again, but you were a part of me for so long that when I left, I didn't know who I was. I didn't recognise myself either. What I should have done was asked for us to take a bit of time apart to think about what we wanted instead of making the decision for the both of us. It wasn't your fault, but I hated who I had become, and the only way I could see out of it was to take myself away from you."

Her words tore my eyes from the photo, and I looked up at Helen again, shadows falling across her face for a moment as a slight breeze disturbed the trees above us. "You sounded pretty sure it was my fault when you left," I said, my jaw clenching slightly as the bad memories attempted to slither back into my mind.

Helen nodded. "I know. But you know me... when I want something, I can't see straight. And I wanted a baby so badly that I had to blame someone. It was easier to attack you than look at myself and what I was doing to us. And I'm sorry for that too because now I've been without you, I can see so clearly how badly I fucked up. How much I wish I could go back and change it."

Yeah, me too. If she'd seen it sooner. If she'd listened to what I was trying so hard to tell her, then we wouldn't be here now. We'd have fixed our relationship and be in a good position to finally bring a child into the world. My heart clenched as my eyes went back to the photo in my hand.

It was all I'd ever wanted. And we'd both pissed it all away.

"I appreciate the apology," I said after a moment or two. "And if we're being honest with each other, I owe you an apology too. I thought I was patient and understanding, but I know there were times when I wasn't. There were times when I lost my temper and got frustrated, and there were a lot of things I couldn't understand. I wanted a family with you, Helen, but I couldn't understand the feelings you were having the way you needed me to, and I'm sorry for that."

140

Her eyes sparkled with tears, but she sniffed and blinked them away. "Thank you. I appreciate your apology too. We'd got ourselves into a rut, and I think mistakes were made on both sides, but I handled it badly. All of it."

I wanted to reach for her hand, but I also didn't want her to take that as meaning more than it did. Rectifying the woman I'd loved with the angry woman who'd walked out on me made it hard for me to know what to do for the best. She wasn't a monster. She'd just let all of the frustration in her build up until she didn't know what to do with it. Yet, I couldn't look back on it and cast it aside because it had hurt to be on the receiving end of all that vitriol, especially when I didn't deserve it. Not all of it, anyway.

"I've really missed you," Helen said, blowing out a long breath. "I've never minded being on my own, but I miss you. I miss your hugs, and your sense of humour, and just... talking to you. And I know we didn't do a lot of that towards the end, but not having it at all... not having you... I hate it, Guy. I hate it."

I'd hated it too, at first. While the peace of not being jumped on at any given moment was a relief, sometimes, it was too damn quiet in my house, and even the fighting felt like it would have been better than nothing at all. But that had passed, even more so when I moved.

I couldn't tell her I still felt that way because I didn't. I'd picked myself back up and started to move on with my life without her. Maybe that was heartless. It had only been six months, and that wasn't much compared to the time we were together, but my alternatives were moving on or wallowing in my part in the break-up. I'd reflected, I'd forgiven myself for the things I'd screwed up, and then I'd done all I could to help myself step away from that closed chapter.

"Helen," I began, "I know it's hard. It's been hard for me too, especially when I thought about how things used to be in the beginning. But the things you said that last day we saw each other... they were hard to deal with, and they weren't fair. Getting over you wasn't easy, but I had to do it."

An image of Gaby popped into my head. The way she looked when I kissed her for the first time. The light blush on her cheeks, her skin lightly tanned, and her blonde hair blowing in the breeze. Her bright smile and the sound of her laugh.

She had been on my mind for weeks. Months, even. Not constantly, like an obsession. Just quietly in the background, a person I wanted to see again and get to know. We had a long way to go before we knew each other well, but I wanted that. I wanted a fresh start.

Even with Helen looking right at me, her eyes showing me the woman who'd been lost to both of us for so long.

A small voice in my head—one that sounded a lot like Helen—told me I was wrong. I was a horrible person for dismissing this so fast after sharing so much of my life with her, but was I really?

"I'm not expecting you to make any decisions right now," Helen said, bringing me back to the moment. "I can't waltz in here and expect you to say we should try again. I know I hurt you, and I know this is a shock. I would actually prefer it if you didn't decide right now. But I would like you to think about it." She reached over and touched my hand that was still clutching the scan photo. There was hope in her eyes that made me uncomfortable for reasons I didn't understand. "But please can you at least tell me you'll consider it? That you'll really consider letting us have the life we wanted? For so long, Guy, it was me and you, and it was meant to be forever. Now, we've got a second chance. I understand that you're seeing someone else, but does it mean as much to you as what we had?" She sighed. "I love you, and I will always love you. Please, just say you'll think about it."

Again, my heart twisted as I looked at her. It was so easy with her touching me, looking at me the way she used to, to see what we were. What we'd planned. How things were supposed to go.

My eyes dipped to her stomach and butterflies actually flapped around in my stomach. No matter what, I was going to be a father.

But did I *want* the entire family unit now?

Chapter 17

Gaby

"GUYS, CAN YOU KEEP things moving for me? I'll be back in a minute."

I heard Cal speaking, but as I watched Guy and Helen get into their cars, my mind seemed to have drifted away from me because I couldn't really feel anything.

"Gaby?"

A hand lightly touched my shoulder, and I blinked a few times and saw Cal standing in front of me, his brown eyes full of concern. Another couple of blinks and I realised the movement around us had resumed again, and my heart was beating wildly.

"Are you all right?" Cal asked, and I nodded.

"Yeah... what just happened?"

I had walked out of the house to ask Guy if he could come back in and help us shift a couple of the heavier boxes, but when I'd reached the doorway, the words died in my throat as I saw Helen.

I was aware that not all women carried a baby the same way, but Helen was tall and slim, so it was glaringly obvious she was both expecting and a fair way along. If my eyes weren't deceiving me, the likelihood was that she had gotten pregnant right before she and Guy broke up, which meant it was Guy's child she was carrying.

And from the look on his face, he hadn't had a clue until she appeared in Shannen and Cal's front garden.

"Come with me," Cal said, gently turning me back around and ushering me through the front door and into the kitchen.

Thankfully, nobody was in there, and I dropped down into one of the chairs around the kitchen table and stared up at Cal as if he might somehow have the answers. Of course, he wouldn't because this was news to him too.

He turned around, took a bottle of water from the fridge, and handed it to me.

"Got anything stronger?" I asked as I took it and put it on the table.

"Yeah, you know what..." Cal turned again and reached back into the fridge, this time pulling out two bottles of beer. He opened the drawer next to the fridge and took out a bottle opener to crack the lids off, then passed one to me before taking a long swig of his and then shaking his head.

His apparent stupor made me chuckle, breaking me out of my own thoughts for a second. I took a sip of my beer, knowing it wasn't smart to drink on an empty stomach, but I wasn't planning to drink the whole thing. I just needed to taste something that was as bitter as the thoughts that had begun to encroach on my mind.

"Hey, where did you..." Shannen's voice trailed off as she peered around the kitchen door and saw Cal and me clutching our liquid distractions. "Really? It's not even half past ten!"

Cal took her arm and pulled her into the kitchen, closing the door behind her. "Too bad you can't drink because you're going to want one." He took another long drink as Shannen's brow furrowed, and she glanced at me.

"Helen's pregnant," Cal said bluntly, then leaned back against the worktop, awaiting her response.

145

Shannen frowned. "What?"

"She was here," I said, looking up at her. "She came to tell Guy, I guess, not knowing he doesn't live here anymore. And she didn't have to actually *tell* him."

Shannen's hands shot to her mouth as the truth of the situation hit her, just like it had me. If she was pregnant enough that it was obvious, the probability of her baby being Guy's was huge. Unless she was cheating on him, but even though I'd heard some not very good things about Helen, nobody had ever questioned her faithfulness to the relationship.

"Where's Guy now?" Shannen asked as she came to sit down opposite me at the table.

"Gone to talk to her," I replied. "I told him to."

My heart dropped at the thought of them together, but what was I meant to do? Tell him to pretend she wasn't there? That this wasn't happening? At some point, they'd need to talk, and there was no point dragging it out.

Jesus. I'd been hoping to speak to him later about the things I needed to tell him, but how was I supposed to do that now? He'd probably had enough bombshells dropped on him for one day.

But at the same time, maybe this was the perfect day for it. Not because he needed anything more to process, but because he was about to have some decisions to make.

In the grand scheme of things, compared to his long-term relationship with Helen, I was nothing to him, especially not with a baby on the way. A family was what he'd always wanted. And for a long time, he'd wanted it with Helen. Maybe the right thing for me to do was to step back so he could try to fix things with her and not have to worry about hurting my feelings. I would never stand in the way of a family, not ever. My biggest regret my whole life was not creating a family for myself when I had the chance, and the pain of knowing I'd thrown the opportunity away never

146

lessened. I couldn't expect someone else to give up the opportunity when I knew how painful it was.

The idea of giving Guy up now was making my chest tighten, but to have him for longer and then have him change his mind and go back to Helen after I'd fallen in love with him? I wasn't sure I could deal with that.

Cal looked me straight in the eye as if he'd heard every thought I'd had. "He isn't going back to her. There's no way."

Shaking my head slowly, I said, "I wouldn't blame him if he did."

Wouldn't blame him, but it would hurt. Right then, though, I just about had it in me to be able to support him. Not easily, but I could do it for him.

Shannen glanced at Cal, then at me, her expression cautious. "I don't know," she said, looking back at Cal again. "Can you really be so sure about that? Being unable to have the family they wanted was the reason they broke up, and now..." She flicked her gaze to me, apology written all over her face. "Sorry. I hope he doesn't go back there, but I'm not sure we can say he won't."

"Don't be sorry," I said, giving her a smile I hoped showed that I accepted her apology. I didn't want that to happen, but I wasn't at all surprised that my mind was already preparing for the possibility. I wasn't an outright pessimist, but my expectations weren't too high that I was the most sensible choice when everything Guy wanted had just been presented to him by someone else.

"Okay," Cal said, straightening up, "maybe there's a chance, but it's really fucking small. You both know how much work he's put in to getting himself back on track after Helen sucked the life out of him. He's got new priorities, a new project to work on, and he's happier now than he has been in a long time." He shrugged. "I can't see him throwing it all away."

"He's still got a responsibility, though," Shannen pointed out, and again, she looked pained when she glanced at me. She wasn't trying to hurt me; she was just saying the things that had rushed through my head since Guy left.

"He doesn't have to be with her to fulfil it," Cal said, coming to join us at the table and taking another drink. "Helen treated him like shit. I can't see him forgetting about that because there's a baby on the way."

That was also a solid point. He *could* still be a dad if he wasn't with Helen. However, he didn't strike me as someone who wanted to be a part-time father. I'd clocked the way she'd looked at me when she saw me in the doorway too. She knew who I was from seeing me at school when she used to pick Aiden up. I couldn't be mad at her for glaring at me like I was the enemy; if I'd given someone as amazing as Guy up and then saw someone else kissing him, I would have been pissed off too.

The thing was, this was not a situation like Shannen had with Cal and Aiden. Aiden's mum was never in the picture. With this baby, there was no way Helen was ever going to be happy with someone else being with Guy and being around her child. There was the chance that becoming a mother might mellow her a little, but based on everything I'd heard about her and how much she would resent me being with Guy, it didn't feel likely that she would be okay with me having any part in her child's life. And that was also going to be a problem.

"I think we're just going to have to wait until he gets back to have any idea what's going to happen," I said with a sigh. "Guessing isn't going to help anyone."

Shannen nodded. "He's going to need us to be here for him." She paused. "Do you think we should cancel the barbecue? I doubt Guy will be in the mood for fun today."

"No," Cal said, taking another drink. He blew out a breath, and it was clear that Guy's situation was weighing on him. He was worried about his best mate, his brown eyes even darker than usual. "He'll probably want a few drinks and to relax. We should do what we planned to. He's better off keeping his mind off it for a few hours."

I agreed with him. Whatever conversation Guy was having as we sat there in the kitchen was probably intense, and the last thing he needed was to have more focus put on it by us telling everyone the barbecue was off. The way I understood it, the guys who worked for Guy would be going home once the moving was done anyway, and that would leave us, Annie, Sadie, Stefan, and Aiden and Alexander, who would probably entertain themselves. There would be enough of us to help him unwind for a while.

"Okay," Shannen said, kissing Cal on the cheek as she got to her feet. "We'd better get back to it before everyone thinks we're letting them do all the hard work."

Cal smiled up at her, his eyes brightening as they fell on her, then he abandoned his still half-full beer and stood up too.

"Come on, Gabs," Shannen said. "Let's go and see how many books we can whack on the bookshelves before lunch!"

Chapter 18

Guy

I RETURNED TO CAL and Shannen's place about two and a half hours after I left. I was still in a bit of a daze after my conversation with Helen. She hadn't been there the whole time. We'd talked for about an hour, and then I'd taken myself up to my flat so I could think.

If I'd known when I woke up that morning that, before lunchtime, I'd have the news that I was about to be a father, I would never have believed it.

So many things had been said. So many things re-hashed and remembered. Not all of them were bad, though. Helen's revelation had, in fact, done a brilliant job of reminding me what we used to have. What we'd always wanted. I'd been reminded of the old Helen, who I'd always believed would one day be my wife. Impending motherhood had shifted her closer to the woman I'd fallen in love with.

And she'd asked me the big question. If I would think about us getting back together and having our family at last. She was so keen to have me back that she insisted that, once the baby was born, I do a paternity test to prove the baby was mine and not the result of a fling directly after we split, or an affair. It hadn't crossed my mind for a moment that the baby belonged to anyone other than me, and when I'd told her that, she still didn't change her stance. She told me she hadn't been with anyone else since we broke up, but she still wanted me to do the test. I figured she wanted me to be completely certain as a way of proving I could trust her, so I agreed, but trust was never an issue.

It was everything else.

When I walked back into Cal and Shannen's house, everyone was on a break, and they had all spread themselves out across the living room and attached dining room. The smell of fish and chips had smacked me in the face as soon as I walked in, and some kind of chippy buffet had been laid out across the coffee table and the dining room table. They were both covered in portions of chips, fish, battered sausages and burgers, and pies.

I figured since it was so hot outside, instead of enjoying the garden, they wanted a break from the heat. Everyone was chatting animatedly, and I could see a lot of progress had been made with Shannen's bookshelves. The boxes Gaby had been working on when I left had been cleared, and stacks of books had replaced them.

True to Cal's word, the TV was on, Sky Sports News playing, even though nobody was really watching it.

Cal was the first to spot me, and he put his plate of fish and chips down, standing up. He weaved his way between Mike and Luke, who were sitting on the floor with their food, as were Aiden and Alexander. Sadie sat beside them, and Annie was sitting on one of the chairs, talking to her daughter.

"Hey," Cal said as he approached me. "Are you okay?"

Concern was heavy in his eyes, and I nodded. "Yeah. I think so." I looked around. "Is Gaby still here?"

She had been on my mind the whole drive back. I could still see the glimpse of concern in her eyes as she'd told me to go and speak to Helen, and even though she'd assured me she would stay, I wouldn't have blamed her if she'd left. I wasn't worried that she was upset with me; I was as clueless as everyone else when Helen had rocked up. But I *was* worried that she'd be wondering what this would mean for me and her.

Of course she would be wondering that. It was the same thing I'd been thinking about for the last couple of hours.

"She's through there," Cal said, nodding into the dining room. From where I stood, I could only see Shannen and Stefan putting food onto their plates, although I could hear them chatting, and as more people realised I was back, heads turned in my direction, offering nods and waves. Those who knew me best had questions in their eyes, but all I could do in that moment was nod back in response.

I needed to see Gaby.

"Is she okay?" I asked Cal.

"She's... okay. Keeping busy. Shannen stayed with her, and I think they've been talking, but I've been in and out, so I can't say for sure. I spoke to her just after you left, though. She was a bit shocked, but... we all were."

That's an understatement.

Before I could say anything else, Shannen turned around, and when she saw me, she smiled then glanced back into the dining room, where I now knew Gaby was. A moment later, Shannen and Stefan stepped aside, and Gaby stood in the archway.

"Hey," she said.

"Hey." My eyes fixed on hers.

If I didn't know her as well as I was beginning to, I would have guessed nothing was wrong at all. She smiled at me as she always did, but that glimmer of uncertainty sat deep in her green eyes. I wanted to talk to her, but I didn't want to do that in front of everyone.

I also knew Cal and Shannen wanted answers as much as she did.

Breaking the tension, because it was building all around us, Gaby said, "Come and get something to eat. There's plenty."

It was as if a collective sigh rippled across the room at her words. I didn't think anyone was expecting us to have some kind of blowout right there, but when Gaby spoke, it eased the heaviness in the air. I nodded, and Cal followed me as I headed for her. Stefan slipped out, offering me a smile on the way, and then it was just me, Gaby, Shannen, and Cal in the dining room.

There was another load of food and some plates, knives, forks, and napkins on the table in there. Just looking at it made my stomach growl.

In the other room, I could hear the conversations had picked up again. We were a good distance from the front of the living room where everyone else was sitting, so at least anything we said here wouldn't be overheard.

Shannen had grabbed a portion of chips and sat down at the dining table, and Cal, who had left his food in the other room, sat down beside her and nicked a chip from her, making her laugh and slap his hand away before he leaned in and kissed her cheek.

Gaby had taken a plate and put some chips and a battered sausage on it, then handed me a plate. "Eat."

She smiled again, and a feeling of normality at being around my favourite people washed some of the fuzziness away from my brain. If I closed my eyes, we could have been back in Cornwall, on holiday, having fun together. Things were too big a deal for me to slip all the way into that delusion, but remembering I was surrounded by a support system I'd rarely had to use helped.

I took the plate from her as she sat down, then I grabbed some chips and a huge piece of fish and lowered my arse into the chair next to Gaby's, pulling off some of the batter from the cod and popping it into my mouth.

"So, what did she say?" Cal asked me from across the table.

He was never one to hold back when it came to Helen. I could only guess what was going through his head because he more than anyone had been there for me during the break-up. He knew how hard it was for me to watch so many years of my life with her go up in a puff of smoke. As much as he hated her, aside from uttering the occasional supportive 'you deserve better,' he'd got through it without calling her all the names that sat on the tip of his tongue. I knew what he really thought, though, and as much as he'd hated what I was going through, me breaking up with Helen was a relief for him because he no longer had to suck up the way she treated him. He also didn't have to keep his mouth shut over the way she spoke to me sometimes. His thoughts on the current situation weren't about how he felt, though, but how it would affect me. What it would change.

It wasn't lost on me that Cal and Shannen were moving into what I'd always believed would be my family home on the same day I found out that I was actually going to *have* a family. Well, a child, at least.

Life is fucking hilarious.

All eyes fell on me, but since Cal had asked the question, I kept my focus on him.

"A lot of things," I said with a sigh. "Things I wasn't expecting to hear."

"What kind of things?" Shannen asked tentatively.

I glanced at her, and she looked tense. I wasn't sure if it was only because she was waiting to hear what had happened or if, in part, she was worried about Gaby and how all of this would affect her.

"She was honest," I said, then blew out another breath. "She found out she was pregnant a bit after we broke up, and then she wasn't sure what to do and how to tell me. And then she... she said the reason she didn't tell me sooner was because she wanted me back, and she didn't want me to just be with her because of the baby. But..." I paused, finally turning my head to look at Gaby. "Helen saw the photo of me and you at the escape room on Facebook, and she..." I trailed off, and Gaby gave me a sad smile.

"She wanted to tell you before you moved on," she finished for me. "I get it."

My chest ached as I looked at her beautiful face. Because I knew she *did* get it. She was so damn kind. Gaby knew a lot of what had happened between me and Helen before she and I had got together, and I always felt like she saw it from both sides. Understood the pain both of us had been through, not just me. She also had the benefit of never having met

Helen officially, so she hadn't seen the worst of her. Gaby could only look at the situation as an outsider, and until we'd started seeing each other, she'd remained impartial.

She still *seemed* impartial, and I knew she wanted the best for me, but she and I had started something that felt... different. Like it was worth exploring. I didn't know how I would have coped if Gaby had an ex who suddenly wanted her back, bringing with him something she'd wanted so badly it hurt sometimes.

There was no comparison between Gaby and Helen, though. Not anymore.

I thought about Gaby a lot, couldn't wait to see her again, and when I was with her, I was *happy*. She'd given me back a piece of myself that had fallen away; the side that wanted to let loose. Gaby didn't give a single fuck if I wanted to sit around and watch football, or if I wanted to go to the beach as a grown man and build a sandcastle. All she cared about was that I was doing what I wanted to do, and it had given me the freedom to figure out what the hell that was.

"Helen wants you back?" Cal asked, and I snapped my head back around to look at him. "After the way she treated you?"

I nodded slowly. "Yeah, that's what she wants."

I expected his next question to be, '*And what do you want?*' but he said nothing. His jaw was clenched, and I could only imagine what he was holding in. It was a testament to how much he'd changed that he didn't tell me exactly what he was thinking. He understood what being a dad meant to me, and as much as he didn't want Helen around again, I wasn't sure even he could tell me that considering it was wrong.

I reached into the front pocket of the shirt I'd put on after Helen went home and pulled out the scan photo she said I could keep. My eyes lingered on it for a moment, my heart ready to explode at the visual reminder that this was happening before I placed it on a tiny space left on the table.

"It's a girl," I said, and Shannen smiled as she looked at the photo. "She's due a couple of weeks after you."

"Wow." Shannen picked up the photo and looked at it for a moment before handing it to Cal. As he took it, his eyes dropping to the image, the corners of his mouth tipped up slightly. He shared a grin with Shannen, and I figured they were remembering the moment they saw their own baby's first scan photo.

"How are you feeling about all this?" Shannen asked as Cal handed the picture back to me.

I dropped my head back for a second as, not for the first time that day, the reality washed over me. It was like a tidal wave of emotions from shock, to panic, to excitement, to disbelief.

"It's surreal," I said. "When Helen was pregnant before, it was the best feeling ever. We were so happy, but then..." I trailed off, as everyone knew how that had ended. "This time, the circumstances are different, but... I'm excited. I'm going to be a dad."

"Excuse me," Gaby said, standing up. She gave me a small smile and squeezed my shoulder as she quickly rounded the back of my chair and left the dining room, slipping out of the patio door into the garden and out of sight.

But I saw the hint of hurt on her face, no matter how she tried to disguise it.

I started to get up to follow her, and Shannen said, "Give her a minute, Guy. This is... it's a lot."

My focus remained on the patio doors as I considered Shannen's words for a second, then slowly sank back into my seat, resting my elbows on the table and dropping my head into my hands, feeling like an insensitive prick.

I wasn't sure which part of the conversation had tipped Gaby over the edge so she felt like she had to take a break. The photo? The prospect that

Helen wanted me back? Had my saying I was excited made Gaby think I'd already written her out of my life?

But I *was* excited about being a dad. Even though it hadn't fully sunk in, I couldn't wait for the day I'd be able to hold my baby in my arms. But that didn't mean what I was sure Gaby thought it meant.

"What did she say to you while I was gone?" I asked, and Shannen sighed.

"I think you can probably guess. It's Gaby. She wants you to do what's right for you and she won't hold it against you, but she really likes you. So, yeah, it's going to hurt if you end things with her." Shannen shot me an understanding smile. "How do you feel about everything?"

"Honestly?" I asked, my eyes wide as I considered the question. "Like I've just been told I've won the lottery, but I can only have the money if I promise to give up everything else in my life that I care about."

The truth of those words rang out in my head. I'd spoken them without thinking, but that had been the conclusion I'd reached in the mess of my thoughts. I'd wanted a kid for so long, but now, it felt like there would be a price to pay somewhere. I didn't want the price to be Gaby, but one way or another, even with my best intentions, I was worried that *would* be the cost. To get one thing I wanted while losing another. And it might not even just be her. Helen being in my life in any capacity would put a strain on Cal and Shannen, and Aiden too.

"Is that how it would be?" Shannen asked. "You said Helen wants you back, but was there some kind of ultimatum attached? What if that isn't what you want? Is she going to try to keep the baby away from you if you don't want to be with her?"

I shook my head. "There was no ultimatum. I think... I think she believed that we didn't need to discuss an alternative because I'll choose to be with her again. I don't know what the consequences might be. I told her I would think about it, but..." I trailed off, shaking my head again.

I loved my friends, and I appreciated them talking things out with me, but Gaby had rushed outside, upset, and I didn't feel right telling Cal and Shannen where my head was at before telling Gaby. She was the one I was seeing. She was the one I needed to talk to.

"Go," Cal said with a tiny smile, jerking his head in the direction of the door.

Standing, I went out into the back garden where Gaby was. I needed to hold her, make sure she was okay.

We were in such a weird position, having not been together for very long. Being friends first, though, had deepened our connection. She mattered to me, and the news that had been dumped on us today had obviously affected her. I had to find out what she was thinking.

She was sitting on the grass beside the paddling pool, and she'd put her feet in the water, wiggling her toes as she leaned back on her hands, soaking up the sun. It would have been a relaxing visual if it weren't for the dejection in her eyes.

"Hey, Gabs," I said as I approached her.

Her head whipped around to look at me, and as her gaze fell on me, she blinked quickly then smiled, sitting up straighter and wiping her hands on her shorts. "Hey. Sorry. I needed a minute. Want to join me?" She gestured to a spot on the grass beside her, and I nodded and sat down.

For a moment, I looked at her, captivated as I always was in her presence. Even now, when she was so unsure of what I would say or what was going to happen next between us, the only thing I could see in her eyes was kindness. There was an apprehension deep inside them, but it didn't come from a place of anger or frustration. She understood the position I was now in could mean the end of us before we'd even got started. The only things I could read in her were well-intentioned, and it only reinforced what I had been thinking.

Before I could speak, Gaby drew in a deep breath. Her green eyes looked brighter than ever as she looked at me, and there was a slight tremor to her lower lip before she spoke. "Guy... I need you to know that I've had the best time with you. I don't want it to end, but I'm also not a dick. If you... if you want to make things work with Helen, I understand. I don't want you to give yourself a hard time if you need to break things off with me. You've been given a gift. So, please, while you're thinking things over, don't factor my feelings into anything. It's your feelings that matter. I want you to do what's right for you."

Closing my eyes, my whole body flooded with warmth at her words. With some people, they would have been just that. Words. The right thing to say to ease my conscience and for her to trick herself into thinking none of this hurt. From Gaby, though, the sincerity radiated from her, surrounding me like a thick blanket on a cold day.

"Your feelings *are* a factor." I reached over for her hand and held it tightly in mine. "*You* are a factor."

Looking at her beautiful face, I knew exactly what I wanted. Truth be told, I hadn't had to do much thinking at all.

Had I considered Helen's request? Of course. She'd asked me to think about it, and I had. Even though I'd seen glimpses of the old Helen while we'd been talking, they were only quick snapshots of the person I used to know. The things I fell in love with about her would always be there, but we were both different people now. Had we not had the issues we had, we'd probably still have been together. She would have been the one. But the issues *had* happened. Instead of fixing what was wrong with us, we'd continued to ignore it until it got so out of hand that Helen actually loathed being in my presence. I believed her when she said time away from me had given her clarity on what she really wanted, and that she didn't only want me back because of the baby. But I'd had some clarity too. I hadn't realised how unhappy I'd been with Helen until she was gone. Yeah, I missed her at first. But now? There was so much else heading my way. New home, new project, my business was running perfectly, I had amazing friends including a couple of new ones in Donovan and Nova.

And then there was this woman in front of me.

I didn't want to go back.

"Guy," Gaby whispered, her head dropping as a tear slipped down her cheek. She quickly brushed it away. "I hate that I'm crying. There's something you need to know about me before you make any life-changing decisions."

As she looked back up at me, I shook my head and brushed her tears away with my thumbs, holding her face in both of my hands. "I know everything I need to."

She squeezed her eyes closed, her tears falling faster. "You don't understand. I-"

I cut her off, pressing my lips against hers because I couldn't stand seeing her so upset. Didn't want to hear her run herself down. The truth was, though, I *couldn't* imagine a single thing that she could say that would change how I was beginning to feel about her.

Gaby's tears made my cheeks wet, and from the position she was sitting in, her feet still in the paddling pool, the only way I could hold her close was for me to shift. I needed to wrap her up in my arms, so I shuffled around, my legs stretched out around her from behind. I wrapped my arms around her middle, her back against my chest, and I rested my chin on her shoulder.

"Gabriella Davis," I said gently, "You are everything I want."

Her tears fell harder, and she relaxed against me for a second before tensing again. "Guy, please... I need you to be sure about this. This is a huge decision, and I don't think you should make it so quickly."

Sitting behind her suddenly seemed like a stupid decision because now I couldn't look into her eyes. On the other hand, though, her gaze stayed fixed ahead, so maybe it was easier for her not to look at me yet.

"I did think," I told her. "My instinct when I saw Helen out there earlier was not to talk to her but to run away somewhere with you so we could talk it out. I didn't feel any kind of pull towards her, and even when she and I were talking, even though she seems like she's back to who she used to be in some ways, I can't forget the mess we made of our relationship." I felt the tension in Gaby's body ease a tiny bit, and I held her tighter. "I know this sounds like a snap decision, but it isn't. You know how I feel regarding a relationship with her. You know I had moved on before you and I started seeing each other. A baby definitely shakes things up a bit, but what it doesn't do is make me want to go back."

"But... she has everything you ever wanted. The family the two of you always dreamed of."

"That's not what it is, though. I wanted a family with the Helen I loved. I wanted to have children with the woman who didn't smother me until I became a walking ball sack to her. I swear all she saw when she looked at me was a gigantic sperm."

In spite of herself, Gaby snorted out a laugh, and I did too. "She loved you," Gaby said. "She still loves you."

I sighed, discomfort filling me for a moment. As little as I wanted to hurt Gaby, I didn't want to hurt Helen either. Telling her my decision was going to be painful after she'd looked so hopeful, almost confident that I would give us a second chance. It wasn't a conversation I was looking forward to, but it had to be done.

"I know she does," I said. "And it would be so much easier if she didn't. But I can't put myself into a relationship I don't want to be in. Being together for the sake of the kids is never a good idea. My own parents tried it for years and it was miserable."

I'd already left home by the time my parents called it quits, and there was still a relief to it. The tension at home had been high for a long time, and I was glad to be out of it.

"But what if you could fall in love with her again?" Gaby asked. "What if all you needed was time to heal?"

I knew why she was doing this. Why she needed me to be sure about what I was saying, about what I wanted. While I was unable to fully see her face, I couldn't make her hear me. My brain was flooding with the cheesiest words I had perhaps ever uttered, but they were the truth, and I needed her to hear and feel them.

I let go of her and shuffled back, getting to my feet. Instead of standing in front of her, I leaned down and lifted her to her feet, making her laugh a little as they were still in the paddling pool, and she turned to face me, about to get out, but I shook my head. I toed off my trainers, and she stepped back as I got into the paddling pool with her.

"What are you doing?" she asked, still chuckling as I pulled her back into my arms, our feet cooled by the water.

"I'm hot," I said with a shrug, smirking.

"Yes. Yes, you are," Gaby said, her arms wrapping around my waist, making me laugh.

"Gaby, please listen to me," I told her, my face turning serious again as I finally got to look into those amazing green eyes of hers. "Helen and I don't need time to heal. When a relationship descends into the realms of hate, as far as I'm concerned, there's no way back. I have spent the first half of this year figuring out not just what I *want* from my life, but what I need. And I found out that I need to have the space to be myself. I need the space to create things, like I'm going to do with the bar. I healed myself so well that there is no room left for her. And then you came along. With your huge personality, and your don't-give-a-shit-what-people-think attitude, and your gigantic heart, and those fucking beautiful eyes. What I want and need in my life is to not go back to a place where I was made to feel like I was there to serve a purpose. *You* are what I want. What I need. You're where I want to be."

A sigh left Gaby that would have made a heroine in a romance movie jealous. She tightened her arms around me and dropped her forehead to my shoulder. "Jesus, Guy. You really know how to make a girl feel good about herself."

With a chuckle, I raised her chin with my finger, then placed my hand on her cheek, wiping away the last of her tears. "Well, you make it easy."

When she smiled at me, I felt it. She was sunshine personified. That didn't mean I couldn't still see a hint of apprehension in her eyes, but that was to be expected. "We should go back inside and get something to eat," I said, kissing the top of her head. "We can talk more later, when we get back to mine, if you still want to come over."

"I do," she said. She tilted her head back, then brushed her lips over mine in a way that made me feel like I was everything, and I dipped my tongue into her mouth, deepening the kiss and blocking out any remaining space between our bodies.

That was what it was meant to feel like. Being with someone you truly wanted. It felt like warmth, and sparks, and comfort, and trust, and honesty. It was meant to make you feel nervous, but nervous like before you get on a rollercoaster, when you know it's scary but you're going to love every second of it.

And I *had* loved every second I'd been with Gaby so far.

In spite of everything that was about to change in my life, I would hold onto Gaby with everything I had.

Chapter 19

Gaby

I'D HAD DAYS IN my life that had totally blindsided me, but I'd never experienced anything quite like the shock of the ex of the man I was seeing showing up to announce she was pregnant. It had sliced open every insecurity I had, every old wound, and they'd begun to bleed out all over me, covering me in their ugly, sticky residue, coating every inch of my skin. It felt visible. Like I was exposed and everyone could see just by looking at me what I was hiding.

Of course, they couldn't. And once again, I was left holding it in. It would only be for a little longer. Just until Guy had a moment to digest this new twist in his life.

After we'd spoken in the back garden, I felt... relieved. But I was also still struck with fear because in spite of his beautiful words, I knew there was still a high chance I could lose him. If not by him realising he wanted a better version of his old life with Helen, then by him hearing the whole of my story.

And he did have to hear it. Soon.

Although a lot of the day at Shannen and Cal's new house had been hard work, we'd spent the late afternoon into the evening in the garden, having a barbecue, chatting, unwinding, and playing with the kids. Shannen's nephew, Alexander, was the cutest, and he and Aiden had formed a pretty solid friendship. It wasn't the first time they'd met, and Alexander was a year younger than Aiden, but Aiden had introduced him to football, and the two of them didn't leave the area around his new goal the whole time.

We didn't stay late because everyone was pretty tired from moving all the stuff in. Sadie, Stefan, and Alexander were the first to leave around half past six, and Guy and I headed out about an hour later. Shannen's mum was staying at theirs for the night so she didn't have to drive all the way back to Plymouth after helping with the move, and I was pretty sure they'd all be glad to have a bit of peace and quiet after having so many people there all day.

Once we were back at Guy's place and settled on the sofa with a drink each—white wine for me and a beer for him—I felt like I was holding my breath. Not physically, but in the sense that I knew Guy and I had more talking to do, and I wasn't sure how and when it would begin.

We sat on the sofa much like we had when he'd found me with my toes in the paddling pool, with him sitting behind me, and me leaning back against him, one of his arms wrapped around my stomach, the other holding his beer bottle.

"Hell of a day, huh?" Guy said, placing a gentle kiss on my cheek.

"Yeah," I said with a small laugh. "That might be an understatement."

"Probably." Guy rested his chin on my shoulder. "It was good to see Cal and Shannen's place all set up, though."

I smiled. "Yeah. I'm so happy for them. It's still weird to me that I've only known Shannen since last September, but in almost a year, we've got so close."

"I forget sometimes that you haven't known her forever," Guy said. "I mean, I've only known her since January, but I can't imagine her not being around. She and Cal have lived a whole lifetime in the last eight months."

Chuckling, I said, "Yeah, they have. Not all of it good, but I'm glad they're settled now."

"She's been amazing for Cal and Aiden. I've known Cal since he was twelve, before his life went to shit, and when I met him again a few years ago... he was a mess. I never thought he'd be able to find someone who was willing to wade through all of his crap and be there with him while he worked through it. I never thought he would let anyone close enough to help either."

Huh.

That was how I often viewed myself. As someone who couldn't find a person who wanted me enough to put up with the leftover parts of my trauma. Wouldn't be able to find someone patient enough to stay by my side while I healed from it. But Cal had found that person for him.

Had I found that in Guy?

"I think maybe the stars aligned," I said, slightly tongue-in-cheek. I wasn't particularly 'woo-woo', that was more my mum's thing, but I couldn't deny how fascinating it was that the puzzle pieces of our lives had fit together so beautifully. "I mean, Shannen was really uptight when I met her. She thought about work and her upper-class friends, and while she was nothing like them, she never liked the idea of taking a chance in case it backfired. But then she met me."

Guy laughed, his fingers gently stroking across my stomach. "You helped her come out of her shell."

"Kind of. But I couldn't have done that if she hadn't been willing to meet me halfway. I still think that even if she hadn't come out with me the night she met Cal, they were supposed to find each other." I placed my hand over his, squeezing it gently.

"Well, maybe you and I were supposed to meet too," Guy said. "We could have met the night Cal met Shannen, but it wasn't the right time."

Is it the right time now, though? With Guy about to be the father of someone else's baby?

Even though it was illogical, a part of me felt as though I was stealing him from Helen. They had been apart for half a year, and I had nothing to do with that. But she wanted him back and she was the mother of his soon-to-be-born child. She outranked me, and I couldn't shift the discomfort of being the 'other woman'.

With a sigh, I said, "Can I tell you something?" I shuffled forward, then turned myself around on the sofa so I was facing him, my back resting against the opposite armrest.

He must have sensed the seriousness in my tone because he set up a bit straighter, drawing his legs towards him so there was a bit more room for mine. "Sure."

Taking a deep breath, I picked up a cushion, stroking the soft material, and said, "The first time I ever saw you, I thought you were the best-looking man I'd ever seen. But I didn't know you, didn't expect to ever get to know you, and that was okay with me. But then our paths crossed again and again, and I *was* allowed to get to know you. And you weren't just the best-looking man I'd ever seen anymore. You were the best man I'd ever met. In every way. I couldn't believe that you were into me, and not only were you into me, but you actually understood what I needed without having to ask." I paused, looking up at him. Most men would have at least had a tiny grin about the flattery I'd heaped on him, but he was simply listening, waiting to see where I was going with this. "I've liked you for a while, Guy, and now I have you... it's hard to believe it's real."

Being this exposed made me want to wrap my arms around myself and hide from him. I hadn't been with anyone who made me feel comfortable enough to be so vulnerable in years, but that didn't make it any less frightening. I had made it my mission in life to always be honest, to be open and say what I felt after so long of having my voice taken away. By and large, I lived that way all the time. Relationships were my downfall, but Guy had eased his way into my life, and that made it easier to open up most of the way with him. I felt like I was on the edge of having something transcendent, and to be so close to potentially losing it made me feel unbalanced.

I *hated* feeling vulnerable. Not because I had a problem with honesty but because it made me feel like I was that helpless woman I used to be when I was with Flynn.

Leaning over, Guy put his drink down on the table, then sat up. He took the cushion from my hands and wrapped his fingers around mine, pulling me towards him. "It's real, Gabs. I know today threw everything off, but what we're starting to build here.... that's real."

I nodded. "Yeah. I just haven't felt like this in a really long time, and that didn't end well. So, now I'm afraid that if I let myself believe in this, then something will go wrong here too."

"I get that. And I understand. Living with Cal for a couple of years gave me a pretty good insight."

I laughed lightly. Cal and I actually had quite a lot in common when it came to trust issues.

"I don't think there's much more I can say right now to make this easier for you," Guy said. "I'm never going to stop reassuring you, but only time will show you that I meant what I said. I just wish there was an easier way."

I smiled softly at him. "You make everything easier."

Guy leaned in, pressing his lips to mine, and before he could pull away, I moved my hand around to the back of his neck to keep him where he was. He smiled against my lips, kissing me again, then he whispered, "Please can I spend the rest of the evening showing you how much I want you?"

I closed my eyes, his words causing flutters through my whole body. "Yes. Please."

He kissed me once more, then stood, pulling me up with him and leading me to his bedroom.

I couldn't think of any place I felt safer. Cocooned in his arms, wrapped in his sheets.

It was my haven.

With every brush of his lips against mine, every gentle touch, every piece of clothing removed, I found myself relaxing, caught up in everything that was Guy. His rough hands, his soft kisses, his eyes blazing with both adoration and desire. Everything about him made my heart race, my breath shallowing as we lay side by side on his bed, our lips dancing lazily together.

This was more than I could have dared to hope for after the fears that had built up within me earlier. I'd always appreciated how lucky I was to have this man in my life, but now, losing myself in him, in his touches, was the only thing that made any sense to me.

Guy's hands drifted down my back, making me shiver. As his fingers reached the top of my knickers, he paused, leaving a light touch there for a moment before dipping his fingers under the material. His rough hands on my ass always made me gasp, and I closed my eyes as I pressed closer against him and held him tighter.

Sliding his hands over my ass cheeks, he took my underwear with them, pushing them down as far as he could reach, and I used a toe to move them the rest of the way down, then flicked them off the end of the bed.

Gliding one hand to my hip, Guy carefully turned me onto my back. Unbidden, my heart rate kicked up a couple of notches as the first flashes of panic licked at my consciousness. I sucked in a sharp breath, trying to focus only on Guy's lips caressing mine and the sensations that caused within me. He moved slowly, hooking one leg across mine and remaining there, not fully on top of me, one hand trailing lightly up and down my waist, settling my unease.

It's fine. You're okay. You're safe.

I said the words inside my head, the words I always used to ground myself, and slowly, my muscles unclenched.

Still, Guy kept stroking my skin, still kissing me as my pulse slowed then found its way back to the moment. My hands moved down his strong, muscular back, and after a while, he carefully shifted his position until his

169

body covered mine. Winding both arms around him, I kept my eyes closed as his lips trailed from my own, across my cheek, and down to my neck.

I wanted to enjoy it. I *always* wanted to enjoy the feel of him because Guy... he was so goddamn sexy, and so gentle and intuitive. Everything he was doing tipped my arousal higher, but my heart... the racing now wasn't just because of his lips on my skin.

I cracked my eyes open, looking down as his mouth met my shoulder, causing another shiver.

It's Guy. You're fine.

Holding on hard to that thought, I closed my eyes again and a small sigh left me as he dusted his lips along my collarbone. I could feel his dick pressing against my thigh, and I wriggled slightly against him as his hand found my breast, the softest of touches that made me let out a low, needy moan.

This is how it starts. He'll make you relax, make you trust him, and then he'll take over. It'll start with sex, and then your clothes, who you speak to, and then he'll dominate every part of your life.

A second voice popped into my head that screamed at the sinister one, *Not now!* Guy was *not* the person. Could never be. Nothing in me believed it, yet I could feel the darkness taking over.

"Hey." Guy's voice was gentle, a welcome intrusion into my thoughts. As I opened my eyes, his were gazing at me with nothing but kindness. "Are you okay?"

It was then I realised my entire body had turned rigid. Shame and embarrassment collided with my momentary freak-out, and instead of offering him any words, I nodded. My body was still tense, so I did the only thing I knew how to do.

Take back the control.

I threw him a mischievous grin that I didn't fully feel yet, and wriggled out from beneath him, pushing him onto his back and climbing on top of him. As I leaned my body forwards to kiss him, my bravado increasing,

Guy's eyes didn't light up the way they usually did. Instead, they looked...
frustrated, and before my lips could meet his, he turned his head away
slightly.

"Gaby."

The sting of rejection was instant, like a slap, even though he hadn't
pushed me away or said anything cruel. He even still had his hands on the
tops of my thighs, where he'd rested them to steady me. He *hadn't* rejected
me, not really.

It wasn't rejection I felt, it was *seen*. He'd seen something nobody else
had ever bothered to see. And the discomfort that slithered through me
consumed me.

All desire slipped away, my body turning cold in an instant.

No, no, no. Why are you like this?

I could feel his eyes on me, but I couldn't meet his gaze. I lifted onto my
knees and then moved back to my side of the bed, feeling a level of ugly I
hadn't felt in a long time as I slipped under the covers to hide myself and
pulled them up as high as I could. I lay on my back and tried to halt the
thoughts rampaging through my head.

You thought you'd lost him earlier. You definitely will now.

I should have known this would happen. That I couldn't conceal anything from him because he was actively looking for ways to get to know
me. To read me.

Maybe I should have just gone home and not piled more on him on a day
when he'd had his fill. I hadn't meant to freak out, for him to have another
thing to add to his already full plate.

I should have known better.

Beside me, Guy let out a quiet sigh. Had I not been on such high alert
about what might happen next, I might not have even noticed. Almost
instantly, his little finger gently nudged against mine, like a tiny knock, as
if asking permission to hold my hand.

And that was all it took to ground me again. Too late to not mess up the moment we'd been having, but it helped bring me back to reality.

I turned my hand so it was palm up, and a second later, Guy rested his on top of mine. He didn't link our fingers, though, just let his hand rest there, and I realised he was waiting to follow my lead. A dance of trust. First him then me making the next move. With no words exchanged, like always, he knew how to handle me. My eyes remained on the ceiling, but I closed my fingers around his, gripping firmly, and he did the same.

"I've already been in a relationship with a woman who wants to control every aspect of sex, and I won't do it again. I can't."

He spoke with no accusation, disappointment, or anger. He simply said the words like a fact, and my insides withered. The last thing I wanted was for my issues to hurt him. Equally, *I* didn't want to get hurt, though. There wasn't a single fibre of my being that thought Guy would do that, but as much work as I'd done on myself, on healing the damage inside me, *this* was what remained. A part I'd never had to navigate before.

I nodded slowly. "I get that," I whispered. "I'm sorry."

"I don't need an apology, Gabs. I need to understand."

Still, his tone was even, and his using my nickname told me he wasn't upset with me, just confused. Of course he was. Because this was a side of me that made no sense for someone who was so confident in every other aspect. It wasn't bravado most of the time. I had put every single grain of energy I'd had left in my body to dig myself out of the dark and make sure nobody ever made me feel less than I was again. To understand my own worth and allow myself to be me. The carefree girl I was before my essence, my vibrancy, my joy were slowly stolen from me until I became empty.

It made even less sense when I'd laid my feelings open for him, let him know how much I wanted him, yet I was showing such a huge lack of trust in him.

"But... what if you do understand?" I asked, somewhat against my better judgement. "You understood Helen's reasons for her actions too, but it didn't make you feel any better or change anything, did it?" I wasn't trying to be harsh or inflammatory, but it was a fact. Helen had reasons for her behaviour, and Guy understood them, but that didn't mean he liked it. Maybe the same would be true for me.

Guy stiffened beside me, though he didn't let go of my hand. "That's not fair. She wanted what she wanted and that was that. Her way or no way. I don't think you're like that. I *know* you're not. But you're going to have to tell me what's going on and whether it's something we can work on before I can tell you if I understand it."

In a weird way, we'd been through a similar thing. Guy's previous relationship wasn't violent, but there was still a level of dominance to it that had worn away at him. He'd deserved better from her then, and he deserved better from me now. I wanted to give him that. And to get there, I had to tell him everything. Perhaps, if I got it out of the way now and he put an end to this thing, I could still walk away without having my entire heart ripped out.

Just some of it.

"I'm not like that," I told him. "I hate that I'm like this, and I want to change it, but I've never had to because nobody else has bothered to ask or stay around long enough to care. I'm scared of how much it will change how you see me."

There was a long, terrifying pause, and Guy's fingers untangled from mine before he shuffled a little closer and turned onto his side to look at me. "I like what we have, and I want to keep it going, but that can't happen if you don't talk to me. We've had sex three times, and each time, you've taken control, and it's been great, but I need to get a say in what happens in here too." I still wasn't looking at him, but I felt the covers move and figured he'd gestured around the room. "Sex is supposed to be between two people. I want to make you feel good. I want to be in control sometimes too."

173

A tiny spark ignited inside me at his words, and yet the idea of someone having control of me still meant my fears overtook the excitement. I used to like it. Being dominated had been my thing until it was taken too far. Now, it only elicited terror, and Guy had seen that.

This was it. It had to be. The day I told him all the things that would make him turn his back on me.

"Guy, there is a lot left to learn about me," I said. "If I could get away with never telling you the worst things that happened to me, then I would because I don't want to re-live it. I don't want to admit it happened to me, and I don't want you to pity me because pity sucks. You will see me differently, and I'm not ready for it. And it *will* change everything."

Before I'd even spilled a word of my story, the tiny remaining cracks in my heart began to tremor and fracture. They'd been pushing their way to the forefront for a while, knowing they'd be called upon with every single day I got closer to Guy. Knowing I'd need to crack them open in order to rebuild the last pieces that had never been able to heal.

I wasn't sure if they ever could.

Chapter 20

Guy

GABY HAD BARELY LOOKED at me since she'd climbed off me. Her bright, green eyes were fixed on the ceiling most of the time. She was talking, her hand still in mine, but she wouldn't look at me.

Her lower lip trembled so slightly it was almost impossible to see. Something had been holding her back from relaxing with me fully each time we'd had sex. It had been fucking fantastic every time, but it had started to become obvious that, while her confidence in the bedroom was valid, it wasn't all real. Any time I even came close to being on top of her, she'd switch it up so she was the one in charge. At first, it was amazing. Women who know what they want are the most fun, and I had no objection to being ridden like a prize stallion. But I wanted to give something back. To be able to explore Gaby's perfect body without her tensing and then taking over. Not because I wanted to control *her*, but because I wanted to do the things to her that she did to me.

She'd told me her last serious relationship was with a man who had abused her. Flynn. I knew he'd beaten her and belittled her, and it wasn't too much of a stretch to think he'd assaulted her sexually too. If that were the case, then her wanting some control made sense to me, and I did understand that. I could tell she trusted me because if she didn't, she wouldn't still have been in my bed, ready to explain and looking so fragile and afraid I almost didn't recognise her.

She knew I wouldn't hurt her, but something was still holding her back.

"Do you want to talk about it now?" I asked carefully. "It's up to you."

A tiny smile tilted the corners of her lips, but her eyes were wet with unshed tears, and I wanted to drag her to me and hold her tight. I wanted to know what she had to share, but I hated how it was making her react. I could feel how scared she was. I wasn't sure if it was of my possible reaction or just having to talk about something she kept locked up so tight.

"I need to do it now," she said, a tremble in her voice. "If I don't, and I leave, then I don't think I'll be able to face you again."

"Why not?" I asked, a little confused. We hadn't had a fight, and she hadn't done anything wrong. Neither of us had.

Finally, she turned her head towards me, and the movement prompted a tear to spill out, trickling onto the pillow. She swiped angrily at her eyes with one hand. "Because who the hell is unable to have normal, missionary position sex, Guy? It's the most basic and natural thing in the world. It's just sex."

Sure, when she put it like that, she was right. But she had to know that there was a lot more to it than that. I didn't think she was trying to be dishonest, more that she was looking at it from a skewed perspective. Over-simplifying something that wasn't simple at all for her.

"I don't think it's about the sex itself, Gabs," I said, wanting to reach up and touch her cheek but afraid to make the move. "You can have sex just fine. It's about..." I trailed off, unsure what the right word was. Dominance? Control? Fear? All of them?

"Power," she said, her voice losing all emotion. She turned her head to look back up at the ceiling again. "It's about power. When you allow someone to take power from you, and for so long, the struggle to find it again is... it feels impossible. I didn't see what was happening to me, but by

176

the time I got out of that relationship, I thought I was stupid, unattractive, fat, worthless, and I couldn't remember anything I used to love, either about myself or interests I had. Piece by piece, it was sucked away. I liked sex. With Flynn, in the beginning, it was the best I'd ever had. Not that I'd had loads of prior experience, but enough to know that I'd been missing out." She huffed out a deep breath. "Sex was the last thing he took without my consent, but one of the first things he used to gain power over me. He'd convince me to stop seeing my friends by offering me a 'cosy night in.' Like everything, it started slowly. I was like an addict, desperate for a hit of affection from him. Because it started with affection, then led to sex, and it made me so high that I'd accept the seemingly minor things he'd done wrong until they became normal, and then he would step it up again."

Her ability to speak about something so disturbing with no emotion was scary. As if she reserved a special compartment in her head she could slip into where all of her warmth and spark disappeared. A cloak of invisibility to cover her emotions, but it didn't mask her eyes. The green depths filled with the memories. Probably more than she would ever usually allow anyone to see.

"Gaby," I said, not wanting to interrupt but unable to watch her internal breakdown without offering her some comfort. Because this, I was sure, was only going to get worse.

"Mmhmm," she said vacantly, acknowledging me but not stepping out of her safe room of stoicism.

"Please can I put my arms around you? You can get dressed first if you want to, I just-"

"Yes," she said, not a second of hesitation. For the briefest moment, her eyes flicked in my direction, and I got as close to her as I could. I snaked one arm under her neck and lay the other across her stomach. She was still almost completely under the duvet, only her head showing, and still naked, but she tucked herself against me, the side of her head resting on my shoulder. I rotated my wrist so my palm faced up on her stomach, and

Gaby put her hand over it, curling her fingers around mine again. I gave a gentle squeeze, encouraging her to continue when she was ready.

"He did a lot of shitty things to me," she said almost as if there had been no break in the conversation. "But you want to know about the sex side of things, so I'll focus on that part. You've probably figured out that he raped me. Some of the time, I didn't realise that was what it was. By the time he started doing it, and it wasn't that often at first, I believed it wasn't that. That I was his, and I had a duty to fulfil." The laugh she let out was hollow. "Even I know how idiotic that sounds now. But I was under the spell. Believed he was the best I could ever do, and I was grateful I wasn't alone."

She could probably feel my eyes on her and didn't like it, but I couldn't stop staring at her.

If I were the kind of man who ranked women's looks, Gaby would have been a solid twenty out of ten. But that was just surface crap. Her personality and how unafraid she was to be herself was the first thing I noticed about her. When I saw her in that wedding dress, the night Shannen had called me for a ride home, it was the first thing to really make me laugh since my breakup. Gaby was utterly ridiculous, and she'd crawled into the back of my car next to Aiden and chatted away with him as if there was nothing weird about it at all. And with her, it wasn't weird; it was sexy. Her confidence was sexy. Knowing the extent of what had been stripped away from her was hard to understand because it was not obvious from talking to her. There was no hint of her past trauma because she had made herself work through it until she found herself again. I knew about some of it before we'd even considered dating, so I expected, to a degree, that she might need some time to trust me. Hearing the details of why was far harder to take.

"I can feel you feeling sorry for me, Guy, and I hate it," she said, another tear falling, this one landing on my shoulder. "Please don't."

"How would you feel if you were hearing this story?" I questioned, my voice steady. I understood her not wanting pity, but I didn't know what else I could do or feel when she'd experienced something so horrific. I just wanted to support her.

She closed her eyes for a moment and sighed. "I know. I know. It's... it's hard to explain. I was in therapy for years to get rid of the feelings that it was my fault and the humiliation of it all. Women get judged for being with abusive men, and they don't deserve it. Unless you've been with someone who messes with your head, you can't know what it feels like. But I do still feel embarrassed that I was in that position, even though it wasn't my fault. The only way to prevent it was if I'd never met him. But I did."

"I'm sorry," I said, placing a soft kiss on her forehead. "I didn't mean to make you feel like I feel sorry for you. But I guess... I *am* sorry you went through those things. It's not pity, it's just... I care about you."

She gave a small sniffle, but I felt her tiny smile against me, her lips tickling against my chest. "I know. But I'm a lot. And this sex thing... it's not like I never had sex after Flynn. It took a while, but I realised that the only way I could feel okay with it was if I was the one calling the shots. I tried dating, but any man I met... I never liked them enough to see them more than a couple of times. There were maybe two in the last ten years who I thought might go somewhere, but they..." she paused and sighed. "It was like they didn't understand me. They said they were okay with taking their time with me, but honestly, they were happy to let me be in control, and while I thought that was what I wanted, what I really wanted was someone who cared enough to help me get past it. And now... you're here. And I still want to get past it, but doing it is so much scarier than just thinking about it."

More tears dripped onto my skin, faster now, and her body trembled again. The only thing I could do was hold her tighter, but as I did, and as I felt her shaking in my arms, I realised how far she had gotten under my skin.

I'd made the decision earlier that I wanted her. I wanted to move forward with my life and not back. But now it was more. I wanted to be with her while she found her way through this thing that was causing her so much pain. To be the one she overcame this fear with.

"Guy... I need to tell you the truth about this one thing," she said, her voice shaking almost as much as her body. Her skin had grown cold, and I reached over with one hand to make sure the covers were tucked all the way around her before slipping my arm back under the duvet and around her again. "This is the one thing that I think will change everything for you, but I need to say it because if you end this now... I might just about be able to handle it. I already like you way too much for something we're supposed to be taking our time with."

My curiosity was piqued because I still couldn't think of a single thing that would change how much I liked her.

"What is it?" I asked, my hand slowly stroking up and down her arm. "Whatever it is, we can work through it."

She buried her head against my chest for a moment. When she had composed herself, she leaned back slightly, finally looking at me again.

"The last time I saw Flynn was the worst day of my life. I'd been out with some friends. We went for one quiet drink, and someone took a photo and put it on social media. I was tagged, and Flynn saw it. I was sitting beside a guy who was a friend of one of the people I was with. His hand was close to mine on the table. Not touching, and I hadn't spoken to him most of the night. He was just sitting next to me. When I got home, Flynn lost it. Accused me of cheating, which was funny, really, because most of the time he told me how undesirable I was. I don't think he even really believed I *was* cheating, he was just drunk and awful." She paused, swallowing, her eyes confused as if she had gone back into the memory and was trying to understand his behaviour. "I can't tell you the things he said to me because I don't want to go back there." Just like that, her tears slowed and her expression changed. She'd slipped back into detachment, and she was able to look right into my eyes as she told me her story. "He raped me. Right in the middle of the living room. On the floor. He held me down and forced me to do things I don't want to talk about. And then..." she paused. "Afterwards, I was completely numb. I didn't even get up from the floor for a while. He usually left me alone once he'd got what he wanted. But this time, when I tried to get up, to get away from him, he grabbed me by the shoulders and slammed my head into the floor. Probably a good thing because I was only semi-conscious when he beat me up. He beat me so badly that I had to go to hospital. I woke up there with no idea what the hell had happened, just that every part of my body felt broken."

My blood ran cold, and my chest felt tight as I listened. I wanted to find that psycho and beat the shit out of him so he knew how it felt to be scared. If given the chance, I would scare him so fucking badly that he would never go near another woman again.

No wonder she was freaked out at the idea of Flynn being out of prison. Knowing what I knew now, I couldn't understand why she wasn't more afraid because what he had done to her was beyond evil.

With the words she was saying, I couldn't understand how she wasn't crying. *I* wanted to cry just hearing it, but she had lived it. She was a hero. A survivor.

"When I came around from whatever had happened to me, I was told that I... he'd... he'd done so much damage to my stomach that they had to perform an emergency hysterectomy, or I would have died."

She said the words quickly, almost as if she wanted it out so she could breathe again. And again, a chill shot through me.

How does anyone survive that? How does someone rebuild their life after having every bit of it violated and torn apart?

"I've never said that out loud before," she said. "My family know because they were there, but I've never had to tell anyone else."

I tilted my head to the side, still in shock from all I'd heard. "Your friends don't know?"

She shook her head. "I want to tell them. I just... I don't really know how to bring it up. Shannen knows a bit, and Nova knows I was in an abusive relationship, but the extent of it isn't something I talk about." She paused, her eyes fixing on mine again as if she was looking for something. "Guy... I'm sorry. I know I offloaded a lot, but I feel like you might have missed the important part of what I said. The one that might change things for us."

I blinked a couple of times because she was right. She'd said a lot, but I couldn't see how anything had changed. If anything, I was more in awe of her than ever because she'd come through the most horrific ordeal and was living her life for her now. How could that change anything?

The idea of her being in a hospital bed all battered and bruised made me feel sick, but it didn't make me see her differently.

'...they had to perform an emergency hysterectomy.'

My eyes widened, and instantly, Gaby wriggled as if trying to get away from me. My instinct was to keep her close, but in light of the conversation we'd just had, I loosened my hold immediately and she shuffled away from me, breathing hard as if she was trying to hold in her sobs.

"Gaby," I began, but she shook her head.

"It's okay. I'm sorry. I should have... I should never have..." She sat up, holding the covers over her as she leaned forward over the edge of the bed to look for her clothes.

"Gaby," I said more firmly, even though my heart was pounding with her revelation. "Stop, please. Can we talk about this?"

Slowly she straightened up, but she didn't turn to look at me. "I think I should go. One of the reasons you and Helen broke up was because of starting a family, and I know that's something you want. And now you could have it, but I can *never* give you that. I should have told you that sooner. I'm so sorry."

Her last words were almost a whisper, and I did need a minute to process, but I didn't want her to go. Not like this.

Should she have told me sooner? She had never told anyone, and we hadn't been together for long. Okay, she knew my situation, and she'd figured that there was a strong chance her being unable to have children might have influenced whether I saw a long-term future with her. But I wasn't sure she owed me that explanation so early into our relationship.

What a day.

I had just found out I was going to have a baby with my ex on the same day I found out the woman I was seeing couldn't have children.

On the same day my best mate moved his family into what I thought would be *my* family home.

Seriously. Fucking hilarious.

Gaby stood up, hurrying around to the end of the bed to grab her clothes, and the movement shook me from my thoughts.

"Gabs, how could you have told me sooner?" I said, crawling across to where she was pulling on her knickers. I knelt on the edge of the bed and took her hand. "You haven't even told your best friends. Why would you tell someone you've only just started seeing?"

Squeezing her eyes closed, she used her free arm to cover her still-exposed chest. There was no hiding how much pain she was in, and I wanted to drag her back onto the bed and wrap her up; she was still so cold. But I wasn't sure if she wanted me to touch her, if the idea of being close to a man right after reliving a nightmare would make her flip.

"I know it's early in whatever this is, but it's important for you to know. I know you want kids, Guy, and I can't give you that. It's not something I can get help with. I just physically can't."

I raked my hands through my hair and let out a growl of frustration.

I didn't see this coming. She actually had hit on the one thing that had the potential to change things for me. I *did* want kids. I'd always wanted my own family. It had always been part of my plan. I obviously hadn't thought about having a family with Gaby this soon into the relationship. I'd thought about being with her long-term, but at that point, long-term for me meant I wasn't having some quick summer thing that meant nothing. I wanted it to be a real relationship, where we fully got to know each other and discussed forever further down the line.

No wonder Gaby had reacted so strongly to Helen's news. No wonder she'd been pushing me to think carefully. This... this was the thing she'd wanted to tell me earlier, when I'd cut her off.

Gaby was absolutely perfect to me. She had every single thing I wanted in a woman. Beautiful, fun, didn't take herself too seriously, willing to try anything, sweet, kind, and sexy. There was nothing about her I didn't like.

But this was a huge deal.

"Guy, please let me make this easy for you," she whispered. "Just let me go."

I looked up at her. Her hand was still in mine, and she was still almost naked, unable to get dressed with me holding onto her. Tears dripped down her cheeks, and she looked utterly broken. From the memories, from the heartbreak, from the overwhelm.

I'd never been the kind of man who needed to save women, but for her... I wanted to storm my way across the country, burning down the lives of all the men who'd dented her self-worth.

And the one who had set it all in motion... the pulsating, raging anger I felt towards him for doing this to her... I would willingly have served time to end that fucker's life.

"No."

At my simple word, her eyes fixed on mine, narrowing in question.

"If you want to leave because you need some space, then you can," I said. "But if you're asking me to end this, then that's not gonna happen. And to be clear, you're not trapped here. You can walk out at any time. But I would much prefer it if you stayed because I'm not okay with you leaving when you're upset and when you haven't given me the chance to respond to anything you just said. This is not about pity, and it's not about me being the good guy who's doing the right thing. Avoiding the hard conversations is how my last relationship got messed up. I'm not starting that way with you."

Gaby wrapped her arm tighter around herself, and I resisted the need to pull her close to warm her until she told me it was okay. "The hard conversations," she repeated. "There are a lot of those to be had. A lot of things to figure out. I don't think I can do it all in one night."

I gently tugged on her hand to see if she wanted to be closer to me, and slowly, she turned to face me and stepped closer. "We don't have to do it in one night, Gabs. We just have to make a start."

Chapter 21

Gaby

I WOKE UP EARLY on Sunday morning, even though Guy and I had been up late, talking. Instead of waking him, I carefully got out of bed and went quietly through to the kitchen to make a black coffee.

Saturday had been a long day. My entire body ached, and not from lugging boxes around. It was the soreness left over from the amount of tension I'd held in my muscles for so long. I'd been rigid for a large portion of the day, and no gym workout could have hurt as much as this. I hadn't experienced it in a long time; not since I lived with Flynn, when I never knew what mood he'd be in, so I was always on high alert.

This latest tension wasn't caused by a man; it was all me. My insecurities and fears had taken a hold of me and sent my thoughts spiralling.

I was still unsettled by how far I'd let myself get sucked back into negativity. It was the culmination of my worry about losing Guy, first to Helen, then to my hang-ups about sex, and the biggest of all... that Guy would see me as something disgusting and dirty when he knew how things ended with Flynn. What he'd done to me.

I curled myself up in one of Guy's armchairs once my coffee was made. I'd thrown his hoodie back on; he'd given it to me the night before to keep me warm when I'd started to shiver after telling him my story. It was clean, but it smelled like Guy since he'd kept me close to him the whole time we were talking. The scent was comforting, and combined with the calming aroma of my morning coffee, the weight of my concerns was a tiny bit lighter.

As uncomfortable as it was, the first thing Guy wanted to talk about was the stuff with Flynn. Not the attack, but he did ask some questions about my time with him. Nothing that was going to push me back to the dark side, just the kinds of things I would have told him over time anyway. He wasn't asking to be insensitive, he was asking so he could understand me better. Guy, I'd discovered, didn't always ask things directly. Instead, he absorbed the information I gave him, and that became his blueprint for how to handle me. So far, that system had worked well because not once had he done anything that made me feel uncomfortable or afraid.

That conversation, though, had naturally led us back to the thing I'd been so scared to tell him. The fact that I couldn't have children. The memory of our talk caused a lump to crawl up my throat because it had taken the last of my strength to explain to him that I *had* once been pregnant. That Flynn had got me pregnant, and because I was so scared of him and too lacking in self-esteem to take my child and run, I'd terminated the pregnancy. I'd told myself at the time it was because I wasn't ready to have a baby, and while there was *some* truth to that, more than anything, fear had driven me.

It was fifteen years ago, and it still hurt like it had happened yesterday if I focused on it for too long.

The crushing guilt, the feeling of selfishness, and the regret once it was over. It was instant. Like I'd just made a colossal mistake. Maybe my subconscious knew what was to come. Where my life was headed, and that, had I made a different choice, if I'd left Flynn behind way before I did, maybe I would still be able to have a family.

I couldn't change it now, though. All that had been left for me to do was accept it, as devastating as it was. It had taken years to come to terms with where my life was at. To forgive myself as best as I could. Day to day, it was a low-level thing I'd learned to live with. But when faced with the memories, it was like nothing had ever changed, but instead of Flynn's fists punching me, it was my own bad decisions relentlessly raining down on me.

"Oh, thank God."

Guy's sleepy voice broke through my musings, and I looked over my shoulder to see him standing in the doorway. He was only wearing his black boxers, and he looked exhausted. His eyes were still sleepy, and his hair was sticking up all over the place.

"I was worried you'd snuck out," he said, shuffling into the room and sitting on the end of the sofa closest to me.

I shook my head. "Nope. Just couldn't get back to sleep." He nodded, yawning, and I said, "You can go back to bed for a bit if you want. I'll be here, mainlining caffeine."

He smiled sleepily. "Nah, I'm up now. Are you okay?"

I nodded. "I think so. I was just... thinking."

"What about?"

"Everything, I guess." I blew on my coffee, hoping to cool it down enough so I could take a sip without singeing my tongue. "After going over the things we talked about yesterday, I always feel a bit... delicate. It's like having a hangover but without the fun beforehand. And I've never had to face so much at once like that." Shuffling slightly, I added, "There's still a lot more to talk about."

"I know. But, Gabs, I don't want all of this to take over who we are. I learned a lot about you yesterday, and along with finding out Helen's pregnant... my head's wrecked. I think yours probably is too."

"Yeah," I said with another nod. "It is. So, should we take a break for today and talk during the week?"

A flash of hurt crossed his features, and I flinched; I felt it. I didn't want to get away from him, it was just that I thought that was what he was going to say. Clearly, I was wrong.

"That's an option," he said. "Or we could do what we had planned. Full English, Premier League highlights, etc." A teasing smirk played on his lips, and I smiled.

That cheeky suggestion he'd made the day before seemed like forever ago now. "Do you think we'll be able to just act like nothing is different?" I asked.

"That's not what I want to do. I don't do denial anymore. What I mean is, we go about our day as we intended. If there's anything we want to ask each other, then we should, but we don't have to make the big conversations the main focus of the day."

That sounded like bliss. Whether it was feasible in reality, though, I wasn't sure.

"I didn't sleep too well," Guy continued, reaching his hand out across the armrests. I placed my hand in his, squeezing it in understanding. I *had* slept, but it had been patchy. "While I was awake, it occurred to me that only two things are actually different than they were yesterday morning. One, Helen is pregnant, and two, you told me the thing you were most worried about telling me. Everything else is exactly the same. I already knew most of what happened in your last relationship, and as for the bedroom stuff... I was aware before yesterday that there might be an issue we needed to discuss."

His view was rather simplistic, although technically accurate. "Except those two new things that have changed are fucking enormous."

He laughed at my blunt phrasing, and his smile encouraged my own. "Yeah. They are fucking enormous. And I'm not trying to play that down, Gabs. I'm not. I just think we need a day to let everything settle, and I would rather pass that time with you than without you."

His words... the sincerity in his eyes...

My fears were far from gone, but with Guy looking at me that way, and me needing to believe him, I felt... safer. The truth was, it was way too soon to know how the next few weeks and months were going to play out. Whether Guy would still want me when he and Helen had re-connected more. Whether he could deal with my re-emerging demons and the fact that I couldn't carry his children. Whether I could allow myself to let go enough to fully trust him with every part of me.

But I still wanted him. I wanted to believe that we could overcome all of the obstacles.

I untucked my legs from underneath me and leaned over to put my coffee cup on the table. Standing, I shuffled through the gap between the coffee table and the sofa, then sat down beside Guy, who immediately wound his arms around me.

Looking up into his eyes, I said, "Will you teach me the offside rule?"

His lips twitched before he burst out laughing, squeezing me tight then kissing me gently. "That might be the sexiest thing you've ever said to me." His eyes sparkled as he looked down at me.

I snuggled into him, chuckling. "I see all that dirty talk was a waste. Should have just reeled off some football stats!"

"Actually, if you could, that would be great," he teased, and I playfully slapped his arm. Grinning, Guy kissed me again. "How about we go and get some breakfast?"

Taking in a deep breath, another of my mantras drifted into my head. *Be a part of every moment.*

I was in no way certain how things with Guy would go, and it was hard to let go of the idea that sooner or later, I was going to get hurt. But in that particular moment, and in the whole of the night before, Guy had shown me nothing but understanding, affection, and reassurance. There was a chance I might lose him, and I couldn't shake that off.

But I still had him now, and I planned to ensure I made the most of every second.

Chapter 22

Guy

As promised, I cooked Gaby a full English breakfast, although she insisted on helping. The two of us in the kitchen together was almost like something out of a cheesy movie, with us moving in sync around the room, passing each other the things we needed and chatting a little more easily now some of the bigger conversations were out of the way.

I'd slept pretty badly the night before, my mind turning over everything Gaby had told me, along with how I felt about everything that had been thrown at me, not just from Gaby, but from Helen too.

It had never occurred to me that I might have to try to make a long-term decision about a woman I had only just started seeing. Gaby had apologised over and over for not telling me that she couldn't have children, and all I could do was reassure her that I wouldn't have expected to get that information so soon into the relationship. I couldn't even begin to imagine how much it must have tortured her, wondering when she should tell me. Had we met in a different way, with Gaby not already knowing what I wanted from my life, she probably wouldn't have been as hung up on it, because who really discusses having children so soon into dating? Okay, maybe some people do, but it hadn't been that way with Helen, nor any of the women I'd been with before her.

What kept me awake was the fact that it *was* something I needed to take into consideration. That if I wanted to be with Gaby, then a conventional family wasn't an option. I pushed aside the fact that Helen was carrying my biological child and focused only on how I would feel if that wasn't the case. If being with Gaby meant I couldn't ever have a child that was mine, would I still want to be with her?

And the only thing that kept circling back around was how my life was before.

When Cal brought Aiden to live with us, Cal was unable to be what Aiden needed, and I'd stepped into the role of a parent, with absolutely no clue what I was doing, until Cal got his shit together. Aiden wasn't mine, but I came to love him as if he was. I'd already had an unconventional family, and while I would have preferred a tad less dysfunction, it had worked, and it was enough.

I knew, in an ideal world, Gaby would have loved to be able to carry a child, but there were other ways to have a family.

I still wanted that. But was wanting that more important to me than the connection I had with this badass woman in my kitchen? What if I ended it and never found anyone else who breathed so much life into me? I'd had half-arsed relationships, and they were no good to anyone. The light Gaby brought into my world, even on the darkest days, was something I was unwilling to let go of. Even if, in the end, it didn't work out, I wanted her now.

And if it did work out... I would choose happiness over perfection every time.

Once we'd eaten and cleared up the dishes, Gaby went for a shower, and I went back to my bedroom to get dressed. Since we weren't planning on going anywhere, I didn't bother finding anything overly special to wear. I slipped into a pair of grey jogging bottoms and a black T-shirt, then went back into the kitchen to make some coffee. I knew Gaby wouldn't be too much longer.

I heard the buzzer sound, and I narrowed my eyes as I went through the living room to the hallway to see who it was. Cal and Shannen both had the code for the main doors to enter the building. Gaby didn't, but she was in the shower, so I wasn't sure who this would be. It wasn't that I didn't have other friends, they just weren't the type to visit. If I hung out with the guys I worked with, it was usually in the pub.

I pressed the intercom button and said, "Hello?"

"Hi, it's Helen."

I should have guessed.

A slight shiver ran through me. She was supposed to be giving me time to think. Okay, we hadn't exactly agreed on a timescale of when we would next speak, but I didn't expect her to come to my flat less than twenty-four hours after our last conversation.

"Hey. What are you doing here?" I asked, trying to keep my voice light. I didn't want to make her feel unwelcome, but I also needed her to go away.

"I bought breakfast. I thought we could have some croissants, coffee, and talk some more."

The feeling that I was a terrible person began to crawl through me because she sounded so hopeful. I knew how she felt about me, while I had another woman in my shower. Something I was entitled to have, but it didn't ease the feeling. Although I didn't want Helen back, I didn't want to hurt her either. I was going to have to at some point, when I told her what I wanted, but it was one thing me telling her and another for her to know that Gaby was with me, while Helen was very literally on the outside.

"Er, yeah. I already had a massive breakfast," I said. "I've actually got a load of work to catch up on this morning, but I can call you later."

There was a long pause, then Helen said, "She's in there, isn't she?"

Shit.

"Helen..."

"Sounds like you've already made your decision."

I huffed out a breath, running a hand through my hair. This was so not what I wanted. I didn't want to have this talk via the intercom, but I doubted she would want to come up. Even if she did, I wasn't sure how Gaby would feel about seeing her either.

"Helen, please," I said. "We need to talk, but not like this. Can we meet up tomorrow after work?"

"What's the point?"

I heard the door that led to the hallway open, and Gaby stood there, wearing denim shorts and an oversized T-shirt with the Chaos In The Courtyard logo on the front. She was drying her damp hair with a towel, and she'd obviously heard the last couple of exchanges as her eyes were full of empathy and a little sadness.

I stared at her helplessly, not knowing what to say to either of them. One day into finding out I was going to be a father, and I was already in the middle of the two women who were both important to me in different ways.

"Invite her in," Gaby said quietly. "I can go if you want, or I can meet her. Whatever you think is best."

I didn't know what was best. Was having them in the same room already going to be too hard? Would Helen even want to meet Gaby? And how could I tell Helen why I'd made the decision I had with the 'other woman' there?

Turning to the intercom, I said, "Helen, please wait there for one minute."

She didn't reply, but I turned back to Gaby and said, "I don't know what to do. What do I do?"

Her eyes softened as she took in my obvious despair, and she threw her towel over her shoulder as she walked towards me and wrapped her arms around my waist, looking up at me. "Why don't you go down and talk to her? See if she wants to come up."

Closing my eyes, I pulled her in closer. "I'm sorry, Gaby. I'm sorry about all of this."

"It's not your fault. It's just got a bit complicated."

"A bit?" I said, quirking a brow, and she smiled.

"Okay, it's a lot complicated. I don't know what you should do either, but one thing I won't ever do is put pressure on you or force you to choose. I don't want this to end, Guy. I don't. But the fact is, your baby is going to always be your priority, as she should be, and by extension, Helen will also be a priority. I don't want to be in the way."

If there was any way I could get her closer to me, I would have. As it was, there was no space between our bodies, but I wanted to consume her, drown in her. I wasn't sure what I'd done to deserve this level of understanding, but I sure as shit wasn't going to throw it away or abuse it.

"Gabs, if she wants to come up, I don't know which version of her you'll get," I told her. "She might be upset, or she might be aggressive. Are you sure you want to do this?"

Gaby shrugged a shoulder. "Our paths are going to cross eventually, Guy. Might as well rip off the band-aid."

Chapter 23

Gaby

WHEN I HEARD HELEN over Guy's intercom after I'd got out of the shower and dressed, my insides had withered. I knew this situation we were all in was never going to be easy, but I wasn't anticipating having to deal with it just yet. At least, not the Helen side of the equation, and especially not on such little sleep.

I believed Guy didn't want to be with her again, but I would still have to share him with her to a certain extent. And I didn't mind that if she was open to getting to know me. The truth was, though, if she decided she didn't want me in her child's life, things would be almost impossible for me and Guy. No matter what he or I wanted, I would never, ever be the reason he didn't have a relationship with his daughter. He wouldn't choose me over fatherhood, and I would never expect him to. The thought that I was going to always be on the edge of losing him—or at least for the next little while, when things were so unsettled—didn't feel good, but I wasn't going to give Guy up if I didn't have to. Maybe that made me selfish. Maybe I should have stepped aside, but it also wasn't all my decision. Guy had asked me to stay. He'd stayed up most of the night listening to me relive some of the worst moments of my life, and he still looked at me like I meant something to him. I'd waited too long to find someone like that to give up on it now.

Guy had invited Helen up, and surprisingly, she had agreed. I sat on the sofa nervously, wondering what would happen, while Guy waited for her by the front door. How would she be with me? Part of me wanted to put my shoes on and run home because I shouldn't have been there when Guy told her he didn't want to have the perfect family unit with her. It wasn't my place, and if they really dug into that, I would, at the very least, have to hide in the kitchen, if not leave altogether.

Voices drifted through from the hallway, and I stiffened, bracing myself for whatever was about to happen. A second later, I heard the living room door open, and I turned around, looking towards the doorway over the back of the couch. Guy looked like he might throw up at any moment, and Helen glared at me. She was clutching a large brown paper bag, which I guessed was full of pastries of some kind.

It could not have been clearer that she wanted me out. The dislike seemed to pulse from her, and there was no sign at all that she was interested in talking to me.

"You know what," I said, standing up and turning to face them fully, the couch a barrier between me and them. "I don't think I should be here right now."

The atmosphere in the room had thickened substantially with the way her eyes were burning through me. Still, I could see how painful this was for her, and even though she clearly hated me on sight, there was a bit of me that wanted to give her a hug and apologise.

I'd never taken that much notice of her when I'd seen her at school the times she'd collected Aiden; I'd had no reason to since he wasn't in my class. And the day before, shock had been the prevalent emotion on seeing her.

Her blonde hair hung straight over her shoulders, which she had straightened up as if she were trying to intimidate me. She was a bit frightening with those eyes shooting daggers at me. She wore a pair of black leggings and a royal blue vest top that stretched over her enlarged stomach.

A slight smirk crossed her lips as my eyes fell to her belly, and my understanding for her began to ebb a little. She was looking at me as if she had something over me, and every word Shannen and Cal had ever said about her began to ring true. Shannen had tried hard with Helen, but she had always said Helen was hard to get to know. Cal didn't mince his words at all. He outright called her a bitch, and knowing some of the things she'd said about him, I understood his feelings.

I started to walk out from behind the couch to head to Guy's bedroom, where I'd left my bag after my shower, but Guy said, "No, wait."

I stopped and turned to him, and he glanced at Helen, who was still eyeing me like I was the devil. His blue eyes held so much conflict, and I wanted to go to him and hold him, but I didn't want to make the atmosphere any more uncomfortable.

He looked at me, then back to Helen and said, "Look, I know this isn't easy, but you showed up unannounced, again. I told you Gaby was here and you still wanted to come up. I'm not asking her to leave."

Even though my heart swelled at his words, internally, my brain was screaming, *'No, please ask me to leave so I don't have to sit in all this tension!'* It was beyond awkward, yet I *had* also agreed to this happening.

Helen nodded slowly, and Guy said, "Do you want a cup of tea?"

"No, thank you."

Without another word, Guy held his arm out, gesturing for her to take a seat. As she rounded the sofa, he reached out his hand for me, and while I didn't hold onto it, I did give it a gentle squeeze once we were close enough, our eyes meeting as we both sat down. Helen and Guy were at opposite ends of the couch, and I took the chair I'd sat in earlier. There was a weird divide, like it was them together and me on the outside, though he was sitting vastly closer to me. But where else was I meant to go? I certainly wasn't going to sit in between them.

Helen leaned over and placed the paper bag she'd brought in on the coffee table, though she didn't offer the contents to anyone. Just as well; I wasn't sure I could stomach anything yet.

After a few minutes of the most uncomfortable silence ever, the ticking of the clock on the wall seemed to get louder, reverberating around my ears then ricocheting against my skull until it felt deafening.

Someone needed to break through the quiet, but it couldn't be me.

"Okay, look," Guy said eventually, rubbing a hand across his forehead, and I wondered if the clock ticking had grated on him too. "I don't really know how to do this. I'm still trying to get my head around the fact that I'm going to be a dad in a couple of months, and I know, Helen..." he paused and turned slightly towards her, "I know you want us to try again, but I-"

"Did you even think about it?" She cut him off, staring him down. "Because I feel like you didn't. I thought all the years we spent together, and now us finally having a chance to have our family, would mean that you'd at least take a couple of days to consider it. And yet, *she's* here. So, how much thought could you really have put into it?"

I might have bristled at her tone if I didn't think she was making a some-what reasonable point. It had worried me that he'd decided so quickly, although, once he'd explained his thought process to me, I understood. Helen, however, didn't.

Guy's eyes shifted to me before going back to her. "I did think about it. But the thing is... it doesn't make any sense to me. If you had told me you were pregnant right away, things would have been different. But even then... I don't know if it would have worked. I would have tried, but, Helen, we were broken a long time before we split up. And you know that."

She nodded again. "Yeah, we were. But I want to try to fix it. I know it wouldn't be quick. I wouldn't suggest us living together right away. I just want us to get to know each other again. To remember how it used to be."

My heart twinged for her because I could feel how much she was hurting, even behind the defences she'd put up.

The longer I sat there, the silence stretching out, the less sense it made for me to stay. Yet, leaving would make me feel like I wasn't being there for Guy. He was obviously struggling because he didn't want to upset her, but seeing them together, the way he was so tense... it was a clear sign that he wasn't going to change his mind on his decision not to go back.

"Helen, the way we used to be was a long time ago," Guy said. "You might not have meant all of the things you said the day you left, but I still hear it. It isn't just that, though. If we hadn't had Aiden holding us together, I think we would have fallen apart sooner. We were so focused on looking after him that we didn't have to focus on us. And every time I tried to suggest a way for us to reconnect, you didn't want that, you just wanted a baby. A baby isn't going to and shouldn't fill the gap between us, though."

Helen blew out a breath and moved closer to him on the sofa, reaching for his hand, which he didn't pull away. In fact, he held it, and all that did was make me like him more because this... it was breaking his heart too.

He didn't have romantic feelings for her, but he used to, and she was the mother of his child. I couldn't begrudge him giving her as much of him as he had left to get them both through this. It just showed me who he was. How safe my own heart was with him.

"I can be better, Guy," Helen said to him, her eyes on his. "In the time we've been apart, I've been trying to find myself again, and I've done that. I've reconnected with friends, and I've made an effort to remember what I enjoyed because I don't want to be this angry, bitter mum who sees her child as a reminder of something I lost every time I look at her. I want to love her the way she deserves to be loved. And in amongst all of that, it became clearer and clearer how much I still love you. Finding myself always brought me back to you."

While Guy found the opposite... He'd found freedom, and he had to tell her that with those eyes burning into him, tears shining within them.

Guy squeezed her hand, then shook his head. "I'm sorry. But I can't tell you what you want to hear. I'm happy, Helen. Since we've been apart, I re-found myself too. I sold the house because it never crossed my mind that you would want me back, I've invested in a new project, and I'm allowed to eat junk food and wear whatever boxers I want without being told they might affect our chances of fertility."

He wasn't actually trying to be flippant. Her control over him had been a genuine problem.

His tight boxers had always been rather appealing to me, though.

Not the time...

"Those concerns are over now, aren't they?" Helen pointed out, nodding towards her baby bump, though her eyes darkened slightly at his words, and her tone shifted to hold a hint of irritation.

Carefully pulling his hand from hers, he said, "And yet here we are. You getting upset whenever I point out anything I was unhappy with. You spent a solid two years pointing out my flaws, but when I did the same, you shut down. You're still shutting down. If there was any chance for us to make it work, it would involve both of us being honest and hearing things we might not want to hear. I don't think you're willing to do that."

"I might be more open to it if Little Miss Perfect wasn't here." She shot a look at me, and that time, I flinched. I understood my being there wasn't helping the situation, but the acidic tone surprised me, perhaps more than it should have.

She didn't know me at all. She knew I was a teacher, and unless Guy had said anything else about me to her the day before, I assumed that was the extent of her knowledge. I was sitting there, makeup free, wearing relatively scruffy clothes, and she spoke about me as if I were sitting on a throne, perfectly poised and smug as hell. Most of the time, I'd been trying to shrink away from the conversation by remaining curled up in the chair, as small as possible so I didn't intrude any more than I already was.

Untucking my legs from underneath me, I stood, turning to Guy. "I'll go. Let you two talk some more."

"No," he said, standing up too and taking my hand. "Please, don't." His blue eyes were still full of apologies, but I didn't need that from him. He wasn't the one being a dick.

"Let her go," Helen said, pulling our focus to her. "This doesn't concern her."

"Yeah, it kinda does," Guy said, the first sign of annoyance tinging his voice. "I was hoping that you would at least attempt to talk to Gaby and get to know her. Regardless of whether I want to be with you again, Gaby was my friend before she was anything else, and she will be in my life no matter what. She's Shannen's friend, and by extension, Cal's friend too. She's going nowhere."

Helen visibly tensed at the mention of Cal's name, the loathing for him coming off her in waves. "This is about me and you and our baby first and foremost," she said. "You and me, Guy. We're the ones having a baby, not you and her."

Even though she couldn't have known why, the declaration hit me like a punch to the gut, and I blinked quickly before any tears had a moment to form.

"For fuck's sake, Helen." Guy turned towards me, but I shook my head. I wasn't about to give her any further ammunition against me; she'd created enough of her own anyway. She had no right to any information about me.

I was too tired, and my emotions were too raw from the night before to deal with her.

"What?" Helen said, either not noticing or not caring about the dip in mood after her words. "It's the truth."

Significantly less concerned about her feelings now my inner demons had been woken, I moved in closer to Guy and rested my hands on his waist. I could feel her eyes on me, more hate permeating the air. "Call me when you're done," I told him. "But I'm not going to be able to sit here with her glaring at me the whole time." I didn't even care that she could hear me. She wasn't the only one who was allowed to speak the truth. "Maybe in time, we can try again, but not today. It's too soon."

I hated the conflict in his eyes. He didn't want me to feel like I had to leave, but he knew this conversation with Helen had to happen and it would be marginally easier with me gone. Leaning up, I placed a soft kiss on his lips, then whispered in his ear, "It's okay. Do what you need to do."

He wrapped his arms around me and pulled me into a hug. "Will you come back later?" he asked quietly.

"Mmhmm." I breathed in deeply, inhaling his scent. "We have a football match to watch."

He smiled gently at me as we pulled apart. "Yeah, we do."

Without looking at Helen again, I squeezed Guy's hands, then turned and went to his room to get my bag, which had my car keys in it. Since I was planning to come back, I grabbed them and my phone, then went back out into the living room to put my sandals on. The silence was so thick I almost choked on it, but I was so close to getting out of there. My heart began to race with the anticipation of getting away.

I wasn't intending to utter anything more to Helen besides a polite goodbye, but as I reached the living room door, she said, "I know you think you've won, but the fact is, you will always come second to our child."

My jaw clenched, not because I was hurt by her words but because I was finding it hard to muster up any empathy for her now. I reminded myself that she was in a crappy position, but she wasn't the only one. This wasn't fun for any of us, and her attitude was not helping.

I wasn't sure if Guy had a reaction because my gaze shot straight to Helen. "Yeah, that's how it's meant to be," I said. "If you had any interest in knowing anything about me, you would know I understand that. Honestly, if he was the kind of man who'd put a relationship over his child, I wouldn't be with him. I'm sorry this isn't playing out how you expected, Helen. None of this was what I expected either. But this is the hand we were dealt. It might not be the way you want it, but there is actually room for both of us in Guy's life. The only thing trying to shove me out is going to do is make him resent you." I shrugged. "The choice is yours, but while Guy wants me around, that's where I'll be. Accept it or don't. I'm open to talking and us finding a way to get along, but don't think I'm going to sit around and take your vitriol, especially when it's undeserved. Keep your fucking insecurities to yourself."

I didn't pause to hear anything she had to say. I wasn't interested. Maybe I said more than I should have, but I didn't do well when people were attempting to grind me down. I'd spent years making excuses for someone else's shitty behaviour, and it had landed me in therapy. I didn't like the way she spoke to Guy either, and guilt clawed at me for leaving him with her, but I had to get out. I knew he could handle her, I just wished he didn't have to.

I gave Guy an apologetic smile, and he nodded in understanding, then I left the room, gasping in a stress-free breath. Once I was outside the apartment, on a whim, I gave my brother a quick call to see if he was home. When he said he was, I made my way over there, telling him to put the kettle on.

Chapter 24

Gaby

IT FELT LIKE AN age since I'd last seen my brother. It had only been a few weeks, but since his call the previous weekend, I knew it wouldn't be long before he started actively asking me to meet up. He had checked in with me a couple of times since he gave me the news about Flynn being released from prison. That was the least of my worries, though. As long as he remained away from me, I'd be fine.

Gavin had decided against boiling the kettle and instead poured us each a glass of orange juice, then he led me out to his back garden. Calling it a garden was slightly ridiculous, though. It was the size of a small field, and he'd created a kind of zen area complete with a koi pond and willow trees that swayed in the breeze. It was very Japanese-style, with lots of rocks and a small fountain. I was secretly jealous of how cool it was. One thing my brother loved was to relax, which was no surprise in his job. He'd always prioritised his mental health, stating that he never wanted to become as cold and cynical as our dad, and he'd succeeded.

He had a house in the fancier area of Exeter, not hugely far from where Shannen's ex-friend Jade had lived, and I always thought he was crazy for splashing out on such a big place when he was the only one who lived there.

Even if I'd lived with him as he'd wanted me to originally, it would still have been too much. Two of us and five bedrooms, two sitting areas, a gigantic kitchen and dining room, an office, and enough land out the back to host a music festival was excessive. There were even a few outhouses off the back of his property standing empty. His theory was that he could afford it, and that he would one day have a wife and kids.

I argued that if he didn't ease his workload, the only partner he'd ever find was someone he worked with, or someone he was representing, and that would be unethical.

The two of us sat at his glass garden table, which was sheltered beneath the trees. The sunlight still got through, but it was cooler there. It wasn't too hot yet anyway, as it was only a little after ten, but I liked the seclusion. It felt safe.

"So, what brings you over here without me having to bribe you with cocktails or food?" Gavin asked, smirking.

"Har-de-har," I said sarcastically, rolling my eyes. "I thought you'd be pleased I came of my own accord."

"I am." He relaxed back into his chair. "But something is obviously on your mind."

There was no point padding the conversation out with small talk. I launched right into what had happened over the last few days, which of course included me telling him I'd been seeing Guy. I hadn't mentioned it to him before because the last time we spoke on the phone, there hadn't really been anything much to tell. Now, though, I threw it all out there, right up to what Helen had said to me before I left Guy's place.

"Gabriella. I cannot stress this enough, but what the fuck?" Gavin said, his eyes wide. His short blonde hair was getting a little long on top, and it was rippling along with the leaves of the trees.

In spite of everything, I had to laugh at his expression. "You know me, Gav. I don't do things by halves."

Shaking his head, he leaned forward. "No kidding. I wish I did have a freaking cocktail after all that. So... you left them to talk?"

"Yup." I reached over to pick up my glass and took a sip. "I don't imagine the conversation will last much longer after the way things were when I left, but I couldn't stay."

"Do you trust him?" Gavin asked.

"Yes. He's given me no reason not to. I mean..." I paused, trying to get the words right. "I don't think he would ever hurt me on purpose."

But I couldn't rule out him changing his mind about me further down the line. After all, there was a time when he believed he'd spend his life with Helen.

"Are you telling the truth? The real truth? Because you protected a psychopath for years, and life would be a lot less complicated if you could just be honest with yourself about the chances of this working out for you."

The words were like bullets flying from his mouth, penetrating my already fragile composure. "Fuck you," I spat, putting my glass back down. "If you can't see the difference between who I was at twenty-five and who I am now at thirty-five, there is no point in talking to you."

Yup, nothing says you're a grown-up like a hissy fit.

That was my entire issue with Gavin, though. I loved him, but I hated how, at any sign of trouble, he viewed me as a victim. Someone who wasn't strong enough to make a good decision. It was as if he equated asking for advice as a sign that I was completely clueless when all I really wanted was to talk things through.

I was so tired, the morning far more taxing than any Sunday should be, and it made me prickly. I already felt as though my deepest fears and secrets were visible to the whole world, and the one person I should have been able to trust was using the most painful thing in my life to make a point. Gavin had always had a tendency to be blunter than he intended to be, but that was a lower blow than was necessary.

"I'm sorry," he said, pushing a bit of hair out of his eyes. "That was uncalled for, but I can see how much this is hurting you already. I just don't want you to be at risk of being hurt any more. He's going to have a baby with this other woman."

He didn't need to end that sentence. It was loud and clear. *And you can't give him that.*

When I'd left Guy's, I'd still held a fair amount of optimism that everything would work out between us. Was I fooling myself? Instead of hanging in there for my own happy ending with him, was I delaying his and Helen's? Was it inevitable that they would get back together eventually and I just didn't want to admit that?

"You've met Guy," I said. "And you pride yourself on being a good judge of character. Do you think I shouldn't trust him?"

With a sigh, Gavin sat back. "I liked him. He's extremely loyal to Cal and Shannen, and I think that's a point in his favour. He's got a good work ethic, and he seems reliable. But he has got this woman dangling a carrot in front of him. And it's the carrot he has been wanting for a long time."

"I know. But I have been really clear about the fact that I won't stand in the way if that's what he wants. Seeing him with her today, though... I'm almost completely certain that isn't what he wants."

"Then what are you worried about?"

I let the question sink in because I wasn't immediately sure what the answer was. I did trust Guy, and I didn't think he wanted to be with Helen again. So, why was I still so on edge?

Was it because I thought Guy might one day want more children that I couldn't give him?

Was it because I didn't feel like enough for him and one day he would realise that I wasn't?

Was it because I hadn't had enough sleep and nothing made sense anymore?

Looking up at Gavin, I said, "I'm worried I'm falling in love with some-one who will only ever be half mine because his ex won't let him go."

A long-held-in tear trickled down my cheek. I'd meant what I'd said to Helen earlier. I believed there was room for both of us in Guy's life. I would have to make room for her because she was carrying his child, but she didn't have to show me the same respect. I understood that she still loved him and hated that I had him. In her position, I would have hated me too. But what if she never wanted me in the picture? What if she continued to make it difficult?

I wasn't the kind of person who let other people's opinions bother me usually, but hers mattered. If she continued to hate my existence, that would filter down to their daughter, and then Guy would be more torn than he was now and I *would* have to give him up. If not now, then one day.

"You really feel that much for him?" Gavin asked, and I nodded.

"I think I started to fall for him when we first began talking," I admitted. "But then the communication stopped, so I figured it was never going to happen. Then we went to Cornwall, and everything was different. He was ready for something new. I don't think I've even admitted to myself how much I liked him because I didn't believe he was interested. But he was. He *is*. I was ready to let myself fall, and then all of this happened."

"Want me to put a hit out on her?"

Gavin's lips twitched, and I gave into a chuckle, even though my tears were still falling. My brother would protect me with every breath in his body, but he would never actually hurt a woman. His words were spoken to lighten the mood, and even though he pissed me off regularly, I was grateful for him. Grateful to have the only family member I was close to living nearby.

"Listen to me," Gavin said more seriously, straightening up. "You've been through enough shit to last a lifetime. I don't think you'd risk having your heart shredded or be this upset if Guy wasn't worth it to you. You're scared, and I understand why, but as much as you want to be with him, you're already writing yourself out of the picture, and for what? To make life easier for the woman who made *his* life a misery. She's the mother of his unborn child, but from what you've said, he continues to choose you. Not over his child, but as the person he wants to be with. Let him. Stop trying to predict the future and let him choose you."

I had experienced almost every emotion over the last twenty-four hours, but nothing ever quite hit me like a pep talk from my big brother. Even though his delivery was sometimes awful, he was usually on the money, even when it was something I didn't want to hear.

Before I could thank him, or hug him, or as was my norm, affectionately call him an idiot, my phone began to ring from the pocket of my shorts. I pulled it out and Guy's name flashed on the screen.

"One moment," I said to Gavin, then stood up to answer the call, wandering over to the koi pond. "Hello?"

"Hey, Gabs. Are you okay?" Guy's voice was a little weary, and I wished I wasn't quite so far away from him, my heart aching to be beside him to give him a hug.

Wiping my eyes, even though he couldn't see I'd been crying, I said, "Yeah. I'm at my brother's place."

"Shit, sorry," he said. "Didn't mean to interrupt. I just wanted to let you know Helen's gone. Call me back once you're done at your brother's, and we can talk."

"It's okay," I said, a couple of the fish catching my attention as they darted through the water. "I can talk now. Are *you* all right?"

He sighed heavily. "I am. I told her that she doesn't get to talk to you the way she did and that I won't put up with it anymore. That she needs to stop acting like you're the other woman when she was the one who left, and it's been almost seven months since then."

"And how did she take that?"

"She didn't like it. And she liked it even less when I told her that there is no chance ever for me and her. I was as nice about it as I could be, but the way she was with you made it difficult. I explained that the baby will always be my first priority, and by extension, she is still important to me. But I was also very clear that you aren't some disposable girlfriend, and she needs to get used to that."

His voice was that of someone who was well and truly done with her behaviour, and while it was good to hear, I knew this ride we had all been thrown on together was going to be turbulent for a long time.

"Guy," I whispered. "Are you sure about this? Because-"

"Don't," he interrupted, but not harshly. "I'll say it again, Gabs. You are not some disposable girlfriend, and she needs to get used to that."

Let him choose you.

With Gavin's advice and what Guy had just said, it was hard to have any other response.

"Please can I see you?" I said. "Can I come back?"

I could almost hear the smile in his voice. "Yes. Please."

"Okay," I told him, a bit of lightness coming back into my body for the first time in hours. "I'm just going to finish my drink and then I'll be there."

"Okay. See you soon, sweetheart."

"See you soon."

As I hung up, a tentative smile spread across my face. For now, for the moment, it felt like maybe we could make this work after all. There were a bunch more hurdles to jump, and I was going to need some sturdy running shoes for a while, but perhaps this really was the beginning of something real.

Chapter 25

Guy

"Oh my God, Guy. Oh. My. God."

Gaby spun around in a circle, eyes wide as she looked around my bar. The bar I'd been fixing up with Cal, various members of my painting and decorating team, and a small team of bar renovation experts over the last month.

It was far from finished, but Gaby's reaction made all of the hard work we'd done so far worthwhile.

"So, you like it?" I asked, smiling.

"It looks incredible!" She ran her hand across the newly fixed and painted wooden bannisters near the door that led up to a slightly raised seating area. The whole of the main floor had also been repaired, as had the bar and the stage in the main room. "I can't believe how different it looks from the first time I came here!"

I'd been waiting for this moment since I'd first bought the place. The time when it started to look like an actual bar. We had worked so hard to make progress, and it was taking shape better than I could have ever hoped for.

213

"It definitely looks like a country and western style bar to me," she said, stomping the heel of her ankle boot down on the floor a couple of times like she might start line dancing, and I laughed.

"It does, doesn't it? I think it's still plain enough that it could be converted into anything, though."

She nodded, her eyes drifting all the way around the room. "It is. I can't get over how far it's come."

The awe on her face filled me with a sense of pride. Some days, it still amazed me that my workers and I had done this. We had a long way to go, but I'd wanted Gaby to see it now. I'd also taken some photos and sent them to Donovan as promised to show him the progress, but I hadn't heard back from him yet.

The other reason for bringing Gaby to the bar that day, though, was to give her something positive to focus on because we were on our way to see Helen.

Since their first meeting, Gaby and Helen hadn't seen each other. I'd met with Helen once or twice, and I checked in with her a couple of times a week on the phone to make sure she was doing okay, but things were still awkward. However, it was the first week of October, which meant there were around eight weeks until the baby was due, and we had made no decisions about how anything would work. No plans for when I would see the baby, if she would be able to stay with me sometimes, and what Helen needed in terms of money. And on the non-practical side of things, what would I get a say in? Could I help choose a name? Would I be consulted to make bigger decisions later on about schools and anything else of importance?

I had tried to raise some of those things with Helen during the times I'd seen her, but she'd continued to say we could figure it out later. Now, we were running out of 'later.' So, I'd insisted on us getting together to discuss it, and asking if Gaby could be there too. Maybe it wasn't the best idea based on how the last time had gone, but I really wanted the two of them to find some common ground so I didn't have to spend the rest of my life in the role of a referee. To be fair, it wasn't Gaby who was causing the problems, but if Helen pushed her too far, she *would* bite back. I needed an end to it.

"Come with me," I said, once Gaby had finished exploring the main room. I held my hand out and she clenched it, grinning with excitement as I led her through the bar, into the hallway, and then into the smaller room; the one that had the piano and retro games machines in.

Those things were still in there, but they'd been taken out and cleaned up when the plain burgundy carpet had been laid and the walls had been painted cream.

"Oh, wow," Gaby said as her eyes fell on the game machines. "This is so cool! Also, it smells amazing in here."

I nodded in agreement. The smell of the new carpet was still strong, as, once we'd finished in there, we'd shut the doors and hadn't gone back in since. The faintest smell of paint also still lingered, and it all combined to make the room feel fresh and new.

"A few tables and chairs would be good in here," I said. "Now all the other junk is gone, it looks bigger, so a pool table could also fit in easily."

Gaby glanced up at me from beneath her lashes, a smirk playing across her lips. "You're putting an awful lot of thought into the space considering you're not keeping it."

I huffed out a laugh, then used her hand to pull her closer to me. The feel of her body next to mine was so familiar now, and I let go of her hand and dragged her hips against mine. "I'm not keeping it," I said. "I just can't help seeing what it could be. The potential is huge."

"It is," Gaby agreed. "You've done a brilliant job, and it's not even finished yet."

I smiled down at her, pressing my lips against hers. "Don't underestimate your role in this. It was always going to be fun to do, but your support and enthusiasm have kept me going too."

Although Gaby hadn't seen the place since the early days, she always asked how it was going, and on the days when it seemed like I'd bitten off more than I could chew, she calmed me down and set me back on the right track. She might have had a wild side, but she could also be practical when the situation called for it.

"It's the least I can do," Gaby said, leaning back slightly so her long hair swung around down her back. She grinned. "After all, I'm only here to profit from your fortune. It benefits me to encourage you!"

"Gold digger," I murmured, kissing her again.

That had been another of Helen's underhanded swipes at Gaby. That Gaby saw me as a businessman with a lot of money behind me, and *that* was what she was interested in. No matter that, if this little bar project went wrong, it could plummet me into a debt I'd struggle to ever get out of. Nope, Helen believed Gaby only wanted me for my bank account, and without it, she'd be gone.

Chuckling, Gaby took a step back from me and clicked her fingers sharply. "Fetch me my vehicle, driver," she said in a fake posh voice. "I can't possibly spend any more time in such an awful environment. My Louboutins will be ruined!"

As she turned, I slung my arm around her shoulders. "At once, my good lady," I said, matching her tone. "Let me take you from this terrible place."

The smile she gave me as she looked up at me made my heart feel like it might jump out of my chest.

In the weeks we'd been together, my feelings for her had only grown stronger, and I was pretty certain she felt the same way. The 'L' word hadn't been uttered yet, but I felt it. More and more with every day.

I was going to tell her soon. But first, we needed to get out of this talk with Helen unscathed. When Helen was involved, there were no guarantees.

**

Helen had moved to a two-bedroom flat in Exwick after living with her sister for a while after we broke up. It was small, but it would be enough room for her and a baby. I'd offered to find her somewhere bigger, but she said she didn't want that. One thing I would say for Helen was that she was independent, probably to a fault, but I would always take care of her if she asked for anything.

I just doubted she would ask.

When we arrived at her place, Helen greeted Gaby much the way she used to greet Cal. A hello because she had basic manners, not because she wanted her there. This was a trend where Helen was concerned; she didn't seem to like anyone who took my time and attention from her. She had obvious reasons not to like Gaby, and Cal, admittedly, was a nightmare when he first moved in with us, but he'd got better and Helen's attitude to him never changed. She didn't much like the guys I worked with either. She felt like I shouldn't socialise with them because they were my employees, but I'd started off as a very small business. I'd told her more than once that I wasn't going to turn into a wanker of a boss just because things had expanded, but she always hated it.

Once we were all in the living room and we each had a cup of tea, Helen said, "So, where should we start?"

I glanced at Gaby, who was checking out the decor. I had been to Helen's once before, so the cream walls and carpets weren't new to me. I figured since it was a rental property, she wasn't able to change much, but as was her thing, she had added splashes of colour in the hot pink cushions on the sofa and chairs and hung bright Jackson Pollock-style pictures on the wall, all paint splashes and chaos.

I sighed, trying to relax in my chair. Being around Helen these days almost always caused my stress levels to rise, doubly so when Gaby was there too because that made Helen extra hostile. It was my choice to ask Gaby to come along, though, so I only had myself to blame, but I *needed* her there. I needed them to get used to being around each other.

"You've refused to talk about this every time so far, but we need to figure out what money you need for the baby and if there's anything I can buy before she arrives," I said. Helen had already set up a nursery with a cot and a whole array of other stuff a baby needs that I would have to learn for myself in the near future.

Helen nodded, smoothing out a non-existent wrinkle in the material of her long, stretchy green top, then rested her hands on her bump. "I guess we will need to think about the money side of things soon, but as for stuff... I have almost everything I need here, so if you want to buy some things, you should get what you need for your place."

My heart almost stopped at her words. That suggested she *would* actually allow me to have the baby stay with me sometimes. It wasn't that I thought she would outright prevent it, just that I felt like I would need to be the one to raise that suggestion.

She smiled softly at my reaction, the bit of her that remembered how much I wanted a family too reaching out to me and easing my tension a little.

"I think for the first couple of months, you should come and see her here, though," Helen went on. "I want to get into a routine, and also... she's going to be so small, and then there's the breastfeeding. I want you to be able to have her overnight, but just not in the first few months."

My eyes shifted to Gaby again. She sat quietly, holding her cup of tea and occasionally sipping it.

"That's fine with me," I said. "Do we need to figure out set days and times for visits, or..." I trailed off, shrugging.

Helen's eyes narrowed slightly as she watched me look at Gaby, but her words remained steady. "I think you need to bond with her too, so you can come over as much as you want to."

"Okay, thank you. Have you thought about... you know... when the baby's coming? Do you want me there?"

An almost imperceptible flinch from the chair next to me made me wish I had actually not asked Gaby to come over for this. I'd thought by including her, it was the right thing because she was going to be in my daughter's life too, but all this talk of giving birth and spending time with the baby... I was an insensitive dickhead.

I reached my free hand across the armrests to take one of Gaby's hands, and she blinked as if she'd zoned out and I'd just brought her back to the moment. Which, again, made me feel like shit. I should have let her tune this out. She smiled at my move, though, and I linked my fingers with hers.

Which, in turn, caused Helen to twitch in her seat.

I was making both of these women uncomfortable without meaning to, and I didn't know what the hell to do about it. Did I offer to take Gaby home and come back to talk to Helen alone? Should I let go of Gaby's hand so as not to rub Helen's nose in my happiness?

"Hey," Gaby said softly, because now I was the one fidgeting. As I met her eyes, she said, "It's okay. I'm okay."

Before I could say anything, Helen said, "If you're going to get upset every time we talk about the baby, you shouldn't be here." Her eyes were cold on Gaby, and Gaby slowly turned her head towards Helen.

"I'm fine," Gaby said calmly.

"You're clearly not, and I understand it's probably upsetting to hear that your boy toy still has a connection to me and that means he won't be able to spend all his money on you, but this is where we are, at least until *you* can give him a baby."

She couldn't have known how damaging those words were, but I shot her a glare as Gaby's grip on my hand tightened.

"My boy toy?" Gaby repeated. "Look, I know you still love Guy, and I'm sorry. But I have done nothing to flaunt the fact that I'm with him, and I've never given you any reason to dislike me. I really want us to be able to get along, or at the very least tolerate each other, but we can't do that if you continue to make assumptions about me and my feelings for him. So, I'm asking you right now to stop it."

"And if I don't?"

Frustration coursed through me because my life couldn't stay like this long-term. Sure, this situation was still pretty new to all of us, but Helen had had a few weeks to accept that I was staying with Gaby. I'd hoped it would be enough time for her to at least consider making Gaby feel more welcome. The day Helen had come to my flat, Gaby had been super open and understanding about Helen's feelings for me, even though this wasn't easy for her either, yet Helen had never taken even the tiniest step to make an effort with Gaby.

"Helen, please," I said, standing up, Gaby's hand dropping from mine. "Gaby's right. You and me... we're having a baby, and as such, you will always matter to me. But our child is not a weapon you can wield to hurt Gaby. I'm not asking you to be best friends. I'm just asking you to not be such a bitch every time you see her!"

"What about her?" Helen snapped, pointing at Gaby. "Sitting there looking all sorry for herself while we talk about the things we need to discuss for *our* daughter. All I said was if she can't handle it, she shouldn't be here!"

I was about to speak again when Gaby said, "Don't, Guy."

I turned my head to look at her, and her eyes filled with tears.

"I don't need you to defend me," she said. "I'm grateful, but I've got this." Although her gaze was soft when her eyes were on me, she took a deep breath, a steely determination taking over. She got to her feet slowly, a calmness to her that betrayed how much this conversation was taking out of her. When she fixed her gaze on Helen, she said, "I have a job, and you know that, so why you think I'm only interested in Guy because I want his money is beyond me. I can assure you, if he lost everything he has, I would still want to be with him. I suspect you know that, though. The only reason you can't stand me is because I have the one thing you want that you can't have. You had it and you threw it away."

Helen became dangerously still, something she did when she was getting ready to explode. I took a tiny step towards Gaby, but even though she didn't look my way, she held a hand up in my direction to stop me. Instead, she kept her focus on an increasingly pissed off Helen. Conversely, Gaby still appeared unruffled, though when I looked at her face, I could see the clench of her jaw.

"We're not actually that different," Gaby continued. "You see, I have the one thing you can never have, but you? You have the one thing *I* can never have. Your place as the mother of Guy's child is perfectly safe, Helen. I can't have children. It can't be easy for you, seeing me with him, but likewise, it's excruciating to know you can give him the one thing I can't. So, I know how much you're hurting because I am too."

The twinge in my chest at her words must have been visible on my face. To hear her say that was like being punched. She'd never said it out loud, but the closer we got to Helen's due date, and the closer Gaby and I got, I knew she had to feel the sting of what could never be for us.

Surprise registered on Helen's face, but it was fleeting, quickly replaced by malice. "So, you resent me? Is that what you're saying?"

Gaby's jaw dropped open. "Oh, you are something else," she said, shaking her head as she turned away from Helen. Then she spun back around to face her. "I don't resent you because I'm not a petty, spiteful arsehole. Just because I can't have something, it doesn't mean I want everyone else to suffer, but you? You lash out when you're in pain because it's the only way you can make yourself feel better! You might want to accept that *you* are the reason you're in the position you're in! Take some responsibility before you poison your child with your toxic bullshit." Gaby shifted to look at me. "I'm sorry, but this isn't going to work. Thank you for trying to include me in all this, but I think it's better if Helen and I stay away from each other." Gaby reached down to the side of the chair where she'd put her bag and walked out before I could stop her.

Helen had been given the perfect chance to meet Gaby in the middle. To bridge the gap between the two of them, but instead, she'd continued to fight. This was how it had gotten with me and Helen. No peace offering was enough. No suggestion was right for her. Everything was someone else's fault.

I couldn't remember the last time I had been so angry, and I took a few steps towards Helen so she could clearly see how serious I was. She looked up at me, a hint of regret masked by satisfaction that she'd pushed Gaby out.

"Gaby laid the most painful thing in her life out there for you, to show you that she isn't the enemy. That this whole thing is hard for *both* of you. And instead of accepting that and trying to meet her halfway, you had to be... you." Shaking my head, I said, "I don't know where you lost the person you used to be, but you'd better find her because you're about to be a mother. I don't want our daughter to be raised by this version of you. She deserves better than the cold-hearted bitch you've become." With another shake of my head, I walked towards the door, then paused. "We will sort out the things we need to sort another time. Call me when you're ready to have an actual conversation."

"Don't hold your breath," she muttered.

Without turning around to look at her, I said, "That's fine. We'll do it the hard way, by talking through solicitors and having other people make decisions for us. If that's the way you want to play it, that's what we'll do. I never wanted this, Helen, but if your ego is more important than making life easier for all of us, that's on you."

I didn't wait for a response. I walked out of her flat, hoping Gaby hadn't already jumped into a cab and disappeared.

Every muscle in my body was coiled because I knew Helen would be far more likely to call my bluff and force us down the more challenging route of custody agreements rather than admit she had been unfair and vile.

As much as I'd always wanted a child, and as happy as I was that I was going to have one, in that moment, I wished more than anything that it wasn't with Helen. She'd put pressure on our relationship. She was the one who'd ended it. She hid her pregnancy from me until a short time ago. Even now, everything was on her terms, and I was sick of it. Of course, some things *had* to be that way because she was the one carrying the baby, but it was like she couldn't cope if she didn't have the final say in everything, including my relationship.

And if she damaged that, she would have a serious fucking fight on her hands.

I spotted Gaby a little way down the road, leaning against my car, a dejected slump to her shoulders, and I jogged over to her. She looked up when she heard my footsteps, and when she saw me, a flash of panic crossed her features before she quickly wiped her face with her hands.

"Hey," she said, her cheeks stained with her tear tracks. "Sorry."

"For what?" I asked, taking her hands and winding them around my waist before putting my arms around her. Her head fell against my chest, though she wasn't as relaxed as usual. There was a row of apartments behind us, but no people in the street, not even a car driving by, and the silence was much needed in that moment.

"For what I said to her. I didn't mean to get so carried away, but... she's awful. I know she's your ex and the mother of your child, but she is impossible, and I can't... I *won't* be around her. I don't know whether this will change anything for me and you, but I cannot be in the same room as her. I'm not putting myself in the position of being someone's punchbag again, neither physical nor mental."

Holding her tighter, I said, "You don't have to see her. I don't even want to see her, and she kind of threw down a gauntlet. Or maybe I did.

223

Either way, I'm fully expecting to need your brother's law firm details again soon."

"Oh, God," Gaby said, looking up at me and shaking her head, her eyes heavy with guilt and anguish. "I don't want this. You don't deserve this. I'm making your life too complicated."

I had been afraid this conversation would come from the second Helen had said she was pregnant. The threat of it had been ever-present for weeks. It stayed in the background because, when the two of them didn't see each other, it was easier to ignore. The reality was, once the baby arrived, there would be occasions when they would have to be around each other, even if just for a short time. I didn't want my life to be split into sides, me in the middle, with Helen and my daughter on one side and Gaby on the other. I was willing to do almost anything I had to do to stop that from happening, but I wasn't prepared to let Gaby go, and I could see her gearing up to give me all the reasons it made sense for me to do so.

"Gaby, listen to me," I said, tilting her chin gently so I could look into her eyes. "If you want to stop seeing me because you've realised you don't have feelings for me or because I hurt you in some way, that's one thing. But if you're about to throw the 'I'm stepping aside' card at me, I'm not accepting it. You aren't making this complicated, she is."

"But I'm the only one who is expendable."

I dropped my arms from around her, frustration seeping from me at her words. Gently, I loosened her grip on me so I could pace. Thankfully, the street was still empty of people, and we were far enough away from Helen's that she couldn't watch us from her window and enjoy this little breakdown.

"Gabs, we've already had a conversation about control. We've both been in that position before, and neither of us want to go back." I stopped pacing and looked her dead in the eye. "Stop making my decisions for me. Yeah, Helen being in my life is not negotiable because she's having my baby, and you and I both understand that my daughter has to come first. That doesn't make you expendable, though. So, let's break this down. Do you have feelings for me?"

My muscles actually tensed. What if she said no? What if all this had become so big that it took over the way she felt about me?

"Yes. I have feelings for you," she said quietly, her green eyes sparkling as she looked at me. A bit of my tension dissipated.

"Have I done something to hurt you?" I took a small step closer to her, standing directly in front of her again.

She shook her head. "No."

"Do you still want to be with me?"

Gaby stepped forward so we were almost toe to toe. "Yes. I still want to be with you."

The last bit of my tension fell away because her eyes had softened, and her body was less rigid than it had been when I first held her. "Then please stop trying to walk away from what you want just to make life easier for other people. I'm not saying all of this is going to be straightforward, but you've already had too much taken from you to be forcing out things that make you happy. Also..." I paused, then sighed. "Helen might be giving me a daughter, but she took a lot from me too. If you walked away from this, it would be another thing to add to her list. She might make this tough for us for a while, but she will get over it. Maybe when the baby turns eighteen," I added with a raised eyebrow, and she let out a chuckle.

Gaby wrapped her arms around me and said, "I don't know what I did to deserve you, but... thank you. For always fighting for me and not just labelling me as 'complicated'."

"Gabs, we're in our thirties," I said, pulling her close to me again. "Nobody gets to this age without racking up some baggage. As long as we keep talking to each other about what we need, there's nothing to worry about."

She offered a slight smirk, her usual, happy self peeking back through. "I still can't believe I have a toy boy."

Laughing, I said, "Thirty-five and thirty-three barely counts as enough of an age gap for me to be a toy boy."

"You're still younger than me. I'm counting it."

Smiling down at her, I said, "Okay, wise older woman, let's get the hell out of here. Fancy a cheeky afternoon drink?"

Gaby nodded. "I think that sounds like a great idea."

Chapter 26

Gaby

MY SUNDAY WITH GUY was exactly the rollercoaster I'd expected it to be. I'd fully prepared myself for the meeting with Helen to be awful. I truly had tried to give her the benefit of the doubt. I'd felt genuine understanding for how hard it must have been to see the man she loved with someone else, especially while carrying his child and wanting him back, but it was a waste of empathy.

I hadn't planned to tell Helen I couldn't have children, but when the words tumbled out, I'd hoped it might go some way into making her see that I wasn't exactly jumping for joy over the situation we were in either. I was happy for Guy, and even for Helen because they were getting what they had always wanted, but it was still a painful reminder that I would never be a mother.

The one thing all of the therapy I'd been through had taught me was that I was still a woman, still worth something even if I couldn't have kids; because sometimes, society still makes women feel like they should be chained to the kitchen sink and popping out kids every couple of years. When you want something, though, something that by rights you should have been able to deliver, it was sometimes so easy to get caught up in self-destructive thoughts. Did bitchy, un-Gaby-like thoughts cross my mind sometimes? God, yes. But I still never wished harm on Helen or her baby. I didn't have it in me. I hated that her immediate assumption was that I resented her.

Hated that when she was such a prickly bitch, I resented her a little. But that wasn't about me wanting her *not* to have what she had, just that I wished I could have it too. Those thoughts, thankfully, were fleeting. It was the constant ache that was harder to deal with, but my feelings for Guy were substantially more powerful than the pain I'd already had ten years to process.

The new school term had started about five weeks ago, and my new class was beginning to slowly settle in to being at school full-time. It always took me a while to get used to seeing the kids who were in my class the previous year being taught by someone different and getting to know a bunch of new names and faces. It was also quite strange not having Shannen there. She'd only worked at Oakwood Lane Primary for one school year, but because we were so close, it felt weird not to have her around. At least I still had Nova, though.

Shannen's replacement was a male teacher, probably in his mid-forties, and his name was Tim Jukes. He was quite serious for a teacher of five-year-olds, but friendly enough. The new school year had also brought us several new dinnerladies, a couple of people on the cleaning staff, and a new caretaker, though I had only officially met Mr Jukes. Most school years saw a change in staff, but because I was usually in my classroom or the staffroom, I rarely saw anyone besides other teachers and those who worked in reception.

As was tradition, Nova and I settled ourselves into a corner of the staff room. Not because we were unsociable and didn't want to talk to anyone else; it was just that there were usually quite a lot of people in there at lunchtime, so we tucked ourselves out of the way. Plus, it was easier to chat without being overheard in the corner.

"So," Nova said as she took a bite of her sandwich, "Helen really is as horrible as Cal said she was?"

"Oh, yeah," I answered with a dark chuckle. I'd just been filling her in on how things went down the day before. She knew about our first meeting, but always the optimist, she'd hoped round two would go better.

One thing that had come from this situation was that I'd had to finally sit down with Nova and Shannen and tell them my story. Well, I didn't *have* to. I wanted to, though my hand was slightly forced once Guy knew. With him being friends with Cal, I figured he might need someone to talk to about how he felt, and he couldn't do that if he had to keep my secret, so once Guy and I had processed things between us, I'd spoken to my girls.

It was a relief to get it out there. In some ways, telling them had been harder than telling Guy because I'd known them for longer. I'd always felt guilty for not sharing this huge thing with them; they were my friends, and they deserved to know. I couldn't even fully say why I'd kept it to myself for so long. Part of it was that I didn't want it to change how they saw me. Not because I couldn't have children but because this horrible thing had been done to me. I didn't want them to suddenly see me as fragile, or someone to feel sorry for. Once they knew, it was immediately clear I'd been worried for nothing. While they had cried when they heard my story, I felt nothing but love and understanding, and it had brought us closer than ever.

"I think I probably said more than I should have to her," I admitted, discomfort rippling through me at the harsh words I'd barked at Helen. "Telling her she needs to sort herself our before she makes her child toxic was a bit much."

Nova shrugged a shoulder. "I mean... you weren't wrong."

Fiddling with my water bottle, I said, "She's exactly like Shannen said she was. It feels like there is a decent person buried deep inside her, but for some reason, she wants to keep her locked up and let Arsehole McBitchbag run the show."

Nova snorted out a laugh. "Well, for what it's worth, I think removing yourself from the situation was the right thing to do. You shouldn't have to put up with her being that way with you. It might make things awkward for a while, but I'm sure she'll get over it eventually. The most important thing is that it's not affecting your relationship with Guy."

Nodding slowly, I gave her a small smile. Leaning down, I pulled my phone out of my bag for a cheeky social media scroll before getting back to work. As I unlocked the phone, I was greeted with a message from my brother.

Gavin: Call me as soon as you can.

Blunt.

I had about fifteen minutes before I had to be back in my classroom, and I sighed. The thing was, a text like that from Gavin could mean anything from, 'Could you drop some food at my place so I can have something to eat when I get home late' to 'the world is ending'. There was no way to know unless I made the call.

"Everything okay?" Nova asked, and I looked up at her.

"Probably," I said, standing up. "My brother wants me to call him, and if I don't, he'll send a SWAT Team to look for me."

Nova chuckled. She was aware of Gavin's dramatic approach to my wellbeing.

"Be right back," I said, heading out of the staff room, through reception, and up the small flight of stairs that led to my classroom. Once I was inside, I hit dial on Gavin's number and waited for him to pick up.

"Hey, Gaby," he said, his voice tense. "Okay. Erm…"

"It blows my mind that you get paid to represent people in court, " I teased.

"Not the time, " he said with a sigh. "Look, I know you need to be back at work in a bit, so I'll make this quick and also say I'm sorry in advance but... not totally." The tension I'd heard in his voice had now taken on a more familiar tone. Guilt. A sliver of worry trickled through me.

"What have you done? I asked cautiously.

There was a short pause, and he muttered what sounded like, 'Fuck,' before he said, "I know you asked me before not to waste time and money keeping tabs on Flynn, but I couldn't deal with not knowing where he was. He was staying in an apartment on the edge of Manchester and I had someone check to make sure he was still there every few days. A few weeks back, he disappeared. I wasn't too worried about it after one week as he did this once before then came back. By the second week, I asked my guy to look for him harder, to stay near his apartment, but he still never showed up. I have people keeping an eye out for him here too, but the issue is, Flynn Burton has vanished. No movement on his bank cards, no sign of him anywhere in the last three weeks So, I spoke to the landlord of the place he was living, and he said Flynn had given his notice and moved out of the area. He didn't know where he was going, but Gaby... all signs of him are gone. It's like he's become a ghost. He hasn't left the country as far as I can tell, but I have no idea where he is."

I wasn't sure what to respond to first. The fact that he'd ignored my request for him to stay away from Flynn, the fact that he'd lost him, or the fact that my heart was hammering faster than I liked. I dropped backwards into the chair behind my desk, trying to figure out what I was feeling.

"I don't have any real reason to believe he's coming after you," Gavin said when I remained silent. "But it couldn't hurt to be alert, just in case."

"Gavin, why..." I began, then stopped. I knew *why* he'd gone against my wishes. He was my brother, and he took protecting me very seriously. It wasn't the why that was the problem, it was that his interference had actually made me more afraid than I had been before. While the possibility that Flynn might try to find me was always a low-lying concern, it rarely crossed my mind because I knew there was no logic to guessing what he was up to and making myself paranoid. Ignorance was, indeed, bliss.

But since Gavin *had* been keeping track of Flynn's whereabouts and then he'd slipped away... now it felt much more like I had something to be worried about. Nobody just disappears and stops using their bank account. Had Flynn realised he was being watched and moved to escape? Or did he always have plans to move somewhere else?

Or...

"Do you think..." I began, hating how much relief my morbid thought would bring me if it were a reality. "His landlord said he gave his notice, but... could he be dead? If he hasn't been using his bank cards and nobody's seen him..."

"It's possible," Gavin said. "But depending on how it happened, his body may well have been found somewhere by now. I don't think that's the case, though. My gut is telling me he's alive."

With a calm I wasn't sure I truly felt, I said, "Well, did you check out his parents' house to see if he moved to be closer to them? He's originally from Bristol."

"I did. His mum passed away a few years back, but after he was sent to prison for what he did to you, they pretty much abandoned him."

"He has a brother and a sister," I said, idly moving some papers on my desk into piles. "Have you tried them?"

"Not yet, but like his parents, they haven't had any contact with him in years either."

"Did anyone go and visit him in jail?" I asked, because he used to have some friends who he was pretty close to. They were equally as disgusting as he was, and anytime they were coming over, I made sure to go out until they'd gone. If anyone had stayed in touch with him, it would be them.

"At first, yes. But after a couple of years, it all dwindled. Nobody was coming to see him by the end, so unless he made a friend inside who got out before him, I can only assume he's doing everything alone. He's got nowhere to go."

"Well, you should still check out his family. It's unlikely, but maybe he wants to build some bridges."

Even as I said the words, I didn't believe them. Flynn didn't have a single redeeming quality about him. There was a chance that perhaps he'd worked through his shitty behaviour while he'd been in jail, but I doubted it. My thoughts were merely a way to deflect from the terrifying idea that he might be somewhere around Exeter because I didn't want to live my life looking over my shoulder, seeing his face everywhere I turned.

"I'm on it," Gavin said. "I've got a couple of people working on it as we speak. But Gaby, while I don't know where he is I'd be a lot happier if you moved in with me."

Slamming my hand down on a pile of newly tidied paperwork, I said, "Absolutely not. For one thing, we don't know whether or not he's even nearby. I could be living at yours forever."

"Well, you know there's plenty of room..."

"No," I interrupted firmly. Flynn would have to have been spotted directly outside my flat before I'd even consider moving into my brother's house. It wasn't that I didn't love him, I just didn't want to feel like I was back living with my parents again. I was edging closer to forty; I did not need to have to be worrying about telling someone where I was going and what I was doing. There was more than enough room at Gavin's for us not to be in each other's way, but I would always be aware that it was *his* space, not mine. "Thank you, Gav, but that doesn't make sense. Not when Flynn could be anywhere. How would we even be able to judge when I was safe again if you don't know where he is? You say you don't think he's left the country, but you can't know that for sure. I lived enough of my life in fear when I was with him. I'm not going back to that again now."

Gavin let out a resigned sigh; he had to have known that would be my response. "Fine. But please can you be extra careful? Keep an eye out for him, and if anything weird or unusual happens, you let me know right away, okay?"

"I will," I promised. There was a lengthy pause between us, then I said, "I have to go, but... I guess... keep me updated if you find anything out."

I hung up before giving him a chance to respond, still caught between irritation that he'd gone behind my back and the slightly increased worry that Flynn might be nearby.

Living in fear of Flynn was supposed to be over. I liked it better when he wasn't in my head, but now he was back with a vengeance, and it was my own brother who had planted him there. Gavin had good intentions, but the result of his good intentions was me starting to feel a little bit like it was going to be the beginning of my unravelling.

Guy

"So, what do you think?" Cal asked me as we got out of my van with the Gregg's steak bakes we'd just gone out to get for lunch.

My other workers had all chosen to go off-site for their lunch break, but Cal and I were headed back to the bar. I was developing strong attachment issues to my project, and I struggled to stay away, even at the weekends, eager to get the place finished up. The truth was, no matter how hard we worked, there was no way it would be complete much before Christmas, but I was buzzing over the fact that we were turning a battered building into something that could easily be a goldmine for someone. It had been exactly what I needed at the right time, and I would be sad to say goodbye to it.

As we approached the doors, I reached into my pocket for the keys. "About what?" I asked. Unlocking the door, I let us in, then locked it behind us again.

"The new guy," Cal said, then took a bite of his steak slice.

I shrugged as we walked further inside and settled ourselves on the edge of the stage. Everything was dusty, but so were we after working in there all morning. "Seems all right. Why?"

"I don't know. There's something about him." He took another bite, and when he'd swallowed it, he added, "He's good at the job, but he's just a bit... quiet. He looks around a lot, like he's planning a robbery or something."

Laughing, I said, "Cal, nothing gets left in here except wood and nails, and he's hardly going to be able to slip the Pacman machine in his coat pocket to smuggle it out!"

"Twat," he said, but he smirked. "I don't think he's actually trying to steal shit, but something is off about him."

"His references checked out and he's had a lot of experience. And as you said, he's been doing a good job. He's probably just getting a feel for who we all are. Most of us know each other, but he's been thrown in at the deep end."

In my eagerness to get the bar ready as fast as possible, I'd hired a couple more people temporarily. One to work the painting and decorating jobs so I could free up another of my permanent men to help me and Cal, and an additional one to also join us in the bar. Over the last few weeks, I'd hired a bunch of people for short-term jobs, but I needed a couple more temporary but longer-term workers. The one Cal was referring to was good with both wood and plumbing; two things we required some extra help with. His name was Ryder; a name I'd never actually heard anyone around my age have, at least not in the depths of South Devon, but he wasn't a local. He'd moved to Exeter from somewhere in the north a while back, and self-employment wasn't working out for him, so he applied for the temp job with me. I hadn't sensed anything off about him, but clearly, he had triggered something in Cal, so I'd keep them apart while also scoping out the new guy.

As I was about to tuck into my own lunch, someone knocked on the doors, and I glanced at Cal before placing my steak bake back into its paper bag and leaving it on the stage. Nobody who didn't work for me had tried to get in since we'd begun working there, but I kept the doors locked as much as possible for safety reasons. I didn't want anyone to wander in and hurt themselves by falling through the floorboards or standing on a stray nail.

The glass panels in the top half of the door were thick and frosted, so I couldn't see who was there without unlocking the doors. As I opened one of them, I saw Ryder standing there, holding a portion of cod and chips.

I wasn't sure what Cal saw in him that was strange because he had a sheepish look on his face as he said, "Is it okay if I eat in here with you? I didn't know where else to go."

"Sure," I said, stepping aside to let him in, then locking the door behind him again.

"I could have gone home," he explained as we walked across the space to the stage. "But by the time I did that, ate, and got back, I may as well have just stayed here."

"Yeah, I get it," I said as we both sat down. Cal eyed him and gave him a nod in greeting, which Ryder returned.

He was a big guy with a large frame and muscles that made mine look pathetic. I figured women probably found him attractive. He had thick black hair and stubble across his chin; Gaby had informed me that was sexy, but when I tried to grow stubble, I didn't look good, I looked like I'd been on a week-long bender.

"Shannen's on her way," Cal said. "She said she has something for us, which I think means food."

I smiled. Shannen had dropped in to see us a few times over the last couple of weeks to bring us coffee or lunch. Since Gaby and Nova had gone back to work and Aiden was at school, she was bored during the day, and with the baby getting closer to arriving, she was also tired more often and couldn't walk around for as long as she usually would have. Coming to see us at lunchtime broke the day up a bit for her.

"Too bad we can't find a job for her," I said. "Keep her busy until it's time to pick Aiden up."

Cal nodded. "She's losing her mind since the summer holidays ended. She wasn't built to sit around all day, or to be a housewife."

"Wife?" I teased, and Cal rolled his eyes.

"Stop it. I think we've gone fast enough," he said, though his eyes brightened at the idea of being married to Shannen. He turned his attention to Ryder and said, "You married?"

Ryder shook his head. "Nah. Haven't had a long-term relationship in a while. I like being a bachelor."

"So did Cal," I said with a grin. "Until he met the love of his life."

"You're making me sound like a loser." Cal gave me a fake glare, but his happiness still shone through. "I'm not exactly leading man from a romance movie material."

I snorted. "Ain't that the truth!"

"Fuck off."

I grinned at my best mate, while Ryder watched us, an amused expression on his face.

A vibration in my pocket caught my attention, and I muttered some curse words under my breath. I wanted to eat, but it seemed like things were determined to get in my way. I pulled the phone from my pocket and saw Donovan was trying to video call me.

I raised an eyebrow. I hadn't heard from him since I'd sent him the photos of the bar's progress, but I'd assumed he was busy. I wasn't expecting a call, though, just a text. Leaping to my feet, I told Cal who it was then walked to the doors that led out to the small, still undecorated, hallway before pressing to answer the call.

After a moment or two, Donovan's face filled the screen. He was at his beachfront apartment, on the balcony, as I could see the sliding doors that led inside behind him. He'd only video called me once before from inside his place in the Philippines, but he had showed me the balcony and the view over the sea. It was incredible.

Lucky bastard.

"Hey," I said, smiling. "How's it going?"

"Good, thanks, mate," he answered, smiling back, although he didn't look completely like his usual, laidback self, and it made me wonder what was going on. "Sorry it's taken me so long to get back to you. I wanted to be sure about what I was going to say before I called you." He paused, then added, "Are you alone?"

Chuckling, I darted my eyes sideways, already knowing there was nobody nearby, and Donovan laughed. "Well, Cal and one of my other guys are in the main bar, but I don't think they can hear me from here. What's up?"

He paused again. "Can you make sure nobody can hear you? What I'm about to say can't go any further than me and you."

Weirdly, my heart rate picked up because, clearly, this was something big. With a nod, I made my way into the smaller room with the gaming machines, closed the door, and then walked across to the back of the room and leaned against the wall. "Okay, now I'm definitely alone. What's up?"

Donovan drew in a deep breath. "Sorry for all the secrecy, it's just, I don't want Nova to know anything about what I'm going to tell you, and if Cal knows, he might tell Shannen, and then she'll feel bad for keeping it from Nova. Same with you and Gaby. It has to stay between us."

"What the hell is going on, man?" I asked, my curiosity well and truly piqued. "And of course. Whatever you say stays between us."

He nodded, exhaling slowly, but now there was the hint of a smile on his face. "Okay. So, before we get to that, I really liked the pictures of the bar. Even unfinished, it's starting to look great."

"Thanks," I said, only slightly pissed that he wasn't divulging his secret yet. "We've just got a new guy who's joined the team to make things move a little faster. We're hoping to have the main bar area done and painted in the next couple of weeks, and then we're going to look at sorting out the heating system and the plumbing, which is going to be a hell of a task. I'm still now getting quotes, but it's not cheap."

239

Luckily, I had some money to fall back on, but that didn't mean I could just hire whoever got back to me first. I stood to make back way more than I spent when I sold the bar, but I had to be careful with my budget until then.

"Can you cover the costs?" Donovan asked, his face serious. "Because... this is sort of what I wanted to talk to you about."

I felt the crease in my forehead. "How do you mean?"

Donovan widened his eyes for a second, then let out a short, slightly surprised laugh. "I can't believe I'm going to say this out loud, and just to clarify, everything from here on out is the bit you can't tell anyone." I nodded, not wanting to interrupt. "So, I'm coming home. My mum and dad asked me and Nova to spend Christmas and New Year in Italy with them, and while Nova is expecting me to go back on my travels after, I'm not, except to finish up any contracts I have outstanding with the people I'm working for at the moment. I'm supposed to be with them until next March, but once I've seen it out, I'm done. I want to be in Devon with Nova, and closer to my nan."

"Wow," I said, my brows arching. I didn't know Donovan hugely well, but I did know how much he loved travelling. He'd been jetting around the world for close to eleven years, and when he talked about it, it felt like he never wanted to stop. On the other hand, it was clear how much he loved Nova, and being apart so much had to be taking a toll on them. "That's great," I said. "And you don't want Nova to know your plans?"

"Not yet." He sighed, running a hand through his hair. "I want this, and I know it's right, but there is a part of me that's used to only having to think about myself. I'm afraid if I tell her too soon... what if I change my mind?" A glimmer of doubt had already appeared in his eyes, but he shook his head. "I love her, and I want to come home. I *am* sure, but it's taking a bit of getting used to. The thing is, while I plan to continue blogging and travelling around the UK, I want a new challenge too. And since you first showed me the bar, although I *do* know someone who might be interested in it... I want it."

I blinked, wondering if I had misheard. "You... want to buy this bar?"

He laughed, his eyes lighting up again. "Yes. Well, sort of. I wanted to ask you if maybe you wanted a new challenge too. I've been thinking about this for a while, and although I don't know the specifics of how much the bar is worth, I do think it could make a lot of money. I've worked in bars, I have a lot of contacts within the industry, both in the UK and overseas, and I've been talking to them about running costs, licences, and any and all legal shit that would need to be dealt with. It would be a gamble to take it on... but I think it would be a risk worth taking. So, I can and would buy it outright, but Nova's told me via Gaby how much you have fallen in love with the place, and I wondered whether you might be interested in running it as a partnership. I could buy into it, and we wouldn't even have to work there. We could hire people to do all of that for us. We would essentially just reap the rewards, and with my social media reach... it could be huge."

"Why are there no chairs in here?" I mumbled as my back slid down the wall as I replayed what Donovan had proposed in my head. "I need to think."

With a chuckle, Donovan said, "I wasn't expecting a decision this second. I just wanted to float it by you and see what your immediate thoughts were."

My immediate thoughts?

I *had* fallen in love with the bar. I'd bought it because I wanted to do something that was just for me, and it had helped me in so many ways. It kept me busy, gave me a new purpose, helped me get away from the shittier parts of my life, and all-around helped me re-build the self-worth Helen had dented. I never intended to keep it, though. As much as I was attached to it, I didn't know a thing about running a bar. The purchase has been as a fixer-upper; the running of it would be on the buyer. I was just there to make it look good.

And it really was starting to look good.

Gaby was right in what she'd said the day before. The building had started to become a part of me, and I *did* spend more time than I should have decorating it in my head. The country and western feel grew stronger all the time, and I kept envisioning it full of patrons, country music playing, fancy cocktails being served, and it being a place where people could let loose and have a good time.

And Donovan wanted in.

With a cash injection from him, we could make it even better, and although the rewards wouldn't be instant, he was right. With his social media reach, he could easily make it the most popular bar in Exeter.

I realised my hands were shaking a bit from the adrenaline, and I was sure my eyes had glazed over while I considered what he'd said.

"I... Yeah. My immediate thought is that I don't want to give the bar up," I said, focusing on his face on the screen. "I will need to think about it. We might need to spend a few hours one day talking it all through, but I like the idea of a partnership. We would need a lot of legal advice, but Gaby's brother's law firm is brilliant. And they would be bound by confidentiality, so we wouldn't need to worry about him telling her."

Clearly, my brain had already got the bar up and running, and I was seeing myself mixing drinks like Tom Cruise in *Cocktail*. Not that *that* would ever be the plan.

I mean... probably. I never thought I would consider keeping the bar, so who the hell knew what unexpected decisions I would make next?

Donovan's smile widened. "I don't want you to rush this, but I like the way this feels like it's going. The good thing is, the place is yours. It's not like anyone can swoop in and buy it out from under you, so take your time. I won't be back in the UK until December, so I'll see you then, before Nova and I head to Italy, but we can talk whenever you want. I just wanted to plant the seed and see how you felt."

My heart was still hammering, but in a good way.

Jesus. My life at the beginning of the year had felt... not empty, but lonely. Like I wasn't sure what the hell would happen to me because I'd been with Helen for so long, I didn't know how to be on my own. Now, I had the best woman in the world, a baby on the way, and now the chance to keep this bar and make this labour of love mean more than it already did.

I had kept everything small while I was with Helen. I didn't blame her for that exactly; I'd made the choice to try to keep her happy without realising how much I was bypassing some of the things I wanted for myself, our whole lives embroiled in the desire to start a family. Now, I was free. Well, sort of. I was about to be a father, and as long as I didn't risk everything I had, I could make decisions that scared me a bit.

And owning a bar scared the shit out of me. But I wouldn't be doing it alone. Besides, before I bought it, I was smart enough to look at what kind of profits it could pull in. I didn't want to be saddled with something nobody would ever want. The potential was there. I just had to be prepared to put the work in.

"I think this could be amazing," I said. "But yeah, let me think about it for a bit longer. I'll be in touch to talk it over again soon."

Donovan grinned. "Okay. Thanks for not shooting me down right away."

I laughed. "You might have given me the perfect excuse to keep this place, so... thanks."

"Even if you don't want to keep it, I still want it, so one way or another, it won't be too far away. I promise I'll take care of it."

Nodding, I said, "I know. Fuck, this was not a call I was expecting today." I shook my head, still a little dazed. "I'd better go and eat before I have to get back to work, but I will talk to you soon. And thank you."

"No problem. Catch you later, bud."

As I hung up, I let out a long breath before getting to my feet. I had a lot of thinking to do, and the hardest thing was not being able to talk about it to anyone other than Donovan. In spite of the short time I'd known him, I was confident he was trustworthy, but it would have been good to have someone else to go over it with.

You don't need to. You want this.

I did. I wanted it so much that my insides were coiled with the anticipation of making it happen. But I had to shake it off for now. Had to get my head back in the game and crack on with the work I had in front of me. With the possibility of keeping my bar forever, every idea I'd had for it sprang to life, making a smile spread across my face as I put my phone in the back pocket of my jeans and headed back into the main room.

As I walked through the doors, I saw Ryder had already got back to work, although he'd taken his fish and chips with him to the other side of the room, where he was painting the bar. Shannen had arrived too, not too long ago either by the looks of it. She was just sitting down on the stage beside Cal and placing a large white carrier bag full of... something down next to her as I approached. It was a good thing Cal had a key, or she would have been left outside waiting for me to finish my call.

"Hey," I said, and she smiled up at me. "How's it going?"

"All good," she replied, though she winced slightly as she moved, and Cal instinctively put his arm around her as she stretched. "I mean, my back aches and my boobs weigh a ton, but I'm okay."

"Can we not discuss your tits with my best mate?" Cal said, rubbing circles on her lower back, though whether she could feel it through her thick, black coat was anyone's guess.

She smiled at him as I chuckled, and she wiggled her eyebrows at him.

Having witnessed the two of them eye-fucking each other many times before, I averted my gaze, sitting down on the edge of the stage again and finally retrieving my steak bake. Cal and Shannen had pretty much always looked at each other like they were about thirty seconds away from ripping each other's clothes off. Not in a sleazy way that made people uncomfortable; it was more intimate, a deep connection that somehow seemed to make it abundantly clear that they belonged to each other whenever they were in the same room.

"I brought cake," Shannen said, swiftly changing the subject, and I turned my head to look at her again. She smiled. "I wasn't sure how many people would be working here today, or what everyone would like, but there's a selection of muffins, cupcakes, and doughnuts, so hopefully there will be enough for everyone."

"Thanks," I said with a grin. "There are six of us in today, so that should do us nicely."

"No worries. I'm getting so bored that I'm considering baking my own next time."

Cal reached over Shannen to take the bag of goodies and began rummaging through. "I wouldn't be sad about that." He pulled out a jam doughnut then passed the bag to me, and Shannen rolled her eyes, laughing.

"Maybe I'll make something with Aiden at the weekend," she said. "It's getting harder to go out for too long now, plus it's getting colder."

Cal nodded as I looked through the bag of treats. "Sounds good to me. As long as I can lick the bowl."

"Why does that sound like a euphemism when you say it?" I asked, shaking my head as I too took a jam doughnut.

Shannen snorted. "Because you know him too well."

Glancing across the room to where Ryder was painting, I called, "Do you want cake?"

As he looked up and saw me holding up the bag, he nodded. Placing his paintbrush down on the newspaper that was on the floor to catch any drips, he got up and walked over to us. As he approached, his eyes fell on Shannen. He would have seen her when Cal let her in, but the way he looked at her made me wonder if Cal had had a point about him. He wasn't leering, but he definitely kept his gaze on her for longer than was necessary, especially as I was the one holding the baked goods.

Unfortunately, Cal had also noticed, and his body stiffened like he was ready to pounce, though he didn't move. I handed Ryder the bag to look through. Once he'd taken it, I looked at Shannen, and she was also eyeing him with unease.

He took what looked like a blueberry muffin, then offered the bag to Shannen, locking his eyes on hers as he did so. He gave her a flirty kind of smile that she didn't return, though she did take the bag.

"If you like having teeth, I recommend you stop staring at my woman right now," Cal said, his voice low, the threat clear. Ryder was twice Cal's size, but in that moment, I'd have backed my best mate. He was territorial when it came to Shannen, and there was not a single man on the planet he wouldn't take on for her.

Ryder held up a hand and took a step back. "Sorry, man." Then he shrugged as if to say, 'But you can't blame me for looking.' "Thanks for the muffin," he said before heading back to where he was working.

"Yeah, don't like him," Cal said once Ryder was out of earshot. He was still glaring at Ryder's retreating back.

"Okay, I get it now," I said. "He's contracted with us until January, but if he keeps that shit up, he'll be out."

Until Shannen had arrived, though, I hadn't seen any sign of weirdness from him. Not in the interview and not during the morning he'd been working with us. Maybe he was one of those men who got creepy around women, and while we didn't have any women working with us, I didn't want Shannen to feel too uncomfortable near him to drop in. I had been wise enough to put a fourteen-day get-out within the contract, so if anything like this happened again before that two weeks were up, I'd get rid of him.

From high on the possibility of going into business with Donovan to the stress of employee drama in five minutes. In all my time of being in self-employment, though, I had never had a single problem. I was pretty selective about my staff. Maybe the rush to get the bar finished had made me a little lax and I'd let someone slip through that I shouldn't have. I would talk to the other guys when they got back from lunch and get their feelings on Ryder and also keep tabs on him myself, but it looked like I'd be searching for another employee before the week was out.

Chapter 28

Gaby

I HAD NEVER BEEN more relieved to get out of work.

After my brother's call earlier, in spite of my best efforts, I found it hard to get the nagging feelings about Flynn out of my head. Where I could usually box my feelings and worries away, Gavin losing Flynn's whereabouts had thrown me. Gavin was meticulous when it came to keeping me safe, and if *he* had failed to find someone, something was seriously wrong. I concurred with his theory that Flynn wasn't dead, though I couldn't say exactly why. Probably because he wasn't someone who went down easily. Or that was how it felt when I was with him. He was stronger than me in every way, which was why, once I was fully in his clutches, I couldn't find a way out.

On the drive home, I had been on the lookout for any vehicles that appeared to be following me, and I drove a long way past my usual route home in case I was being tailed. I even circled past my apartment building a couple of times to look for any unusual cars in the car park or on the street outside. The whole time, I fluctuated between internally berating myself for being on edge and telling myself I was okay. That I was just being careful.

It was an hour after I left work that I finally parked and went into my flat, exhausted from the anxiety I had let rise inside me.

No caffeine today.

I almost chuckled at the thought, but really, the last thing I needed was another stimulant.

Damn you, Gavin. And fuck you, Flynn, for still being able to live inside my head like this.

I wasn't really angry with my brother. More... peeved with his interference because it had triggered this meltdown. And Flynn... he hadn't lived in my head for a long time. I just hated how easily he'd got back in there. How easy it was for the fear to amp up.

I should have gone to the gym to use up some of my excess adrenaline, but once I left work, I just wanted to be inside, in an enclosed, non-public space.

As I stood in the middle of my living room, surrounded by my belongings and my wall of books, I took some deep breaths, centring myself in reality.

Yes, Flynn was untraceable. But there was a whole world out there, and he could have been in any part of it.

Okay, he might have been able to find out where I was, but that didn't mean he had any interest in finding me or seeking to hurt me again.

For all I knew, he was a fully reformed character with a new outlook on life.

That might have been too much to hope for, but the fact was, catastrophising wasn't helping anything. All I could do was be alert to the possibility that he *could* be around while also understanding the likelihood was low. After all, it would be particularly dumb to get out of jail and then risk going straight back in for committing another crime.

Of course, that *did* happen. But it didn't mean it would happen to me.

Once I felt a little more grounded, I headed to the bathroom and took a long, hot shower, trying to wash the rest of my doubts away. When I was done, I was drying my hair with a towel after getting dressed into some comfy lounge pants and a long-sleeved grey top that buttoned up at the bust when someone knocked on my door.

Knowing it was Guy, I smiled to myself and rushed from my room to let him in, still rubbing my hair dry on the way.

Seeing his face smiling at me was exactly what I needed.

"Hey, come in," I said, stepping aside so he could get in. Once the door was shut, he wound his arms around me and dragged me to him for a kiss, making me drop the towel.

Swept up in the warmth of his kiss and the safety of his arms, it was the first time I'd felt relaxed since Gavin's phone call, and I held Guy tightly.

And to think you were ready to give him up yesterday.

Well, my head was. My heart, however, was a *very* different story.

"I missed you," Guy said, brushing his lips over mine again, his eyes sparkling as they met mine.

"Missed you too," I told him. Technically, it was less than twenty-four hours since we'd last seen each other, but that didn't make it any less true. "Do you want a cuppa?"

"Please," Guy replied as I led him through to the kitchen area. "I went home, showered, and came straight over here, so I haven't sat down yet."

Glancing up at him, I realised his hair looked damp, a fact I hadn't noticed immediately because I was too caught up in the kiss.

"I haven't either," I said, flicking the kettle on to boil, then turning to face him again. "How was your day?"

He grimaced slightly then said, "A mixed bag, but we made some good progress with work today, so I'm happy enough."

I nodded. "Any word from Helen?"

I wasn't trying to deflect from my own day; I just needed a minute before going into the stuff about Flynn.

I wondered if part of the mixed bag of Guy's day involved a conversation with Helen because, typically, when Guy had had a rougher than usual day, her name almost always came up. They had left things in an awkward place after I'd walked out, and sooner rather than later, there would have to be some kind of resolution.

"Not yet," he said, reaching up to pass me some cups from the cupboard, as he was closest to it, and I watched the stretch of his T-shirt over his muscles as he did so. "I expect it'll be on me to make the next move." The usual frown crossed his features when he spoke about her, and as I took the cups from him with one hand, I used the other to squeeze his arm, feeling a little guilty for ogling him while he was being serious.

"I wish this was easier for you," I said. "Do you really think she'll take this down the legal route?"

"I don't know," he answered with a sigh. I put the cups down on the side and went to grab the milk from the fridge. "I hope not. I'm still not ready to talk to her, though, so maybe it would be easier if someone else made the decisions for us, or at least mediated our conversations."

"Maybe. But overall, it would be better if she could be an adult and you could sort it out between you."

"I just wish she would stop taking pathetic shots at you every time you're mentioned." I opened my mouth to speak, and he cut me off before any words could come out. "I will not stop mentioning you, Gabs. It's not like I bring up all the things we've been doing together. But when things like the baby staying over at mine and you being there come up, you are going to be factored into those conversations. And I also need to talk to you about them because with her dragging her feet on discussing it, I haven't even asked you what you want."

He lowered his gaze from me. It wasn't only Helen's lack of discussion that had stopped him from asking me what I wanted. He was afraid of upsetting me, knowing this was a topic that tore at my soul. But Guy was my man, and I wouldn't let him feel bad over something that wasn't his issue to worry about. I loved that he was so thoughtful, but part of that meant he'd beat himself up over things he shouldn't.

"I can tell you what I want right now," I said, walking over to him, and taking his hands. "I want you, and if you want me to be a part of your daughter's life, I would like nothing more. But I don't expect to be involved right away. I want to meet her, of course, but she needs you and her mum first and foremost. I would never overstep or try to make decisions that aren't mine to make, but I absolutely want to be there for her if that's what you want. And if Helen can stand me being around. I can't promise not to call Helen out on her attitude at every opportunity, but I'll do my best to make this as easy for you as I can."

Guy chuckled and squeezed my hands. "You're incredible. I want all of that too. I want you to be a part of my daughter's life. I also..." He paused, shaking his head, then went on, "I should have also asked you this before I mentioned it to Helen yesterday, but... if she wants me to be there at the birth... are you okay with that?"

I laughed softly, linking our fingers together, a surge of adoration for him filling me up. "If you want to be there, I don't have a problem with that. I wouldn't expect you to miss the birth of your baby. Please don't worry about this stuff. I'm not here to hold you back, Guy. I'm here to support you in whatever decisions you make."

Difficult as it would be knowing he had a child with someone else, there wasn't a single part of me that wanted him to miss out on any of this journey to fatherhood. It hurt that we could never do it together, me and him, with our own baby, but I wanted him to have as much of what I couldn't give him as possible because this was his dream.

"Fuck, Gaby," he said, pressing his forehead to mine. In the second before his eyes left mine, I saw a depth of emotion in them I'd been seeing more and more of lately, and it made my stomach flutter. "Thank you."

I gently nudged my forehead against his, encouraging him to lift his head so I could look at him. When I did, the intensity on his face almost took my breath away.

He was truly beautiful, and he looked at me like he'd had the exact same thought as me. My mouth dried out as I stared at him, everything I was feeling swirling around inside me. I couldn't force out any words because I was lost in his gaze, in the sensation of both comfort and need surrounding me and filling me simultaneously.

"Gabs," he murmured, his mouth hovering close to mine as he pulled me against him.

"Mmhmm?" Speaking still felt impossible, and the air had become thick and charged around us.

"I need to…" he trailed off and swallowed, brushing the tip of his nose against mine, his breathing shallowing. "Can we…"

From how the conversation began, I hadn't expected things to take this direction. Maybe it was me. Maybe I was needy because of the stress I'd felt all day, and I craved the connection with Guy.

Even as I thought it, though, I knew that wasn't true. It wasn't anything I did or said. It was the underlying level of commitment we showed each other in the confessions and promises we'd uttered. It was the sheer depth of what we were building together and hadn't expressed out loud.

I peered up at him from beneath my eyelashes and nodded, offering him a small but flirty grin. His blue eyes shone as his own smile broke out, and, already knowing the way, he let go of me and took my hand to lead me to my room.

I didn't waste any time tugging my top off over my head, and Guy let out a low growl at my exposed breasts. I hadn't bothered with a bra after my shower, and the fire in his eyes let me know that was a good call. I reached out and dragged his T-shirt up, and he helped me pull it off before sliding his hands down the waistband of my lounge pants and pushing them down my legs a little way until they fell down to my ankles. I stepped out of them, and he was already taking off his jeans and boxers.

My gaze trailed up and down his body, across every defined muscle in his chest and stomach to his dick that was clearly eager for me, and then down his toned, strong legs.

My tongue darted out to moisten my lips, and he circled his arms around my waist, lifting me as I wrapped my arms around his neck. He carefully laid me down on my bed, then covered me with his body, his mouth on mine. As he always did, he kept himself propped up on his forearms so his weight didn't overwhelm me, but he pressed his hips against mine while I slid my hands down his back.

I loved the feeling of him on top of me, but I still hadn't been able to quite overcome my fear of letting him be in control. I wasn't always the one on top, but I also couldn't deal with *him* being fully on top either. We'd had fun finding creative positions that meant I didn't feel 'trapped' beneath him, but the longer I was with him, the more I wanted him to take me over. To let myself submit to him; not in a dom/sub way, just enough to show him how much I trusted him, and how ready I was to push past this final barrier.

Guy's lips trailed down my neck, over my collarbone, and down to my breasts. His mouth was hot, his breath dusting across my skin. He circled my nipple with his tongue before sucking it into his mouth, flicking at the bud with his tongue before capturing it again, his teeth lightly gripping and pulling gently. The sensation shot lightning to my core, and I moaned as his mouth tugged at the delicate nub then released it, his lips wrapping around it again.

My hips bucked towards him, my thighs growing damp as his expert tongue fluttered across my chest. As he kissed across my other breast, he shifted slightly so he could hook his fingers down the side of my knickers and he rested his hand on my pussy gently, the heat of his hand making me gasp.

Too much!

The warning sounded out in my head far earlier than it usually did, and I knew he felt me stiffen because he stopped moving immediately, moving his hand back to my hip and looking up at me.

Shaking my head, I said, "Please, don't stop."

I said the words, but my brain was still arguing, my body remaining tight as the battle between internal and external raged on.

My body and my heart wanted this, but my brain screamed out, trying to protect me from a danger that didn't exist.

Moving back up my body so our faces were level again, Guy said, "What do you need, Gabs?"

The worry in his eyes settled me a little. I knew with every part of me that he was safe to be with. Knew that I trusted him in a way I had never trusted anyone else, and I took a deep breath.

"I want you to stay right where you are," I said, looking deep into his eyes, tethering myself to him. "On top."

His eyes widened. "Gaby, that's..."

I shook my head, interrupting him. "Please," I whispered, almost begging him with my stare. With his eyes so soft, so caring, still so full of need, my body was already coming alive again, the tension in my muscles easing. "I want this. I trust you."

Not giving him a chance to respond, I pulled his mouth down to mine, kissing him in a way I hoped showed him how much I meant it.

Even though we'd been sleeping together for weeks, I had always held this part of myself back; the part that wanted to give in and let him have domain over my body. The voice of fear had lurked in the corner of my mind, warning me that nobody could truly be as amazing as Guy, that it was a trick, and he was just waiting for my guard to drop so he could hurt me. Start to snake his way into my brain until he had total control over my life.

But he *was* that amazing. He was real and genuine, and the only thing he wanted from me was... me. Not power, not dominance, and certainly not pain. He just wanted me.

"Gaby," he whispered against my cheek. "Promise me..." He brushed his lips against mine again. "If you want to stop." Another kiss. "You tell me right away."

I nodded. "I promise."

He smiled as he pulled back slightly, then rolled off me and onto his side, causing me to frown. He tugged at my wrist to turn me to face him and said, "I need you to relax a bit more first, okay?"

He wasn't wrong. I was ready for him to be inside me, but I was almost positive that if he went too fast, my legs would clamp shut, and I would ruin it.

At my nod, he ran his hand down my thigh, and said, "Turn onto your other side, Gabs." My brow furrowed again, and he chuckled. "Please."

Focusing on how much I wanted to feel his hands on me again, I did as he said, an unfamiliar ripple of arousal flowing through me that I was actually doing this. I was letting him take control.

It was okay right then because I wasn't trapped. I could move, I could stop anytime, even though I didn't want to.

Once my back was to his front, he tucked me in tight against him, his lips finding my neck from behind. He had both arms around me, one underneath and the other over the top, free to move and explore me.

At first, his fingers traced slow circles across my stomach, so slow they were barely moving, but I could feel the slight tickle, and I took a couple of deep breaths, settling myself. Once he sensed I was ready, he slid his hand upwards, gliding his fingers across my breasts. The touch was so light, and I found myself leaning into him, arching my back because I wanted a little more.

His breath was warm against my neck as he whispered, "I've got you, okay? I've got you."

I nodded, tears springing to my eyes unexpectedly. I knew he had me. It was the fact that he understood how much it was taking for me to leap over this hurdle, the last hurdle of trust, that caused the emotion. He wasn't just saying the words to get me to do what he wanted. He'd taken the time to learn what I needed; what was going to make this possible for me.

"You're beautiful," he murmured against my skin as his hands moved back down across my stomach, then onto my hip, and back to my thigh. "You're beautiful, and sexy, and you're safe, Gabs. I promise."

"I know," I whispered back, emotion clogging my throat. "I know I'm safe with you."

He let his fingers stroke back to my stomach, moving lower, and I lifted my top leg, even though my body was already preparing to fight, to shut down. He kept his hand perfectly still on my stomach as he waited for me to settle, as if he could hear the demons swarming into my brain.

Placing my hand over his, I moved it downwards, slowly, so slowly, until it covered my pussy, then I moved my hand away, letting his rest there. After a moment, I lifted my leg a little more, giving him more access and slightly opening myself to him.

My heart began to pound, the panic going up another couple of notches as the tips of his fingers lightly nudged at my entrance.

"Stay with me, Gabs," he said. "Right here. Stay in the moment."

Safe, safe, safe. I chanted it in my head, urging the ever-present monsters to slink back into the shadows because I was done listening to them. Done letting them control me.

Guy carefully eased a finger inside me, moving slowly enough that I could stop him if I wanted to, and as he did, he said, "Me and you, Gabs. It's just me and you."

With each word he spoke, I found it easier to stay focused on him, on what he was doing to me instead of getting sucked into the abyss of dark thoughts.

"Guy," I said, opening my legs wider so he could get deeper. "Keep talking to me."

"Okay, sweetheart," he said, sliding another finger inside me. "I can do that. Just tell me you're okay."

"I'm okay," I said, my breath fluttering in my chest as his fingers began to move in and out.

I was more than okay. I was letting go, and I felt myself shaking as the realisation hit. It wasn't that he'd never put his fingers inside me before, it was that I knew what was coming. That instead of me fighting to take back control, I was going to give in. Surrender myself to him completely, and as my core muscles began to clench and my stomach tightened, I cried out as the pleasure coursed through me. I felt his dick twitching against my back, and as he withdrew his fingers, I shuffled over, willingly turning onto my back.

My body was hot, and I was sure my cheeks were flushed from my orgasm. Guy stared down at me, shaking his head slowly as if in awe. "I can't believe you're mine."

"Make me yours," I said, my eyes on his. "Please, Guy."

Carefully, he moved his leg over mine so he was on top of me, still always moving slowly to allow me to change my mind at any point.

Now his weight was all on me, the beginning of the feelings of suffocation began in my chest, oppressive and heavy, but Guy gently cupped my cheek. "We can stop," he said. "Any time, we can stop."

I nodded, parting my legs for him, even while the volume was turning back up, the voices telling me I was in imminent danger of pain. That he was going to hurt me, take something he shouldn't.

I blinked, forcing myself to look at him and see who was really above me. That it was Guy. That no harm was going to come to me.

He lined himself up at my entrance, and even though I knew he wasn't going to move yet, my core tightened as if it wanted to keep him out.

Instead of speaking, he kissed me. With each brush of his lips, I replayed the words he'd already said over and over.

Beautiful. Safe. Would never hurt you.

They circled around like a mantra until, eventually, my muscles uncoiled, and I lifted my hips upwards, silently letting him know I was ready.

This time, when my body started to shake, it *was* partially because I was afraid. Not of him but of what this meant. Of how big a step it was to allow someone to hold me under their weight. How much it messed with my head to give someone an opportunity to hurt me because, even though I knew he wouldn't, drowning out that worry was the hardest thing I'd done in a long time.

I felt him gently nudge inside me, and instinctively, I held my breath, bracing myself.

"Breathe, sweetheart," Guy said, stilling immediately. "I'll go slowly."

At his instruction, I let the breath out, and wriggling my hips to try to relax, I said, "I'm sorry. This is hard."

I heard the tremble in my voice, and I felt like the world's biggest loser. I didn't want to cry. Crying during sex was not sexy at all, and I turned my head to the side while I tried to contain it.

His fingers pushed my hair from my eyes then rested on my cheek again. "You don't have anything to be sorry about. This is a big deal."

He was still only slightly inside me, unmoving, and I felt kind of like I was in the middle of my first time, trying to sidestep the awkwardness. Except it was worse. The man on top of me meant everything to me, and even though I knew he understood why, I didn't want to be a sobbing mess. I wanted to be brave, the way I always imagined I one day would be if I got to this point with someone.

I breathed in deeply, turning my head to look at him again.

Guy had dropped into my world and made every part of it better. He'd made me laugh and shown me understanding and patience. He'd shown me consideration and fought to keep me with him, regardless of the hot mess I was. He looked at me the way Nova said he did. Like he was captivated, and I was pretty sure I looked at him the same way.

He was gorgeous. Not just physically, but in every way a person could be.

I trusted him.

"I love you," I whispered. "I love you."

The smile that spread across his face made my heart leap. It was as if hearing that made him feel the way his protection made *me* feel. Like nothing or no one could ever feel as special. Like we were each other's person.

"I love you too," he said.

Staring at him for another moment, I said, "I'm ready."

"Promise?"

"Promise."

Slowly, he began to move his hips again, and once he was fully inside me, it was like something had finally fallen away. All of the tension left me, and I clung to him, relief, and need, and love, and freedom colliding within me as I allowed myself to get lost in him. To let go of the things I'd clung to to protect me because Guy protected me now.

Moans tumbled from my lips as he worked my body into a slow frenzy until I writhed beneath him and finally exploded, holding him tight and crying out as he followed me soon after.

As he pulled out of me, he rolled onto his back, pulling me with him so I was on top. He was holding me so tight I almost couldn't breathe.

"This might be a weird thing to say after sex, but thank you," he said, still breathless. "Thank you for trusting me."

My heart was still hammering, but I said, "Thank you for not pushing me. For letting me take the time I needed."

"Every single minute I waited was worth it. I love you so much."

It *was* worth it. Every time my hang-ups took over, I was terrified he would think I was too much. More hassle than he needed. But instead, he'd just waited. I believed he would have waited forever if that was how long it took.

And that was how I knew this was right. How I was able to trust him.

"I love you too."

 Chapter 29

Guy

IN MY LIFE, I'D been in a few relationships, and I'd always preferred long-term over meaningless flings. Helen had been my longest, but before her, I'd been with women for three or four years before things ended. Women who had meant a lot to me, but that it hadn't worked out with.

Meeting Gaby told me why that was. I'd loved all of those women at the time, but they never felt like Gaby. Helen aside, I had never so badly wanted to make a relationship work. But Gaby was still different from Helen. I'd always viewed Gaby as sunshine. She was so vibrant; even in the cool of autumn, she lit everything up, made it feel warmer and brighter.

I had been with her for weeks, watched her wrestle with things from her past that wouldn't leave her alone. Sex with her was always great, but it destroyed me to see her struggling with what she wanted and what she felt able to allow. She rarely talked about it even when I asked, but it was obvious in the way she tensed, her facial expressions, how often she had to pause to take deep breaths. I hated that she'd been hurt so badly by someone that something that should have been fun and easy was a source of such huge stress for her.

Recently, the struggle had become harder, not because she wanted to overcome it less, but because she wanted to overcome it more. It was as if the more she wanted me to take control, the louder her worries became. When it became clear that discussing it made her feel weak, I changed my tactics and continued to let her do things the way she needed to.

With everything that had been happening with Helen and the baby, I knew Gaby's insecurities were letting loose in her head, but she never once stopped supporting me, and she never asked or expected me to do anything that would tip the delicate balance I had to walk between her and Helen.

I had fallen in love with Gaby, and I had been ready to tell her, but when she said it first, in a moment when she was fighting her way through the turmoil in her head... it was something I would never forget. To have her love, her trust, and for her to understand that I wanted to be with her whether she overcame the things she fought with or not, whether we could have children together or not... it meant everything.

Once we'd dragged ourselves out of bed, we showered, dressed, and ordered a takeaway. While we waited for food, Gaby sat on my lap on the sofa, snuggled against my chest while I stroked her hair, and it was perfect.

It was almost an annoyance when the delivery person knocked on the door with our food.

With a groan, Gaby kissed me on the cheek before climbing off my lap to answer the door. I got up to grab plates and cutlery from the kitchen, and I heard voices drifting down the hallway, but it didn't sound like a delivery. I couldn't quite hear what all the words were, but I caught a male voice saying, 'check who it is first,' and Gaby saying, 'takeaway.'

I got the things we needed and put them down on the coffee table as I heard the door shut and two sets of footsteps padding towards the living room. I assumed it was Gavin and was proved right when he and Gaby walked in.

"Guy," he said with a nod, and I was glad I'd got dressed fully again. I wasn't sure how he would have felt about seeing me half-naked with his little sister. He had obviously come straight from work as he was dressed in a dark grey suit with a white shirt and a black tie.

"Hi," I said as Gaby came all the way into the room and wrapped her arms around my waist. "Are you joining us for food?"

"He is not," Gaby said, looking at Gavin. "He's here to pour cold water all over my good mood again."

Even though what she'd said was sharp, her tone was light, though I did catch the hint of sarcasm and I wondered what she meant. She hadn't said anything about her brother when I'd arrived, but then, we hadn't really been focused on talking.

"Gaby, come on," Gavin said with a sigh, his shoulder slumping. "I just wanted to make sure you're okay."

"Okay or alive?" she asked, holding me tighter, and at that, I leaned back from her slightly.

"Why wouldn't you be alive?" I asked, my eyes pinballing between her and Gavin. As far as I was aware, he didn't consider me a threat to her. The three of us had been out together once, and he'd invited us over for dinner one night too, so I wasn't the one he had a problem with.

Gaby sighed, glaring at her brother before looking at me, "There's something I was going to tell you tonight, but then..." she trailed off, smiling softly at me, and I pulled her against me again and kissed the top of her head to let her know I understood. "And I just wanted to enjoy tonight without anything ruining it, but..." She gestured to Gavin, who closed his eyes as if he regretted coming over.

"I don't know what I've interrupted, but I'm sorry," he said. "I should have just called, but after ringing you earlier, I wanted to see you."

"Gav, I love you, but I'm not living like this again, like when you first followed me to Exeter. I don't need to be checked on all the time. I know you want to look out for me, but if you're going to start dropping by every five minutes, I'll find somewhere else to live and not tell you where it is."

"There is nobody I can't find," he said firmly, and she let out a bitter-sounding laugh.

"If that were true, you wouldn't be here."

"Okay," I said because I sensed things were about to get out of hand. "Can someone tell me what's going on?"

At that moment, there was another knock on the door, and Gaby sighed. "You can tell him since this is all your fault," she said to Gavin, then untangled herself from me to greet what was, hopefully, the delivery person this time.

Gavin dropped his head into his hands before looking up at me. "I'm so sorry I've ruined your evening. That wasn't my intention, but today... look, I assume Gaby told you that her ex is out of prison."

I nodded. "She did."

"Well, she asked me to not get involved, but I needed to know where he was." He looked me in the eye as if imploring me to understand his actions. And I did. "I just wanted to be sure he was nowhere near her. And he wasn't, but the people I had tracking him lost him, and now I don't know where he is. I had to tell Gaby because I want her to be aware that there's a chance he could be somewhere local now. I mean, he could be anywhere, but if there is even a small possibility he's in the area, I didn't want to have Gaby wandering around unaware. Unfortunately, Gaby thinks I'm an interfering dickhead and I've scared her. When she didn't know where he was, she wasn't worried, but now she knows I've lost all trace of him, it's freaked her out. But I couldn't *not* tell her."

Gaby had told me a few times that Gavin was overprotective, and she found it frustrating and smothering, but in this case, I could see why he'd done what he did. He loved her and wanted to make sure that bastard never got near her again. But in doing so, he'd uncovered something that had put her on edge again.

Before I could speak, Gaby returned, holding a white carrier bag full of our Chinese food. The smell made my stomach growl, but I doubted we'd be eating immediately as now we had something else to deal with.

Gaby stood in the doorway and said, "You could have just done what I asked, Gavin."

He turned to face her. "Tell me right now, if you had the means to protect someone you care about, that you wouldn't do it. I know you would, Gaby, so being angry at me isn't fair."

"I know why you did it," she said, her words clipped. "And I do appreciate it, but now, everything feels scary again. I just wish I didn't know." Her eyes shone with tears as she fixed her gaze on me. "Guy... what happened tonight... what I said... it didn't happen because of what Gavin found out. I don't want you to think that I was just trying to forget about it or use you to..."

I crossed the room to her in a couple of long strides, taking the bag from her and putting it on the floor so I could hold her. "I don't think that," I said, looking into her still damp eyes. It had never crossed my mind. She didn't tell me she loved me because she was afraid her ex was out there somewhere. How we felt about each other had been getting stronger for weeks, and her confidence had been growing with it. But I could see why she would think I'd considered it. "Let's just sit down so we can talk about it."

"I don't want to talk about it," she said, pulling from my hold and picking up the bag of food. "I want to eat."

She walked past me and Gavin and sat down on the sofa. I exchanged a worried glance with him because her avoidance and sharp change of mood was a sure sign that she was burying her head in the sand.

But I also didn't want to call her out on it because I knew she would talk about it when she was ready. She needed time to run through her thoughts and feel her feelings. Once she had got it straight in her own mind, she would open up. Tonight might not be the night, though.

As she set about pulling the food containers from the bag and putting them on the coffee table, I nodded towards the hallway, gesturing for Gavin to come with me. He followed me out and I closed the living room door over and walked towards the front door with him.

"I messed up, didn't I?" Gavin said quietly, but I shook my head.

"You didn't. You did the right thing in finding out where he was and telling Gaby you don't know where he is now. She knows that, and you know it too. She needs to get her head around it. It might be best if you go home, and I'll talk to her. I'll call you later or tomorrow and let you know how she's doing."

Gavin nodded. "Thanks." He took a step towards the door, then stopped and looked back at me. "I don't know what Gaby's told you about our family, but it's dysfunctional as fuck. Our mum lives in her own world, and our dad's a work-obsessed prick who cares very little for anything other than his business. It's a miracle me and Gaby have a shred of decency between us. Probably because we figured out how we didn't want to be by watching them. *She* is my family. The only member of my immediate family I would risk my life for. I just don't want anything to happen to her."

If I knew him better, I'd have given him a man hug. Instead, I gave him a supportive slap on the shoulder. I felt for him. I didn't know a whole lot about their family. Gaby had said more or less the same as Gavin had, though she was a bit nicer about her mum. I didn't know about how any of them got along or if they kept in touch much. I assumed not, though, because Gaby hadn't once said she'd spoken to either of her parents in the whole time we'd been together.

"I get it," I told him. "I'll look after her. Keep trying to find that dick and make sure he's miles from here."

He nodded. "I will."

Gavin opened the door looking deflated, then gave me another nod before he left.

With a sigh, wondering why, just for five minutes, things couldn't be simple, I went back into the living room. Gaby was sitting on the sofa, her legs crossed, and her head in her hands, all of the food laid out on the table in front of her.

I heard a small sob slip from her, and I walked over and sat beside her. Without a word, I pulled her onto my lap and cocooned her in my arms.

"I hate this," she said into my chest. "I hate that I'm such a fucking mess! I'm trying so hard to just be myself, but since I met you, I've... there's all this stuff I've had to confront. I want to be happy, but the closer I get to it, the more stuff comes along that I have to deal with! I can't keep balancing between safety and danger all the time. I'm tired of getting so close and then having something try to snatch it away," she paused, burrowing herself further into me. "I'm tired."

As much as it killed me that she felt this way, I couldn't help also feeling relieved that she wasn't pushing me away as she usually did when things got too much. I wished there was a way for me to get her closer to me, but she was nestled in so tight, my arms a barrier from the pain that kept coming for her. There was no more physical space between us, but it still didn't feel like she was near enough.

"Gabs, when I said you were safe earlier... when I said I'd got you... that means always. Not just in a moment when you need me, but all the time. So, tell me, what do you need right now? What can I do to make all of this easier for you?"

She shifted slightly, freeing an arm so she could cling to me, but I could feel her cries making her body shake. "You're already doing it."

Am I?

If I was, would she be sobbing in my arms? I knew this wasn't about me, but she *had* just said that being with me had made her confront things. Had I really done enough to support her? It wasn't just this stuff with Flynn and the bedroom stuff she'd had to contend with, it was me having a baby with someone else, knowing that we could never have our own children. Had I talked about it too much? Not talked about it enough and made her think her opinions didn't matter?

In spite of my rising doubts, deep down, I knew that wasn't it. It was more like she'd been so eager to bulldoze through her issues that she hadn't properly allowed herself to admit how she really felt in case it showed weakness. She'd had to fight for her own survival while she was being abused, and maybe she'd forgotten that she didn't need to do that now.

"I'm scared," she said quietly. "For the first time in ten years, I'm scared, and I don't like it. There is no reason for me to believe Flynn is anywhere near here, but what if he is? I don't want to be afraid to turn a corner in case he's there or even slightly think that maybe he's around, watching me because I can't afford to let those feelings take over. He could be *anywhere*. From the city centre to Australia. I cannot live my life wondering if he's going to drop back into my world, but that is how I feel right now."

Her fear was almost tangible, and I couldn't stand how my confident woman had shrunk back inside herself as if that would hide her from him. That if she made herself small, he'd just walk right on by her.

That was how he'd kept her in line when they were together. By reducing who she was until she became insignificant in her own mind. Until she believed that was just the way things were meant to be.

"Gavin found him once," I said. "He'll be able to find him again."

"Maybe. He still has some places to check out, but what if he can't? I'm going to find it hard to feel safe anywhere until I know where he is. I'm already worried about being on my own here when you go home, even though I scoped the street out before I came in."

"Then I won't go home." I gently ran my fingers through her hair. "I'll stay here with you."

"Thank you, but what about tomorrow night? And the night after?" She shook her head. "No. I need to stop being stupid and go on as if I didn't know anything at all."

"But you do know," I pointed out. "And I'm not going to be able to relax knowing that you're worried." My fingers continued their soothing motion through her hair, and I said, "Come and stay with me."

She stiffened in my arms and slowly looked up at me, her green eyes red-rimmed and tears staining her face. "What?"

"Come and stay with me," I repeated. "Even if it's just for a few days until Gavin checks out the last few places he knows to look. I mean... if Flynn was coming for you, he's had plenty of time to do so already. Maybe if you get out of here for a bit, it'll give you time to figure out how you feel without worrying that he knows where you are."

I loosened my arms a little so she could shuffle backwards. "You don't know him," she said. "If he were looking for me, he wouldn't strike right away. He'd be on the periphery, looking in."

Her words stirred discomfort inside me. She was right, I didn't know anything about the man except that he was a piece of shit. I knew that abusers were manipulative, but I also imagined after being imprisoned for ten years, he'd have had enough of being patient.

But what if she was right?

Like I'd been kicked in the gut, I thought about Ryder, and Shannen and Cal's reaction to him.

Now who's being paranoid?

I had interviewed him myself and checked out his references. There was a gap in his work record, but it wasn't ten years long.

Anyone could get fake references, though.

Cal had said Ryder had been 'scoping out' my bar, but what if it wasn't really the bar? What if it was me? What if he knew where Gaby was, and who I was? Maybe he was staring at Shannen because he'd dug up enough info on her to know they were friends?

"What's wrong?" Gaby asked, her eyes heavy with concern because I'd just jumped on my own crazy train of thought.

"No, nothing," I said, shaking my head. I sure as shit couldn't tell her what I suspected or she would flip. Plus, it was way too far-fetched. And what was he going to do, wait for Gaby to visit me at work one day and snatch her out of my arms.

No. I was wrong. But I was also going to text Gavin the second I got to work in the morning with Ryder's details to see if he could look into it, just in case.

"So, what do you say?" I asked her, putting my focus back on her face. "Why don't you come home with me? At least that way you'll get some sleep. My building is more secure than this place, Gabs. And you'll have me."

She sighed, wiping her eyes with the heels of her hands. "I don't know. I don't want people to know anything about this stuff with Flynn, and if I'm staying with you..."

"It's because we can't keep away from each other," I interrupted, smiling at her and breaking through the weight of the atmosphere that had been hanging over us. "You're my woman, and I want you in my space. What's so weird about that?"

She shrugged a shoulder. "What about everything that's going on with Helen? Won't that make it worse if she finds out?"

"Gabs, your safety means more to me than whatever tantrum she wants to throw. This is not about her. This is about what you need. So, if you want to come and stay with me, you can."

 Chapter 30

Guy

THE LAST FEW DAYS since my evening at Gaby's could best be described as... bumpy. Gaby had agreed to stay with me until at least the end of the week, so after we'd finished our takeaway, we'd packed up some of the things she would need and then went back to mine.

There's always a bit of an adjustment period needed when people are getting used to living in the same space. It was harder for Gaby than me because she was the one who wasn't in her own home, and she'd been living alone for a lot longer than I had too. We'd managed because we liked being around each other, and she was at ease in a place that was more secure than her own building, but I was super conscious to let her have her own space when she wanted it. That wasn't often, though, and I loved having her around.

It wasn't the living together that caused the turbulence. The turbulence wasn't even between us, really, it was more that we were both now always wondering if Flynn was nearby. We didn't talk about it, but it felt like it was always hanging over us, a possible threat that, unless he was found, would never fully go away. It was crazy to me how that had literally always been the case, but we wouldn't have been obsessing over it if we hadn't known Flynn had disappeared from his last known location. Now, we were constantly alert when we were out of the house, and Gaby had come home from work every day exhausted from the additional worry of it.

Gavin had checked out Flynn's family and it didn't look as though he'd been anywhere near them. He was having a harder time tracking down his friends, but he was still working on it, and he said he would let us know as soon as he had news.

I had also informed Gavin of my suspicions about Ryder, the new guy I'd hired. Against my better judgement, we'd both kept this from Gaby. She was stressed enough without her considering that I had invited the enemy onto my property. She would probably have wanted to do something mad like come to the bar to check for herself, and if it was him, I wasn't sure how she would handle it. Gavin had also considered coming to the bar to have a look, but he didn't trust himself not to commit murder. I wrestled with it too, only calming myself by remembering that Ryder might be exactly who he said he was.

If he wasn't, he would need to get out of my sight really fast.

On top of that, Helen refused to speak to me. I'd text her to ask if we could talk, and she hadn't responded. I'd tried to call her, but she didn't pick up. I left it for a day, then tried again with the same results, at which point I began to worry that something had happened to her. So, I'd asked her to at least let me know if she was okay, which she did. But she still refused to answer my questions or my calls. So, I'd eventually sent her a text telling her that if I hadn't heard from her by October 31st with some definitive answers about how this co-parenting thing would work, I would assume she wanted to go ahead with getting solicitors involved. She was probably going to wait until the last minute to respond, but that was on her. I was done chasing her. The only thing I knew for sure was that she would never keep me away from my daughter.

While I was at work on Thursday morning, my phone rang, and I braced myself because I'd been expecting a call from Gavin any time. He hadn't fully updated me on his findings on Ryder, but he'd told me he was close to having answers, so I'd been anticipating it. Sure enough, Gavin's name was on the screen, and my breath hitched because this was it. Ryder would either be an innocent worker who I'd placed my paranoid suspicions on, or he was Flynn, and I would break his legs.

Instead of answering while inside the bar, I shouted over to Cal that I had to take a call, then jogged outside.

"Hey, Gavin," I said, and I heard the nerves in my voice. "Any news?"

"Yeah," he said, his own tone less frayed than mine. "Good and bad."

I unlocked my van and jumped into the front seat, shutting the door when I was in. I wanted to be out of the way in case someone came out and overheard.

"I'm guessing it's definitely not Flynn," I said, relief rushing through me. If it was, I suspected Gavin would have knocked my doors down to get to him.

"Definitely not Flynn," he confirmed. "His name *is* Ryder Norton, like he said. And he wasn't lying about his skills or where he said he came from. He does, however, have a criminal record."

"For what?" I asked cautiously.

"Drink driving. About six years ago. It was recommended that he go on a drink-driving rehabilitation course, and beyond that course, he continued to seek help for his drinking problem." Gavin paused. "Now, this could be a complete coincidence, but given the things you told me about his shifty behaviour, it's unlikely. While he was going to a local group for alcoholics, he met a man there. Ian Lewis."

Ian Lewis? No way.

"Okay," I said, tightening my grip on the phone. "That's probably a common name. Can you be more specific?"

I needed to hear confirmation, even though he said he doubted any of this was coincidental, so my gut instinct was probably right.

"Cal's dad," Gavin replied. "I wasn't able to get a lot of information, but I had someone go through Ryder's social media and he unearthed some photos that tagged Ian Lewis. Even before double-checking, it was obvious who he was. Cal looks like him. Well, sort of. His dad looks way older than he really is because of all the drinking, but the resemblance is there. So, Ryder Norton isn't at your place for Gaby, but based on his staring at Shannen and him showing interest in Cal, I'd say he *is* there to gather info for Ian."

Rage simmered under my skin, and I dropped my head back against the headrest. "Why would he suddenly want to know what Cal's doing? It's been like ten years or something. He just fucked off and left him."

"I don't know, but it might be worth finding out."

"You think I should talk to him? See if he'll tell me anything?"

"Yeah. Because if you tell Cal, who already doesn't like him, he's going to end up in a cell again."

Gavin hadn't spent that much time with Cal, but it was enough that he understood how volatile he could be, and I couldn't disagree. But if I spoke to Ryder and found out why he was sniffing around, then what? Would I need to tell Cal myself?

He was finally in a good place. He had a new house, a baby on the way, and everything was right. What the hell would finding out his father was trying to creep back into the picture do to him? Cal's father had only ever done one good thing for Cal. Well, maybe two if you counted him disappearing from Cal's life. The rest of the time, though, he'd been a violent, abusive prick.

"Jesus Christ," I said with a sigh. "I'll deal with it. Thank you for letting me know."

"No worries. How's Gaby doing?"

Gaby and Gavin had spoken since the night he gatecrashed our takeaway, but she'd asked him for space. He found that easier to give knowing she wasn't on her own, but she hadn't been exaggerating when she said he worried about her. He was almost paternal towards her, though given what both of them had said about their relationship with their own father, it made sense.

"She's coping," I told him honestly. I couldn't tell him she was fine because she wasn't her usual self at all. "I think she just wants you to find Flynn so she can get her life back. She's using all of her energy to get through work, but it's draining her to feel so restricted. When she's at mine, she's okay, but she doesn't want to go out other than for work like she used to. We're having dinner at Cal and Shannen's tonight, so that's something, but she won't go to the pub, or out to eat, or even to the cinema."

A pained growl left him. "I should have kept my mouth shut. At least until I'd exhausted every avenue of where he could be. I'm sorry. I wanted her to be careful, but I didn't mean to make her *this* careful."

I thudded my head lightly against the headrest. "I get it. Honestly, if I was in your position, I probably would have done the same. I've hated keeping the fact that I thought Ryder might be Flynn from her because I was afraid it looked like I was protecting him more than her when what I was really trying to do was not scare her."

"Welcome to my world," Gavin said with a sharp laugh. "I know she wishes I would butt out, but, Guy, if you had seen what he did to her... you'd understand."

"I don't need to see it to understand," I said. "She's your sister, and he destroyed her confidence and hurt her so badly that she almost died. Even seeing how she's been this week is enough to make me want to kill him."

"I'm glad she met you." His tone changed to one that told me how fully he approved of me being with Gaby. He'd always been welcoming and supportive, but with the two of us working to keep her safe, it was like he understood the depth of my feelings for her now. "I promise I will find out where he is so you can have your lives back."

"I know you will. But now, I have another possible fire to put out."

"For fuck's sake." Gavin sighed. "I'm sorry. Again. Let me know how it goes. I'm going to get back to work and meddle in people's lives who actually want me to do so."

With a chuckle, I said, "Okay. Talk soon."

"See ya later!"

As I sat in my van, I wondered if there was some kind of metaphorical baton that had been passed from Cal to me. For the last six months, he'd been swamped in drama, fear, and danger. Did I take that from him when I moved out of my house and into the flat I'd bought for him?

It's not like the last six months were so great for you either. And with this latest revelation, it seemed Cal's issues might not be over yet.

Swearing to myself, I opened the door to my van and jumped out, ready to get this over with now, while I was still riled up enough to deal with it. I was protective of Gaby, but equally, I'd been looking out for Cal most of his life too.

As teenagers, he was the slightly younger kid who played football with some of my mates and me, the cocky little shit who had a horrible dad and stayed out of his house as much as he could so he didn't have to be around him. He stayed at my place a lot back then, but after his mum and brother died, he pulled away. I still had his back, but from a distance. Once I left school and Exeter, we lost touch, but the second I was back in town and I ran into him, I stepped straight back into the big brother role and had been doing it ever since.

I didn't consider myself to have a saviour complex exactly, jumping in to help anyone who crossed my path and was having a bad time, but once I cared about someone, I *would* move mountains to protect them.

Walking back into the bar, I made a beeline for Ryder, who was once again working alone. Or he had been. It was about two minutes until his lunch break, so he was dusting himself off and tidying up the area he'd been working in.

"You got a minute?" I asked, though it wasn't a question. He was going to talk to me whether he wanted to or not.

"Sure," he said, wiping his hands on his jeans. "What's up?"

I jerked my head towards the corner of the room, even though there was nobody near us. My other guys were blaring their radio over by the stage. I wasn't sure they'd even seen me come back because they were pissing about, using paintbrushes as microphones and pretending to be in a boyband. Usually, I would have been laughing, or telling them to get back to work, but I had more important things to do.

Ryder followed me, and we stood slightly behind the bar. He didn't show any sign that he thought I was on to him. He just rested a hand on the top of the bar and waited.

"Okay," I said, too irritated to waste time beating around the bush. "What's your deal?"

"What do you mean?" he asked, tilting his head, but watching him closely, I saw a flicker of concern pass over his features.

"I'm really particular about who I give work to, and you won out because of your experience and your references. It checks out, and you're doing a great job. The problem is, you have been showing a lot of interest in this place, but more so, your interest in Cal and his other half has been noticed. You don't pay anywhere near as much attention to anyone else as you do him, and it got me wondering why. So, do you have anything you want to tell me before I tell you what I know?"

He dropped his head back and let out a sigh before straightening up to look at me, rubbing at the scruff on his chin. "Look, mate, I wasn't lying when I said I needed a job, okay? I need it. But it's not completely random that I came to you. I've been waiting for something to open up with your company for a while."

"Because...?" I prompted.

He turned his head to look across at where Cal and the rest of my team were howling with laughter at their own antics, and in spite of whatever was coming, I smiled. They were idiots, but they were my idiots.

"I came here knowing Cal worked for you," Ryder said, looking at me again. "I met his old man a few years back while we were both trying to get off the drink. We got talking, and seeing each other week after week, we started hanging out outside of the meetings, and I got to know him. He'll be the first to admit he was scum. Bad husband, bad father, wallowing in his own self-pity and using alcohol to make himself feel better. He'd been in relationships and fucked them up, all because of his temper and his drinking problem, and when I met him in rehab, it was because he'd met someone new. He was a high-functioning alcoholic, and he really wanted to kick the habit and be better. We helped each other."

It was obvious that Ryder had managed to stay sober, but I was still waiting to hear where this was leading.

"Ian thinks he's irredeemable, even though he *did* manage to stop drinking," Ryder said. "He is still with the woman who inspired him to make the change, and they live together in Bovey Tracey. The last two years, all he's talked about is wanting to find Cal, but he's been too afraid to do it, thinking Cal won't have anything to do with him. I told him I would look for him, but he kept saying no, to leave it, so I did." Ryder paused, shaking his head. "The thing is, last year, Ian was diagnosed with cirrhosis of the liver. It's pretty serious, and it's going to kill him. The likelihood is, he won't see out another five years. It's looking more like two to three at the most with treatment. So, although he doesn't want me to tell Cal who I am, he did ask me if I could find out where he is and if he's okay."

I leaned back against the wall, shaking my head. I wasn't sure what I was expecting, but that wasn't it. I couldn't imagine anything would make Cal have an interest in his dad's wellbeing. He'd often told me he presumed alcohol had killed him years ago. It was as if that thought made life easier for him because his father had brought him nothing but pain.

If Ryder was telling the truth—and he appeared genuinely upset about his friend's illness—it sounded like Cal's dad had finally got his life on track, but would Cal even care now? More importantly, was it now on me to decide what to do with this information?

"So, what's the conclusion?" I asked. "Do you think Cal's okay?"

Ryder smirked, in spite of the seriousness of the conversation. "I've seen his woman. He looks like he's doing great to me!"

I rolled my eyes. "Yeah, you made her uncomfortable with your staring."

He held his hands up, and said, "I didn't mean to, but she is smoking hot. They do look happy, though."

"They are," I confirmed. "So, I guess you can tell his dad that."

Ryder nodded. "I will. He knows I work here, and he knows I'm around Cal, but he hasn't asked any questions yet. I think he's afraid to know the answers in case he messed up Cal's life so badly that he couldn't recover."

"That was almost the case. But listen, I can't have you here now I know why you came. I get why, but if his dad wants to know about Cal, then he needs to be the one to ask. Maybe knowing Cal is happy will be enough for him, and the way I see it, he doesn't deserve to know much else. I'm sorry he's not well, but he had years to sort his shit out and try to make things right, but he didn't."

"I understand." Ryder blew out a breath. "And he knows that. I guess he's missed his chance." Slapping his hand down on the bar, he added, "Thank you for giving me the chance to explain, and for giving me the job. And I really am sorry if I made anyone feel uncomfortable. I just wanted to give Ian the answers he was looking for." He began to round the bar, then he stopped again and said, "I don't know if you plan to tell Cal why I was here, but if by any chance he does want to see his dad, you or he can call me and we can figure it out. You have my number."

I nodded, and he wandered over to his things that were still waiting for him and picked them up before heading out of the bar.

As far as everyone else knew, he was going on his lunch break. Whether I told them why he never came back, I wasn't yet sure.

Chapter 31

Gaby

"GABY! CAN YOU PLAY with me!"

In a week where there had been little else but stress, Aiden's enthusiasm made me smile.

Shannen had invited Guy and me over for dinner because Shannen and I hadn't seen much of each other lately. I was positive Guy had been delighted at there being an excuse for me to get out of the flat for a while for something other than work. We hadn't told Cal and Shannen that I was living with him in the short-term, nor did they know about Flynn and his amazing disappearing act. I didn't want anyone else worrying about me. It was bad enough knowing my brother was frantic and Guy, although calm on the outside... I was sure he internally felt the strain too.

"Of course," I told him. I had barely got through the door and taken off my coat before Aiden pounced on me with his request. "What are we playing?"

"Jenga!" He grabbed my hand and tugged me down the hallway and into the living room, the scent of lasagne fading as I was pulled further away from the kitchen. I turned my head to look back at Guy, Shannen, and Cal with mock horror, and they all laughed.

Aiden had set the game up on the coffee table, and we sat down at opposite sides. As I looked up, I saw Guy was looking around the living room a little wistfully. He'd been part of the team that had redecorated his old house before Shannen, Cal, and Aiden had moved in, but it had looked a certain way for so long that, even after visiting several times, it still probably looked a bit strange to him. I preferred Shannen and Cal's setup to the way Guy and Helen had it. Guy had admitted to me that he hadn't loved the small touches Helen had added when she lived there, but having spent some time with her, I understood why it was perhaps easier to let it go than have a fight over it.

The phrase, 'pick your battles' sprang to mind.

"Do you want a drink?" Shannen asked everyone. "We have tea, coffee, a range of fizzy drinks, beer, pink gin, and wine."

"It's only us," Guy said with a laugh as he sat down. "No need to go to so much trouble."

"This is our usual selection," Shannen told him, chuckling. "And the wine? That's there for me to have a glass of as soon as this baby pops out." She cradled her bump fondly, and I smiled.

"Pink gin would be great," I said. Guy was driving, so I was okay to have a glass or two. I wouldn't have any more as I had work in the morning.

"Guy?" Shannen asked, looking over at him, where he sat behind me on the sofa.

"I'll have a beer, please."

Shannen took a step backwards as if to go to the kitchen, but Cal put his hands on her hips to stop her.

"Go and sit down," he said. "I'll be serving up in a minute anyway. Relax."

When she smiled up at him, I noticed she did look a bit tired, but I figured, with the size of the human growing inside her and getting closer to her due date, she had to be more uncomfortable now. She reached up and pecked him on the lips before sitting next to Guy.

"Gaby, come on!" Aiden urged. To be fair to him, he'd been patient while we discussed refreshments.

"Okay, okay," I said, shuffling around to face him and the game he wanted to play. "You go first."

He reached over and carefully removed the first block, letting out a triumphant cheer as he hadn't knocked the tower over.

I took my turn, choosing one that would, hopefully, keep things balanced, and placed it down in front of me once I'd freed it.

"So, how was your day, Mr Aiden?" I asked as he took his next turn, and he laughed at the name I'd used for him.

"It was okay. Mr Jukes told me off today because I wouldn't sit still. He called me Aiden Fidget Bum."

"Sounds right," Shannen said, and I could hear the smile in her voice.

I laughed as he did a celebration dance at his successful removal of another block. Behind me, Shannen, Cal, and Guy were chatting after Cal had returned with our drinks, and I felt Guy's hands rest lightly on my shoulders. Before taking my next turn, I looked around at him and smiled.

Honestly, this was the most relaxed I'd felt all week. I'd loved staying with Guy; it had been easier than I expected. However, there was no denying that my internal fight to stay on top of my fear had been prominent. The best thing about Guy, though, was that he didn't push me to talk about it. He knew that if and when I was ready, I would. It was one of my favourite things about him, that he offered this place of security. Not just in his home, but with *him*. He was so attuned to what I needed that I never really had to ask for anything. Not space, not understanding... nothing. I knew that he would be there for anything when the time was right for me.

"Okay," Cal said, "I'm going to put the garlic bread in the oven, so, Aiden, once that game is done, it'll be time to eat."

Aiden nodded in response.

As Cal left the room, Guy said, "What training method did you use on him?" and Shannen laughed out loud. "How have you domesticated that Neanderthal?"

I turned slightly, so I could see both the game I was playing and Guy and Shannen.

"He's not *that* domesticated," Shannen said, though fondness shone in her eyes. "He leaves the toilet seat up, he never knows where to find any of his stuff because he doesn't look properly, and he complains about washing up, even after I've cooked. I'm also not sure he knows where the hoover is. But the more pregnant I get, the more help he gives me. And when he cooks, he gets cocky because he knows how good his food is."

"Yeah, I remember the first time you came over and he offered you his lasagne. Seems like forever ago now."

Shannen nodded as I reached over to take my turn, the Jenga tower now beginning to wobble slightly.

"Hands down, this has been the most ridiculous year of my life," she said. "This time last year, I'd just met Gaby and Nova, and now look at us. I've aged about ten years since January!"

"Pah," I said, chuckling. "You haven't at all! But it is weird how different everything is."

It was as if someone had hit a fast forward button when the clock struck midnight on January 1st because in that time, Shannen had met Cal, Nova and Donovan had maintained their relationship long distance, and I had met Guy. Shannen and Cal had survived lies, betrayal from family and friends, an accidental pregnancy, and a house move, all while juggling a handful of a five-year-old. Guy and Cal and Shannen had swapped homes, Guy had split with his long-term partner and bought a new business, then met me—also a handful—and found out his ex was pregnant.

And I had recently had to face up to the bits of my past that I'd tried to avoid, and in doing so, gotten closer to my friends and Guy because, without ever telling them, I'd needed them all more than ever.

There were still two and a bit more months left of the year. God only knew what they would bring, but I hoped they would be kinder.

The tumbling of the tower caught my attention, and Aiden growled. "I'm rubbish at this game."

"No, you're not," I told him. "You did really well! It's just that when the blocks get too loose, eventually, the tower has to fall."

He shrugged. "Can we play again later?"

I nodded. "Sure. And we'll see if everyone else wants to play too."

Aiden grinned. "My dad is no good at Jenga. Mum said it's because his hands are too big. Then Dad said that's why she likes him, but I don't know what that means."

I cackled because I could feel the embarrassment pouring from Shannen, and sure enough, as I glanced up at her, her cheeks were red.

"And on that note," she said. "Let's move to the dining room!"

Aiden jumped up and ran on ahead while I got to my feet, picking up my gin, and Guy helped Shannen to stand.

"I love that kid," I said, still laughing.

"You won't be saying that when he's a teenager and we're sending him over to stay with Auntie Gaby so we can get a break!" Shannen poked her tongue out at me.

"Anytime," I said as we walked across to the dining room. "I'll probably be the one taking him to get his first tattoo!"

As we reached the dining room, Aiden was already sitting down, waiting patiently, and we all took a seat, Shannen next to him, and me and Guy sitting opposite them. After a couple of minutes, Cal came in with a huge dish of lasagne and placed it in the middle of the table.

"Oh my God," I said. "That smells incredible."

Cal grinned. "It is."

Shannen swatted his arse as he left the room and headed back to the kitchen. Once Cal had returned with the garlic bread, we tucked in, chatting easily as we ate. Shannen hadn't been lying when she said Cal's lasagne was the best she'd ever had. I couldn't disagree, and I was gutted we ate it all and I couldn't pinch any to take home to eat later.

When we'd finished eating, we remained in the dining room, aside from Aiden, who had gone to play in his bedroom, when Shannen said to Cal, "So, what happened with that guy at work? You started to tell me that he walked out, but then Mum rang and you didn't get to finish."

I frowned. I asked Guy every day about work, and he always told me what had been going on, but he hadn't mentioned anything about anyone walking out.

"Oh, yeah," Cal said, and I turned my attention to him. "He went out for lunch and never came back. He messaged Guy and said he quit, no explanation."

"Who was this?" I asked, surprised Guy hadn't mentioned anything.

"Some temp," Cal replied, glowering as if just the memory of the man pissed him off. "It's a relief if you ask me."

Once again, I shifted my gaze to Guy. He'd mentioned that he'd interviewed some temporary staff, but he hadn't said they'd started work. The low tinkling of alarm bells began in my head. Guy told me about the most random things while working in the bar, so why hadn't he mentioned this?

He'd stiffened very slightly beside me in a way that suggested he was holding something back, but before I could question him, Shannen spoke.

"Gaby, he was so weird," she said, and she shuddered slightly. "I mean... he didn't *look* weird, but he kept staring at me, and it creeped me out."

"I still wish I'd knocked him out," Cal said, and the alarm bells grew louder. This was definitely something Guy would usually have mentioned, and the fact that he hadn't looked at me was enough to set my heart skyrocketing.

"I didn't know you had new people working for you," I said, my eyes on the side of Guy's head and trying to keep my voice steady, and he slowly turned to look at me.

"Yeah," he said, his voice tight. "But he's gone now. Nothing to worry about."

Something about Guy keeping this from me didn't sit right. Also, he was not a liar, so his poker face was crap. There was only one reason I could think of that he wouldn't have talked to me about it. He was almost begging me with his eyes not to say anything else; a silent warning that we were trying to keep the Flynn stuff away from Shannen and Cal? In my already frayed mental state, I couldn't bite back my irritation. Guy *must* have thought the man was Flynn.

"Can I talk to you for a second?" I asked sharply, standing up.

I was vaguely aware of puzzled glances watching me from across the table, and Guy gently took a hold of my wrist. "Please sit down. We can talk later."

"Was it him?" I demanded pointedly, staring him down. When he didn't answer, I snapped, "Guy!"

"What's going on?" Shannen asked, confused eyes moving between us.

"Nothing," Guy said, standing up, clearly realising I wasn't going to shut up. He glanced at Shannen and Cal. "Excuse us for a second."

He gestured for me to leave the room, and I did, walking through the living room to the hallway, Guy right behind me. Once the door was closed, I rounded on him.

"Why didn't you tell me you had new staff, one of whom Shannen was totally creeped out by?" I asked hotly, looking up at him with a challenge in my eyes. I could feel it burning into him.

Guy held up a hand, and in a low voice, he said, "Gabs, it was nothing. This bloke started working with us on Monday, and on Monday night, me and you... we didn't talk about work." He tilted his head to the side slightly, reminding me of what a lovely night it had been until my brother had arrived. "And then, when we were talking about Flynn, you said something about how he might circle around you. With Cal thinking the new guy was weird and Shannen not liking him either, it made me wonder if it might be Flynn. So, I got in touch with Gavin, and-"

"Gavin?" I hissed. "Why didn't you tell *me*?"

"Because, Gaby, you were already on the edge. I didn't want you storming over to the bar in case it was him. I didn't want you to have to see him. So, I asked Gavin to check out the guy's info, to see if he was who he said he was. And he was."

In spite of my annoyance, relief shot through me. However, with Guy knowing how little I liked Gavin interfering and going behind my back, I was still pissed off, and I shook my head.

"Guy, I understand your reasons for not telling me, but don't ever do that again. I already have a brother who treats me like a delicate little flower, and I don't need that from you too. And I also don't need you trying to control what I say. I chose not to tell anyone else about Flynn, but it's my story and I'll talk to whoever I want about it."

I breathed deeply, both glad I'd said it and feeling awful for snapping at him. I stood by my words, but I'd never had a need to get angry with Guy before, and I didn't like it. I swallowed down the emotion that had begun to clog my throat and turned away from him in order to compose myself.

"I'm sorry," he said, and I felt him step closer to me. "I knew not telling you was wrong, but I've seen how hard this week has been for you. And also... I felt guilty. I was worried I might have been the one to accidentally bring him closer to you, so I wanted to check it out before I said anything. And then, if, as was the case, it wasn't him, I would never need to mention it because it wouldn't be relevant."

The remorse in his voice exacerbated my discomfort at snarling at him, and I slowly turned towards him again.

"Also," he added, "I would never stop you from telling people whatever you want to tell them."

I shook my head. "You were looking at me like you wanted to shut me up."

"I did, but it wasn't because of the Flynn thing." He rubbed his forehead with a sigh.

I felt my eyebrows draw together at his change from apologetic to concerned. It was as if tiredness had suddenly taken over him, and I reached out for his hand, my self-absorption with my own drama melting away in an instant.

I looked up at him, not speaking, just silently asking what was wrong, and he dragged me into him, holding me tight like he *needed* the hug. "The man who quit today... he wasn't there for you. He was there for Cal." Guy said the words quietly into my ear.

"What?" I asked, keeping my voice lowered as I slipped my arms around his waist. He relaxed against me, and I held him tighter.

"I don't like secrets either, Gaby, especially when I'm the one who has to decide whether to keep them. Keeping what I kept from you might have been wrong, but I was trying to protect you. There was a possible physical danger. But the thing I found out today... it could have an effect on Cal. I don't want to hide things from him, but I know that telling him could lead to a spiral neither he nor Shannen needs right now."

"Can you tell me, or would you rather not?"

"I don't know." He sighed. "I think if I'm going to tell anyone, it should be Cal, but I'm not sure it's right."

"What do you need to tell Cal?"

Fuck. Cal's voice from behind Guy caused us both to stiffen, Guy's decision now taken from his hands.

Even though I didn't know what it was, from Guy's concern, it must have been pretty big. I slid my hands down his chest then kissed him on the cheek before stepping away from him and slipping past Cal back into the living room.

Chapter 32

Guy

I'D HAD A DAY of it. A week, really, what with thinking I'd accidentally employed Gaby's ex for the first four days of it. I wondered if that might have been the easier thing to deal with rather than the secret I'd been burdened with instead. At least with Flynn, I could have warned him off. Worst case scenario, we could have looked at getting a restraining order to keep him away from Gaby, but this? I hadn't been prepared for it, and I couldn't decide whether holding it back was better than the chance that his dad might push harder to see him, taking him by surprise.

When we went back to work after lunch and Ryder didn't return, questions were asked. I'd told my men he'd quit and didn't say why, and while most didn't have any thoughts on it, Cal had looked relieved. I'd then spent the rest of the day debating what to do about what Ryder had revealed. The constant back and forth had driven me crazy, and I could barely look Cal in the eye.

Was it even my place to decide what was best for him? *Was* I really keeping a secret from him by keeping my mouth shut?

Yes. Yes, you are.

Slowly, I turned to face Cal, who was now leaning against the doorframe. He didn't look suspicious or annoyed, just curious, and I sighed.

"Fuck's sake," I muttered, running my hand through my hair. "This is..." I turned away from him, pacing as I realised I was really going to do this. Okay, I could have made something up, but lying wasn't my strong point; I couldn't think fast enough to come up with something plausible.

"What's going on?" Cal asked, straightening up and taking a couple of steps towards me, confusion on his face.

"Okay," I began, puffing out my cheeks before speaking again. "Erm, you might want to get a drink for this. Can we go in the kitchen? We should sit down."

Cal nodded and raised an arm to gesture for me to go ahead. I did, the smell of the food we'd just eaten still strong. I took a seat at the kitchen table and waited for Cal to sit opposite me. I placed both elbows on the table, then folded them down on the flat surface in front of me. Cal sat quietly, waiting for me to begin.

With one more long breath, I gave Cal the truth about Ryder. How he had taken the job with us to check on Cal for his dad, and how his dad had turned his life around but was now seriously ill.

"I wasn't sure whether you needed to know this," I finished with a sigh. "You've spoken about your dad as if he was already dead for the last few years, and you've never shown any interest in finding out for sure, but I didn't want to pretend I knew nothing because... what if you found out he'd died and I hadn't told you I knew he was dying?"

Cal wrinkled his nose and sniffed, shaking his head. "Doesn't make a difference, mate. Dying or dead, I don't give a shit. His creepy little buddy can tell him I'm fine, and that's the end of it."

If I didn't know Cal as well as I did, I would have believed he meant that. But I saw the shadow of emotion ghosting across his eyes. "You sure?" I asked. "Because... a lot of time has passed. Isn't there anything you'd like to say to him?"

As if a switch had been flicked, Cal slammed his fist down on the table and stood up. "Oh, yeah," he said sarcastically. "A lot of things. Starting with why he was such a shitty excuse for a father, and why, instead of getting a job and being an adult, he chose to blame everyone else for the fact that his voice failed him and he could no longer do the thing he loved! Why his family wasn't more important than his fucking misery! But you know what? None of it matters because knowing won't change it. It won't make up for the years he beat my mum, and the years after she died when he beat me and made me feel useless. I don't care if he's turned his life around. It's too late. Just because he's dying, that doesn't give him a free pass, and I don't and won't forgive him. The best thing he ever did for me was leave me the fuck alone!"

Cal had raised his voice, but he wasn't shouting. He was pacing the kitchen, his reaction explosive, like it used to be before he'd been in therapy, and that was the very reason I hadn't wanted to tell him anything. He'd learned to process a lot of things, but I didn't think his dad would ever be a topic of conversation he would handle well.

"Cal," I said, standing up and stepping in front of him to stop him from wearing down the kitchen tiles.

He shoved me back, but I knew it wasn't me he was angry with. He was just pissed off at having the most painful part of his life dragged into the present.

"I don't want anything to do with him," Cal said firmly, his eyes fixed on mine. "Lose that twat's number, and we'll go back in the other room and pretend this didn't happen."

He attempted to push past me, but I blocked his way, my hands on his shoulders to stop him. "Cal, wait." He breathed in deeply, and I waited for him to settle. "I'll destroy his number. I'm sorry."

Cal shook his head, his shoulders dropping and his jaw unclenching. "Don't be. I get why you told me, and I'm sorry I lost my temper. But I don't want to talk about it again."

"Not even to tell Shannen?" I questioned with a tilt of my head.

"Does she need to know?"

"Yeah, I think so. If nothing else so she understands why Ryder was watching the two of you so closely."

He bristled at the memory of Ryder staring at Shannen. "She'll probably tell me to talk to him while I have the chance. She's nicer than me."

Once again, knowing Cal well meant I could read his thoughts. There was a chance Shannen might say that, but it was the fact that *he* had that thought that made him bring it up. A year ago, that hint of compassion for his dad wouldn't have happened. This was an indication of how much he'd changed, even if he ultimately reached the same decision to stay away from him.

"Nah," I said. "She's barely speaking to her own father. She isn't going to lecture you on how to deal with yours."

Cal put his hands on his head, scrubbing his hands over his hair as he turned away from me. "You're right. I'll tell her, but... once I have, just like I'm saying to you, I don't want it brought up again. The line is being drawn right now."

I was impressed by how easily Cal appeared to push our conversation aside when we returned to the dining room. It was as if he'd shoved it away in a drawer in the back of his mind, but I knew it wouldn't be so easy. Once Gaby and I left, when he was trying to sleep, it was going to jump back out of that drawer and the questions would come. Even though he wasn't upset with me for telling him, there was still a level of guilt inside me, but that would have also remained if I *hadn't* told him. At least now I could appease myself with the knowledge that he knew the truth about Ryder's reasons for inserting himself into our workplace.

When Gaby and I left Cal and Shannen's place, after a couple more games of Jenga with Aiden, Gaby seemed a lot brighter than she had for most of the week. As we got into my car, Gaby said, "Guy... I think I want to go home."

I opened and closed my mouth a couple of times before I spoke. She *did* seem more relaxed, but I hadn't expected that. "To your place?" I asked, making sure I hadn't misunderstood.

She nodded. It was dark in the car, but there was enough light coming from the streetlamp that I could make out her features. "Yeah." She sighed and reached over for my hand. "Being here tonight, with Shannen, Cal, Aiden, and you... it felt normal. Like there was nothing to worry about, and that might actually be the case. While I shut myself away in your flat, whether Flynn is nearby or not, he still wins. It means he gets to take up space in my head that he should have vacated a long time ago." She paused, pushing a few strands of hair out of her face. "I swore to myself I would never live in fear again, and look at me. Just the mention of him, and I ran." She shrugged. "Staying with you has been great, and so easy, but we aren't ready to be living together long-term, and how long am I meant to wait to see if Flynn appears? A few more days? Weeks? Months? He *could* show up at any time. Equally, he might not show up at all, and I can't rearrange my life over something that is so uncertain. I need to go home."

I stared at her in the half-light; my beautiful girl. She'd been dragged to hell and clawed her way out, never losing an ounce of her kindness, never becoming bitter, and certainly never making herself small. What had happened recently had been an adjustment. Once she knew her ex was free, although she'd taken it in her stride, it must have played on her mind, and Gavin then telling her that he'd been tracking Flynn, only to lose him, had tipped her over the edge. But Gaby wasn't designed to sit quietly and do as she was told. It was one thing to be careful when there was a genuine threat, but that wasn't the position she was in. The threat was, until given a reason to believe otherwise, nothing more than a theory. Boxing herself up and being afraid was crushing the essence of who she was. She *had* come alive while we'd been at Cal and Shannen's place. She was more like herself amongst friends, and it had taken that to tell her what she probably knew all along. That she needed to not be smothered by what-ifs.

"Okay," I said, my thumb stroking across the back of her hand. "But can it be tomorrow? It's getting late to go to mine and pack up your stuff and then take you home."

She smiled softly. "Thank you for understanding." Gaby leaned forward and brushed her lips over mine. As she pulled back, she smiled teasingly. "I suppose... since tomorrow is Friday, and then it's the weekend, which I would probably spend with you anyway... I could go home on Sunday."

The corners of my lips pulled upwards, and I kissed her again. "I like the way you think."

Her own smile widened, her green eyes lighting up. "I appreciate everything you've done for me this week. Not just for letting me stay, but for not forcing conversations and not staring at me as if I'm about to crack. You've just acted like we were having a week-long sleepover, and even when you knew things were getting on top of me, you sat quietly until I wanted to talk. I didn't understand how much I needed that until I met you. I didn't even know men could *be* patient and not try to fix everything immediately." She chuckled, shaking her head. As her eyes connected with mine, she said, "I love you so much."

Those words had never meant more.

"I love you too," I told her, bringing her hand to my mouth to kiss the back of it, then kissing her lips again. "So, shall we go home, drink coffee, then have the best sex we've ever had?" I raised an eyebrow, and she laughed, her mouth close to mine.

"Maybe we can skip the coffee."

I dropped a kiss on her forehead, grinning. "If you insist."

As she settled back into the passenger seat, I smiled to myself. I was a bit gutted that she wanted to go home because it had been good sharing my space with someone again. But she was right, and I never wanted her to feel forced into anything with me.

Also, I was one hundred percent certain that one day, she would move in with me for real.

And that day was worth waiting for.

Chapter 33

Gaby

Two Weeks Later

"Is there a bloody ghost in here today?" Iris, Oakwood Lane Primary School's headteacher, said as she wandered into the staff room during morning break. The woman was usually unflappable, but her grey hair was coming loose from her tight bun, and although there was a hint of resigned amusement on her face, she looked like she was ready to go home. "I know it's the day of the Halloween disco, but I think there might be actual demons in this school with all the chaos going on, and it's not even lunchtime."

I was just grabbing a cup of tea from the vending machine, and my fellow teachers Tim Jukes, David Carr, and my classroom assistant, Gemma, were also in the room, having a snack and a drink.

"What happened?" Tim asked, looking up from where he was sitting. I turned all the way around to look at Iris, tea in hand.

With a dramatic eye roll, she said, "When I got here this morning, there was a message on the answerphone from an angry parent who said some kids from this school have been trespassing on their property and could we send out a message for parents to control their children. Also, the heating wouldn't work first thing, but luckily someone came out right away and sorted it. Then one of the kids in Year 4 fell in P.E and broke her arm. The sink in Nova's classroom then sprang a leak, so we had to move her class to a different room while the caretaker fixed it, and when I went out to my car to get some paperwork I left in the boot, I saw someone has made a hole in the fence at the back by the car park which will need fixing immediately before anyone notices it."

That was a *lot* before lunch, but before anyone could speak, Nova walked in, also looking a little frazzled. She was putting her hair back up in a ponytail, and she eyed the vending machine like it was her new best friend.

"Is the sink fixed yet?" Iris asked her, and she nodded.

"Yeah. All done."

I sat down in the chair next to Tim and took a sip of my tea. "Maybe that's all of the bad stuff out of the way now," I said. "Plus, there are only three days until half term!"

"Not a moment too soon," Iris said as she came in and sat down too. We only had ten more minutes before we had to be back at work, but she looked like she needed a moment to compose herself.

I, on the other, was the most relaxed I'd been in a while, greatly helped by the week-long break that was rapidly approaching.

After the evening at Shannen and Cal's, I had moved back to my own flat. Gavin was still drawing a blank on where Flynn was, but as I'd told Guy, I refused to spend my life in fear, especially when there was no indication that Flynn would come anywhere near me. It had only been two weeks; well, a week and a bit, but making the decision to live my life had helped the stress fall away. My brother was still trying to figure out a location for my ex, even though I'd told him to stop. Deep down, I was annoyed with him for not letting it go, but I also understood. I hadn't felt this conflicted about Gavin since he'd moved to Exeter. He was my big brother, and I loved him, but the fact that he continued to go against my wishes in the name of caring about me grated. However, we'd got over our issues before, and I was sure we would get over this too.

I was additionally buzzing that day because, as Iris had mentioned, it was the day of the Halloween disco. October 31st was still a week away and fell during half-term, so we held the event the week before, but it was one of my favourite days in the school year. The kids got so excited about dressing up, and they were also adorable as they danced with their friends. I always volunteered to be one of the teachers who 'chaperoned,' and so did Nova. David, and the deputy head, Bryan Nash, would also be on duty, and some of the parents on the PTA would be helping out with refreshments and the general running of things.

"Hey, what are you wearing tonight, Nova?" I asked as she sat down next to me with a cup of coffee.

She grinned at me. "I'm going to be a bat. I have black flared trousers, a black long-sleeved top, and the bat wings you let me borrow for New Year's Eve."

"Cute," I said. "I'm going for a classic witch this year."

Because we were working in a school, we had to be super careful not to wear anything deemed too 'sexy' or scary. Anything tight, revealing, or terrifying was a no-no. As someone who loved dressing up, a lot of my clothes fell a bit too far on the side of sexy for a kids' disco, so I planned to wear a long, loose-fitting black dress and a witches' hat that had little lights in that I could turn on and off.

"As much as I love this place," Iris said, "I'm glad I don't have to come back this evening." With another head shake, she added, "I'd better go and get on to someone to fix that fence."

We waved her off before Nova turned back to me as Gemma was chatting with Tim and David.

"Are we still having drinks tonight?" Nova asked, and I nodded.

Because she lived in Dawlish, she was staying at my place for the night. We'd arranged to go out straight after the disco ended—in our costumes—for a drink or two before going back to mine, and Shannen was joining us too since it had been a while since we'd had a girls' night. We wouldn't be out late with it being a week day and with Shannen now two weeks from her due date, but she'd wanted to come out, citing as it her last chance, as the baby could come any time now.

"Yup," I said. "Drinks tonight, three more days until half-term, and no matter what Guy says, I'm dragging him away for a couple of days next week before he works himself into an early grave."

With a grimace, Nova said, "That bad?"

I laughed. "I'm being a bit dramatic, but the last week or two, he has been staying later at the bar. I don't know why exactly, but he seems even more driven than ever to get the place finished. I honestly think he's planning to keep it because instead of keeping it neutral, he seems to have begun to lean into a theme. He's mentioned it having a more country vibe, but overall, it seems to be heading towards some kind of retro feel."

"Huh." Nova tilted her head slightly, reaching up to readjust her ponytail. "Donovan said he'd spoken to Guy about the bar the other day, now you mention it. Donovan had a friend who he thought might want to buy it, but maybe things have changed."

I shrugged. "Whatever he does with it is cool with me, but I do like the idea of it being a new place for us to hang out. Regardless of whether he keeps it, Guy has worked a miracle on the place, so whatever it becomes, it's going to be worth checking out."

I took another drink of my tea. I hadn't yet worked out how I was going to get Guy away from work for a couple of days, but he needed it. Since we'd been to Cornwall in the summer, life had heaped piles of shite over both of us. In spite of the external noise, Guy and I were doing well, not letting any of it seep into our relationship, but it circled us. The stuff with Flynn, Guy working so hard, my own mini meltdown, and the drama with

Helen... a moment to breathe, to be on our own away from everything was most definitely in order.

"We'd better get back," Nova said, her eyes falling on the wall clock.

With a sigh, I stood up. "Let's hope we can get through the rest of the day with no more disasters!"

Chapter 34

Guy

I WAS SITTING AT one of the newly installed barstools while the rest of my guys were doing their assigned tasks. I wasn't slacking off. I'd been answering some emails, but once I was done, I started looking online for decor for the bar and got pulled into a rabbit hole of neon sign options.

I had confirmed with Donovan the day before that I wanted to keep it. We'd spoken on the phone several times to discuss financial stuff, ways in which we could make it work with both of us part owning it, and I'd already been in touch with a solicitor to find out what we needed to do to make it happen. We were a long way from finalising things, but a verbal agreement was in place, and we were planning to be in regular contact while we got things moving. The excitement coming from him increased my own. When he'd first mentioned coming back to the UK permanently, although it was only a couple of weeks ago, there was still a hint of doubt lingering there. The more we'd talked about it, though, the more I could feel him loving the idea. It had to be weird for him to consider giving up his nomadic lifestyle that earned him a lot of money to be rooted in one place, but he missed Nova, and the pull to be closer to her was outweighing his desire to keep travelling.

Donovan and I had agreed that making it a country and western-style bar was the way forward, but we were both gigantic children, and we wanted to keep the games machines in the smaller room too, so we'd decided that the bar would have an overall retro feel. Since country was making one hell of a comeback, we were going to push the nineties angle, when line dancing was popular, and we were also intending to have karaoke nights; something else that had fizzled out a bit over the years but evoked nostalgia in people. Then, the smaller room with the gaming machines would have an eighties and nineties aesthetic, and we were going to move the piano into the main bar, as it would fit better there.

For two people who were only in the early phases of negotiations, we had a lot of ideas, and I was buzzing with how great it was going to be once it all came together.

The buzzing of my phone on the bar caught our attention, and the name *Jeanette* showed on the screen.

Helen's mum. I didn't even realise I still had her number. I hadn't heard from Helen since I'd set my ultimatum for her to get in touch before the end of October about sorting everything out for the baby's arrival, so I wasn't expecting to hear from her mother.

I wasn't sure I wanted to answer, though. If she was calling me, it was either to give me a mouthful or because something was wrong, and I didn't want to hear either of those things.

Cursing under my breath I picked up the phone and answered it.

"Hello?"

"Guy, it's Jeanette." She sounded frantic, and the sound put me on immediate alert. "Helen asked me to ring you. She's at the hospital. Her waters have broken."

I felt as though all of my blood was draining from my body. The baby wasn't due for four and a half weeks. Cal and Shannen's baby was even due first. This was too soon.

"What?" I said, hearing the panic in my tone. "Is she okay?"

"I think so, but her dad and I are on holiday up in Scotland, so we can't get to her. She rang me first thing this morning to say she wasn't feeling good and she was having pains, and I told her to take it easy, but her waters broke about an hour ago. She got a cab to the hospital, but she asked me to ring you and tell you because she has to get herself checked in and seen to, and she wanted you to know as soon as possible. She's scared, Guy. Can you go and be with her?"

My heart began to pound. This wasn't supposed to happen yet. We were supposed to have more time. There was still so much we had to figure out.

Was this dangerous? I knew babies born prematurely could sometimes have health problems. Was four weeks going to mean our baby might not be okay?

"I... does... does she want me there?" I asked, trying to pull myself together and not asking the more terrifying questions in my head.

"She asked for you. Listen, I know my daughter can be difficult, but she's on her own, and her sister is at work and won't pick up her messages until later. With us being so far away, there's nobody else. Regardless, though, she wants you there, Guy."

I wanted to say she hadn't spoken to me for weeks, that she'd shown no sign that she wanted me anywhere near her, but it didn't matter right then. My daughter was arriving, and whether Helen liked me or not, I would be there by her side like I said I would be.

"Okay," I said, standing up, a hand running through my hair. "Okay. I'm on my way. Is she at the RD&E?"

There were a few hospitals in the city, but I presumed she would be at the Royal Devon and Exeter. However, I didn't want to waste time by accidentally turning up at the wrong place.

"Yeah," Jeanette answered. "And Guy? Please can you keep us updated when you can?"

I nodded. "Yeah, of course. Thank you for letting me know."

"It's fine. And thank you for going to her. I know she's been... challeng-ing."

That was an understatement, and I huffed out a laugh. "Well, that's Helen. But this is my baby too, and I won't let her do this alone. I'll call you as soon as I can."

"Okay. Talk to you later."

I hung up the phone, slipped it into my back pocket, and then walked across the room to where my team was getting ready for their break.

"What's wrong?" Cal asked, noting my probably ashen face.

"Helen's waters have broken. She's at the hospital now, so I need to go. Erm... you lot all know what you need to be doing this afternoon, so just carry on. Cal, I'll need you to lock up for me, and I'll figure out tasks for tomorrow later. I'll ring you tonight."

"Okay," Cal said. "Do you want a ride to the hospital?"

I shook my head. "It's okay. I'll take my van. I don't know how long I'll end up being there, so it's easier if I drive myself." My limbs were twitching with the need to go, adrenaline flooding me as the mix of worry, anticipation, and excitement collided within me. "I have to run. I'll see you later."

A chorus of goodbyes and good lucks followed me as I raced to the door. On the way, I took my phone out and dialled Gaby's number. I knew she wouldn't be on her lunch break yet, so I waited for the voicemail message to kick in, then said, "Hey, Gabs. Erm... I've just spoken to Helen's mum, and Helen has gone into early labour, so I'm on my way to the hospital. If you haven't heard from me again by the time you finish work this afternoon, can you call me? Then I can fill you in on everything." I sighed, unlocking the door to my van. "I'm scared, Gabs. I have to get going, but I'll talk to you later. I love you."

Hanging up, I put the phone back in my pocket and got into my van. This was it.

My baby was coming. I just hoped and prayed everything would be okay.

Chapter 35

Gaby

AFTER GETTING GUY'S VOICEMAIL at lunchtime, my heart had been in my throat all afternoon. I could hear the fear in every word he'd spoken. I'd wanted to call him right away, but I realised that in the twenty minutes since he'd left the message, he would barely have got to the hospital, so he wouldn't have an update yet anyway.

The time seemed to drag on like never before in class, even though we were doing fun things. I tried to stay focused, but it was hard when I knew Guy and Helen's baby was on the way and Guy was stressed.

Four weeks early wasn't great, but it also wasn't the worst-case scenario from what I understood. The baby would be small, but hopefully, that would be the only issue. I had to believe that because Guy and Helen had gone through so much to get to this point already. Helen had been horrendous to me, but nobody deserved to lose a child. I wasn't sure how either of them would recover if that was the case.

When the school day finally ended, I did my duty of seeing the kids in my class were all collected by their parents, then rushed back up to my classroom to grab my phone from my desk drawer to call Guy, hoping he would pick up on my first attempt because waiting for news was killing me.

Even though I shouldn't have, I'd checked my mobile several times through the afternoon, just in case he tried to ring again, but he hadn't.

The phone only rang twice before he answered. "Gabs," he said, a relieved-sounding sigh falling from his lips.

"Hey," I said, my own relief pouring out of me at the sound of his voice. "Are you okay? How is everything going?"

I held my breath, bracing for whatever he would say next.

"I'm okay. Everything seems to be going in the right direction. I'm actually at my flat right now, but I'm going back to the hospital shortly. Helen made me come and have a shower because I was all dusty and covered in paint from rushing out of work. The nurses were also pretty adamant about me showering and changing too because... hygiene."

I chuckled, letting out my breath. When Guy came home from work, he was rarely in too bad a state, but in a hospital, where new life was coming into the world, I could understand why they'd made him clean up.

"Is Helen all right?" I asked.

Guy let out a low groan. "Health-wise, she's good. Everything is going as it should be, although obviously earlier than planned. Labour could still take a while, so she's a bit up and down. She wants me to stay with her, but her friendliness slips in and out depending on how much pain she's in. Which, under the circumstances, I will let her off for."

"Have you managed to get any further with how everything is going to work when the baby arrives? It seems a bit more pressing now."

"Yeah, just a little." He sighed. "Honestly, in between me getting there and her being looked at, and nurses and doctors being in and out, we haven't been able to say much about anything important yet, but I'm probably going to be there all night, so we have time."

He sounded tired already, and he'd only been at the hospital for a few hours. Dealing with Helen was always a good way to become exhausted quickly, and even giving her leeway for the strain of childbirth, it was going to be a long night for him.

"Guy, do you want me to come to the hospital?" I asked quietly. "I know I can't be in the room with the two of you, but I can sit in the waiting room if you need a breather. I can just be there for you."

There was a long pause, and I could feel his gratitude down the line. "I would love that, sweetheart, but you'd only be bored here. Also, don't you have the Halloween thing tonight at school? Plus, you have plans with Shannen and Nova after."

"I do, but I can find someone to cover if you need me." As much as I loved the Halloween disco, I would give it up if it gave Guy a bit of sanity on what was going to be a stressful evening. Nova was staying at mine, but I could always give her my key so she could get into the flat later. "I won't be able to stay all night because I have to work tomorrow, but I can stay until around nine or ten."

"I love that you want to be here for me, but I don't want you waiting around when you've already made arrangements for tonight. Plus, Shannen might not forgive you if you pull out of her last night out for a while."

We both laughed, and I said, "You know she would understand but you're right. This will be the last time the three of us go out socially for a bit, so I'll carry on with things as planned, but I'll ring you later. And you can call me too if you need to."

"Thank you. I will." There was another pause, then Guy said, "Gabs, this is really happening. This time tomorrow, I'll be someone's dad."

Hearing that, even though I'd accepted it, always caused a ripple of envy to pass through my body. I doubted it would ease when the baby arrived, but in spite of it, I *was* excited for him. Happy he would have a child. It might always sting that we couldn't make our own babies, but that man was made to be a dad, and I knew watching him raise a child would only make me love him more.

"You're going to be a brilliant father," I told him. "The best."

"That remains to be seen," he said with a small laugh. "But I'm going to try."

"You can't do much more than that."

A comfortable silence fell between us, and my chest ached because I wished I could see him. Even if just for a minute, to give him a hug. We rarely went more than two days without seeing each other, but even that felt like too much sometimes. We were still very much in the early part of our relationship, yet we'd already been put to the test a few times. Regardless, I hadn't been so certain of having something that was for the long-term in many, many years.

"I miss you," he said, as if he had a direct line to my thoughts.

"I miss you too, but I'll see you... well, whenever you can," I finished with a smile.

"We have plans for tomorrow, and I'm still going to see you. Even if it's only for an hour or two."

I heard the promise, but if he couldn't make it happen, I wouldn't hold it against him.

I noticed Nova standing in the doorway of my classroom and smiled at her, beckoning her to come in.

"I'd better get going and let you get back to the hospital," I said reluctantly as Nova approached my desk.

"Okay. I'll speak to you sometime tonight. Love you."

"Love you too," I said, warmth spreading through me. As we hung up, I looked up at Nova. "Everything is good so far," I told her. "Thank God."

She smiled. "That's good news. Is Guy okay?"

I nodded. "He seems to be. As long as the baby is all right, I don't think anything is going to be able to rattle him today. Not even Helen."

With a chuckle, Nova said, "Well, at least we'll be kept busy tonight. And hopefully, by the morning, the baby will be here."

The realness of that remark hit me hard. This new addition to our lives was going to change a lot of things forever. I had to believe that it would be for the better, even though Helen seemed to hate my very existence and I couldn't imagine her wanting me anywhere near her daughter.

I thought I'd have a few more weeks to deal with those thoughts, but life often had a way of doing things I hadn't prepared for.

Inhaling deeply to push that aside for now, I stood up. "Until then, we have a disco to get ready for!"

Even though I'd attended almost every Halloween disco since I'd worked at Oakwood Lane Primary, I was always impressed by the effort made to decorate the school's assembly hall for the event. The moment the kids were out the door at the end of the day, the volunteers from the PTA came in and set things up. *Happy Halloween* banners were hung up on the walls, and the ceiling was adorned with paper cutouts of bats and witches, all decorated with paint and glitter; every one made by the kids. It was fun to watch them looking up to see if they could find their own creations. At the side of the room was a long table of refreshments, again manned by members of the PTA, and the DJ had set up at the back end of the room. Some chairs were lined up on the opposite side to the refreshments, which left the rest of the floor free for the kids to dance and play. The main lights were off, and the room was lit mostly by the lights from the DJ's booth and some additional smaller ones that he'd brought and set up around the room. The vibe was suitably spooky, and by six o'clock, everything was in full swing.

My job for the evening, along with the other teachers, was simply to keep an eye on things, make sure everyone was behaving, and to be around in case anyone needed anything.

My colleagues had excelled themselves in the costume department this year. Nova, who I had already known about, was dressed as a bat, and

David was Beetlejuice, though he didn't go as far as face paint in case it scared the children. Bryan was a vampire; again without face paints, and some of the PTA were also dressed up. I'd seen another witch, Wednesday, and a skeleton.

I was standing at the back corner of the hall, watching Aiden, who was spinning around in circles, making Aria and Avery laugh hysterically, especially when he stopped spinning then over-exaggerated falling over because he was dizzy. That kid was five years old and already popular with the girls. I would have bet good money that, when he was older, he was going to be a real charmer.

All around the room, the children were having a good time. Some dancing, some just being silly with their friends. There was a queue for drinks and snacks, and even though there were things on my mind, it was easy to put them to one side and bask in the festivities, especially knowing I'd be seeing my own friends once this was all over at seven-thirty.

My phone was in my pocket, and I risked a quick look at it while I was standing in the shadows. No messages, but I hadn't been expecting any yet. It had only been a few hours since I'd spoken to Guy anyway. I planned to text him before Nova and I went to meet Shannen to see if he was free to talk.

Above the volume of the music, I heard a shout and looked up, shoving my phone back into my pocket and looking around the room to see where the sound had come from. Nothing was immediately amiss, but just as I was putting it down to someone's overexcitement, a loud scream pierced my ears. I stepped forward a couple of paces to see if I could figure out what was going on, and then all at once, kids started to rush to the edges of the room. I watched, confused, as David acted immediately and began to usher kids quickly out to the hallway that led to some of our classrooms, getting them out of the way of whatever had shattered their good time. I still couldn't see what it was in the poor light, and neither had most of the children if their confused faces were anything to go by. They'd just heard the scream and dashed to find safety.

I'd been so busy watching them, unable to see much else in the dark anyway, that I didn't realise what was really going on until gasps and shouts became audible even over the music, and standing in the middle of the room, I saw... a man dressed in a devil costume.

He was holding a knife to the throat of Amy Ward, one of the parents who had been volunteering at the refreshments stand. Even from across the room, I could see her trembling, the movement making her ginger curls shake. The darkness, with them only being illuminated by the disco lights, was creepy, but nobody attempted to turn the hall lights on, and I slunk backwards into the corner.

I didn't recall seeing a devil around earlier. Had someone just stormed into the school to hurt Amy, and why? She was an older mum, always one of the first on hand to volunteer and make cakes for bake sales. Who could possibly have a grudge against her?

Or maybe it wasn't personal. Maybe he'd bust in here like some horror story you see on the news, but since the children were all evacuated, she was the first person he was able to grab and threaten.

Shit. This was not the kind of scared anyone wanted, and nobody seemed to know what to do, everyone taken over by their own silent sense of dread.

Finally seeing what was happening, the DJ cut the music, his face paling.

The other parents who had volunteered were wide-eyed and frozen, and I frantically looked around for Nova, who was close to the DJ; her mouth had dropped open as she took in the scene that confronted us.

Thank God the kids had been taken out before the knife-wielding maniac put himself in the spotlight. David had returned, which meant the children were probably wondering what the hell was going on as they had no adult supervision, but at least they were out of harm's way. David remained by the door he had let the children out of, preventing them from getting back in or the intruder from getting to them. He must have been the first to spot the threat, and I was so relieved he had, or the potential for this to be worse than it already was could have been huge.

"Okay," a voice said across the room. I recognised it as Bryan, the deputy head. "Let the lady go, please, and we can talk."

The man dressed as the devil spun around to where the voice had come from, still clutching Amy in his grasp, and I could hear her sob. My heart cracked open. She must have been petrified, but I figured the reason nobody had made a move to grab her was because it would likely only put her in more danger. Whatever this arsehole wanted, we were going to have to tread carefully. It wasn't merely common sense holding everyone back, though. Shock that someone had come into our school, to an event meant for children, seemed to permeate every corner of the assembly hall.

"Please," Bryan said, as he stepped forward, closer to the middle of the room. "Let her go."

Under different circumstances, the sight might have been amusing. A vampire in confrontation with a devil was the stuff of either fantasy movies or comedy sketches, but unfortunately, this was neither. It was real, and the room held its breath as we waited to hear what this man wanted.

"Where is Gabriella Davis?"

My head swam as a voice I hadn't heard in ten years bounced off the walls in an angry snarl. I'd heard him growl my name a million times in anger. Still heard it in my nightmares sometimes. It was distinctive in the same way radio presenters have distinctive voices, with a naturally gravelled tone, which, when I'd first met him, was sexy as hell. It was only later that it sent a very different kind of shiver down my spine.

I shook my head. Was the fear coursing through me making me hear things? I'd only just realised I was trembling.

"Where is she?" he spat at Bryan.

Suddenly, all eyes searched the room for me, and my chest tightened because there was only one way this would end. There was a woman, a mother, with a knife to her throat. I didn't doubt he would hurt her or worse if I didn't move, but my feet felt stuck, and I was struggling to breathe.

He'd found me.

I'd hoped against hope that he wouldn't care to know where I was now. Wouldn't need to seek me out, but a tiny part of me had always believed he would. I just hadn't been able to tell if it was born from old fear, or if it was a true, gut instinct that still knew him well enough to understand how his mind worked.

As if it was bothering him and impeding his vision, he tore off his mask like a villain in *Scooby Doo*, and my worst fear was confirmed.

But how had he got in? The school was secure.... unless... he was the one who had damaged the fence...

"If someone doesn't tell me where the fuck Gaby is, this woman won't be going home tonight!" As if to emphasise that he wasn't kidding, he moved the knife from Amy's throat and sliced it sharply across her shoulder, making her cry out in pain before holding it back at her neck.

"I'm here," I said, finally finding my voice and taking a couple of paces out of the corner into the middle of the hall.

His eyes lit up as they fell on my shaking form. Not with fondness, but with the kind of sick delight that always came before a beating.

He hadn't changed much. Flynn was 'president of a motorcycle club' hot. He wasn't nearly as muscular as he used to be, but it was clear he was still strong. He had thick, dark stubble across his chin, perfect lips, and eyes that were beautiful but hard to pin down to one colour. They could range from deep brown to hazel depending on his mood, and for years, I had stared into them, loving him, thinking him to be my saviour while he wore me down until I believed I was lucky to have his mistreatment because, without that, I would have nothing. Nobody else would ever love me. He twisted my brain to make me think that violence paired with occasional affection was better than being on my own with my 'overweight, disgusting' body and hideous looks.

I felt like I was shrinking, reverting, just seeing him there.

"Flynn. Let her go and I will do whatever you want." I shifted my eyes in Nova's direction for the briefest moment, imploring her to understand, and when her orbs widened, I knew she did. She had the real name of the person to report, and knew to make the police see the urgency since he was known to me.

My entire body was quivering, and my legs weakened as I walked towards the man who had once destroyed me, offering myself up to him.

I thought about Guy, totally oblivious, on what was meant to be the best day of his life, my heart stuttering in my chest.

I thought about Gavin. He was going to lose it when he realised Flynn had been right under our noses.

Soon, everyone would realise how fitting Flynn's costume was because he was definitely flung out of hell. Spat out because he made Lucifer seem like a wuss.

Keep it together, I told myself, even though I felt sure I was going to collapse. *You're not the same woman he used to know. You are not those things he made you believe. You never were. You are strong.*

Those thoughts, however true, struggled to hold when I knew what I was likely to face.

I finally dropped to my knees, my legs giving out, triggering Flynn's laughter.

As I looked up, Flynn shoved Amy to the side, and she fell on the floor, crawling to the side of the room as best as she could while trying to stop the flow of blood from her shoulder, and Nova picked her up and wrapped her tight in her arms.

"This is what's going to happen," Flynn said to the room, though his words were beginning to sound distorted, as if I'd had too much to drink and everything was sliding out of focus. "I'm taking her, and you are going to let me. One of you takes a single step towards me, and I will not hesitate to slit her throat in front of you. And when I'm done with her, I'll make sure I take out as many of you as I need to. So, do yourselves a favour and let me out of here."

As desperate as I was to be saved, I inwardly prayed everyone did as he said because he was going to hurt me anyway. I was done no matter what, and at least if it was just me, I could take some comfort in that. I didn't want anyone else getting injured trying to rescue me when my fate was sealed.

While I struggled to get to my feet, Flynn marched towards me and grabbed my hair to drag me up. I didn't give him the satisfaction of making a sound. Although his appearance had rendered me weak, I was still too stunned to fully comprehend that this was happening. It was as if some well-hidden part of my brain had always been ready for it. Like a smoke alarm; you don't expect to ever need it, but you always have an idea of what you'll do if a fire breaks out. That was what this felt like. A pre-rehearsed hostage situation, except once it had become reality, the script was torn up, and all I could do was toe the line. He wrapped an arm around my middle, using his other hand to hold the knife at my throat before pulling me towards the doors.

With each step, my eyes found another person I knew. A parent, a colleague, Nova. Each one of them showing fear, shock, and horror at what had unfolded.

Once we'd made it into the cold evening air, Flynn shoved me against the wall by the door, my head slamming against the brick and dazing me.

"Well, look at you," he said, a deranged grin on his face. "Ten years. New life. New boyfriend. Friends. Still too fucking stupid to know I was watching your every move." Dropping the knife from my throat, he wrapped his hand around it instead, forcing my head up to look at him and squeezing lightly. "We're getting out of here, and I'm going to tell you all about how fun prison is. Might even show you some of the treatment I got in there. And then... well... the rest depends on how well you behave."

Before I could force a response from my lips, he slammed my head against the wall again...

Chapter 36

Guy

A YEAR OR SO ago, a lot of my time had been spent imagining this moment. The moment when Helen and I would be in the hospital, our baby on the way, and how excited we would be.

Even if we were still together, though, no amount of excitement could have counteracted the boredom of labour.

I'd been at the hospital, aside from an hour's break, since just after twelve that afternoon, and it was now quarter to seven. While Helen's contractions were slowly getting closer together, we were still a long way off the baby's arrival.

In the time I'd been there, the tension between us had eased. She'd apologised for not answering my messages, and we'd had some of the conversations we were supposed to have the day Gaby and I had gone to her place.

Because of her previous silence, I still hadn't bought anything practical for my place, not knowing what I would need, especially if it came down to court rulings, and knowing decisions might be made that meant I couldn't have my daughter at my home.

We had killed a bit of the time by looking on my phone for the things I would need because Helen agreed that after a few months, I *would* be able to look after our baby. I understood why she wouldn't want to part with her early on; I also wasn't confident in my ability to take care of a newborn on my own. I was sure I'd figure it out if I had to, but I didn't think taking a baby away from its mother overnight was right until she was a bit older. We'd also discussed money, which meant I'd explained everything to Helen about the bar, including my plan to keep it, and that while my finances might be tight for a short time, I would provide exactly what she needed to support them both. I would reassess and up any necessary payments every time I could afford to, and Helen was appreciative of that.

"Bloody hell," Helen said from her place on the bed, dropping her head back against the metal-framed headboard. "The fact that women go through this multiple times blows my mind."

I chuckled. Her blonde hair had been thrown up on her head, but loose strands were falling free, and she looked tired. Not surprising since she'd been having pains since eight that morning.

"You don't think you'll want more children one day?" I asked, pouring a cup of water from the jug on the table at the side of her bed and taking a sip.

She fixed me with a deadpan stare. "Not in a million years." As if to emphasise the point, she winced slightly, and I put my cup down and offered her my hand. She breathed in deeply, then grabbed it, closing her eyes tightly while she let out a low groan of discomfort.

"You're okay," I said gently, stepping around the table so I could stand right beside her, gently stroking her hair as she breathed her way through the contraction.

Once it had passed, her forehead sweaty, she turned her head to look at me. "Thanks."

It was a strange situation to be in, with the woman I used to love, who I was pretty sure still loved me, trying to do what I could to make this easier but both of us knowing our feelings no longer matched. I'd been so pissed off with her because of the way she'd treated Gaby. I knew this wasn't what Helen wanted, to see me with someone else, but it wasn't as if she hadn't been a huge part of the reason we'd split up. It wasn't like I was seeing Gaby behind her back and this was all on me. I didn't expect her to be happy that I was with someone new, but I *did* expect her to respect it. To respect Gaby. But she hadn't.

Regardless, though, Helen was the mother of my child, and she was in pain, getting ready to deliver the most incredible gift we could have ever asked for.

"It's okay. I'm sorry your mum couldn't be here."

Helen shook her head, more of her hair slipping free. "I'm not. She would have driven me up the wall. It's going to be bad enough when she comes to stay with me for a few weeks. I did want my sister here, but I *had* to go into labour on the one night of the year she had nobody to watch the kids for her!"

Apparently, her husband was working away for a couple of days, and the people she would have normally called to look after her children were all unavailable. I had never much cared for Helen's sister, so it would have been even more awkward with her there. Still, it would have helped Helen to have extra support.

Giving her hand a final squeeze, I said, "Do you want some water?"

"Please."

Once I'd given her the drink, I said, "Will you be okay for a minute? I need to ring Cal and talk to him about work tomorrow as I probably won't be going in."

With another grateful smile, she said, "I'm fine. Go."

I nodded, then went outside the room Helen was in and stood in the corridor, blowing out a breath. Somehow, being out of the confined space made me feel like I was back to reality, Helen's hospital room a kind of cocoon where time was all jacked up and the rest of the world had paused while we waited for the most important moment of our lives.

Now, though, seeing people wandering up and down the corridor, some rushing, others taking it slowly, I remembered there *was* life outside, and I pulled my phone from my pocket so I could take care of some business.

As I looked at the screen, I saw eight missed calls from Cal, three from Shannen, and one from a number I didn't recognise.

I'd had my phone on silent, not even on vibrate because I didn't want any interruptions while Helen and I were actually communicating.

If Cal needed something, he would usually call twice at the most, then leave a message. The fact that he'd tried so many times, as had Shannen, all of which had occurred in the last ten minutes made my pulse pound.

It was still early evening. He'd probably only left the bar half an hour or so ago.

Oh, Christ. What if something had gone wrong?

Picturing my project going up in flames, I hit the button to return Cal's call, my heart hammering in my ears.

"Guy! Where the fuck have you been?" Cal asked frantically.

I presumed that was rhetorical because he knew exactly where I was. "What's wrong?" I asked. "What's happened?"

There was a long silence, and I could hear his heavy breaths down the line, which did nothing to ease my nerves. "It's Gaby."

My legs seemed to fold without my instruction, and thankfully, there was a chair behind me, which I sagged into. I hadn't been expecting Gaby's name to come from his mouth, and it didn't make me feel any better to hear something was wrong with her and not the bar.

But wasn't she still at the school disco? What could be causing Cal to sound so anxious?

"What about her?" I asked. "Is she all right?"

There was another pause before I heard some muffled voices in the background, and then Shannen's voice hit my ears. "Guy, something awful has happened, but I'm going to need you to stay calm until I've finished, okay?"

"I don't think I can promise that." There was an ominous air to this entire call, their voices afraid and serious. My heart was now banging so fast it was beginning to ache, and I put my hand over my chest, hoping it would slow down before I passed out.

"Fuck," she said, which told me exactly how concerned I should be. Shannen hardly ever swore. "So... Aiden was at the school disco tonight. The parents were meant to pick up the younger kids at half past six, ready for the bigger kids to come in later, but Nova called me at a bit after six because... while the disco was going on, there was... a man. He grabbed one of the volunteers, and he was threatening her with a knife if Gaby didn't come forward. Guy, it was... it was her ex. He came into the school in a Halloween costume, and... he's taken her."

Blinking, I tried to understand everything I'd just heard, but it was hard with blood roaring in my ears and my heart trying to rip its way out of my chest.

If he was so close, why Gavin hadn't been able to find him, though?

"Where?" I said quietly.

"I don't know," she answered, her voice cracking. "I don't know. I... I went to the school to pick Aiden up, and I spoke to Nova. She's a mess. All the staff are. But there are a lot of police there, taking statements and trying to find out as much as they can. I just... I'm so sorry."

She began to cry, and I could only imagine how horrific it must have been to get the call that her best friend had been taken, the call from her other best friend, who had seen it happen. They were supposed to be going out in a couple of hours. They were supposed to be in the pub soon, laughing together.

My entire body was stiffening, tension and anger filling every muscle until I let out a roar that made a passing doctor jump and hurry away.

"What do I do?" I snapped. "I... what do I do?" Gaby had been snatched from her workplace by her ex, and Shannen knew as well as I did what he'd done to her before. What he might do again. How much worse it might be after ten years of stewing on the fact that she'd got him locked up.

"I don't know," Shannen said again, her sobs breaking my heart further. "I'm scared. I don't know how to help you or her, and Cal's trying to take care of Aiden because he doesn't understand what's happened. He just knows the place he goes to school is swarming with police. Neither of us has the heart to tell him the truth."

Standing up on less than steady legs, I said, "I can't sit around not knowing what's going on. Should I go to the school? Do I call her brother?"

Fuck. That was what I needed to do first, but there were still more thoughts in my head that I needed to purge.

"How do I get updates?" I asked. "Who do I need to speak to?"

"I think... me," she said softly. "The police aren't going to be able to keep everyone updated, so Iris, the headmistress, has gone down to the school, and she'll be the one they liaise with. She will tell me what she can, when she can, but even that's going to be limited."

I growled again, frustration bubbling inside me harder.

Gaby had been missing for almost an hour now. He could have taken her anywhere. Be doing anything to her.

I knew way too much about the way he'd mistreated her in the past. He'd almost killed her once. Had he come back to finish what he'd started?

My throat began to close over. I'd seen Gaby afraid recently, and that was minimal compared to what she used to endure from him. How was she going to handle being with him again now? Was she going to go back to how afraid she used to be, or would her inner fire kick in? And if it did, would it do her more harm than good with someone as nasty as Flynn?

I felt like my insides were caving in, like the rage and fear forming internally was crushing me. I was helpless. I wanted to run. To jump into my car and drive around the city until I found her, but where the hell would I even start?

Moreover, Helen was in labour. How could I leave her?

"Shannen," I said, my voice coming out croaky. "I need to let her brother know what's happening, but once that's done... I'll call you back in case you have any updates. Please ring me if you hear anything before then, okay?"

"Of course," she promised. "I know this is a nightmare, Guy, but let the police handle it. They'll find her."

I wasn't sure *she* even believed that, but I knew she was only trying to help. She likely felt as useless as I did, and as much as it was my instinct to snap that I had little faith in the police, I just said, "Yeah. I'll talk to you in a bit."

She uttered a choked goodbye, and as I hung up, I squeezed my phone hard in my hand, wanting to throw it, to smash something, but I needed it to stay in touch with Shannen. I began to pace, thinking about what hell I was going to say to Gavin; this was going to destroy him. He'd spent weeks trying to track that prick down, looking into Flynn's family and friends, only to find out he was here the whole time. Right in front of us. Right in front of Gaby. Should I wait to tell Gavin? Leave it until I knew more?

No. The chances were, the fact that someone had abducted a teacher from a school disco was already making its way onto social media, and what if he heard about it before I could tell him?

I swore under my breath and pulled up Gavin's number, not giving myself time to back out, and whacked the call button.

It rang and rang until the voicemail kicked in. Maybe he was still working. I knew he worked past eight a lot of evenings. I wasn't sure leaving a message about this was the best way, so I sent him a text asking him to call me when he could. I scratched my head, my brain no longer my own.

I couldn't decide what to do for the best. Five minutes before, I was about to call Cal about work, and now, none of it mattered. I would have taken my bar burning down, my entire livelihood going up in smoke if it meant Gaby would get back to me unharmed. No matter how I looked at it, though, I couldn't see how that could be the case. Flynn didn't take her so they could have a cup of coffee and reminisce about their—minimal—good times. He had gone into that school with a knife. He only had one intention, and that was to hurt her.

"Guy?"

Turning, I saw Helen standing in the doorway to her room, and mentally shaking myself, I rushed towards her, taking her gently by the arm. "What are you doing? Get back on the bed."

"I heard you shout. What's wrong?" She seemed genuinely worried, so Christ knew what the expression on my face was. As I attempted to steer her back into the room, she planted her feet firmly, looking up at me.

I didn't even know what to say. My heart was still thundering, a heavy, stifling tension threatening to suffocate me because while I'd understood what Shannen had said to me, I was still struggling to accept it. I didn't want to accept it.

"I... it's..."

Before I could finish, my phone lit up in my hand, Cal's name on the screen.

"Helen, go back in and sit down. I need to get this."

It was only the fact that she was so tired that made her feet shuffle back to the bed. If she could have stayed and stared me down, she would have. I moved further into the room to make sure she actually did sit down, then answered the phone.

"Hey," I said, my heart rate notching up again at the prospect of news.

"Hey," Cal said, his voice lowered as if he was trying not to be overheard. "Look, I have a lead and Shannen will kill me if she finds out I'm doing this, but we can't wait for the police to get their shit together. I need to be quick because she's upstairs with Aiden and I don't know how long she'll be. Shannen, Nova, and Gaby have their Snapchat locations shared with each other. Shannen thought of it after she hung up with you. She's messaged Nova to pass the information along to the police since she's still at the school, but by the time she's spoken to someone…" He trailed off, not needing to finish.

"Tell me where she is," I demanded.

"No."

"No?" I hissed. "He's fucking taken her, and the longer he has her, the less chance there is of someone finding her alive! I can't lose her, Cal. I can't lose her." In spite of the anger, emotion took over, the very idea of never seeing Gaby again making me want to simultaneously throw up and collapse into a heap and never get up again.

"Hey, take it easy," Cal said. "I'm coming to get you. I'm not letting you rock up to this place on your own, but I need to go now before Shannen comes back downstairs and stops me."

"You can't just walk out. She'll be worried sick about where you've gone, and she's already worried enough."

"Then I'll tell her I'm going out to pick up a takeaway. She hasn't eaten because she was going to eat when she went out. Look, the longer you argue with me about this, the less chance there is of me getting out, so shut the fuck up and meet me in front entrance of the hospital. I'll be about ten minutes."

He hung up, and I stared at the phone, wondering what the hell just happened.

What happened is that Cal stepped up. Knowing the risk Gaby was at, knowing the police could drag their heels, knowing that Shannen, Nova, and I were all going out of our minds, he was willing to put his own ass on the line to help me get my girl back.

"Guy… what…" Helen said, then paused, taking in a sharp intake of breath and slamming me back to the moment. She moved her hands onto her baby bump and slowed down her breathing, and I went to her side and took her hand again until it passed. Once it was over, she said, "Tell me what's going on."

"It's Gaby," I said, still holding her hand because, ill-advised as it might have been, I actually needed her support right then. "Her ex... it's a long story, but he used to... he hurt her. He's been in jail for ten years for what he did to her, but now he's out, and tonight... he took her. From the school's Halloween disco. But Cal has managed to get her location, or at least the location of her phone..." I paused.

What if that was all it was? What if, when we got to wherever it was, she wasn't there, and Flynn had tossed her phone away to make her untraceable?

I couldn't let myself finish the thought. She had to be there. She had to.

Her eyes widened. "Jesus. I... I..."

Sentences with everyone I was speaking to were becoming harder and harder to finish, and I said, "Helen, I have to go. I have to get to her. I'm so sorry."

Helen's eyes filled with tears, but she swallowed hard. "I... Guy... I don't want to do this alone."

Closing my eyes, I let go of her hand and wrapped my arms around her. "I'm sorry," I said again. "I don't want you to do this alone either, but..."

"Go," she said against my chest. I could feel how little she wanted to let me leave when her arms squeezed me tight, but as much as she disliked Gaby, I knew she understood. She was a bitch sometimes, but underneath all of that, she had a heart.

I kissed the top of her head. "I'll be back as soon as I can," I promised.

"You'd better be," she said. "Be careful, please. Do not leave our daughter without a father."

Until then, I hadn't considered that I might be putting myself in danger because Gaby was all that mattered. I *had* briefly considered Shannen's concern that something might happen to Cal if she knew where he was going, but my own safety hadn't crossed my mind. The adrenaline was making me reckless, and as I felt Helen shaking against me, the enormity of it all washed over me.

Getting hurt was not an option. I had to get Gaby, and I had to get back here to support Helen and meet my baby.

I nodded, no longer able to speak through the lump in my throat. Hugging Helen one more time, I rushed out the door, almost positive I heard her sob, "I love you," as I left.

Chapter 37

Gaby

BLINKING, I WAS VAGUELY aware of a dull ache at the back of my head.

Was I... asleep?

No. I was blinking.

Why can't I see anything?

The pain in my head intensified, but I forced myself to widen my eyes, just to ensure they were definitely open, but I still couldn't see anything but total blackness. I couldn't sense anything covering my eyes either, and I gasped in panic. In my state of utter horror, I had no idea if I was sitting or lying down. I tried to move my limbs, but my arms, I realised, were bound behind me. My legs were free, but I was, from what I could gather, tied to a chair, and I cried out, wriggling so frantically and suffocating in the blackness that the chair tumbled sideways, and I hit the hard ground, my left shoulder taking the brunt.

I tried to take in some breaths, but my heart was pounding so wildly that all I could do was gulp at the air, my chest wheezing with the effort of attempting to fill my lungs. It was all too much; the inability to breathe and move my arms, the pain in my head and shoulder, but mostly... the lack of vision.

There was nothing. I wasn't sure even the darkest room I'd ever been in had been without the tiniest chink of light somewhere. Usually, when you wake up in the dark, after a minute or two, your eyes adjust, but nothing was changing.

And that was when I remembered.

I'd hit my head. Well, no. Flynn had smashed it against the wall...

Flynn.

He'd taken me. He'd had a knife pressed against my neck, and he'd abducted me in front of my colleagues in the school hall.

He wasn't here, though, was he? Because if he was, he would have almost certainly let me know when he saw I'd woken up and tipped the chair over.

The thought heartened me for a second because if he wasn't in this place with me, then maybe I could get out. I assumed it was inside because it was reasonably warm. Warmer than outside, anyway. It had been windy earlier, and I couldn't feel a breeze or anything that suggested I was outdoors.

Would be easier if you could see!

The thought jolted my terror to life again, but there had to be a door somewhere. If I could get my hands untied, then I could crawl around, feel my way out.

Telling myself over and over that I wasn't blind, it was just the fear, or maybe a temporary result of hitting my head, I wriggled my hands, but the bindings were tight. Rough; probably rope.

But I did still have the use of my legs.

Like an injured worm, I pushed my side into the floor, the chair still attached to me, and used my legs to inch me forwards. I wasn't sure where I was going, but the fact that I was going anywhere ignited a small spark of hope. My shoulder was agony, and my head was still thumping, but I had to push on and see where the exit was.

Breathing hard, I cried out with every tiny push towards what I prayed was an escape, the only thing on my mind in that moment my safety.

"It won't do you any good."

I screamed when Flynn's voice shattered the silence, and then again when a torch flicked on. He was holding it up so it illuminated only his face, like we were in a horror movie. I barely had time to register my relief that I could see before he charged towards me, grabbing me by the arm and then lifting the chair so I was upright again.

Quick as a flash, he flicked the torch off, and we were plunged back into complete darkness. I'd barely managed to regulate my breathing when my pulse began to race again. I could feel him near. Could hear his breathing now, but I was still so disorientated that I couldn't work out exactly where he was. Then, I heard footsteps, sounding as if they were pacing away from me, and finally, a light came on overhead, making me flinch from the shock of the brightness. I couldn't cover my eyes, so I squeezed them shut, blinking slowly to allow my sight to adjust.

When I could bear to fully open them, I let my gaze flick around the space. The floor was stone, the walls well-maintained brick, and although there was absolutely nothing in there apart from me, Flynn, and the chair I was sitting on, there were traces of what looked like hay on the floor. Maybe an old barn of some kind? It didn't smell of animals, though. It didn't smell of anything, so maybe it had been empty for a while. It was a long-ish building, and Flynn stood at the far end, near the light switch and the doors. Still in his devil outfit.

"Where are we?" I asked, even though there were a million more things rushing through my head.

What time was it? How long had I been unconscious? How did he know where to find me? Why had he come?

Was anyone going to be able to find me?

My body was trembling now I could see him, adrenaline, terror, confusion, the blazing of my shoulder, and the pounding in my head all fighting for first place in the race for what I should try to deal with next. It was too much, and as Flynn slowly, with calculated steps, strode towards me, I couldn't get any of it under control. All I could see was the monster before me. The one I'd spent years purging from my brain, unpicking his taunts and learning how to live again.

"Where are we?" he repeated as he stood in front of me, cruel smirk in place. "That's the first thing you want to know? Not why you're here? Why you're only half tied up and not completely bound? Why I've been watching your every move since September? How I got into the school? Why it took me so long to get my hands on you?" He laughed, shaking his head as if there was something funny about any of this. "You never did have much of an imagination."

My jaw was beginning to ache from trying to bite back a response.

During my time in therapy, I was once asked what I would say to him if I had the chance. That day, I'd roared out words of rage and deep-buried pain until my throat was sore and I felt empty, collapsing and sobbing so hard that there wasn't an inch of me that didn't hurt.

The thing was, even though I hadn't told *him*, I'd said it. All the things I needed to release from my mind and heart to move on were left in a safe, warm therapist's office.

Now, I was no longer safe. And I didn't want him to hear how much he'd ruined me. He knew, and hearing it would only increase his enjoyment of this situation.

But I also didn't want to allow him to crawl under my skin. I could see it happening already.

He hadn't tied my legs up for two likely reasons. The first being that he wanted me to feel that hope I'd felt as I'd tried to crawl away to find a door, only for him to snatch it away at the last minute. The second was because he was planning to violate me, but I would not allow that thought to take hold. If I was paralysed by notions of what might be, I wouldn't have enough strength left to fight.

And I *would* fight.

With another quick move, he rushed forward so he was right in my face, grabbing my chin in his fingers and squeezing hard. "You know what the best thing about this is, Gaby? I'm untraceable. Even if I did tell you where you were, it's not going to matter in a few hours anyway." His smile was nothing short of pure evil, his eyes wide and manic. "But until then, let's catch up, shall we?"

Untraceable...

My phone. My phone was in the pocket of my dress, and I had my location turned on. A small sliver of hope slid into my psyche again, but as quickly as it appeared, it vanished, because what if nobody remembered? Nova knew we shared Snapchat locations, but I saw her face as Flynn dragged me away. She'd been petrified. What if it didn't occur to her that she was the key to helping me?

Flynn delivered a sharp slap to my cheek, then a harder one, and although it stung, I refused to flinch, somewhat buoyed by the fact that there was a chance someone could find me.

"Oh, good," he said, smirk back in place. "You think you're tough again now, don't you?" He reached forward for my throat, but not harshly. His touch was gentle as his fingers stroked lightly against my skin, and I tilted my head back, trying to move away. "What's up? Afraid you might like it?"

I wanted to lurch forward and rip his fingers off with my teeth to keep him from touching me again, and as he barked out a laugh, he said, "As I was saying... this bravado is great for me. It means I'll enjoy it even more when I break you again."

Chapter 38

Nova

I SAT IN THE school staff room, a blanket around my shoulders, my hands wrapped around a rapidly cooling cup of tea. Police officers were talking to my colleagues and the parents who had been volunteering at the Halloween disco.

About two hours ago, said disco had been hijacked by a psychopath with a knife, and chaos had taken over Oakwood Lane Primary School.

I'd watched, heart in my throat and motionless, as Gaby was pulled out of the school hall by her ex. I'd never known silence like the aftermath. In my arms, Amy was crying after being Flynn's first victim. He'd sliced her shoulder, and she'd needed medical attention, but it took a solid five minutes before any of us was able to comprehend what went down.

And then, several people moved at once. I heard someone shouting directions to others, people rushing around, but I just kept holding Amy until she was eventually taken from me to see to her wound.

At that point, Bryan came over and asked me to help as we needed to call the parents of the children at the disco to get them collected. Unable to even speak, he instead asked me to accompany David in seeing to the kids, and that was what shook me out of my daze.

Innocent children needed taking care of, probably confused about why they'd all been shown out of the hall, away from their disco, and left alone in the corridor.

That whole time was a blur, but I helped David talk to them, told them there was an accident, and that their parents were coming to get them. We'd had no direction on what to say, we just knew we couldn't say, "Miss Davis was kidnapped." It wasn't really up to us to traumatise them; we just had to reassure them until they were collected and taken home.

We had all been interviewed about what happened, and I made sure to pounce on the first police officer on the scene, slightly hysterical, to explain who had Gaby and the danger he posed.

I'd given them the information about Gaby's Snapchat location too, and while they didn't exactly head out in a rush, they had gone to check it out, and I hoped we'd hear something soon because my stomach was churning. That was why my tea was getting cold. I wasn't sure I could keep it down.

"Hey, Nova. How are you doing?"

I looked up as Iris sat down beside me and wrapped an arm around my blanketed shoulders. She looked exhausted. Her day had already been fraught with fires she'd had to put out, and this was the icing on the horrific cake. Iris hadn't been at the disco; she'd come in after she was told what had happened, and although it fell on her to stay strong, the worry lines on her face gave away her true feelings.

"I don't know," I answered. "I'm just sitting here, praying to hear good news."

With a soft smile, Iris said, "You and me both. You know, if you want to go home, I can call you the second I get word from the police."

I shook my head. "I was meant to be staying at Gaby's tonight." The words caught in my throat, visions of her, Shannen, and me having dinner and drinks out and catching up filling my head. "I'm not leaving until I know where she is."

But the longer our phones stayed silent, the less confident I was that we would hear anything good, my heart sinking further into my stomach with every tick of the clock. I'd checked her Snapchat location every ten minutes since she'd been gone, unsure whether to be heartened or afraid by the lack of movement. If she still had her phone, then she would be found soon. If not...

"I understand," Iris said. "I think it's going to be a long night."

"What will we do about school tomorrow?" I asked, turning my cup around in my hands. "What will we tell the kids? Will we even be able to open?"

"It really depends on how long the police are here. Technically, it's a crime scene, and they're having a good look around now and still talking to a few people. It also depends on..." She sighed, and I nodded.

If Gaby was safe and well, we'd probably be able to carry on as normal in the morning. If not, though... I wasn't sure what the protocol was if a teacher was murdered. Would we have to just suck it up and get to work?

I moved a hand to my stomach as it churned, bile creeping up my throat at the idea that that might be the outcome.

As if the thought was too much for her, Iris let out a small whimper, covering her mouth with her hand, her head bowed. I'd never seen her anything other than totally put together, and I put my cup on the table and turned so I could hug her, triggering my own tears.

"You know, Gaby was one of the first new teachers that joined the school after I became the head," she said, her voice cracking. "She breezed in here, all confident and bubbly, and I knew right away how much the kids would love her. And they do."

"Everyone does," I said, my mind leaping to Guy as it had several times over the past couple of hours. "I-"

"I found this!"

David rushed into the staff room, turning the sombre mood to one of anticipation as he held a backpack aloft between his thumb and forefinger, as if afraid to get his fingerprints on it.

"Put that down carefully!" a male officer said. He'd been standing by Iris's office door talking with another officer, both of them panic-stricken at David's discovery.

David whipped his head around to look at him, and the officer held up his hands as if to ask for calm.

"Seriously," he said. "It's probably nothing, but please lower that down carefully."

Did he think there was a bomb in that bag or something? I leapt out of my seat, as did Iris, and we both backed away slightly, a new threat suddenly presented.

"I don't think there's much in it," David said as he very gingerly placed the bag on the floor close to where the officers stood then took a few steps backwards. "It's really light, and it's a bit open too. It looks like it's just clothes."

The male officer, whose name I hadn't caught, moved towards the backpack. "Where did you find it?" he asked.

"In the toilets," David answered. "The ones just beside the hall. I went in to make sure all the lights were off, and it was under the sinks. None of the kids have backpacks that big, and the teachers wouldn't leave stuff there."

"Why would the devil leave it there?" one of the female parents asked, a frown on her face. Because most people had no idea exactly who Flynn was, everyone had been referring to him as 'the devil,' and they weren't wrong. "Is he trying to get caught?"

"Not necessarily," the officer said, tentatively unzipping the main compartment of the bag. "If it is just clothes, he probably didn't care about them being found. It's not like we can track him down just from that."

The room seemed to hold its breath as he carefully opened the bag and put his hand inside. He pulled out first a light blue T-shirt and placed it on the floor. Going in again, he took out a pair of jeans, belt attached, and put them on top of the T-shirt. His hand went into the bag a third time, and he slowly moved it around as if checking for anything else, and then he pulled out a handful of photos. He laid them one by one on the carpet, and as if we'd decided a bomb threat was no longer a concern, Iris, David, the female officer, and I all moved forward to inspect them.

The first I recognised as Gaby's social media profile picture. How had he found her through that, though? She didn't use her real name online. She went by Davina Gabriel, a name she'd picked because it used many of the letters from her legal name, but not one easily guessed. As my gaze fell on the rest of the photos, it was clear to me he'd been looking at her profile because he'd taken photos she'd been tagged in too. One was of her wearing the bat wings I had been sporting earlier when she'd dressed as a bad for a charity run with some people from the gym. Another was of me and her from the previous year's carnival; I'd had it as my own profile picture for a time, and I'd forgotten to make it private once I'd changed it. The other photos were of her at various events, and in each one, she was beaming in that very Gaby-like way that made everyone adore her. What was most striking, though, was that the eyes of each picture of Gaby had been stabbed through, vacant holes in the place of her pretty green orbs.

Blinking back tears, I moved away, unable to bear looking at photos of her, the concept of never seeing that face again making nausea rise again. I moved right away, standing by the window and looking out. The lights of the police cars were still bright in the front car park, and I saw a couple of our volunteers leaving.

I wished more than anything that Donovan wasn't so far away. I could have used one of his tight hugs, hearing his voice reassuring me things would be okay. To have his comfort to help block out some of the worry. I missed him so much. He still wasn't sure if he'd be able to come home next week, but I'd kept my fingers crossed. Now more than ever, I needed to see him and be grateful that I had him, while Guy... he didn't know if he was ever going to see the woman he loved again.

At least Shannen had Cal... well, she would have if he hadn't slipped out of the house to look for Gaby.

Christ, I hoped he and Guy were safe. So many people were at risk, and why the hell had we heard no word about the Snapchat location? Someone must have got there by now to check it out. I was considering calling Shannen to check in when Iris said, "Nova, over here."

There was an urgency to her tone, and I turned to see her beckoning me across the room. The police officer was holding a well-crumpled piece of paper in his hand, and I walked over, brow furrowed.

"This was in the bag. Do you know what any of this means?" he asked, handing it to me.

I wrinkled my nose as I took it. The paper looked as though it had been in that backpack for a while. It wasn't just crumpled; bits of it were ripped, and it felt weird. A bit damp, like perhaps a bottle of water had leaked near it at some point. Some of the blue ink had run, but it was readable.

Written in scruffy handwriting were four addresses. Three of them were in Exeter, the fourth in Sidmouth.

"The first one is Gaby's address," I said, my hands shaking a bit as I tried to work out what the others were. "I don't know about the other Exeter addresses but... the Sidmouth one might be close to the Snapchat location." I'd stared at it often enough to know the street name.

"We still haven't had any information from our team out there yet," the officer told me, and I tried hard not to glare. It wasn't his fault, but couldn't he just radio them or something?

"Would Shannen know what the others are?" Iris asked, hope beginning to bloom in her eyes.

I shook my head. "Not sure. Do you want me to phone her?"

I glanced at the police officer, and he said, "If you know someone who might be able to shed some light, by all means, talk to them."

Or you could just send someone to each location to check them out, I snarled inwardly, but aloud I said, "I'll try."

Chapter 39

Guy

THE POLICE HAD SHOWED up at the abandoned property about fifteen minutes after Cal and me. Cal had explained what we'd found, which was pretty much nothing, while I was sitting, leaning against the outhouse wall and trying to dig up some optimism from the toxic pit my brain had turned into.

"Mr Danielson, I'm Officer Allen."

I looked up to see a uniformed policeman standing in front of me. I guessed he was a lot younger than me; he had a youthful face, one not marred by years on the force. His smile was empathetic, and although it was his job to look that way, I kind of wanted to punch it off his face. I didn't want empathy, I wanted answers.

"There is no evidence that your girlfriend was here for any significant period of time," he went on. "As this is private property, we need to leave."

"And where would you like me to go?" I asked, trying to keep the anger out of my voice. "Because from what I can tell, you don't have any idea where we should be looking next."

"Sir, I think it would be better if you went home. We-"

"Home?" I snapped. "Gaby is missing, in the hands of a man with a knife, and you want me to go home, and what? Try and watch a movie and relax?"

"Guy," Cal said, hurrying over. He'd been speaking to the other officer; four had showed up, but two had already left. Probably back to the station for a cuppa because they'd hit a dead end here.

"I'm not going home! We need to keep looking!"

"We will," Cal said.

"Actually," Officer Allen said, "this is a police matter. If you have any thoughts on places we should look, then you need to tell us and let us handle it."

Cal stood directly in front of me at the speed of light, sensing I was about to erupt. I got to my feet anyway, once again overcome by an adrenaline spike, my muscles coiled and ready to spring into action.

"You can't expect us to sit around and do nothing," Cal told him. "There must be something we can do to help."

Static crackled through his radio before he could answer, and then my phone rang from my jacket pocket. For a second, the deluded hope that it might be Gaby made my heart leap, but of course, it couldn't be. Her phone was broken and now in the hands of the police, who'd taken it away as evidence.

I didn't recognise the number on the screen, so I assumed it was probably going to be someone wanting some painting and decorating done.

But what if it wasn't?

I unlocked the phone to answer the call, moving slightly away from Cal and Officer Allen. "Hello?"

"Is that Guy?"

The voice was female, nervous, but again, not a voice I recognised immediately. "Yeah, who's this?"

"It's Nova."

344

My heart sank, not because I didn't want to hear from her but because I knew she was as distraught as I was. It was laced into her words.

"Hey, Nova," my tone softened. "Are you okay?"

"Erm, maybe ask me an easier question." A bitter chuckle left my lips, understanding exactly what she meant. "Are you with the police?"

"I am." I glanced at them, and they were watching me as I paced around. "Why?"

She sighed. "Okay, so we found Flynn's backpack in the school." The mention of his name caused fury to shoot through me. "Right at the bottom, there was a piece of paper, and it has some addresses on it. One is Gaby's, one is the place in Sidmouth that you checked out, and the other two I didn't know, so I spoke to Shannen. One of the addresses is yours, but we don't know who the last one belongs to."

What the fuck?

Flynn had our addresses? How and why? And if he had Gaby's address, why go to the trouble of breaking into the school to get her?

Trying to understand the workings of a criminal was a pointless task, so I said, "Have the police sent anyone to the addresses?" There was no way Flynn could have got into my building, but what if he was actually holding Gaby at her own flat?

It was a twisted notion, but not beyond the realms of possibility for someone like him, who had clearly had a plan in place.

"Not yet. We just want to see if you know where this last address is first. See if anything makes sense." She reeled the address off, and before she even finished, I interrupted.

"That's where Gaby's brother lives."

Nova relayed the information to whoever she was with, then said, "Thanks, Guy. This might not lead to anything, but it's all we have right now. I have to go, but... be careful, okay?"

I promised her I would before hanging up.

345

My brain couldn't comprehend why that arsehole had made this so difficult for himself. Why take Gaby at an event where people would quickly report her missing? Where he had revealed who he was? Why not just take her from her place? Or even when she was leaving mine or Gavin's if he knew where we all lived.

Unless… it didn't matter who knew because he wasn't planning on being around to face the consequences.

The incessant racing of my heart fired up once more. What if this was sensationalism for him? He'd been stuck behind bars for a decade. The only thing he'd had in there was time. Time to plot revenge.

His life was already over with his family discarding him and likely his 'friends' too. If he had nothing left to lose, why not go out with maximum attention? Especially if he thought nobody would be able to find him anyway.

An additional thought struck me.

Gavin's property was huge. The first time Gaby took me there, she'd showed me around the grounds. He had the most impressive garden, and a fair amount of land at the back that…

The outhouses.

Gavin had outhouses on his property set way back. Gaby had said he'd never decided what to do with them, so they just sat there, unused. They were accessible from the road that ran behind the house, but they weren't visible from Gavin's home because of the trees that lined the fence at the back of his garden. I'd questioned the security because there was a gate that led out onto the rest of his land, and Gaby had said it was all protected with cameras. But the field beyond wasn't.

I hadn't heard back from Gavin yet. It wasn't impossible that he was still at work, but it wasn't like him not to call me back, especially when I'd asked him to.

Shit. I hoped nothing had happened to him.

But the addresses had to mean something. Maybe places to scope out. This place had obviously been some kind of decoy, just in case her phone was trackable. He could have just flung it anywhere, but perhaps it was deliberate, to send us miles out of the way while he got a head start on whatever he was doing to her.

"She's at Gavin's," I said, more to Cal than the police officers, my pulse beating a dangerous rhythm. "That's where he's got her."

At the same time I spoke, the officers were getting a message through their radios with the information I'd just shared with Nova. That they had addresses, and who they belonged to now they had a complete picture.

I didn't wait for any further instructions or listen to the shouts to come back. I ran towards the car, Cal hot on my heels.

Chapter 40

Gaby

MY HEAD.

It felt like someone was constantly banging it against a wall, the ache thudding through me and draining my energy.

Time was no longer real. I could have been tied up for hours or days.

Flynn had said he was going to enjoy breaking me, but my will to prove he couldn't was dwindling more and more.

Nobody had come for me yet. Which meant either my phone battery had died, or nobody had remembered about Snapchat.

But they would. I had to keep that tiny grain of belief close. Without it, it would be game over. Someone *would* come, even though Flynn had made it clear that nobody cared about me enough to try.

Flynn had said we were going to 'catch up.' I'd believed that to mean he was going to re-introduce me to his fists. Weirdly, though, since the slaps and the stroking of my throat, he'd backed off. He sat on the ground in front of me, knife in his hands, telling me about his time in jail. It was eerie. I felt like I was a counsellor and he was my patient, processing his ten years behind bars.

I knew what it really was. It was a trick. His words weren't fabricated, but in acting so calm, he was trying to lull me into a false sense of safety.

Unfortunately for him, I'd spent long enough around him to know I was never safe with him. Or maybe *that* was what he was banking on. Setting me so on edge that I was too exhausted to fend off an attack.

That was his superpower. Unpredictability.

Now, he paced around me. He'd slipped his knife into the waistband of his trousers, the handle visible to remind me he was armed. His silence was unnerving. When we were together, he would do this. Sometimes, he wouldn't speak to me for days. Back then, I was so desperate for him to love me that I begged him to say something, to show me some ounce of affection, even though I knew it wouldn't come in the form I wanted. I was fucked up enough to think that his insults were better than no words at all.

"You're different," he said, his voice harsh. "But not so different that the silence doesn't bother you."

"It doesn't bother me," I said, the first words from my mouth in forever. It was a lie, but at least my tone sounded confident.

"No?" he challenged. "So, at any moment, you aren't going to offer to suck my dick, just so I'll talk to you?"

The suggestion made me want to vomit "You put your dick anywhere near my mouth and I'll bite it off."

He laughed darkly, and without warning, he grabbed a handful of my hair from behind, tugging hard so my neck snapped backwards, and the sting from where I'd hit my head made me cry out. "You're not fun anymore. I liked you better when you did what I wanted you to."

Sensing it wouldn't be wise to speak, I clamped my jaw shut, holding back my response and trying to pretend he wasn't hurting me. He yanked harder, increasing the pain in my head.

"Earlier, you asked me where you are," he continued. "It proves how stupid you continue to be that you don't recognise it."

His insult was another chip at my resolve. One of his old favourites was attacks on my intelligence. This was his warm-up. Small digs until he'd hit me with enough that I began to weaken.

"It's an empty structure," I said through gritted teeth. "It could be anywhere."

"But it's not just anywhere." Flynn let go of my hair, shoving my head forward as he released his grip. "It's somewhere you know well." He walked around so he was in front of me again, and I slowly raised my head.

His eyes were dark but with a glint in them that told me how much he was enjoying this. I wouldn't have been surprised if he was getting off on it, but I refused to look anywhere other than his face.

Before that day, the last time I'd seen him was when he was looming over my semi-conscious form, my eyes swollen from his hits and my body screaming for some respite from the pain he'd inflicted. Even dazed and confused, I'd wondered what I saw in him. Physically attractive as he was, I'd stopped seeing that long ago, yet I'd still craved his love because I thought I'd made him do those awful things to me. That if I was a bit thinner, studied harder, worked harder, wore things that would please him and ensured he was satisfied, he would go back to showing me the good kind of attention. Affection.

The truth was, he was a bully, and nothing would have ever been enough.

Looking at him now, that was still all I saw. The monster trying to get his claws into me. Into my head.

He wanted me to ask where I was. He wanted me to give him a reaction, to beg, to plead with him to let me go. But I wouldn't.

Because eventually, when he was ready to end this, I'd need my strength. To fight him now would be a waste of my effort. I was already drained. I needed to conserve what little energy I had left. My insides were trembling, and I knew he wouldn't have missed the shake of my hands, the small, involuntary signs of fear that ballooned and contracted with each of his movements.

In a swift move I didn't see coming, he lunged forward, his fingers tightening around my throat. "You want to know how I know you're still an idiot?" he snapped as I struggled to breathe. He'd come at me so quickly that I hadn't had a chance to inhale. "You think I don't know you're afraid of me? You think, if you can just get to your phone, you'll be able to press some buttons without me noticing and call for help."

A horrible sound left my throat as he squeezed harder; the sound of me trying to gulp in air as my blood rushed around my body, my head growing light.

Just like that, he let go with a mocking laugh, while I leaned forward as far as I could, coughing and breathing hard, my body trying to regulate itself. Still dizzy, I flinched when he kicked the leg of my chair and then knelt in front of me. His fingers gripped the bottom of my long dress, and he flapped the skirt up and down, prompting me to recoil back against the back of the seat, my heart galloping.

"Have you figured it out yet?" he shouted, and in that moment, I did. A smile crossed his face. "Only just realised you can't feel it in your pocket? That's because I tossed it away hours ago, before we came here, to your final destination. So, if anyone *was* able to track you... you're not there!"

My whole body seemed to slump at his words. I *was* a fucking idiot. I'd held onto the hope that my phone would be my saviour, but I hadn't even noticed it was gone. The pockets were lower down on my skirt, than they would be in regular clothes, and because of the loose fit, I couldn't feel it against my hip, but I should have realised that the weight of it was missing.

Or maybe I did know and I'd continued to pretend, just to con myself into thinking there was a way out.

But there wasn't. It was me and him.

Keeping a hold on the bottom of my dress, he caressed the material between his fingers, then slowly lifted it, exposing my legs as a flash of desire ignited in his eyes. He let the material drop when my underwear was on display, and I swallowed hard, knowing this was it. The time I'd need the fight I'd been holding on to.

Chapter 41

Guy

CAL WAS SPEEDING DOWN the country lanes towards the back of Gavin's property so fast that if anything was coming the other way, we were dead. I was already maxed out on feeling terrified, though, and I hadn't said a word other than to offer directions since we left the abandoned property in Sidmouth.

My head was running through an unhelpful selection of thoughts ranging from whether Gavin was hurt because he still hadn't called me, to whether I was right and Gaby was really at his place, to what that sick fuck had done to her.

Louder than ever, though, was the deafening question drowning out all the others. *Is she still alive?*

Because the police were able to run through red lights with their sirens on, the cops who were with us had overtaken us a while ago, but I knew other officers, who were closer, had headed to all of the locations on the list they found. What I didn't like was the silence. It had only been just over half an hour since we'd leapt into action, but someone had to have found something by now. I would have taken the tiniest clue Gaby was alive over nothing at that point, but we were getting closer to Gavin's property now.

I could see flashing lights, and I began uttering prayers in my head, my fists clenched tight as Cal began to slow the car and then turned us onto the field Gavin owned, stopping at the side of the three police cars that were already there.

I jumped out without a thought, and as I did, I saw three police officers wrestling with a man who was wearing red trousers and a long-sleeved red top. He was struggling, screaming incoherent words, and I knew with everything in me that that was him.

Flynn.

I felt Cal grab my arms and hold them behind my back because I'd been ready to charge at the prick and beat the shit out of him. I didn't care that the police I had him; I needed to get to him, to hurt him.

"Get off me," I growled, trying to get free, but Cal held firm.

"I know you want to kill him, but you do not need to get yourself thrown in jail. Not when you have so much to lose. So, calm down."

"Is that what you would do?" I asked, knowing full well he would have moved to strike before anyone had a chance to stop him if Shannen had been in danger.

"Of course not, but you're not a reckless pillock, so get it together."

Normally, I would have laughed, but as Flynn was being stuffed into the back of a police car, I still didn't know if Gaby was okay, or if she was even here.

The second Flynn was out of my reach, Cal let me go, and we both ran towards the fence that separated Gavin's 'garden' from the end of the field. I was ready to leap over it when two things happened at once. First, a couple of uniformed officers on the other side of the fence tried to halt us to ask who we were, and then... I saw her.

Trembling, held up by two officers, Gaby was being led out of the outhouse and towards the fence where Cal and I stood.

She looked awful. Her eyes sunken and red, tear stains down her cheeks and her hair lank and messy. Her lip had been split, and as she got closer,

I saw her throat was discoloured, bruised, as if a hand had been wrapped around it.

But she was alive.

"Gaby," I murmured, even though I knew she wouldn't be able to hear me. I didn't care about anything else, or whether it would get me into trouble. I shoved past Cal and leapt over the fence, and as I did, she saw me, her mouth dropping open before she pulled out of the officers' hold and ran for me. On her weak legs, she stumbled and landed on the grass, and I rushed over to her, falling to my knees in front of her and dragging her into my arms.

"You came for me," Gaby breathed, holding me tight, her fingers digging into me and bringing me back to the moment.

"Of course I did," I whispered into her ear. "I have never been so scared in my life. But you're okay. You're safe now, and he's gone."

"I thought I would never see you again, Guy. I really think he was going to kill me."

She began to cry against me, and I rested my hand on the back of her neck, keeping her close to me as my own tears finally gave way. I'd been holding so much in, trying to focus on Gaby's wellbeing, but now I had her in my arms, I could finally feel all the feelings I'd shoved down.

"I had to find you," I told her. "There was no other option. I would have ripped every bit of this county to pieces if that was what it took."

So wrapped up in each other, I didn't see the female police officer approach us until she said, "Miss Davis, we need to talk to you about-"

My head snapped up. "Can you please give us a minute?"

A sheepish expression covered her features, and she nodded. "An ambulance will be here in five, Miss Davis."

"I don't need an ambulance," Gaby muttered. "I just want to go home."

"Miss Davis, you've been through a lot tonight and suffered a severe blow to the head. You need to be checked over properly. You might also need some stitches, so you're going to the hospital."

I hadn't had a second yet to ask her what he'd done to her. I could already see some of the evidence on her face, but... he'd been alone with her for a long time. The now-familiar anger stirred again as I wondered if she was hurt anywhere else. If he'd...

Gaby's hand on my cheek drew me back to her, finally allowing me a chance to actually look at her. I'd needed to hold her before anything else, but now I needed to see her.

Her beautiful green eyes were exhausted and sparkling with tears, but she smiled softly. "I'm okay," she promised, but then her chin wobbled. "Another few minutes and I might not have been, but I am."

Physically, that might have been true, but her worst nightmare had just come to life. She needed to be taken care of, and I didn't intend to leave her side. I would go with her to the hospital and...

Helen.

It had been close to four hours since I'd left Helen to come and find Gaby, and I'd promised her I would get back to her as soon as I could. I'd made that vow not knowing what the hell I would find, or if I would find anything. I would have spent hours trawling every inch of the local area if I had to, but no matter what the result was... I did still need to get back to Helen. I had a responsibility to see out. A baby to welcome into the world.

But I also had a woman who needed me not to run out on her on one of the worst days of her life.

"Cal," Gaby said, and I turned my head, not realising he was behind me.

Cal smiled down at her. "Thank God you're okay," he said, then with a mischievous smirk, he added, "This one has been a pain in my arse all night." He nodded towards me, and Gaby chuckled at his playing down of the situation, the sound mixing in with the sobs as relief and residual fear seemed to wage war in her head.

Cal took his car keys from his pocket and held them out to me. "I'll go with Gaby in the ambulance. You take my car and get back to Helen."

I shook my head. "I can't leave her."

I glanced down at Gaby, completely drained now, but she smiled gently. "You need to go."

"Gabs-"

"Guy," she interrupted, fixing her gaze on mine. "I'm a mess, yes, but Cal is here. You need to go and see your baby being born, and I'll be coming to the hospital anyway. I'll be right behind you, but you have to go now before you miss it."

Even at such a horrible time, she was able to take it upon herself to do what was right over what she needed. If it had been any other time than the birth of my baby, I would have stayed. I *wanted* to stay.

I hugged her tight one more time, pressing my lips to her forehead and soaking in the knowledge that I hadn't lost her. "I'm so sorry I have to leave you already." The idea of being away from her after only just getting her back was breaking my heart, and I wished I could take her with me. I didn't want to let her out of my sight.

"It's okay," she whispered. "Once tonight is over, I'm not letting you go for at least forty-eight hours. I'll come to work with you if I have to. But I'm not going anywhere."

She sounded so damn tired, and I wanted to take her home, put her into my bed and just cling to her.

But Helen needed me too. She was alone.

"I love you," I said, giving her one last squeeze.

"I love you too. Now, get out of here." She smiled up at me, and it took every bit of strength in me to break the connection between us.

As I got to my feet, the policewoman, who I'd forgotten was there, said, "Are you insured to drive Mr Lewis's car?"

"Of course he is, Officer," Cal said, smiling brightly at her. "Do you really think I would encourage someone to break the law in front of a police officer?"

Cal, charming as ever, had clearly won her over with his grin, and she rolled her eyes but smiled. Looking at me, she warned, "Drive carefully."

357

Nodding, I said, "Will do." Turning to Gaby and Cal again, I said, "Cal, look after her, please."

"I will," he promised. "Now go!"

Guy

AT ELEVEN P.M., AN hour and a half after an intense labour that made me wonder why women put themselves through it, I sat next to Helen on her hospital bed as she held our daughter in her arms.

It was also two hours since I'd sped back here, my heart aching at leaving Gaby behind after her ordeal with Flynn. The guilt was heavy, even though I knew she understood, because I wanted to be the one taking care of her. I knew Cal would look after her, but it should have been me

They were somewhere in this hospital. I'd called Gaby when the baby came, and she was still waiting to be seen, but she said she would let me know once she was done. She'd told me that while they'd been waiting, she had spoken to Nova, Shannen, and her brother, who, in the end, had turned out to be working extra late. I was actually slightly envious of the fact that he'd been oblivious to what had happened while it was happening. He was still livid about it and felt awful for being unable to track Flynn down, but we could all sleep easier knowing Flynn was out of the picture.

Helen's head nodded forward slightly as she dropped off, but the movement, as well as catching my attention, woke her back up, and she looked down at our daughter

She was tiny. Four weeks early, she only weighed five and a half pounds, and she had scared us shortly after we'd been left alone with her for the first time when her breathing stopped for a few seconds, then she began breathing rapidly before calming. The nurse reassured us this was normal in newborns, something called periodic breathing, but because she was premature, we were to call for assistance if it happened again to ensure there was nothing more serious underlying.

For the moment, though, everything was calm. Nobody buzzing around us, just me, Helen, and our daughter, who was wrapped in a white blanket, cradled against Helen's chest.

When I'd held her for the first time, I'd broken down completely. This tiny miracle had arrived on one of the most emotionally distressing days of my life, all soft skin and the tiniest scattering of blonde hair on her head. She had the cutest little button nose and blue eyes.

And I had never felt love like that before. It consumed me, made me want to be a better man, to always be the dad she would need. To make sure she was never afraid to ask me for anything, to turn to me when she needed help or someone to talk to. Having her in my arms changed my entire world, and I felt like I was floating, high from the euphoria of becoming a first-time father.

The one thing I had always wanted.

Helen had been incredible. She may have almost crushed my fingers to pieces and sworn at me a few times, but she'd delivered our baby safely, and there was a shift the second she'd arrived, like the moment she became a mother with a child in her arms, nothing else mattered.

"Do you want me to take her?" I offered.

She shook her head. "Not yet. I want to... I want to talk to you about something."

"Right now?" I asked. "Because you look like you need to sleep."

"I do," she said, finally pulling her gaze from the baby to me. "But before that... there are a few things I want to tell you. And I need you to not interrupt while I say them or I won't be able to finish, okay?"

Her eyes glazed over with unshed tears, and I shuffled a bit closer to her, putting my arm around her and waiting.

"Gaby," she began, and I immediately stiffened, afraid of where this was going. "I didn't get to ask properly if she's okay. With the labour and all." She gave a half-smile, and I returned it with one of my own. Helen was halfway through birthing the baby when I'd rushed back into the room, and the relief on her face was something I would never forget.

"She's as okay as she can be," I told her. "I don't think it will hit either of us properly for a few days, but she's all right for now."

Helen nodded, then swallowed. "You know how I feel about you. I've never made a secret of that. Somewhere, deep down, I hoped that maybe you would change your mind and want to be with me again at some point, but tonight... the answer was obvious. Guy, you are a good man, and you always try to help the people you care about, but I saw the look on your face when you heard Gaby had been abducted. And it broke my heart." She paused as a tear ran down her face. "Because I knew for sure then she wasn't just some girl you were seeing. I could see how terrified you were of losing her and that... that you love her." Closing her eyes, she took a shuddered breath. "I have been horrible to her. Some of the things I said to her the last time I saw her..." She shook her head. "And just like that, tonight, her life could have been over."

Helen's tears were racing down her cheeks now, her eyes puffy and her chest stuttering with her sobs. A lump formed in my throat, and I wanted to speak, but she'd asked me not to yet, so I stayed silent.

"I love you," she said, looking me right in the eye. "And I needed to say that to your face one more time. Not because I want you to feel bad for not loving me back anymore but so you know that all those times I took my shitty moods out on you and said things in the heat of a moment... it

361

wasn't a reflection on you. You didn't deserve it, and if I ever made you feel like you did, I'm sorry. So, I guess this is me letting you go."

Her head dropped back against the pillow as she cried, and I tugged her carefully against me, my own tears falling now too.

This was a form of closure. Not just for her, but for me too. While I knew the times she'd blamed everything on me were unfair, it still ate away at me, allowing the doubts to remain and make me question whether I was a good person to be in a relationship with. I'd spent hours and hours going over things, checking and re-checking my behaviour in my mind, and even when I managed to placate myself, I *still* questioned it. A lot of second-guessing had occurred, but what she'd just said resolved those things I'd struggled to let go of.

"I loved you, Helen," I said quietly. "I will always love you. It's just different now. Can we please try to fix some of the damage done over the last few months and focus on this little one?" I stroked our baby's super fine hair gently.

"I would like that," Helen said.

We sat quietly for a while, both of us letting her words settle. Helen had done something she hated. She'd apologised, and it felt like she meant it. I didn't expect her to keep her sharp tongue completely under control because she was so used to lashing out. But I believed she was going to work on it, and that was more than I'd expected from her. She'd managed to see what happened to Gaby as an eye-opener, and while I would have preferred it hadn't taken a kidnap to wake Helen up, it was reassuring to know that she could see the bigger picture at last.

"There's also this one really big thing we didn't get around to talking about yet," Helen said after a while. "I thought we could do it now."

"What's that?" I asked, transfixed on the tiny form of our daughter as she breathed gently.

"Her name. Did you have any ideas?"

I hadn't. Not seriously, anyway. A few had drifted in and out of my head, but I didn't think I would actually get a say in it, so I gave up thinking about it. After what Helen had just confessed, though, she didn't need to hear my reasoning on why I had no options for her.

I shook my head. "No. I didn't have any ideas. If she were a boy..."

"No," she interrupted. "We would not be naming our child after Bruno Guimaraes!"

I narrowed my eyes but grinned at her shooting down us naming a baby after my favourite Newcastle United player. "What about... Antonia?" I offered, a nod towards Anthony Gordon.

"Stop it!" She laughed, and it was good to see her smiling again, even though the tiredness was kicking in. "Do you have a serious suggestion?"

"No," I replied with another smile. "What about you?"

Helen looked down at the precious bundle in her arms and said, "I was thinking about Mila. I looked up the meaning, and one of them is 'miracle.' I think the name is pretty, but the meaning fits well too. What do you think?"

Mila. I let it simmer for a moment. It was cute, and it kinda suited her. She was a miracle as far as I was concerned, coming along at a time when both Helen and I had all but given up on ever having children. But there she was, living and breathing. Our beautiful baby girl.

"I like it," I said, smiling again. "Mila."

"Mila Danielson. It's perfect."

Chapter 43

Gaby

I HAD BEEN OUT of Flynn's clutches for four and a half hours, most of them spent sitting in the hospital with Cal, waiting to be seen by a doctor. If Guy couldn't be with me, I was glad it was Cal at my side. He'd risked Shannen's wrath to come and look for me, and I would never be able to repay him for that. I *had* thanked him approximately a million times, though. My brother had wanted to come to the hospital to be with me, but it was after eleven when he'd contacted me after finishing work. He'd apparently gotten a ton of missed calls from the police, letting them know they were on his property; the last thing he needed after a long day. I told him to go home and deal with that since I was fine with Cal, and Cal spoke to him too, which had calmed him down somewhat.

The thing was, I wasn't ready to face the barrage of questions Gavin would have, along with his apologies for letting me down.

The second the police had slammed through the doors of the outhouse, I had already begun to push down the memories of what Flynn had said and done in the time I was conscious with him. I wasn't delusional enough to think those memories would stay buried. In fact, I would dig them up myself to process them eventually, but with it so fresh in my mind and with so much else going on around me, I wanted a break.

Cal wasn't big on discussing feelings, so although I caught him looking at me with concern a few times, he never asked, never pushed for me to talk. Once or twice, he did reach over and hold my hand for a short time, and I liked that he still didn't try to force me to open up. He just noticed when I had zoned out and brought me back. The times we did talk, it was about the phone calls we'd had; with Gavin, with Shannen, and with Nova. Nova had been especially shaken because I'd been taken right in front of her, and she had been crying the entire time I was missing, completely inconsolable until she heard I had been found.

Truthfully, while I was always fully aware of how lucky I was to have such a great group of friends, I never felt it more than that night.

Nobody is going to look for you. Just like when we were at uni, you're nothing but the good time girl. You were fun, yeah, but nobody cared about you. That's why I was able to make you rely on me so easily. And nobody cares about you now. That guy you're with only sees a fit body, but there's still nothing in your head. And your friends? A week of fake concern about your whereabouts and it'll be over. They won't think about you again. Maybe they'll come to your funeral out of duty, but that'll be it. Nobody will remember you in a year.

He said those words to me while he was crawling over my body. While he was touching me. Some epic headfuck to make me feel like a nobody yet turning himself on by belittling me and staring at me like he wanted me.

What he wanted was for me to die thinking nobody loved me.

Bile rose in my throat at the memory, and I forced it all back down.

He had just started to get under my skin, to wear me down, and he could easily have got his wish because he always knew how to get to me. Armed with understanding as I was now, it still didn't stop him from forcing himself through the barriers I'd put up to keep him out. He always found a gap, a small place to wedge his seeds of doubt before pouring the water on and allowing me to let them grow.

But he was wrong. I had everything I needed, and if I had never returned, people *would* have cared. Seems an odd consolation in the face of death, but it was how I'd been able to hold on.

"Are you ready?" Cal asked me, and I dragged myself free of my thoughts and focused on his face.

I'd been examined a short while ago. I'd had to be checked for signs of concussion since I'd been knocked out, and while I was tired, the doctors had surmised that was to be expected after what I'd been through. They'd told me to make sure I had someone with me for the next twenty-four hours, and I wasn't to go back to work until after half term. They'd also given me a whole list of other things to watch out for, and told me to come right back to the hospital if any of them occurred. The only thing I was currently dealing with was a dull headache, soreness where the hit had occurred, and a little discomfort around my neck, but again, that was to be expected.

Because Guy was going to be busy for the next few days at least, I was going to stay with Shannen and Cal since Shannen was on maternity leave and wasn't going very far at the moment. Nova was also there because she'd wanted to be with Shannen after what had happened. We were still going to get our night together, but not quite in the way we'd anticipated. What we needed was a good rest, but none of us would do that until we'd had visual reassurance that everyone was okay. I was exhausted, my body depleted, but my mind was still too wired to switch off.

Before that, though, Cal and I were about to head for the maternity unit. Guy had called a short time ago and told me Helen had invited us to see the baby. I sensed from Guy's tone that this wasn't going to be as uncomfortable as the other times I'd seen her. He sounded calm, and it felt like more than just happiness at becoming a father. That didn't stop the nerves, though, and they fluttered inside my stomach the closer we got to the room Guy had said Helen was in.

Having been convinced mere hours ago that I wouldn't see the next morning, I wasn't sure there was much Helen could have said to bother me now. I was alive, and while, once the relief and shock had passed, I was sure the realer feelings of sadness at not being able to have my own children would come back, right then, it wasn't as important as the fact that my heart was still beating. Mostly, though, I was going to see Guy.

The thought of him was another anchor when Flynn was trying to provoke a reaction from me. I'd sat there honestly believing I would never see Guy's face again, but what I did know was that I had found something special with him, and it elicited a little extra bravery amongst the terror.

I hadn't had enough time with him when he'd found me. I could feel how badly he wanted to stay with me, but I couldn't let him miss the birth of his child, no matter how much I wished he could stay. Now, though, albeit with Helen in the room, I could go to him.

"Are you ready for this?" I asked Cal as we approached the door.

He chuckled, shaking his head. "I'm not going in there."

"What?" I asked, stopping him and pulling on his arm. "You're going to make me go in there by myself?"

Laughing again, Cal said, "I'll be out here, but this is your time to meet Guy's baby."

"But you're his best friend." My brow furrowed, feeling guilty that I was going in and he wasn't. "Don't you want to meet his daughter?"

"I do," he confirmed with a nod. "But two things. Firstly, one way or another, you are going to be a parent, even if it's just at the weekends for now, so you need to go first. Secondly, I'm sure Helen is happy she's a mum, but she will never be in a good enough mood to be nice to me, so I'll wait."

At that, I giggled. I wasn't certain she would be nice to me either, but he was right. I had to go in. She had invited me, after all.

"Okay," I said with a sigh. "I guess this is it."

Cal winked at me. "You'll be fine."

I gave his arm a gentle squeeze full of thanks for being with me all evening. For everything he'd done for me. Then, I tapped lightly on the door and peered around it.

Guy was sitting in the chair next to Helen's bed, baby in his arms. His eyes lit up when he saw me.

Helen looked like she was ready for a twenty-four-hour nap, her face pale, her hair resembling a bird's nest, and there was something like nervousness on her face.

"Come in, Gabs," Guy said, and I tentatively stepped inside. "Where's Cal?"

I jerked my head towards the door I'd just closed. "He's out there. He said I should come in on my own first, but please know, he is dying to get in here for a cuddle."

He hadn't said that, but I knew he was excited to meet the new arrival, and Guy laughed. "Probably ready to get some practise in."

I nodded with a small smile, and then took a few steps closer, eager to look at the baby but aware I hadn't spoken to Helen yet. As I looked over at her, I said, "Hi. How are you feeling?"

With a shake of her head, a tear I hadn't expected to see dripped down her cheek. "You're asking me how I'm feeling? You've just been kidnapped."

I shrugged. "And you just pushed a human out of your body. I'd say we're even."

For the first time ever in my presence, she laughed, even though another tear fell. There was a noticeable change in her demeanour towards me, but I wasn't quite ready to let my guard down all the way yet.

"Are you okay?" she asked.

"I've got a headache," I admitted. "But it could be worse." I glanced at Guy, who was looking lovingly at his daughter, but I knew he was listening. He was just giving us space for... whatever this was.

Helen looked over at Guy, a soft smile on her lips as she watched him staring at their child before saying, "Guy, could you give us two minutes, please?"

He raised his head. "You want me to keep hold of this one, or do I have to put her down?" His expression screamed that he did *not* want to put her down yet.

It was as I'd thought. Seeing him, all muscly-armed and sexy, holding a baby so gently made me love him even more.

"Go introduce her to Cal," Helen told him, rolling her eyes good-naturedly.

Guy's grin widened at the idea, and he heaved himself to his feet. As he reached me, he kissed the top of my head. I couldn't resist taking a peek, and I gasped at how tiny she was. I couldn't see her very well, as she was tucked up in a blanket. My eyes filled with happy tears, though. She was really here.

If I was allowed to, I would do everything in my power to ensure she grew up feeling safe and loved. One glimpse, and she already had a little piece of my heart.

"You can meet her properly in a bit," Guy said. "Back in a few."

His eyes pierced mine with a look so full of love that I wanted to wrap myself around him, lose myself in him. Instead, I mouthed, 'I love you,' and he winked at me before heading out of the room.

Once Helen and I were alone, I turned to her, taking a deep breath and trying to get a grip on my trepidation. She had been friendly so far, but I had no clue what she wanted to say to me. We'd never been together without Guy before.

Swallowing hard, she ran a hand across her face, swiping away a few stray tears on the way. She dropped her head back for a second then looked at me again. "I'm going make this as quick as possible because, well... it's been quite a day."

A small chuckle left me. "You can say that again." I raked a hand through my hair, wincing slightly as I accidentally pulled at the sore part at the back of my head.

"I talked to Guy earlier," Helen began. "I told him all the things I needed to tell him, but now I need to do the same with you. I'm not so good at apologies, and while I owe you that, I think there's probably a lot that I'm about to say that you already know. Things like how I feel about Guy, and how I took that out on you instead of dealing with it. The more understanding you were, the more scared I was because I realised that you are everything I had stopped being a long time ago." She paused, screwing up her face for a second. "This will be hard to believe, but I never used to be a dick."

I snorted at her choice of words, and she smiled weakly because I could see her facade beginning to crumble, and her tears fell again. My instinct was to hug her. In spite of her behaviour towards me, she was still a woman who was in love with a man she could no longer have, and I had never forgotten that, even on the days I was angry with her.

But I wasn't sure she wanted a hug from me, so I just waited, standing where I'd been the whole time.

"I'm sorry for the way I treated you," she said, wiping her tears again. "None of it had anything to do with you. I had played out in my head what I thought was going to happen with me and Guy, and when it didn't, I projected it onto you as if it were your fault. The thing is, even though I knew that the whole time, there was still this part of me that thought once the baby came, he would fall in love with both of us because of all the history we have, but..." Her words faded out as she shook her head. Not in disappointment or even sadness. It was more acceptance. "I don't imagine Guy has ever left you questioning how he feels about you, but if you ever had cause to doubt it, you shouldn't. Because he looked like his entire world had ended at the idea of anything happening to you."

It must have taken every bit of strength she had to tell me that, and I took a couple of steps closer to her. When she didn't look horrified, I sat down on the edge of the bed next to her.

"Helen, you meant everything to Guy," I said. "I first met him not too long after you broke up, and he was... lost. Why do you think he sold his house and moved somewhere else? It wasn't to get all memories of you out of his life. It was because it hurt to be there on his own. That house used to be full, and then it wasn't. Just because he's with me now, it doesn't lessen how he felt about you."

Squeezing her eyes closed, Helen let out a sob, as if everything she'd been holding in was finally free to come out.

"Thank you," she said quietly. "Thank you for putting up with all of this and for letting me apologise."

Flashbacks of Flynn circling me in the outhouse, playing with his knife, snarling in my face, and climbing on top of me rushed to the front of my mind, and I shoved them all back. I didn't need the threat of my life ending to be a good person; I would have heard her out anyway. But I couldn't deny that staring a madman in the face made it a little easier to let go of stuff that didn't matter now.

"I only ever wanted things to be civil between us. Maybe even be friends eventually."

"Don't push it," she said dryly but with humour in her tone, and we both laughed. "Seriously, I do want to get to know you. I know Guy was worried I would try to keep you on the outside, but you are who Guy wants to be with, and he has a daughter now. I can't and won't be someone who says you can't be a part of that."

Maybe her emotions were all jacked up because she was tired, but I could feel that she meant it. I wished this Helen had been around earlier. It would have saved so much pain. However, she was here now, and it felt like the beginning of a less dysfunctional relationship for all of us.

"Thanks," I said. "I promise I will never overstep. I just want to be able to be in her life."

Helen nodded, tears still falling. "Well, in that case, you'd better get Guy to bring her back in here so you can meet her."

Standing, my heart felt full.

Fuck you, Flynn. You didn't win this time.

He would never win while I had something to fight for.

I opened the door and peeked into the corridor, where Cal and Guy were sitting in the seats outside, Cal holding the baby and staring at her, spellbound.

"From hero to pile of goo in two minutes," I teased, and Cal and Guy turned around.

"I bet you fifty quid you fall in love with her the second she's in your arms," Cal said, looking back down at her with a smile.

"I don't doubt it."

Guy stood up and pulled me into his arms. "Everything okay?" he asked as I leaned into his strong warmth.

Yup. That is what I needed. He was always my safe place. My comfort. He meant everything to me.

"Mmhmm," I answered, though tiredness was beginning to fully kick in now. "All good." Reaching up, I kissed him lightly on the lips.

Cal stood too, and Guy let go of me to take the baby from him. "I'll let you get acquainted. Gaby, you ready to go home soon?"

"I am," I said, and a yawn slipped from me. I couldn't wait to dive into a comfy bed and sleep away this half-amazing, half-horrifying day. All thoughts of talking to my friends all night dwindled, but being near them would be enough.

"Cool. I'll ring Shannen and let her know we won't be long." With one last glance at the baby, and then me and Guy, he stalked off down the corridor.

I pushed the door to Helen's room open again so we could go back inside, and as we entered, a soft snore came from her direction.

Her head turned to the side, she finally drifted off.

Smiling down at me, Guy said, "Gaby, I would like you to meet Mila Danielson." He handed her to me, my arms shaking a bit as I took her.

"Oh my gosh," I whispered, feeling how truly tiny she was. She barely weighed a thing, but she was so cute. She had lips that would have made teenage girls jealous, all pouty and sassy-looking. Her nose wiggled in her sleep, and my heart melted as I stared at her. "Hi, Mila," I said quietly. "You know, there's a little girl in my class called Mila. She told me that her name means miracle, and I think that's why your mummy and daddy chose it for you."

Guy wrapped his arms gently around both of us, and I looked up at him.

"Let me tell you something else," I said softly, looking back at Mila again. "You and me and your mummy... we are the luckiest girls in the whole world because nobody will ever love us as much as your daddy does. One day, precious girl, when you're bigger, you'll understand."

Guy's hold tightened a bit more. "I'm the lucky one. Fuck, Gaby. I almost lost you."

I snuggled into him, happy to let denial cover up the reality of his comment for a bit longer. "But you found me. You raced around until I was back where I belong. And that's how I know that I'm the real winner here."

I had once been beaten, broken down, left as an empty shell. Then, I'd built myself back up.

As I stood there, in that hospital room, with the most important people in my world, I was painfully aware of how close I'd come to never having this moment. To becoming another statistic.

But I was given a reprieve. A chance to have a family.

What was clearer than ever right then, though, was that I'd already *had* the family. Not just with my brother, but with Shannen, Cal, and Aiden.

With Nova and Donovan. With the work colleagues who had been so upset and afraid for my safety.

With Guy.

Mila was just the last piece in the beautiful puzzle of our lives.

For as long as I was breathing, I would protect it with everything I had.

Epilogue

Three Weeks Later

GUY

Usually, when people put plans in place 'just in case,' they never actually need them.

So, naturally, when Cal had called me late on the Friday night before Aiden's birthday party to let me know Shannen had gone into labour, those plans were put into action immediately.

Gaby had been staying at my place, so just before midnight, we got out of bed, dressed, and rushed over to Cal and Shannen's place to watch Aiden so they could go to the hospital.

And that was how Gaby and I ended up overseeing Aiden's sixth birthday party.

His actual birthday wasn't until Tuesday, Shannen's due date, but knowing how unpredictable the arrival of a baby could be, everything had been organised down to the finest detail.

Aiden had originally wanted to go and play mini golf with his friends, but Shannen felt it better if she stayed at home because standing up for a long time was a challenge now, so Aiden changed his mind because he wanted her to be at the party. Eventually, they decided they would have a 'traditional' party for him at home with simple food that Gaby and I had put together that morning, games, and Nova had made him a birthday cake in the shape of a Newcastle United shirt.

Aria, Avery, and Maxwell from school had been invited, as well as a couple of boys he had made friends with at football training, plus Shannen's nephew, Alexander, with Shannen's sister and brother-in-law Sadie and Stefan, Shannen's mum Annie, and Nova. It was only small, but that was all Aiden wanted. Helen and Mila had been invited, having spoken with Cal, Shannen, and Aiden over the last couple of weeks, but while she was a little more at ease with our situation now, that was a lot of people for her to face three weeks after having a baby, so she'd declined.

Things between Gaby, Helen, and me were better. Gaby and Helen would never be best friends, but the hostility had melted away after their heart-to-heart in the hospital. It was as if they'd reached an understanding, and while both women had their own pain to deal with, the sniping was over, and they could talk to each other more easily now.

Being a dad was the best gift I'd ever had. I visited Mila every day, and Gaby came with me a few times a week. She had helped me turn my spare room into a baby/kid room. It had a cot and a changing table, and a little chest of drawers where we could keep clothes for Mila, but there was also a bed in there. It meant that there was still a place for Aiden to sleep if he wanted to stay over sometimes. Mila hadn't slept at my place yet, and I knew she wouldn't for a while, but it was ready for when she did. Helen had stayed true to her word about the paternity test too, and while I never had any doubts, the results showed that Mila was definitely mine.

She was perfect. I couldn't believe how quickly she was changing. She was still tiny, but growing, and I had also delivered on my promise to get her a little Newcastle United kit. She was so small that it would be way too big for her for a while, but Cal and Shannen had got her a specially made onesie with the logo on the front, much to my delight.

Gaby had been signed off work until after Christmas. While her head injury had cleared up well, her mental health had been shaken. Plus, with her being snatched directly from the school, it was felt that it would be better for her to take a few additional weeks to come to terms with what had happened.

For the first week, she'd pretended she was okay, even though it was clear she wasn't. By the beginning of week two, though, she finally broke down, like everything she had tried to push down had exploded inside her, and Gavin and I had spent an entire day with her, helping her to pick up the pieces. Breaking down that barrier, her spilling out everything Flynn had said and done to her, had been awful for all of us. For Gaby reliving it, and for Gavin and me hearing some of the vile things he'd said to her, and the fact that he had been dangerously close to violating her when the police barged in.

As harrowing as it was to hear it, though, it was nothing compared to knowing how terrified Gaby must have been at the time.

The nightmare was over because Flynn had done more than enough to ensure he was shipped right back to jail, this time locally, unfortunately. He didn't yet have a court date, but abduction, bringing a weapon into a school, slicing someone with a knife, attempted sexual assault and the fact that he'd been using a false identity, not to mention trespassing on one property and forcibly breaking into another on the back of a ten-year sentence for the things he'd done to Gaby years ago meant he wouldn't be bothering us anytime soon.

But that didn't stop the nightmares. The rehashing of the old trauma. My girl was strong, but she knew when she needed extra support, and she was seeing a counsellor twice a week to try to help her move on.

Day to day, though, she was doing okay. And she was having way too much fun being the DJ as the kids played Pass the Parcel in Cal and Shannen's living room. The coffee table had been pushed to the side, and they sat in a circle, excitedly passing the wrapped gift around.

Aiden was restless, understandably, because although he was excited that he was having a party, he asked every half an hour if the baby had come yet.

I figured it wouldn't be too much longer now.

The party had started at one and was finishing at four, and it was just past three now, so the kids' parents would be coming to collect them in less than an hour. But right then, everything was in full swing.

"Aria!" Maxwell sang as the music stopped while the parcel was in her hands. The adults were sitting around on the sofas, watching with amusement, and I slunk away into the dining room to make a start on tidying away some of the food. Annie, spotting what I was doing, came to join me, and she grabbed a plate of crisps and leftover ham rolls, and I grabbed the now-empty bowl of cut-up hot dogs, and stacked up a bunch of paper cups to carry through to the kitchen.

"You've done a good job here today," Annie said as we set the dishes down by the sink, ready to wash later, and I binned the cups.

"Thanks." I smiled at her. "I wasn't expecting to have to do this, but it wasn't so bad, and all the kids have behaved."

"Yeah." She swiped a crisp and popped it into her mouth, and I leaned forward to grab a roll. It would have been a shame to waste it. "They've all been really good."

"How are you doing?" I asked. "Must be weird being here and knowing Shannen's having a baby right now."

She nodded. "It's strange, but Cal's calls have helped. At least we know she's doing okay, but it had been a couple of hours since he checked in. I hope that means we'll get some news soon."

"Didn't you want to go and be with them?"

Shaking her head, she said, "Those two have been through so much. I would love to be there, but I also know that they need this to be just for them."

Annie had been through a lot too. She was starting divorce proceedings, and she had lost people she thought were her friends. But she did it all with her head held high, and I understood why Shannen was so level-headed. Annie was calm, even in a crisis. I'd always liked her, and she'd kind of become a second mum to me and Gaby lately too. She was going to stay with Cal and Shannen for just a few days to help them with the baby and Aiden, and I suspected we would go over and visit during the week.

That was the other thing. I'd halted all work on the bar since Gaby was abducted. My guys all had other work they could do, and I needed time to take care of Gaby and bond with Mila. Cal would now be taking a couple of weeks off too, so it made more sense to me to hit the pause button; something Donovan was in full agreement about.

Annie and I wandered back through to the dining room, still chatting as we cleared more dishes out of the way.

"Guy!" Gaby called. "Your phone is ringing!"

I'd left it on the windowsill, out of the way, and as she pressed play on the music on her own device so the kids could keep playing, her eyes widened with anticipation as she nodded towards my phone. She couldn't see who it was from where she sat, but like me, she was hoping it was Cal.

I felt a weird surge of nerves as I hurried over to pick it up and saw it was, indeed, my best mate. I answered while heading out into the hallway, grabbing Annie's hand as I went and taking her by surprise as I pulled her with me.

"Hey," Cal said, and I put him on speaker so Annie could hear. "We did it. We have a baby boy."

Annie's eyes filled with happy tears, and she clapped her hands together in excitement.

A boy. A little brother for Aiden. He couldn't have asked for a better birthday present.

"Congratulations," I said. "Is everyone okay?"

"Yeah, everyone's great. I know you said childbirth makes you appreciate the woman in your life, but... I had no idea. Shannen was incredible. He weighs just over seven pounds and he looks really little, but Shannen still had to push him out, and she didn't threaten to kill me once."

Annie and I laughed. "I'm so happy for you, my darling," Annie said. "What time did he arrive?"

"Two-twenty-two," he said, chuckling. "Nice and easy to remember. Is Aiden there? I want to tell him. Shannen can't wait to see him, but she's just resting before you all descend on us."

"Are we allowed to come this afternoon?" I asked. "Or do we have to wait until visiting hours?"

"So, Aiden is allowed to come in for an hour any time before eight o'clock tonight, so obviously, someone will have to bring him, but if he wants to come as soon as the party's over, he can. Everyone else can come between six and seven. We might be allowed home tonight, but there's a whole gross checklist of things that need to happen first."

The disgust in his voice made Annie and me burst out laughing again. Helen had to complete the checklist too, but because Mila was so tiny, the doctors wanted them to stay in for twenty-four hours to ensure all was well.

"You'd better get used to baby poo," I said. "You'll be seeing a lot of it!"

"Yeah, thanks for that. It's been a long time since I changed a nappy."

Still chuckling, I looked at Annie and said, "Why don't you take Aiden? They might let you in if you're lucky."

"Are you sure?" she asked, and I nodded. "Thank you. I'll go and get him so he can hear the news."

With a grin, she left the hallway, and I said to Cal, "How do you feel?"

He laughed, disbelief ringing out. "I never had this with Aiden. I missed out on all of it, and to have it now with Shannen... I can't believe it. I can't believe it's real."

"Best feeling ever."

I knew it because I still felt the same way.

Before I could say more, Aiden hurtled into the hallway, and said, "Dad!"

"Hey, buddy," Cal answered. "So, do you want to hear some good news?"

"Yes, please!" He bounced on the balls of his feet as he waited.

"You have a baby brother."

The squeal of excitement he let out made Annie and me cover our ears.

"Happy about that?" Cal asked with sarcasm.

"Yes!" Aiden shouted, jumping up and down. "Can I see him?"

"Course you can. Nanny Annie's going to bring you to the hospital in a little while, okay? So, go back and enjoy the rest of your party, and then it'll be time for you to come."

Aiden was still bouncing like a kangaroo as he went back into the living room, and I said, "I think you've made his day!"

Cal

As I stood in the doorway to Shannen's hospital room after speaking to Aiden, Guy, and Annie, there was no getting rid of the smile on my face.

Happiness still held some discomfort for me, a small part of me always waiting for the thing that would take it away, but this moment would always be my anchor. My reason to fight every damn day to keep what I had.

Without letting Shannen know I was there, I just watched her, her eyes tired but bright as she held our son.

That woman had grabbed hold of my heart from the first day, and I hoped with every piece of me that she never let it go because I loved her and our family more than I could ever tell her.

How could anyone walk away from this?

I'd been a dad for almost six years, and for a lot of it, I was a waste of space. A deadbeat dad who scraped by. But I loved Aiden, even when it scared me to care so much about another person. Even when he was taken from me. It was always a struggle between wanting to love him like he deserved but being scared I would turn into my own father. Scared I wouldn't cope. Scared I would be selfish.

Just frightened of it all.

Since Guy had told me my dad had sent someone to check up on me, I'd thought a lot about him. About the dad he used to be before he lost his livelihood. The one who showed my brother and me that he loved us. That was what I'd missed when he changed. I had the memory of a father who was good, and then he turned into a bitter, alcoholic, violent mess. Someone I was afraid of.

Now, he was older and ill. Dying. And somewhere inside me, the little boy who loved him was devastated for who he once was and what we missed out on because of what he'd done to my mum and me.

But adult me? Adult me couldn't rectify the damage he'd done with the old man who was no longer a drinker. Why couldn't he have got over himself for the family he had and not for some new woman, so many years later? My mum had done everything she could to support him, to help him. As much as I tried to understand what he might have been feeling over losing the career he loved, I couldn't understand why he refused to see how lucky he really was. He could still walk, talk, do anything else in the world, and he had a wife and two sons who loved him. But he'd let himself drown in his misery and become the bastard I'd been left with.

Why weren't we enough? Why did he take his pain out on us?

As low as I'd sunk when I'd been left with Aiden, I never hurt him, even on the days when I resented the position I was in. And as I stood there, looking at Shannen, who was gazing at our baby like he was everything, I couldn't see a day when I would do anything other than love and protect them. No matter what.

I didn't have anything left to give my dad. Even if deep down, it hurt to know he was ill, anytime I thought of him, all I could see was my mum, bruised and bleeding after an attack, how she lost her spark more and more every year. His behaviour was what caused her to rush out of the house with my brother the night they were killed. And beyond that, I heard his cruel words to me. The things he said to me when I was grieving at fourteen years old, feeling like nobody would ever give a shit about me again. How he beat me down in every way possible, then walked out and never looked back. Until now.

There wasn't a single word he could say that could fix any of that or take away the issues I'd fought so hard to overcome that stemmed from being abused by him for so long.

I was happy now. I refused to re-open old wounds when I'd said goodbye to him a long time ago.

Shannen

"I might not be looking at you, but I can still see you," I said, my eyes on my newborn son. I couldn't recall ever being so at peace. Even though I was tired and felt gross, I didn't care that I looked like crap because I had never been happier.

Except that Cal was lingering in the doorway, and I could sense his gaze on me. Something was on his mind; he gave off an energy when something was bugging him, and the sensation was coming at me, thick and heavy.

I heard him laugh lightly, and I looked up to see him walking into the room. As he sat down on the bed beside us and wrapped his arm around my shoulders, he said, "I spoke to Aiden, Guy, and your mum. Aiden's very excited and your mum's going to bring him here once his friends have gone. Guy and Gaby will come later, and I'm sure Sadie and Stefan will want to come too. Maybe Nova too."

I smiled as I looked into Cal's expressive brown eyes. I'd always loved them, found they grounded me. Our baby boy looked just like him. His eyes were the same chocolate brown, his face shape the same, although tiny. He had black hair like both of us, and although he didn't have a lot, what he had was curly. I was aware that every parent thought this about their child, but he was the most beautiful baby I'd ever seen, and already, I wanted more. A house full of brown-eyed, curly-haired kids. A family that would fill our home and our hearts.

"I can't wait to see everyone," I said, "especially Aiden. I feel so bad that we missed his party."

"Me too." Cal kissed the top of my head. "But he's so glad to have a brother that I don't think he'll mind."

I chuckled. He would have been a good big brother regardless, but he had expressed his wish for us to have a boy. I could only imagine how much of a handful he had been at his first ever birthday party, full of sugar, and then with this news on top. Poor Gaby and Guy, having to try to calm him down.

Still with the feeling Cal had something on his mind, I said, "Are you okay?"

He nodded. "Yeah. I was just thinking about the stuff with my dad."

Since Cal had told me about the creepy man Guy had hired being a friend of his father's, he hadn't mentioned it again, and where his dad was concerned, I knew not to push. Any conversation around him rarely ended well because it sent Cal into either a rage or made him withdraw. So, I never brought him up first. It had to have been on his mind, though. Not constantly, but with us welcoming our own child into the world... it makes a person think. I'd certainly thought about my dad a lot lately.

Since Mum had said they were getting a divorce, I'd spoken to my dad on the phone twice and seen him once. We used to get together whenever we could, but I still struggled to forgive him. I wanted to let go of it, but just like my mum, I couldn't understand anyone setting out to hurt their own child, no matter the intention. It was a move that had done damage on a wide scale, rippling out into other people's lives too. The consequences of his decisions had hurt more than just my immediate family, and I wasn't sure if I could get past it.

When I'd heard Cal's dad was ill, it made me think about what would happen if that were the case with my own father. Wasn't life more important than a grudge?

I still hadn't made a decision on what to do regarding him having a relationship with his grandson, but I hoped clarity would come with time.

In the position I was in, I couldn't reach for Cal's hand, but instead, I rested my head against his shoulder. "What were you thinking?"

"That I don't get how anyone could do what he did to his family. I feel guilty if I even shout at Aiden. The idea of hitting him makes me feel sick. Look at us, Shan. This has been a fucking whirlwind, but I have you, and we have a baby. I would kill to protect you, but the idea of hurting *you*?" He shook his head. "Never gonna happen. So, I guess I was just thinking that my decision about whether I want to see him is definitely made, and it's a no."

"Okay," I said simply. I figured that would be his choice, and that he was already set on it, but it had been reconfirmed now. Lifting my head so I could look into his eyes again, I smiled. He looked tired, the stubble on his chin thick because we'd rushed out before midnight, and he hadn't had a shave the day before either. He was still gorgeous. In fact, I found him more attractive in that moment than I had the day I met him, and that was saying something.

We'd had a lifetime of craziness in eleven months, but it was worth it to be with him now, like this. The three of us, and Aiden coming to join us soon.

"Cal, I wanted to ask you your thoughts on something," I said, and he tilted his head slightly. "We had a list of names picked out, and we haven't had a chance to settle on one yet, but the thing is... I've been sitting here, looking at him this whole time, but there's a name not on the list that keeps coming to me every time he looks at me with those big eyes. How would you feel about calling him Luca?"

Cal's own eyes widened, and a small gasp left him. "Luca," he repeated.

His brother's name. I'd, of course, never got to meet him. From the stories Cal had told me, they were close, and more than anything else, he wondered about what his brother would have been doing if his life hadn't been cut short. But our baby... the name Luca almost called to me every time I looked at him. If Cal didn't want to name him after his brother, that was okay with me, but it just felt like he was telling me that that was the name he wanted. Maybe I was still high on medication and exhausted, but it felt right.

"What do you think?" I asked, watching as Cal stared at our son, his eyes filling with tears.

"I think it's perfect." He looked up at me, and I smiled as he leaned in to kiss me gently. "You're perfect. I love you so much, Shan."

"I love you too," I whispered, my heart fuller than it had ever been.

Gaby

Waiting for the news of Shannen and Cal's baby had felt like the longest wait ever. But the few hours before we were allowed to go to the hospital? That was torture.

It had been a strange few weeks, first spent faking okayness, then letting everything I'd stored up spill out onto Guy and Gavin. Shannen and Nova had also been amazing through that time too, and it only compounded how I'd felt once I'd got away from Flynn that night. That I was the luckiest woman in the world to have such exceptional people in my corner.

Even Helen had mellowed since my near-death experience. And Mila... I adored her. I never thought I would be able to even hold her if Helen had anything to do with it, but I'd had many snuggles, and while I thought it would be painful to be around Mila, knowing I could never have a baby of my own, it was strangely okay. Did I sometimes get sad about what I couldn't have? Yes, and I probably always would occasionally. But being around Mila didn't trigger it. I was fortunate to be part of her life, and I would never take for granted that I would be there to watch her grow up.

As Guy and I entered the ward Shannen had been moved to, with Aiden in tow, emotion swept over me. I'd been with Shannen when she found out she was pregnant. Sat with her while she figured out how she felt about it. Been excited over every scan photo, and waited for this moment with everyone who loved her, Cal, and Aiden. I knew Guy felt it too; his best friend had just had a baby with the woman he adored, and it was the most special time.

Hand in hand, we approached Shannen's bed. Cal sat beside her on a chair, holding their new baby, who Aiden had informed us was called Luca. Nova would have joined us, but she'd already made plans for the evening with her parents, so she was going to visit the next day, when Shannen would hopefully be at home.

Shannen's face lit up as she saw us, and Aiden rushed over and clambered up onto the bed to give her a hug.

"What about me?" Cal asked with mock indignation, and everyone laughed.

Aiden grinned at him. "Hi, Dad. Hi, Luca," he said, but he snuggled into Shannen, and she wound her arm around him. She looked good. A little pale, but there was a glow coming from her, and I guessed she might have had a tiny nap before we arrived too.

Once we'd all greeted each other with hugs and kisses, Cal looked up at Guy and me and said, "So, who wants the first cuddle?"

As much as I wanted a snuggle, I nodded for Guy to go first. Cal got to his feet, bringing Luca towards Guy, and the two of them exchanged a look that blatantly screamed how much they cared for each other. It brought a lump to my throat, and as I glanced at Shannen, she smiled at me as a tear slipped down her cheek, her arm still around Aiden.

"This is your Uncle Guy," Cal said, handing Luca to Guy. "If you ever want anything, ask him because he's a pushover."

We all laughed again, and Guy said, "That is, sadly, true." I stood closer to Guy to have a peek at the baby in his arms, and my heart felt like it might burst.

All of the stuff we'd been through seemed so insignificant as new life had come into the world. Luca was sleeping in Guy's arms, unaware of how we were all in awe of him. Unaware of anything but the comfort of his warm blanket, which was how it should be.

I reached over and stroked his soft cheek. "Hey, little one," I whispered. I grinned at Shannen, just as Cal sat down on the other side of the bed beside her, his arm winding around her. "He is beautiful."

She nodded. "I'm biased, obviously, but I think he's a cutie."

"He is," I agreed, then looked at Guy. He gazed at Luca with the same affection he had for Aiden. They weren't related by blood, but I could already tell another strong bond was being created.

That was the very thing I'd come to realise more and more lately. My real family was intact, but we weren't really close, aside from me and

Gavin. I had a better connection to the people in this room, and Nova and Donovan, than I had to my own family. It didn't matter who was related to who, only who was there for each other when times got tough.

The family I'd created for myself wasn't made up of a husband, a wife, and some children. It was made up of a man who would have died to rescue me, his baby daughter, and the kind of friends who had each other's backs through anything.

I was still a mess. Still had more to overcome, but with my arm around the best man I'd ever known, surrounded by the family I'd chosen, the overriding feeling coursing through my veins was peace.

My ex had tried to take what I'd built for myself, make me doubt it was even real, but ultimately, I knew better.

I was Gaby freaking Davis. The woman with a wedding dress in her closet, a man at my side, and a heart full of gratitude.

Was it all a bit unconventional? Perhaps.

But it was mine, and that was the only thing that mattered.

Author's Note: There are just two more books remaining in the Oakwood Lane Series as it stands, and as you know, there are still a few things that need tying up!

Rest assured, your questions will be answered, but to tie in with reality for police procedures, to allow time for the dust to settle, AND because Gaby and Guy deserved their time to shine, I wanted this book to focus mostly on them.

If you are ready to sink in to Book 4, Back To You, you can pre-order it here!

Clare Dugmore and Clare Bentley – Thank you for your dedication to getting this book read and tidied up! Couldn't have done it without you!

Sophie Mitchell - My beautiful Soph, thank you for always being there. Not just in your capacity as a marketing guru, but as a friend. Your support means everything.

Richard - For plying me with sugar while I got through the stress of edits, and for ordering that Chinese and new boots to celebrate the end of the book. You continue to be the best partner a girl could ask for!

And of course, my readers. Thank you for continuing to read this series and coming on this journey with me!

RAZES HELL SERIES

Nobody Knows

Everybody Knows

Chaos and Consent Series

Hear What You Want

Say What You Feel

Take What You Need

Oakwood Lane Prequel

Re-Writing Christmas

Oakwood Lane Series

All Of You

Only With You

Over You

Standalones

Reasonable Doubts

Picture (Im)Perfect

Unintended

About the Author

Kyra Lennon is a UK-based romance author who writes love stories with heart, heat, and emotional depth. Her books often feature small-town settings and characters navigating real-life challenges on their way to their happily ever after. Kyra's stories are full of raw chemistry, complex emotions, and the kind of romantic tension that lingers long after the final page.

A lifelong storyteller and unapologetic daydreamer, Kyra believes in messy feelings, imperfect characters, and the magic of a well-timed kiss. When she's not writing, you'll find her chatting with writers in her online community, overusing heart emojis, and plotting her next book with a latte and loud music!

If you would like to keep up to date with all of Kyra's latest news, you can follow her on <u>Facebook</u> or sign up to her <u>newsletter</u> for news, book recs, and freebies!